Praise for Tim Maleeny

BOXING THE OCTOPUS
The Fourth Cape Weathers Mystery

"*Boxing the Octopus* is a colorful gem of a book with sharp, funny dialogue and a crowd of dangerous characters, one of whom is startlingly well-armed."

—Thomas Perry, #1 *New York Times* bestselling author

"Maleeny moves his colorful cast around with giddy panache. His detective's fourth caper is a Hiaasen-esque delight."

—*Kirkus Reviews*

"Maleeny produces some fast-paced, cheeky fun, along with a splash of social consciousness."

—*Publishers Weekly*

"*Boxing the Octopus* reads like a surreal blend of Raymond Chandler and Carl Hiaasen as the story winds its delightfully bonkers way through San Francisco's underworld... If comic crime fiction is your thing, Maleeny delivers in spades."

—*Irish Times*

"*Boxing the Octopus* is a great mystery novel, but it's also great literature. One cannot read it without appreciating how sharp a writer Maleeny is."

—*Bookreporter*

"A complex plot worthy of Leonard's heir, Maleeny bursts back onto the crime fiction stage with a surefire winner. Can't wait for Cape and Sally's next adventure."

—bestselling author J. T. Ellison

GREASING THE PIÑATA

The Third Cape Weathers Mystery
2009 Winner of the Lefty Award, Best Humorous Mystery

"Maleeny smoothly mixes wry humor and a serious plot without sacrificing either in his third Cape Weathers mystery...an appealing hero, well-crafted villains, snappy dialogue, and an energetic plot."

—*Publishers Weekly*

"Maleeny is the kind of writer that makes you want to jump in the passenger seat and go for the ride—okay, maybe with eyes jammed shut and your hands gripping the armrest—but then you want to go again."

—Don Winslow, #1 *New York Times* bestselling author

"Tim Maleeny nails it with this new installment from Cape Weathers. It's an intriguing murder mystery crossed with a fast-paced political thriller. The whole thing is tied together with a witty protagonist and a finely tuned sense of humor. In *Greasing the Piñata*, just as in Mexico, anything can happen, and most of it does."

—Bill Fitzhugh, award-winning author of *Pest Control*

"A cracking good mystery definitely not for the faint of heart but just right for readers who like a gritty crime novel with a labyrinth of plot twists."

—*Library Journal*

"The Cape Weathers novels are smart, snappily written, energetic mysteries starring an engaging hero."

—*Booklist*

BEATING THE BABUSHKA
The Second Cape Weathers Mystery

"The snappy writing and a parallel plot of drug-dealing Italian and Chinese mobsters keeps the pace lively and will resonate with Elmore Leonard fans."
—Publishers Weekly

"Maleeny does a nice job of showing us the cutthroat side of the movie industry. Keep 'em coming."
—Booklist

"*Beating the Babushka* goes a long way toward establishing Maleeny as one of the new princes of detective fiction."
—Bookreporter

"A plot that sizzles from page one and keeps cooking until the twists at the end."
—Crimespree Magazine

STEALING THE DRAGON
The First Cape Weathers Mystery
2008 Macavity Award Finalist, Best First Novel
IMBA Killer Book of the Month

"Tough, original, compelling—a perfect thriller debut."
—Lee Child, New York Times bestselling author

"Readers will want to see more of Cape and Sally."
—Library Journal

"Maleeny gives readers a fresh and fast take that enthralls."
—Crimespree Magazine

JUMP

"If you threw in the air the pages of Agatha Christie's *Murder on the Orient Express* and Elmore Leonard's *Get Shorty,* and then invited Monty Python to stitch them back together, you might end up with something like *Jump,* Tim Maleeny's hilarious novel."

—*Boston Globe*

"We're firmly on darkly comic terra Hiaasen. Fast-paced and funny, this is a perfectly blended cocktail of escapism, with or without the beach towel."

—*Publishers Weekly*

Also by Tim Maleeny

The Cape Weathers Investigations
Boxing the Octopus
Greasing the Piñata
Stealing the Dragon
Beating the Babushka

Standalone Novel
Jump

HANGING
THE
DEVIL

HANGING
THE
DEVIL

A CAPE WEATHERS MYSTERY

TIM MALEENY

Poisoned Pen
PRESS

Published by Poisoned Pen Press, an imprint of Sourcebooks
P.O. Box 4410, Naperville, Illinois 60567-4410
(630) 961-3900
sourcebooks.com

Cataloging-in-Publication Data is on file with the Library of Congress.

Printed and bound in the United States of America.
SB 10 9 8 7 6 5 4 3 2 1

For Kathryn
a truly original work of art

"Good artists copy. Great artists steal."

—Pablo Picasso

1

Grace stared at the Buddha, but the Buddha didn't blink.

His eyes focused on something beyond Grace, a distant vision of an unattainable future. He looked serene, but Grace thought he was being stubborn. She knew a lot about being stubborn.

The Buddha was eleven hundred years old. Grace was eleven.

Her eyes started to water, and Grace blinked first. She was annoyed, convinced this particular Buddha would come to life and smile, if only she could outlast him.

It was the second-oldest statue in the Hall of Buddhas and the tenth to face her in a test of wills. Grace was working her way through the Asian Art Museum one exhibit at a time, a game designed to keep her restless imagination occupied while her uncle, Han, patrolled the building.

Grace chose a different exhibit to explore every night until she got tired, then she slept on a couch in the main hall until her uncle's shift ended at dawn. Technically, only her uncle was allowed to be in the museum after hours, but his supervisor said it was okay until they made new arrangements. Han had been the night guard for two years and had a sterling reputation. He assured Grace that no one would know as long as she didn't break any priceless artifacts.

Han didn't feel comfortable leaving her alone in his small apartment. Not until they got word from her father.

Grace let her gaze drift to the placard set into the column below the statue. This particular Buddha was from northern China, near a town unknown to Grace. The red dot on the little map seemed incredibly far from her home in Hong Kong, a world away from where she stood now.

It had been a week since she arrived in San Francisco to stay with her uncle, but a lifetime since she held her father's hand in Victoria Park. Grace's eyes stung at the memory. She told herself it was from the staring contest and blinked away the tears as she read the Buddha's quote inscribed below the map.

Even death is not to be feared by one who has lived wisely.

Grace wondered if her parents lived wisely. She wondered if they were even still alive.

Her father said a million people were gathering in Victoria Park that day, the biggest protest Hong Kong had ever seen. When Grace was older and Hong Kong was independent, she could say she had been there. Her stepmother told him to stop saying such things aloud, that they shouldn't have come.

Her father shrugged and laughed. He took out his cell phone and held it at arm's length, mugging for the camera as they rode a wave of humanity into the park. Grace asked her stepmother why so many people were holding umbrellas.

When the tear gas canisters started falling like rain, she understood.

Now, standing in a museum half a world away, memory of the tear gas made her eyes sting all over again. The Buddha looked at her with infinite compassion, but that didn't make Grace feel any better. He still refused to blink.

Grace exited the gallery. She would conquer the Buddha another night.

She turned left and stepped onto a glass walkway, a translucent path to the escalator that would take her downstairs. To her right, a wall of glass rose seamlessly to fuse with a massive skylight supported by green copper bands. Grace imagined she was walking through a dragon's rib cage.

Through the glass was an outdoor patio one floor below on the roof of the adjacent building. Small tables had been arranged for an event tomorrow night. Umbrellas were set at regular intervals. At street level was Civic Center Plaza, a rectangular park at the center of the city, and beyond that, San Francisco City Hall. The building loomed over the park, its dome and spire illuminated in a soft red glow.

The red was new. Last night it had been blue. Grace figured the person in charge of lighting the building must change the color depending on their mood. She stood staring out the window, grateful for the distraction, cheeks crackly from drying tears.

An enormous shadow swept across the sky and eclipsed the dome. Grace recoiled from the window, thinking it was a giant bat. Maybe a dragon.

Then she heard the rotors.

A helicopter flew low across the square. Grace pressed her hands against the window to steady herself as the glass floor began to vibrate. The helicopter was matte black, flickering in and out of existence as Grace tried to track it against the night sky. It tilted suddenly, like someone rocking on their heels, and spun halfway around to approach the museum.

Grace realized it wasn't going to land in the park, it was angling for the patio directly below where she was standing. As the helicopter rotated sideways, Grace could see inside the cockpit.

The pilot stared back at her. He looked scared.

Grace called to her uncle as he bounded up the escalator holding a walkie-talkie in his left hand. Han waved her away from the window and grabbed her by the hand to drag her back inside the Hall of Buddhas. As they reached the threshold, Grace looked over her shoulder.

The body of the helicopter was spinning wildly. Something was wrong.

Grace felt her uncle's hand slip from hers as a metallic scream penetrated the glass, sounding almost human. The helicopter seemed to freeze in midair.

The pilot couldn't see the steel cable that ran from the top of the main building to the corner of the patio, but Grace could. It tore free of the building in an explosion of plaster as the helicopter blades bit into the cable. The frayed end wrapped around the main rotor shaft like a string on a spinning wooden top. The helicopter lurched sideways as the main rotors seized in place while the back rotor kept spinning.

Grace stood transfixed as calamity unfolded. Uncle Han grabbed her roughly by the shoulders and shoved her through the doorway. Grace slid across the marble floor as the helicopter crashed through the glass wall where she'd been standing.

She came to a halt near the column where the Buddha rested as glass shards flew like dragonflies, a thousand steel bolts screamed, and marble turned to shrapnel. She pressed her face to the floor and wrapped her arms around her head. Bits of stone pelted her hands and plaster fell across the floor like snow. She felt a sudden surge of heat and opened her eyes.

Smoke filled the room. Grace shouted her uncle's name but couldn't hear over the din. She scrambled to her feet and looked around. The broken tail of the helicopter dangled over the edge of the walkway.

The mangled cockpit squeezed into the gallery entrance. Flames were licking the floor.

The head of the Buddha lay on the floor. The tail rotor that beheaded the statue was embedded in the wall behind Grace. Blood was dripping from the blade.

Her uncle's body lay a few feet away. His head was nowhere in sight.

A scream caught in Grace's throat and she turned away, but what she saw then terrified her even more. Men silhouetted against the flames. Three shadows moving toward her.

Grace blinked smoke from her eyes and felt tears burning her cheeks, but she forced herself to look at her dead uncle. The only person she had known in this strange city.

Then she turned and ran.

2

The monkey ran along the top of the wall, its tail held high as it skirted the barbed wire and security cameras. It was a macaque, with gray fur encircling a round, pink face that was pinched and angry. Its yellow eyes were twin spotlights that tracked Wen with every step.

Wen suspected the monkey was following him but realized how paranoid that sounded. Besides, a menacing macaque was the least of his problems. He had tried to stay positive since arriving in Xinjiang, grateful he managed to smuggle his daughter, Grace, out of the country before he was arrested.

It had taken the police almost a week to round up all the protestors, matching surveillance footage with known addresses. Wen worried what Grace might do if he couldn't get word to her.

He compartmentalized all other feelings, especially for his wife. His last memory, his wife lying on the grass, eyes staring at nothing, blood streaming across her forehead from where the baton struck her temple. Wen lost sight of her when the riot police swarmed around her prone figure. That's when he threw Grace over his shoulder and started running.

Grace never saw her stepmother fall onto the grass at Victoria Park, but that didn't make it any easier to tell her what happened once they got home. His first wife dead from cancer, his second lying on the grass. Only his daughter safe, for now.

Wen felt his resolve fraying daily, terrified that Grace might leave San Francisco and return to China to find him. His worst nightmare was Grace being apprehended and sent here.

The northwest corner of Hell.

He marched along the wall, another worker in an endless line. None of them locals, all sent to Xinjiang for what the Central Committee euphemistically called vocational training and reeducation. Wen recalled newspapers in Hong Kong, articles written by the state news agency celebrating the region's poverty-alleviation programs like the factory where he worked now.

Eleven-hour shifts, six days a week. Building mobile phones.

If only he could make a call.

Each shift included two hours of supplemental training consisting of sitting in a classroom listening to lectures on the importance of national unity. One day, while a film was projected from the back of the room and the lights were dimmed, Wen noticed one of his fellow workers nodding off from exhaustion. By the time the lights came up, the man was snoring so loudly the other workers couldn't stop laughing.

Wen hadn't seen the man since. Other workers told Wen the man had simply been sent for personal instruction. They called it tutoring. It took a beat before Wen realized they meant torture.

Many of his fellow inmates were Turkic-speaking Uyghurs, Uzbeks, and Kazakhs from former Soviet states close to China's border. They communicated in broken Mandarin, the only language allowed and a mandatory part of their instruction.

Wen was surprised at the number of Chinese workers. Mainlanders, mostly, but some from Hong Kong. On his second day, Wen met an older man named Bohai who used to be a bookseller in Causeway Bay. They stayed close, taking comfort in being able to converse in Cantonese, if only out of earshot of the guards.

"What did you do," asked Bohai, "before you came here?"

"I teach art history at the university in Hong Kong." Wen wasn't ready to use the past tense to describe his life of a week ago. "But that's not why I'm here."

"No one knows why they're really here," replied Bohai. "But we have our suspicions."

"What are yours?"

"My customers' taste in literature veered westward," said Bohai. "Nabokov, Ayn Rand, Orwell, even Stan Lee. Comic books are wonderfully subversive." He smiled and shook his head. "When government officials started coming by the store, I should have packed up and moved to Taiwan. Instead, I removed the covers from party-approved books and used them to wrap my customers' favorite novels. It was only a matter of time before I wound up here."

"For how long?" Wen had asked.

Bohai held up his left arm to reveal a naked wrist. "There are no watches in purgatory."

Wen had to ask, "When did you stop counting the days?"

"Seventy-nine days ago." Bohai winked. "Do yourself a favor and stop asking dumb questions."

"I have a daughter."

"Then do her a favor," said Bohai, "and pray that she forgets all about you."

3

Grace remembered her father and what he had told her about fear. It helps you prioritize.

Her immediate priority was to become invisible. The three figures had emerged from the smoke and were getting closer. If she tried to reach the escalator, she would definitely be spotted.

If I can see them, they can see me.

Grace dropped to her stomach and swept her arms outward like a swimmer, propelling her body backward across the marble floor. She scooted twelve feet on her belly until she could squeeze behind the largest standing Buddha in the gallery.

The statue was from Thailand and once flanked the entrance of a temple damaged during the Burmese-Siamese war. Grace knew the history from having read the placard on her first night in the museum, but right now she cared more about its height than heritage. Six feet tall and three feet wide at the base, it was the best cover she could find.

Grace peered around the statue and saw the silhouettes take shape.

Three men, the first slightly built, the second short and stocky. As the smoke dissipated, Grace could see they were

Chinese. Both were dressed in loose-fitting, black coveralls. They paused in their advance and glanced at the figure on their left, as if awaiting orders.

The third man was still a shadow, tall and ephemeral. Wrapped in tendrils of smoke, as if the fog had accompanied him inside. Grace craned her neck to get a clearer angle, but the figure blurred as wind poured through the broken window.

Someone was yelling.

Cries mixed with the moaning wind and metallic groans from the shattered face of the building. A human voice clearly discernible and impossible to ignore. The three intruders turned toward the broken shell of the helicopter, and Grace edged her way around the statue.

Grace would have to get closer to exit the gallery and reach the main hall, then slip down the escalator before the men turned around. She hoped that once she reached the escalator, she was small enough to keep her head below the railing and not be seen.

Grace took a deep breath and scampered in a crouch until she reached the arched door of the gallery. Cold air swirled around the hallway as the smoke cleared.

Grace got her first good look at the third man and felt a sudden chill.

He was dressed all in white, pants loose in the leg but tight at the ankles, sleeves long and open. What struck Grace most was his hair, long and flowing, pale as the moon. He extended a hand toward the man on his left, and Grace glimpsed the bone-white skin of his arm and the gaunt fingers devoid of color.

Guǐ.

A ghost. The word came unbidden, and Grace stood, frozen, as she realized the screams were coming from inside the cockpit of the helicopter.

Someone was trapped. Her brain told Grace to run, this was her chance.

Her feet were more stubborn.

Being closer to the gallery than the escalator on her left, Grace knew she was exposed, but the shouts were an undertow pulling at her conscience. She inched forward to get a better look as the wind shredded the last of the fog and smoke.

The pilot was pinned in the cockpit, his legs trapped under the flight console.

The cockpit was a broken eggshell, the windscreen cracked, the aluminum doors mashed like a discarded can of soda. A translucent panel separated the pilot from the main cabin of the helicopter, which was surprisingly intact. Wooden crates of various sizes filled the cramped space near the passenger seats.

The pilot was louder and more insistent, but Grace couldn't make out any of the words. An angry blend of Russian, English, and something else. She saw a ruddy face with angular features, short black hair, and a long, sharp nose. Spittle flew from the corners of a wide mouth as the man shouted at his former passengers.

It was a face twisted by fear, and Grace could see why.

The ghost took a short cylinder from the man to his left. With a movement as graceful as a ballet dancer, he bent both legs and swept his left arm in a broad arc, striking the tip of the tube against the floor. The road flare sputtered to life. The flame was red, orange, and angry.

The ghost shrugged in apology, then tossed the flare underhand at the helicopter.

The fiery baton spun end over end before landing at the edge of the wreckage, where a thin trickle of fuel ran across the marble floor.

Shouts turned to screams as the pilot convulsed in a frantic effort to free his broken legs. He strained to reach the flare, slapping his nearest arm repeatedly against the mangled door, as a river of blue fire ran straight at him.

The stocky man threw a second flare. It landed among the wooden crates and turned the cockpit into a crematorium. The roar of the flames muffled the last of the pilot's screams.

Smoke poured from the broken body of the helicopter like a fleeing soul.

Grace gasped and took a shaky breath, tasted salt and realized she was crying again. She bit down on her lip and forced her legs to move. As she began to turn away from the inferno, she heard sirens. The ghost said something to his companions, and Grace saw them shift their weight and adjust their stances.

She wasn't going to make it. She stood in no-man's-land, between the gallery and the escalator. Grace dashed back to the gallery as the three men turned their backs on their victim.

She would hide until they left, then she would run. As far and as fast as she could.

She didn't expect them to head for the gallery where she was hiding.

Grace willed herself to become invisible and wished she was four again, when closing your eyes made the monsters go away. Her guardian Buddha was in the middle of the hall, so her back was exposed if they came into the heart of the exhibit. She remained in a crouch in case she needed to run. Between her hiding spot and the exit was an uneven forest of pedestals and tables displaying other Buddhas of various sizes.

The ghost walked directly toward the first pedestal after the entrance, which held a sitting Buddha about fifteen inches tall and ten inches wide.

Grace knew this statue. It was the first artifact her uncle had shown her the night she slept in the museum for the first time. A patina of gold covered a bronze figure that looked not only serene but mischievous, as if Buddha was keeping a secret. It was the oldest Buddha in the gallery. Her uncle said it was priceless, then smiled and looked around at the other statues, reminding her they all were. Then he put a hand on the side of her face and told her even the oldest statue in the museum wasn't as precious as family.

The ghost extended his pale arms and lifted the Buddha unceremoniously from the table. As he turned to hand it over to his men, his eyes swept the room. Grace was too slow, and too curious, to stay hidden.

Before she could shrink behind the column, the eyes of the ghost found her. His eyes were bloodred. His features were Asian, his face long and elegant, his skin bleached parchment, so pale he seemed to glow.

Grace vaulted from her hiding spot like an Olympic sprinter.

The two men in black were slow to react, the shorter one careful to not drop the Buddha. Grace cut diagonally across the gallery and crossed the threshold before they took a single step. She kept her head down and made it halfway to the escalator before she spared a glance over her shoulder.

The helicopter burned like a funeral pyre, and directly behind her, the ghost was walking after her. Walking, not running. As if she could never hope to escape.

Grace closed the distance to the escalator and went into a slide, letting her legs skid across the floor until she reached the top step. She scampered down, skipping steps whenever she could, heart pounding.

When she reached the bottom, she spun on her heel to look up the escalator. The ghost stood at the top, making no attempt to ride down the steps. Grace kept moving backward toward the main entrance without taking her eyes off him. As she neared the main doors, the pitch of the sirens got higher.

Police would arrive any minute, but Grace wasn't going to wait to be rescued. She would save herself. Grace stared at the ghost, who was watching her like a cat tracking a mouse. When their eyes met, he smiled and waved.

For the second time that night, Grace turned and ran.

She spun through the revolving door and leapt down the steps two at a time. She hit the street and sprinted into the darkness of a sleeping city. It was a city she didn't know, but it was also a city that didn't know her.

Grace hoped that made it the perfect place to get lost.

4

Sally almost lost the man she was hunting when he took a sudden right turn and cut across Jackson Street. She ran along the rooftops of San Francisco, tracking her quarry between buildings.

She had followed him from the moment he exited the bar on Stockton Street, a tourist dive where over a dozen women had been drugged. Weeks of surveillance eliminated most of the likely suspects after Sally spent countless hours in clubs drinking watered-down cocktails and declining invitations to dance.

She knew it could be anyone. One in five women living in San Francisco will be drugged by a stranger, or by her date, by the time she turns thirty. One in ten for men. It was a nightly occurrence almost impossible to track, but recently there had been a disturbing spike at Chinatown bars.

Rumors spread from emergency rooms and twenty-four-hour clinics, stories of women carried by friends who thought too much alcohol or something recreational had made them tipsy. They were the lucky ones, women whose friends stayed close when their knees started to buckle. Few would come forward because most couldn't remember what happened.

Sally suspected a lone actor who got a taste for control. A fetish became an addiction.

Young drinkers traveled in packs, and half their friends were digital acquaintances, so victims often assumed a new face at the bar was simply a friend of a friend. Sally could only search for a pattern.

Bartenders' descriptions were consistent with women's fractured and half-remembered tales. Male, early thirties, with short black hair and close-cropped beard. Nice clothes. Someone who worked in an office, good salary, nice watch. Athletic, with a great smile and perfect teeth.

Sally knew she could never catch all the men spiking drinks, but she'd settle for this one. No one knew his name, but Sally knew he looked an awful lot like the man she was tailing.

Her business partner, Cape Weathers, would have approached this very differently. As a private detective, Cape worked the streets more than rooftops. Gathering evidence, building a case to hand over to the police. Cape might bend the law, but he didn't disregard it entirely.

Sally had been raised in a school run by the Hong Kong Triads, where lessons included reading, writing, and killing with your hands. She had a code but wasn't big on laws. And the day she arrived in this city, Sally had made a promise to herself.

As long as she lived in Chinatown, she would keep it safe.

Cape was working a case of insurance fraud, straightforward and boring. No need for a trained assassin, so Sally had time on her hands. Maybe not time to kill, but enough to stir up trouble.

Sally waited for a passing car to mask any noise as she leapt from the roof to the fire escape. Though only five feet tall and as lithe as a gymnast, she didn't want the groan of rusty bolts to give her away. She hopped from one landing to the next until she reached the lowest platform, where a ladder was suspended eight feet above the ground. Sally bypassed the ladder and did a somersault over the railing. She landed on the sidewalk in a crouch as her target strolled east on Stone Street. Sally closed the gap, blending into the shadows as he turned down Washington. She waited until he passed the Chinese Independent Baptist Church, a modernist building of white stone with a twenty-foot cross cut into the facade. The perpendicular lines etched into the stone foreshadowed the intersection up ahead, which gave Sally an epiphany.

She knew where this guy was heading.

The Li Po cocktail lounge was a Chinatown fixture, famous for mai tais and popular with locals and tourists. The club stayed open late, and the hidden bar downstairs remained open even later. Sally guessed her predator wouldn't risk getting trapped in the basement, but at this hour plenty of twentysomethings and college students with fake IDs would be crowding the bar upstairs. If the guy had struck out earlier, Li Po was a good place for a nightcap attempt.

The street was quiet. A lone streetlight was a poor sentry against the darkness. A few feet beyond the light was a garbage dumpster, and set back from the curb, a residential building which must be the source of the trash. This street opened onto a wider avenue at the corner, which meant more lights, cars, and late-night revelers. Assuming this was the right guy, Sally would have to wait until he made another attempt in the bar. Unless she forced an encounter.

Take him now.

Sally could hear the man whistling as she closed the distance. She had spent her childhood learning to become invisible, and the sound of her footfalls was as absent as her shadow. She matched his pace and stayed close.

He was almost a head taller than Sally. His topcoat looked very expensive.

"Hey, sailor."

It was something Sally would never say in a million years, which made her want to say it all the more. The man turned, startled, a look of irritation evaporating as he got a better look. Even dressed for concealment, Sally was striking. Green eyes set wide in a face that blended East and West, long hair braided and draped over her shoulder like an ebony scarf.

Testosterone took over, and the man squared his shoulders to assert his height, then ran a hand through his hair to conjure his charm. His lips parted in a tentative smile as his brain scanned a vintage catalog of opening lines.

Sally had to admit the rumors were true. This asshole had perfect teeth.

Her right arm shot forward, wrist perpendicular so the heel of her hand struck his sternum at an upward angle. She aimed for the xiphoid process, the point where cartilage fuses the rib cage, directly above the diaphragm. Too gentle, and she would knock him on his ass, but too hard and the cartilage would shatter, shards flying into his heart and lungs.

Sally tried for the Goldilocks hit, a short punch, arm snapping like a piston. The goal was knock him down, knock the wind out of him, and knock that smile off his face. It did all three.

A trifecta of nonlethal violence.

Prince Charming landed on the sidewalk like a frog. A look of shock appeared, his eyes watering as a thick, whistling sound emanated from deep in his chest. Sally bent down and reached under his topcoat. She rummaged through his jacket pockets and wondered idly if perhaps she had hit him too hard.

When she found the glass vials, Sally decided she hadn't hit him hard enough.

There were three small tubes the size of perfume samplers given out at department stores. Sally guessed they contained GHB, liquid ecstasy, or another drug like Ambien or scopolamine. The original date-rape drug, Rohypnol or roofies, had lost market share to more potent synthetics. Overdose wasn't a concern as long as you thought of your victim as a piece of meat in a dress.

The handsome stranger gaped like a koi fish and sucked in air.

He appeared incapacitated, but Sally learned at a young age to take nothing for granted. Crouching so her shoulders were level with his, she shaped the fingers of her right hand into a flat blade and struck his left shoulder at a point just beside the collarbone. He wheezed like a broken accordion as his shoulder slumped, eyes wide, then Sally shifted the vials to her right hand and performed an identical strike against his other arm.

For the next five minutes his arms would feel like overcooked pasta.

Sally brought her left hand behind his head and clutched his hair, almost gently, and pulled him to his feet. She figured one dose would do the trick. Guiding him along the sidewalk, Sally turned his head like a joystick to steer him over to the dumpster. She scanned the windows of the apartment building, but lights were dim and curtains were drawn.

"Bottoms up." Sally pulled his head back and thumbed the top off one of the vials. Poured the contents down his throat, shaking the vial to make sure he got the full dose. "You probably won't remember much after this, but hopefully you'll remember me."

The man gargled something that sounded to Sally like thank you, but that was probably her imagination. Maybe profanity was involved and gratitude wasn't on the tip of his tongue.

"Sweet dreams." Sally patted him on the cheek and slipped the remaining vials into his pocket. When the police got the call, they would find him in possession. Guilty as found, soon to be charged.

Sally widened her stance, dropped a shoulder and, with an effort, hoisted him onto her back just long enough to roll him into the dumpster.

He landed in a fetid jumble of garbage bags and corrugated cardboard, his expression a dreamy look of panic, pupils dilated and a thin line of drool running down his cheek. In the wan light of the dumpster, his lips parted as if he was about to say something in his defense. His perfect teeth gleamed like a perfect lie.

Sally brushed her hands together like someone who just finished a household chore.

I love taking out the trash.

The sun would be making an appearance soon. There was a building with a fire escape only a block away, and she could make better time across the rooftops. She strolled past the streetlamp toward the main intersection, the shadows welcoming her like an old friend.

Sally heard the footsteps as soon as she reached the corner.

Someone running, out of breath. Not a late-night jogger, the footfalls were too uneven and hard, shoes smacking against concrete. Sally stood and listened a moment longer. Someone running from something, with no destination beyond escape.

Sally reached the corner in time to see a young Chinese girl sprinting toward her.

Maybe she doesn't see me.

Sally braced herself as she realized the girl was accelerating. Whatever might be chasing this girl made Sally look like a safe alternative. That was a new feeling to examine later. Sally caught the girl in her arms and lifted her off the sidewalk.

The girl's legs kept kicking as if she was too afraid to stop running. Sally held tight until the feet stopped, then lowered the girl onto the ground.

Arms locked around Sally's waist as the girl's face buried against her chest. Sally could feel a heart beating at twice the rate of her own. She gave the girl a squeeze.

It was the first hug Sally had given to anyone since she was five.

A stream of words poured from the girl in a torrent of English and Cantonese. Sally spoke both fluently, but the verbal waterfall was beyond translation. She waited until the girl ran out of breath, then untangled her arms and took a small step backward until their eyes met.

Neither one of them blinked. After a long moment, the girl inhaled and tried again.

"I saw a ghost," said Grace.

5

"A ghost."

Cape Weathers looked both skeptical and open-minded, which wasn't easy. Being inscrutable was one of the few things that made him qualified to be a private investigator.

Being stubborn didn't hurt.

Cape glanced at Sally. "Maybe we should call the police and tell them to be on the lookout for Jacob Marley...or Beetlejuice."

"I believe her," said Sally.

"Never said I didn't." Cape behind his desk in a chair that was more tragicomic than ergonomic. Scarred leather on a wooden frame, wheels that squeaked every time he rolled back and forth across the hardwood floor, which he did incessantly.

Grace sat in one of the client chairs with no wheels. Sally leaned against a bookshelf that ran the length of the wall. The early morning sun struggled to penetrate the fog and break through the window at the back of the office.

Grace looked over her shoulder at Sally and said something in Cantonese.

"No police." Sally shifted her gaze to Cape. "We need a plan B."

"She can't go back to her uncle's apartment," said Cape.

"The thieves might have checked his wallet for an address." He watched the girl's reaction at the mention of her uncle. She was remarkably stoic, a frisson of fear passing over her face as fleetingly as a cloud.

Sally locked eyes with Grace, which seemed to instill instant calm.

Cape reminded himself how young Grace was and made a mental note to refrain from thinking out loud about all the dreadful, horrible, unimaginable things that might happen. He would be neurotic on his own time.

"A friend of her father got her into the country on a charter flight from Hong Kong," said Sally, "but we don't know if she's got a visa or was smuggled in under a false name."

"We can check that without making waves." Cape stared at the ceiling. "That's the least of our troubles."

Sally nodded. With the uncle dead, Grace had no sponsor or legal tether to the country.

After Grace ran into her hours before, Sally got her to stop hyperventilating and took her to an all-night diner. Sally wasn't inclined to call the police, so she called Cape and woke him up, then asked to meet at his office. Now the only man Sally truly trusted was half-awake behind his desk, tracing the cracks in the ceiling as he replayed the story in his head.

The normalcy of the diner had been jarring. Sally wanted to shock Grace into recounting the robbery as if it were a bad dream fading with the rising sun. A stack of pancakes and a chocolate shake can distract even the most traumatized kid for a few minutes. That was all the time Sally needed.

People bustled in and out of the diner. Executives getting a head start, factory workers from the night shift, waiters and waitresses smiling, grabbing plates, and accepting tips. Normal people doing mundane things. No air of menace, no apparitions coming through the window. The more chocolate she gulped, the less Grace frowned, and eventually she told Sally everything. Sally listened without interrupting, then ordered more food and had Grace tell it all over again.

After the third retelling, and the second shake, Sally brought her to Cape.

Cape rolled back and forth, watching Grace, trying to phrase his next question carefully. Grace had been studying the office, eyeballing the books and glancing at the worn leather couch. She scrutinized the clutter on the desk.

"Are you really a private detective?"

Cape stopped rolling and tried to look professional. "Yes."

"Do you have a magnifying glass?"

"Like Sherlock?"

Grace nodded.

"I used to." Cape searched his desk. "I might have lost it."

"Aren't you supposed to find things?" asked Grace. "And not lose them?"

"I'm better at finding people than things," said Cape. "Always have been."

Grace seemed to give his answer the consideration it deserved. "Could you find a ghost?"

Cape glanced at Sally, whose mouth twitched at the corner, a half smile of recognition at the girl's grit. Most people would ask to run away, but this kid was asking if they could hunt down the men who killed her uncle.

"Grace, do you have any money?" asked Sally.

Grace was nonplussed, but after a moment scrounged in the right pocket of her pants and found some cash. A ten, five, and two singles, plus two quarters. The money her uncle had given her for snacks, or in case she ever needed to take a cab to the apartment.

"Give him the fifty cents," said Sally.

Brow furrowed, Grace placed two quarters on the desk in front of Cape.

Cape looked into her eyes as he picked up the coins, wanting Grace to know he was taking this seriously. He took one of the quarters and, using his thumb and forefinger, launched it at Sally in a spinning arc. Light broke through the window and hit the coin in mid-flight. Reflections danced across the shelves like a drunken fairy.

Sally caught the quarter in her right hand and slipped it into a pocket.

"You are now our client," said Cape.

"Which means we have to do whatever you ask," said Sally.

"That is not what it means." Cape frowned. He had fired more than a few clients over the years, but he wasn't about to dump an eleven-year-old. And if he did, Sally would kill him.

"Then what does it mean?" asked Grace.

"It means I'm going to visit a museum," said Cape.

6

The museum was a circus.

The fire truck painted the surrounding buildings red and white with its lights. Staccato flashes lit the morning fog from below, turning the amorphous gray ceiling into a festive tent. Cape searched the scene for peanuts and pachyderms, but all he saw were police.

Two patrol cars, one unmarked sedan, and a fire truck.

This wasn't the first time Cape had visited the Asian Art Museum, but the helicopter dangling from the front window was definitely a new addition. Smoke rose listlessly from a twisted fuselage. The blaze must have been extinguished a short while earlier because the fire crew stood idly by the truck, smoking cigarettes and talking among themselves.

Cape approached across Civic Center Plaza, having parked illegally on Polk Street, tight against another vehicle, a red Mini Cooper facing out from the curb. It hadn't been towed, and with none of the government offices open this early, he figured his chances of getting a ticket were slim.

He crossed the broad park that separated city hall from the museum and headed toward Larkin Street, sidestepping fecal hazards along the way. Cape counted eighteen tents and forty homeless people sleeping or sitting on the grass by the time he reached the middle of the square. One woman nursed a baby, ten feet from a man with his head pressed into the grass and ass in the air like an ostrich hoping this would all go away. Cape wondered if the mayor's office overlooked the park, or if he worked from his house in Napa Valley. More likely, all the city officials simply kept their blinds drawn.

The walkway was flanked by long benches on either side. Cape noticed a pile of clothes on the bench to his left. Brown and black fabric intertwined with swaths of blue denim, a torn beige sheet and a frayed green blanket. The rags moved and Cape realized there was a man underneath, as shapeless as his camouflage. Brown eyes tracked Cape with a haunted hunger.

Cape looked across the road at the museum stairs. The morning sun had punched a few holes in the fog, spotlights of warmth on a cold tableau. The officers on the steps gravitated toward the shafts of light, subconsciously aware they stood on a public stage.

Cape recognized one of the cops and breathed a sigh of relief.

Beauregard Jones was half a head taller than everyone in his vicinity. As a senior inspector in the Robbery and Homicide Division, Beau wouldn't be here if Grace's story didn't hold some truth. Something was stolen or someone was dead. Maybe both.

Dispatch wouldn't wake up Beau for a helicopter crash.

The helicopter was only recognizable by the bulbous shape of its shattered cockpit and a single rotor, bent back on itself like a paper clip. The tail jutted from the concrete at an impossible angle as if it wasn't a part of the same helicopter. Cape used his phone to take a photo, then zoomed in on the fuselage and took another.

He glanced toward the bench on his left, then looked across the street at the wreckage.

That must have made one hell of a bang.

Locking eyes with the man on the bench, Cape took a slow step in his direction. The mound of clothes contracted, muscles coiling before a jump. Cape did the least threatening thing he could think of—he sat down on the grass next to the bench. The man studied him for a long minute. Cape held his gaze, letting the man know he was visible, acknowledging that so many passed this bench without sparing a glance.

"You were here last night," said Cape. Matter-of-fact, not a question.

The man's voice was a baritone wheeze. "I live here."

Cape jerked his chin at the museum. "Must have woken you up."

The layers of fabric swayed in dissent, the eyes impatient. "Don't sleep at night. S'when I gather, find stuff. Get my fix."

Fix. Cape thought about the irony of the expression and wondered how this man got broken in the first place. He could have been an athlete with a torn Achilles, or a stockbroker with a bad back. A construction worker with a torn meniscus. A few weeks on OxyContin turned into a few months before the insurance company started asking questions or the money ran out, at which point shooting heroin became the fiscally responsible choice, like going to Costco for paper towels.

Buy more for less, until you realize that more is never enough.

"Mornings for sleep, but not today." The fabric rippled. "Too many sirens."

"You talk to the cops?"

"I'm talkin' to you."

"I'm not a cop," said Cape.

"Cops don't see me," said the man. "S'what are you?"

"I'm...curious."

"That'll get you killed." The man's eyes ducked below the

covers. "Killed the cat." There was a rustling before he asked, "You got nine lives?"

Cape shook his head. "Just the one."

"Was kinda hoping you had one to spare."

"Sorry."

"What else you got?"

"A question."

"Am I s'pposed to do with a question?"

"Up to you," said Cape. "What's your name?"

"Not tellin'."

"Mine's Cape."

"Funny name."

"Yeah." Cape looked toward the steps, where Beau was talking to a woman Cape didn't recognize. Tall, with dark hair running down her back. Too well-dressed for the department, too stylish for a reporter. Animated, talking so close that Beau took a step backward and held up his hands. She advanced as he shook his head and pointed at the museum doors.

Cape turned to the bench and tried again.

"After the crash, what did you see?"

"Frank."

"What?"

"M'name's Frank," said the man as his face reemerged. "Don't use it much, but it's still mine."

"Nice to meet you, Frank."

"Is it?"

Before Cape could answer, Frank said, "Heard the bang, then the boom."

Cape waited.

"Screams." Frank's deep vibrato faltered. "Then quiet, 'cept for the crackling of the fire."

Cape shifted on the grass but didn't say anything.

"Then the girl."

Cape sat up straighter.

"Little girl, down the steps 'n into the dark."

"What did she look like?"

"Kid was fast," said Frank.

"Who else?" Cape saw a flicker in the eyes and pressed. "Who else did you see, Frank?"

Frank withdrew into his cloth cave. Cape was talking to a shapeless pile, someone's dirty laundry thrown onto a bench. No face, no fingers, no toes. No sign Frank had ever been there.

Cape rose, his right knee crunching and popping like Rice Krispies. He opened his wallet, removed all the bills, and laid them gently on the corner of the bench. A hand scuttled into the daylight, and the money disappeared into the cave.

Cape knew cash wasn't the answer either of them needed, but it was all he had to give. He was six feet closer to the street, his back to the bench, when Frank's voice caught up to him.

"Three of 'em."

Cape turned, took a step back. "Three men?"

"Two men." The wheeze downshifted to a whisper. "And a ghost."

Grace doesn't have an overly active imagination after all.

"These men," said Cape, "did they run after the girl?"

"Went the other way." Frank shook his head. "Didn't run and didn't walk."

"They drove?" Cape chewed on a contingency plan, a stashed car nearby.

"They got picked up," said Frank, "in a limo."

Cape looked east on Larkin Street and ran the probabilities. If they kept going straight, they might end up in Russian Hill or veer left across the Golden Gate to wine country or the mansions of Marin. A hard left meant Golden Gate Park and the beach, a U-turn meant the Mission District.

Cape considered the contents of the museum and the value of a stolen Buddha. They could be anywhere, but he had to start somewhere. Drive a few blocks north and then take a right on Bush Street, and very soon you're passing through the Dragon Gate into Chinatown.

It was time to cross the yellow tape and see if the police had anything to share.

After that, Cape knew where he was going.

7

"Where are we going?"

"Home," replied Sally.

"My uncle lives near Chinatown," said Grace.

Sally caught the present tense and let it go. Her own parents had died when she was five, but she often felt they were still with her. Grace could get there on her own schedule.

"I live in Chinatown," said Sally.

"Is it safe?"

"You decide when we get there."

They passed through the Dragon Gate on Bush Street, then past lanterns strung across Grant before turning right and then left, then right again. Grace looked around in an attempt to get her bearings, clearly new to the back alleys and shortcuts.

Chinatown covered over twenty-four city blocks, the most densely populated urban area west of Manhattan. Sally deliberately took a byzantine path, glancing at store windows to check their reflection and make sure they weren't being followed. She walked quickly but not hurriedly, a stride that gobbled up sidewalks.

They circled back to Stockton and paused in front of New Luen Sing Fish Market.

Grace wrinkled her nose at the scent of seafood, which took her back to Lei Yu Mun fish market in Hong Kong and shopping trips with her parents. She resisted the riptide of memory and the urge to cry, fearful she would melt into the sidewalk, a puddle of tears flowing down the drain, straight to the ocean until it found its way home.

Grace blinked rapidly and tried to focus on what Sally was saying.

Sally was speaking Cantonese to an old woman sitting on a folding chair. The woman's skin was dark and wrinkled from sitting in the sun all day, wrinkled canyons cut deep across her forehead. Her eyes were mischievous but warm, and her hands were animated as she gestured at rows of plastic containers on shelves, buckets on the floor, and circular tanks on tables. Each held an aquatic menagerie of edible creatures. Octopus, shrimp, frogs, and sea cucumbers.

Tilapia swam in circles, their motion hypnotic. Grace found it oddly soothing.

"What's good today, Āyí?" asked Sally.

The old woman glanced across the street. "Everything is good today, Little Dragon." Her gaze shifted to Grace. "Hold out your hands."

Grace looked at Sally, who nodded. The old woman reached behind her chair and grabbed something from a low shelf. The woman's wrinkled fingers danced over Grace's open palms, a gentle rain of color falling.

Ten candies, brightly wrapped. The woman pointed at each in succession. "These are pineapple, those orange. Plum...apricot...and strawberry." She pointed at two bright blue wrappers. "I've never figured out what flavor that is, so you'll have to tell me later."

"Xièxiè," said Grace, with a respectful nod.

"This is Grace," said Sally. "She's a friend."

"I am Rushi," said the old woman. "Any friend of Xiǎolóng has a friend in me."

"Thank you, Aunty," said Sally. "May you live as long as the southern mountain."

Rushi laughed, a sharp cackle. "I'm already much older than any mountain."

"And for that I am very grateful."

With a gentle tap on the shoulder, Sally turned Grace around and guided her across the street. Next to a grocery, an open stairway led to the top floor of the building. They climbed the stairs silently until Grace came to a breathless stop on the broad landing.

"That woman," said Grace.

"Rushi."

"Yes…she said everything was good, but you didn't buy anything."

Sally considered telling Grace the old woman was speaking in code. With a simple greeting, Rushi informed Sally that no one was watching her apartment or waiting upstairs.

Sally decided it could wait. Grace clearly wasn't done asking questions.

"She called you Little Dragon."

"It's a nickname from when I was a child," said Sally. "At school."

"Where did you grow up?"

"Hong Kong," said Sally. "Like you."

Not like her. Grace was probably studying art. Not the art of war.

Grace looked around the landing. "Why did you leave?"

"I'll tell you about it later," said Sally, "after you help me get inside."

Directly in front of them was a wooden wall, a massive pocket door that ran the length of the landing. The heavy teak surface was scarred, hairline cracks in the wood closest to the right wall. The door was divided into six panels, three across the top and three on the bottom.

Grace wondered how heavy it was and noticed there wasn't a handle. As she studied the door, the grain, knots, and patterns in the wood took on the form of faces and figures, bodies swirling around each other in combat. Demons' faces leered at rival warriors in a war that no one could win because this battle, petrified in the wood, would never end.

Sally stepped to the second panel along the top and pressed her thumb against a knot that resembled the frowning face of an old woman. Sally flexed her hand, extending her index and pinky fingers until they rested pressed against two other twisting figures.

Grace heard a loud click as a section of the lower right panel recessed into the door. The recess was a square hole big enough for a hand.

"Reach inside and grab that handle," said Sally. "Turn it clockwise."

Grace knelt in front of the square opening and peered inside. A brass handle was connected to an elaborate mechanism, steel gears resembling the inside of a bank vault. Grace gripped the handle and looked at Sally.

"Clockwise?"

Sally nodded.

Grace twisted the handle one complete turn. The door unlatched from the wall and shifted three inches to the left, leaving enough space for Sally to insert her hand and push it sideways.

The door was perfectly balanced and didn't require much effort to move. It slid inside the left wall with a clack, revealing a Japanese-style shoji screen in front of them. A door consisting of a simple wooden frame with panels of translucent paper instead of glass.

Sally slid the screen aside and led Grace inside a vast loft.

"What would have happened if I turned the handle counterclockwise?"

Sally gave Grace an appraising glance. "Most people wouldn't have asked that question."

"I'm curious."

"Clearly." Sally stepped back onto the landing and pointed at a narrow rectangle outlined against the ceiling. "Weighted nets fall onto anyone standing here, and then..." She indicated a column of holes in the wall spaced four inches apart. Each was half an inch in diameter. "...tranquilizer darts shoot from the wall."

Grace's eyes doubled in size. "What is your job?"

"I'm a teacher."

"What do you—" Grace stopped short as she stepped into the loft. The space was enormous, hardwood floors and exposed beams overhead. Racks lined every wall—collections of wooden swords, face masks, body armor, gloves, and other practice equipment. Some displayed recurve bows and quivers of arrows, Japanese katanas, and Chinese jian swords which gleamed in the dim light. "—teach?"

"Philosophy," said Sally.

Grace started as she felt something brush against her legs.

A cat looked up at her, tail raised. Grace dropped to her knees.

The cat was entirely black save for a white streak along its right foreleg. Its green eyes were expectant, and Grace held out her right hand and tentatively scratched behind its ears. A deep purring filled the room.

"Does he belong to you?"

"Of course not," said Sally. "He's a cat."

Grace sat on the floor, and the cat climbed into her lap. "What's his name?"

"I haven't asked."

Grace looked at the streak on the cat's leg, a jagged scar covered by fur that had lost its pigment. "This looks like lightning."

Sally glanced from the cat to the young girl, hearing echoes from her own childhood. "I had a teacher with a scar like that."

"What was his name?"

"I'll tell you another time." Sally extended a hand to help Grace stand. The cat hopped from her lap and padded across the floor. "We need to rest."

"I'm not tired."

"That's what tired people always say," said Sally. "Come, I'll make us tea."

They passed from the main room into a short T-shaped hallway with doors on the right and left. Sally turned right to open another shoji screen which revealed a small chamber whose floor was covered in tatami mats. A low table sat in the center of the room, and a small kitchenette was visible through an adjoining door.

"Sit."

Grace sat by the table as Sally took a cast-iron kettle from a shelf near the sink. Soon the rich aroma of matcha filled the air along with the familiar sound of a whisk. The rhythmic *swish swish* was hypnotic, and Grace felt herself falling through time.

Her father carried Grace over his shoulder to her bedroom, her head resting in the crook of his neck. She could feel him breathing in time with her. Grace wondered how she could be so light that he could carry her and yet feel so heavy at the same time.

Sally laid Grace on the small bed in the last room at the end of the hall. She brushed the girl's hair away from her eyes and pulled the covers over her legs. The cat snuck into the room and climbed onto the low mattress, then circled around before finding the perfect spot near Grace's head, where it curled into a ball and started purring.

Sally remembered the simple wooden cot she had at Grace's age. Her roommates sleeping only a few feet away. Classes began at dawn and instructors kept them training into the night.

Lessons that lasted a lifetime. Scars that would never heal.

Sally had been up all night but felt restless. She poured herself a cup of tea and brought it to her room. A long sword that looked like a spear was mounted on the wall above her bed. It was a *naginata*, a cavalry weapon eight hundred years old.

Sally sat cross-legged beneath the sword and drank her green tea, its sharp bite a bitter taste of memory. She pulled the layers of Grace's story apart again and again. She was looking for the ghost, but he disappeared before she could see him clearly.

Rumors and whispers from her days in Hong Kong clouded her memory and obscured her vision. She knew the answers were hidden in the shadows of the museum.

Sally wondered what Cape was doing to find them.

8

"What do you think you're doing?"

The uniformed policeman spotted Cape as he ducked under the yellow tape. The officer was too far away to stop him. Cape deliberately picked a spot in the perimeter guarded by the greenest-looking cop, and without breaking stride flipped open his wallet to flash his license. He snapped it closed with a wave that he hoped was both assertive and reassuring.

Cape climbed the stairs two at a time, hoping the rookie might conclude he was with the Feds. Halfway up the steps, Beau spotted him and scowled.

Cape wondered if his old friend would wave him up the stairs or arrest him. With a look of exasperation, Beau gestured for Cape to join the circus.

Beau said something to a uniformed cop nearby. The officer hurried to the top of the stairs and pulled another patrolman from the door before going inside the museum. Now the only person next to Beau was the woman Cape had seen from across the street.

Cape didn't recognize her and definitely would have remembered if they'd met before. She was probably five-six but was close to five-nine in a pair of boots that looked both elegant and dangerous. The heels could definitely be weaponized. Her profile was a smooth line with gentle curves. The rest of her clothes looked like the national debt put to good use.

Her skin was olive, eyes chocolate, her hair a blend of caramel and licorice. Cape couldn't decide between cherry or strawberry for the lips and realized he was getting distracted. Either way, Willy Wonka would approve.

She was half a head shorter than Beau but had him on his heels. Very few people could get Beau to take a step back, which he did as Cape joined them.

Beau gave him a considered look before glancing at his watch. "You're up early."

Cape pointed at the flexi-straw tail of the wrecked helicopter. "I wanted to see the new exhibit."

"Museum's closed." Beau tilted his head toward his visitor. "I was just explaining that to—"

"Isabella Maria Diaz y Angelos." She extended a hand as her eyes gave Cape a head-to-toe appraisal. Her voice was deeper than he'd expected, and the way she said her name suggested her Spanish was much better than his. "Call me Maria."

"Cape." He shook, noticing the callouses on her thumb and forefinger. "I'm a p—"

"—pain in the ass," said Beau. "And a private investigator."

"I thought we were friends."

"That we are," said Beau. "Which is why you're standing on this side of the yellow tape."

"My supervisor calls me that all the time," said Maria. "He says I'm a stone in his shoe."

Beau held up a hand. "Turns out Ms. Diaz—"

"—Maria."

"—*Maria* came all the way from Spain," said Beau, "to visit the museum on official business. Except it's not official—"

"—yet—"

"—because her supervisor put her on an unpaid leave of absence."

"A vacation," said Maria.

"She works for Interpol."

"Cultural heritage crime division," said Maria.

"Art heists." Beau jerked a thumb over his shoulder. "Except nothing was stolen."

"*Mierda*," said Maria. "I assure you, something was stolen."

"Someone was killed," replied Beau.

"A Buddha," said Cape. "And a security guard?"

Maria and Beau both stepped sideways to stare at Cape, who shrugged.

"Just a hunch."

Beau did the math. "You have a client."

"No comment."

"My ass," said Beau. "Why else would you be here...at this hour?"

"I'm an art lover."

"Uh-huh." Beau gestured past the security tape at a van from one of the local television stations. "Even the press doesn't know anything—they just think a helicopter crashed."

"It looks like they're right."

"What did happen inside the museum?" asked Maria.

"Maybe we should go inside and find out," said Cape.

Maria smiled. "What a good idea."

"You are not going inside," said Beau. "Neither one of you. The medical examiner just got started on the bodies."

"Bodies," said Maria. "was that plural?"

"I forgot about the pilot," muttered Cape.

"Dammit," said Beau. "Can I get back to work?"

Cape turned to Maria. "How do you like San Francisco?"

"I thought it might be boring compared to Barcelona, but so far...not bad."

Beau rubbed his temples. "Maria told her boss the museum was going to be robbed—"

"—but he said I was paranoid," said Maria. "I bet him a hundred euros I was right."

"What's that in dollars?" asked Cape.

"About the same," said Maria. "The EU's in a slump."

"Since she's on leave," said Beau, "my chief of police did not get a phone call from her boss, which means I can't let her into the museum—"

"—yet."

"Yet." Beau nodded. "And since you clearly didn't come to our fine city to sightsee, I'm sure we will talk later." Beau's onyx eyes bored into Cape. "As for you—"

"It's been too long."

"Not long enough," said Beau. "On your last case, you destroyed half of Pier 39."

Maria gave Cape another appraisal. "You don't look that dangerous."

"You'd be surprised," said Beau, eyes still on Cape. "What I'm saying, you seem to know an awful lot about this train wreck—"

"—it's a helicopter—"

"—that just happened," said Beau. "So what I'm asking is... who's your client?"

Cape cocked his head to one side. "Sorry, I'm a little deaf in this ear."

Maria gave Beau a thousand-kilowatt smile. "Maybe he could hear better inside the museum."

"What a good idea," said Cape.

Beau looked from Cape to Maria and back again. "So that's how it is."

Cape and Maria shrugged simultaneously.

"I'm going inside the museum," said Beau. "Alone. By myself...to talk to my partner and see what's going on."

"Tell Vinnie I said hi," said Cape.

"We can talk later," said Beau, "as long as you don't do something stupid like talk to your pals in the press." He turned to Maria. "I want to hear all about your conspiracy theory."

"It's not a theory," said Maria.

"We'll see," said Beau.

Cape turned to Maria. "May I buy you breakfast?"

"I thought you'd never ask."

9

"Never ask about the monkeys."

Wen didn't immediately respond to Bohai. He kept his eyes on the macaque as they trudged along the perimeter fence. The monkey hopped from one fencepost to the next, skipping over strands of barbed wire, all the while keeping its yellow eyes on the prisoners below.

"They give me the creeps," said Wen.

"That's their job," replied Bohai. "Keep your voice down."

"Job?" Wen made a face. "You talk as if—"

"—one of the other prisoners kept asking the guards about the monkeys," said Bohai. "The next day he got sent to Doctor Loh for a physical."

"So?"

"We don't get physicals," said Bohai. "The only reason we see Doctor Loh is if we're too sick to work or injured. Anyway, this fellow wasn't the same when he came back."

"How do you mean?"

"He was...docile." Bohai ran his index finger across the top of his forehead, near the hairline on the right side of his skull. "And had a little scar right here."

Wen didn't say anything for a few paces as they approached the corner of the fence.

"You recognize the doctor's name?" asked Bohai.

Wen shook his head.

"Over a year ago, a doctor by that name made international news by successfully creating the first transgenic primate."

"Which means—?"

"—he spliced human genes into a monkey's brain."

Wen almost stopped in his tracks but knew dropping out of line would attract the guards' attention. "I never saw that story."

"Most Chinese papers didn't carry it." Bohai shrugged. "One of the perks of running my own bookstore was carrying foreign papers. The experiment was a collaboration with Western scientists, including one at a Texas university who condemned Loh, but only after it worked. Everyone backpedaled from the backlash."

"Why would anyone—"

"—to make them smarter." Bohai shrugged. "More useful maybe."

"And Loh came here?"

"You think that monkey is keeping tabs on us?" asked Bohai. "I suspect you're right but don't care enough to end up like that other prisoner."

"What happened to him?"

"He died two weeks later."

The line stopped as the guard at the front of the line raised his hand. The prisoners were handed shovels or pliers, the guards alternating tools as they walked down the line.

Bohai was given a shovel. Wen got pliers.

The nearest guard indicated a section of fencing about ten meters wide. Coils of wire were loose along the bottom, and one of the fenceposts listed to the left.

"Pangolins," said Bohai. "They dig at night for termites, loosen the fence."

"I thought the fence was electrified," said Wen. "They told us that on our first day."

Bohai glanced at the guard, who stood just beyond earshot. "Ever notice how the lights flicker at night, sometimes during the day in the factory? The power is erratic out here." He kicked at the dirt, sending a clump through the fence. "But don't be surprised if you find a dead pangolin."

Two hours later they were still on their knees, rebuilding a fence designed to keep them inside. Wen reflected on the simple psychology of their task, its complete lack of subtlety. Their only choices were made for them.

Shovel or pliers.

Fingers raw from twisting wire, Wen sat back on his heels and noticed a dust cloud on the horizon. The ground trembled as the cloud became a cirrus smear across a clear sky. Wen and the other workers stared as a massive army formed in the distance. Even the guards stopped and stared.

The army was on horseback.

Red banners unfurled as riders galloped. Spears glinted in the sunlight. To Wen it looked like a scene from one of the fables he'd read to Grace at bedtime when she was little.

A helicopter roared overhead and broke his reverie.

The side door of the helicopter was open and Wen could see the cameraman in his harness. The camera swiveled on a rig as the helicopter banked toward the oncoming horde.

"It's a movie," said Wen. "They're shooting a battle scene."

"It's not the first time." Bohai rubbed his chin. "Big, open plain with natural light, a landscape that hasn't changed for thousands of years."

The approaching army split as the cavalry swept to the right and left, flanking the infantry as it advanced. Archers held their positions and drew back their bowstrings.

Horns trumpeted as a lone rider broke away from the main force.

It was a young woman on horseback, hair wild in the wind, sword raised defiantly in her right hand. The sun seemed to swell with pride as she galloped headlong toward the imagined enemy, the air around her shimmering with midday heat.

An air horn sounded abruptly and the infantry shuffled to a chaotic halt, horses circling back to their starting point. The sound came from somewhere behind the archers. The woman's horse reared as she pulled the reins, then turned and trotted back toward the disbanding warriors.

A high-pitched squeal, electronic feedback from a bullhorn, then a sharp male voice echoing across the plain. Wen couldn't make out the words, but as the army scattered he could see through the dust and glimpsed production vehicles and trailers.

"They're filming a movie...here." Wen shook his head in disbelief.

"You notice the cameras aren't pointed in our direction." Bohai smiled ruefully and jutted his chin at the helicopter as it banked over the plain. "Recognize the logo?"

Wen squinted against the sun and tracked the helicopter as it headed toward the trailers. On its tail was the name of a studio he'd seen at the beginning of countless American films.

"China's a big market for Hollywood now," said Bohai. "If the studio films here, or casts a Chinese star, it gets better distribution and guaranteed box office. A good showing in China can recoup production costs in a week, so the rest of the world is all profit."

"But the helicopter," said Wen, "they saw us..."

"Did they?" asked Bohai. "Or did they see a factory, or a training facility?"

Wen didn't respond. He knew he was a prisoner but didn't realize he was invisible. If he didn't escape, he would be all but forgotten.

He thought about the woman warrior on horseback and knew the movie was based on the fable he'd read to Grace. A lone woman fighting impossible odds, her only weapons her sword and her bravery. Her loyal companion was a dragon sent by her ancestors to protect her. Grace loved that story so much.

Wen prayed she was safe and silently asked his ancestors for a dragon to protect her.

10

"I can't protect you," said Sally. "Unless you learn to protect yourself."

Grace looked both sleepy and defiant as she rubbed at her eyes and yawned. "I just woke up."

They stood in the center of the dojo, the large open space where Sally taught martial arts.

"Assailants usually come at night," said Sally. "Besides, it's the middle of the day."

"I was up all night."

"Do I care," asked Sally, "if I'm a burglar?" She almost said ghost but knew that wouldn't help. She would hold fear in reserve until it was needed.

"I took karate lessons after school," said Grace.

"Show me."

Sally took a step back, turned sideways and flexed her hand in a come-hither gesture. Grace adjusted her stance and raised her hands in a defensive position. She shifted her weight but remained where she was.

"Good," said Sally. "You didn't attack first. That's smart when you don't know the strength of your opponent, or if you think they're stronger." Sally lowered her hands. "But you already made your first mistake."

The corners of Grace's mouth contracted. "How?"

"You didn't use your legs."

Grace looked at her feet. "But you just said—"

"—to run away." Sally waited until Grace met her gaze and added, "What you did at the museum is exactly what a wise person does whenever confronted by violence. Ask yourself, why am I in this fight? Did you come here to hurt me?"

Grace's brow furrowed. "No, you said—"

"—did I want to hurt you?" Sally paused. "If I was a burglar, a mugger, or worse?"

Grace nodded.

"Remember," said Sally, "'he who fights and runs away, lives to fight another day.'"

"Is that from *The Art of War*?"

Sally shook her head. "It's a quote from a dead Roman named Tacitus."

"Do you speak Latin?"

"*Non si vitare possum.*"

Grace's eyes widened. "What does that mean?"

"Not if I can avoid it." Sally took up her stance. "Now, what if you have to fight?"

Grace raised her arms again. "I let you attack first."

"Unless you have an easy opening. Maybe you're close enough to kick me in the shins, or jab your thumb into my eye, or if I'm a man, kick me in the—"

"—but that's cheating."

"That's survival." Sally's tone was flat. "This isn't a karate match, Grace. The only ribbon you'll get is a tourniquet."

Grace blinked. "I understand."

Without warning, Sally stepped forward and swung her right

arm at Grace's head. Quickly enough to be a threat, gauging her speed to see how Grace would react.

She didn't disappoint. Grace ducked under the swing, and instinct took over. Inside Sally's reach, she took half a step forward and punched with her right fist, targeting Sally's sternum. Sally slapped the hand away.

The girl's teacher wasn't bad.

Grace pivoted from her failed strike and, keeping her hands up to protect her face, swung her left leg around in a snap kick. Instead of twisting away from the kick or blocking, Sally turned into it and grabbed Grace's leg with both hands.

Grace tried to pull away but it was too late. Sally lifted Grace off the floor, using the captured leg as leverage to toss Grace onto her back. There were mats on this part of the floor but they were thin, and the fall knocked the wind out of her.

Sally didn't move to help the girl, since no one outside these walls would, either. Grace stared at the ceiling and caught her breath, ragged at first but normal by the fourth exhalation. As she climbed onto her elbow, Sally asked, "What did you learn?"

Grace didn't reply. She wrapped her arms around her knees and remained on the floor. Sally could see how tired she was. After what she'd endured, Grace probably wanted to sleep until she could wake up and discover her night at the museum had been nothing but a bad dream.

All the more reason to push her now.

"Your kick was too high." Sally paused for a moment. "If it caught my knee, or even my shin, it would have hurt more and been harder to deflect. They tell you in class to kick high, because it helps with flexibility and makes you look like a badass."

A half smile found the corner of Grace's mouth. "Did I look like a badass?"

"Right up until you ended up on your ass, yes." Sally's mouth twitched, a hint of a smile. "In a real fight, you get no points for style."

"You're stronger," said Grace.

"Exactly," said Sally. "And I'm barely taller than you. What if I were six feet tall and outweighed you by fifty or a hundred pounds?" Preempting any rebuttal, she added, "Always assume your opponent has training. Even fat, stupid men may know how to fight."

Grace stood. "So how can I win?"

That was the right question.

Sally gestured at the walls. "If outmatched, grab a weapon." Grace started to move to the nearest rack, but Sally held up a hand. "Sometimes that's your nails, or your keys. Something within reach, like a stick or a rock. Understood?"

Grace nodded.

"Eyes, nose, fingers, face." Sally touched each part in turn, ending on her cheek. "Spots that trigger an instinct to recoil, to pull back."

"So that I can run." Grace's mouth turned down.

"Winning does not mean defeating, it means escaping." Sally brushed a stray lock of hair away from Grace's eyes. "That is today's only lesson." She waited until Grace gave a short nod. "If you get away, you've won."

"If I get away, I've won."

Sally waved at the wall. "Now find a way to hurt me."

Grace surveyed the weapons. Double-edged jian swords hung next to single-edged dao, the Chinese sabre. Japanese katana and wakizashi caught the light and winked at her, the folded steel rippling as if alive.

She moved to the practice weapons and almost grabbed a wooden kendo sword until she got closer and realized its length. Taking a step back, she scanned the racks of weapons and body armor as they diminished in size, until she came to a row of wooden sticks about twenty inches long and two inches in diameter. Each looked like a policeman's billy club.

A third of the way along the length of each stick, a wooden handle was set perpendicular to the main shaft. Grace grabbed two and turned to face Sally.

"Those are tonfa," said Sally. "It's a melee weapon. Interesting choice…do you know how to use them?"

"No," said Grace. "I saw them once in a movie. I just thought I could hold them without losing my balance."

"Not a bad reason." Sally was going to ask why she didn't choose one of the real swords but let it go. Even Sally's childhood had turned things into a game. The blood and scars came later, when she was old enough to understand the real purpose behind her school. "Throw one to me; I'll show you."

Grace tossed a stick underhand. Sally caught it with her right hand and twirled it like a baton. She held the handle so the shorter piece of wood extended just beyond her closed fist. The longer section was braced along her forearm.

"If I punch…" Sally straightened her arm. "…the front of the stick extends my reach. If I raise my arm…" She squatted as if under attack. "My opponent's strike hits the stick and not my arm." She stood and swung her arm slowly, leading with the elbow. "On the offensive, I let my arm guide the stick, using my momentum so the wood takes the impact."

Sally tossed the tonfa back to Grace. "Last thing, if you're not sure of yourself, lock one in place along your weak arm, and only attack with your strong arm. Use it for defense, but never let it throw you off balance."

"Aren't you going to choose a weapon?" asked Grace.

Sally's mouth twitched. She bowed but kept her eyes on Grace, who did the same before raising her sticks in a defensive stance.

Sally closed the gap, leading with her left leg as she brought her right arm in a smooth arc toward Grace's neck. She slowed her swing only marginally, without telegraphing her strike. Grace saw it and moved one of her sticks above her head before Sally could connect. Sally pivoted for her next assault, but before she could attack, Grace did something unexpected.

Grace attacked first.

Instead of staying on defense, Grace stepped into the opening left by Sally's turn and swung her right stick upward. Sally smiled as the tonfa swept toward her jaw. Grace might not be ready to grab a real sword from the wall, but she clearly understood this wasn't a game.

Sally snapped her arm back to catch the stick against her palm with a smack that echoed across the room. Grace's eyes went wide as Sally held fast and twisted the tonfa with a flip of her wrist. She lost her grip in the same instant Sally raised her right leg to ninety degrees, bent her knee, and kicked Grace in the stomach.

Grace flew backward, one stick poorer. She landed on her backside, her momentum rolling her in a backward somersault that ended on her knees, facing Sally from ten feet away. Grace still had one tonfa stick, held tightly in her left hand. Her chest heaved as she caught her breath.

Grace wobbled on her knees and watched Sally's eyes.

Sally had kicked a spot that would give Grace a brief bellyache, well below her sternum. Fracturing a rib or puncturing a lung the first day wasn't going to help the cause. Grace rose to one knee, her other leg bent in front of her, as if she was about to stand. Sally took a deliberate step forward to show that she wouldn't stop coming.

She took another step. Then Grace surprised her again.

Without changing position, Grace hurled the tonfa in an

overhand swing that would have impressed any pitcher in the World Series. It flew end over end directly at Sally's head.

Sally turned sideways and used the stick she'd taken from Grace to deflect the airborne missile. It clattered to the floor and smacked against the wall. Before Sally could turn to face her young opponent, she heard the slap-slap-slapping of Grace's feet as she ran away.

Grace had used the opening she'd created to scramble to her feet. Now she was running toward the far door without looking back. As she cleared the threshold, she yelled triumphantly over her shoulder.

"I win, I win, I win!"

Sally's mouth surrendered to a full smile as she tossed her tonfa after the first, her eyes on the empty door through which Grace had vanished.

She won't be easy to kill.

Grace wasn't what Sally was expecting, and that might give her the edge when she needed it most.

11

"You aren't at all what I was expecting."

Cape glanced up from his breakfast with a quizzical expression. He wanted to ask Maria if that was a compliment or an insult, but his mouth was full. He'd ordered a lot of pancakes.

"I've only known one private detective." Maria selected a strip of bacon from a shared plate in the middle of the table and bit it in half. "An ex-policeman who'd been on the force with my father."

"And?"

"*Gilipuertas.*" Maria smiled. "A real asshole."

"You just met me," said Cape. "Give it time."

"Fair enough," said Maria. "What's your story?"

Cape shrugged. "I was a reporter, back when there were newspapers."

Maria nodded. "Same thing in Europe…it's all opinions now…so?"

"So, a long time ago…"

"…in a galaxy far, far away?"

Cape laughed.

"We have *Star Wars* in Spain," said Maria. "We even have bacon."

"Then I'm definitely booking a trip."

Maria gestured at their table, which had far more plates than people. "Do you always eat this much?"

"Only at breakfast."

"What do you eat for lunch?"

"Usually another breakfast."

They were sitting in a booth at a diner on Van Ness. Not Cape's first choice but easy to reach from the museum. The Mini Cooper parked next to his car had been Maria's, and after navigating the minefield of scatological obstacles across the park, they got in their respective vehicles and drove here. The food was solid, the decor loud, and the service serviceable. Most importantly, the place was noisy enough to talk without being overheard.

"So you worked for a newspaper…" Maria prompted, snatching another piece of bacon. "But you left."

"Had a disagreement with my editor," said Cape.

"Over a story?" asked Maria. "Or was it personal?"

"I found a connection between some local politicians and organized crime. Rigged bids for a renovation project downtown. The paper broke the story, everybody seemed pleased."

"That's good, no?"

Cape shrugged. "Some mid-level officials got indicted, the paper sold a few more copies, everybody got a pat on the back. My editor said the story was closed."

Maria's eyes smiled over the rim of her coffee cup. "You disagreed."

"I pulled on that thread a little harder and found it was tied to some very bad people." Cape flexed the fingers on his right hand. "Prostitution network specializing in underage girls, doing business out of massage parlors and nightclubs. The girls weren't from around here so nobody made any noise."

"Trafficked?"

"Mostly from Asia, some from Guatemala and Mexico, but their clients were all local—"

"—and tied to the other end of that thread?"

"Ran all the way to city hall." Cape flexed his jaw, memory's aftertaste fresh on his tongue. "Naive jackass that I was, took it to my editor, who said drop the story."

"He was one of their customers?"

"I think he was just on the payroll," said Cape. "Whether he succumbed to political pressure or his monthly checks came from somewhere else, I couldn't care less. So I quit, figured I'd take the story to a rival paper, but they wouldn't touch it either." Cape cracked the knuckles of his right hand. "Until a local girl went missing."

Maria put down her cup. "She had a family?"

"Exactly," said Cape. "Her aunt came forward, and a local TV station picked it up, showed the girl's photo on the seven o'clock news. Once crime has a face, it's a lot harder to pretend it doesn't exist."

"Did you go back to the paper?"

"I slammed that door on my way out." Cape gave a half smile. "But I found the girl."

"*¡Reivindicado!*" Maria's eyes flashed. "You were vindicated."

"I was arrested."

"What?"

"I traced the girl to a brothel, but I wasn't the only one looking. I entered as a potential client, then arrived in the girl's room at precisely the same time as someone else." Cape smiled at the thought of Sally climbing through a window. "Someone I thought was just an urban legend."

"Who?"

"Today, she's my business partner," said Cape. "Back then, she didn't know me. I was just another guy in a brothel."

"She was suspicious?"

"She threw me out a window."

Maria sat up straighter. "I think I like this woman."

"Don't get on her bad side." Cape laughed at himself. "As I hung from the edge of the roof, two stories up, the police raided the place. I climbed back through the window and found myself staring down the barrel of a very big gun held by a very large policeman."

"Who arrested you."

Cape nodded. "The policeman you were talking to at the museum?"

"Inspector Jones."

"Beau, yes," said Cape. "He's the one who arrested me."

"You keep interesting company." Maria rubbed her hands together. "Why didn't you get your old job back?"

Maria's tone suggested she already knew the answer.

"You mean, after being thrown out a window and getting arrested," said Cape. "Why do this for a living?"

"Because you were bored to death!" Maria's eyes were alight with amusement. "*¿Es cierto, que no?*"

"Maybe." Cape shrugged. "What's your excuse?"

"My father was Policia Nacional," said Maria. "Mother was an artist. I decided to combine the two." She sipped her coffee and added, "Mamá was furious."

"With you?"

"With my father," said Maria. "I said that it was her fault for buying me the Spanish-language editions of Nancy Drew when I was ten." Maria set her coffee down. "I didn't mention that Papá took me shooting at the police range while she was at work."

"What led you to Interpol?"

"Cape, I think you are good at this dance." Maria's eyes flashed again, and Cape wondered if it was a trick of the light or if she lived in a constant state of mischief.

"I'm not much of a dancer."

"Oh, but you are. I asked some questions—"

"—and I answered."

"You gave me just enough to trust you," said Maria. "Then you spun us around and started asking me questions—"

"—because I'm curious."

"About why I'm here."

"Well, I already know why I'm here."

"See, we are doing the tango," said Maria. "Give and take."

"So what would you like me to give," asked Cape. "Or take?"

"You believe your inspector friend...Beau...will help us?"

"He'll talk to us, eventually," said Cape. "He plays by the rules, so I can't say whether or not he'll help, but he will share, especially if you share with him."

"Give and take." Maria held her arms as if dancing. "It's how people who don't know each other come to trust each other."

"Beau's a better dancer than I am." Cape signaled the waiter for the check.

"I doubt it," said Maria. "Are we going somewhere?"

"I am," said Cape. "Want to come, or would you rather wait around until your supervisor stops being a bureaucrat and lets you do your job?"

Maria grabbed her jacket off the back of her chair. "Is this you giving?"

"This is me trying to stay ahead of the police," said Cape. "Once they check the museum's security tapes, they'll know most of what I know, maybe more. So I need something to barter."

"Where are we going?"

Cape took the check from the waiter and laid some bills on the table. After replacing his wallet, he pulled out his phone and opened the photo app before handing it to Maria. "Zoom into the tail section."

"The helicopter." Maria spread her thumb and index finger across the screen to enlarge the image. A series of letters and numbers were painted in white, distorted by the crimp in the tail. "Is that a *Z* or an *N*?"

"Not sure," said Cape. "But we can narrow it down, and find out who the pilot was..."

"Was, not is..." Maria returned the phone. "At the museum, you mentioned the pilot."

They emerged from the diner into the watery light of San Francisco, the city where the fog holds the sun hostage. Cars sped along Van Ness in both directions. An articulated bus lumbered past as they reached their cars.

"The pilot," said Maria. "You think he's dead."

"I think he's Russian," said Cape. "And dead."

"So are we going to talk to a live Russian," asked Maria. "Or a ghost?"

"Funny you should ask."

12

"Funny," said the ghost. "I don't remember hiring the helicopter pilot. Wasn't that your job?"

He sat on a low couch in a dimly lit room, his long arms stretched across the red upholstery, his legs extended and crossed at the ankles. In the half-light of the nearby lamps he seemed to glow, and his eyes flashed red whenever he turned his head to look across the desk.

The man across from the ghost was barely visible through the fog of smoke curling toward the ceiling. He was on his third cigarette, and the meeting had only begun moments ago. Freddie Wang concluded a long time ago that his unseemly profession would put him in the grave before cancer could spread its fingers through his lungs. Somehow he defied the odds long enough to grow old, bitter, and suspicious.

"You blame your mess on me?" Freddie's voice was a snake slithering through ashes.

"Stockholm was smooth as clockwork."

Both men spoke Cantonese, but the ghost's voice had a sepulchral chill that gave Freddie the creeps. He sucked the cigarette down to his fingers and used the butt to light another.

"You used a boat in Stockholm, in a city full of boats." Freddie waved a hand dismissively. "Helicopters are too flashy."

"The local help was more accommodating in Sweden," said the ghost. "That's all."

"Help...help?" Freddie came halfway out of his chair. "Let me be clear, my albino friend. I am helping you, but I am not the help." Freddie's left eye was a milky cataract but his right was as black and clear as night. "As far as you're concerned, I am this city."

"You run the tongs, which are connected to the Triads." The ghost smiled and his eyes flashed. "As far as you're concerned, I am the Triads."

Freddie felt another chill but didn't back down. "Bullshit." The word in Cantonese sounded like fi-*wah*, and Freddie punched the last syllable into a squawk to show his irritation. "I've heard about you—"

"—rumors," said the ghost. "Whispers in the dark."

Freddie shook his head. "You left your clan and became an independent operator. Dangerous business, with no house backing you."

"I have the Middle Kingdom behind me," said the ghost coolly. "I'm backed by Beijing."

Freddie snorted. "What do communists care about lost art?"

"It wasn't lost," said the ghost. "It was stolen." His long fingers traced a seam on the couch. "And we are stealing it back."

"For profit," said Freddie.

"For patriotism," said the ghost. "Don't be so cynical."

"You sound like someone trying to sell me something," said Freddie. "Sound like a capitalist, and I bet you're getting paid plenty of money."

"So are you, Freddie." The ghost rubbed his hands together. "So how can we continue our arrangement—"

"—so nobody goes to jail?" Freddie blew smoke rings at the ceiling. "If you had blown the back door instead of going through a skylight, nobody would know you were there."

"It worked in Norway."

"You been outside?" Freddie cackled. "Norway is clean, the people are polite—this isn't Norway. Police start investigating, checking security tapes—"

"—I'm not worried about the tapes," said the ghost.

"My men were with you," said Freddie. "Comes back to me."

"Get them alibis," said the ghost. "I'm more concerned about a witness."

Freddie nodded. "The girl."

"Find her."

"Who's going to believe her?" asked Freddie. "Another whisper about a Chinese ghost. The museum should make it part of the tour."

"I don't care that she saw me." The ghost leaned forward and rested his long arms across his knees. "I care that she saw what I was holding."

"They have the helicopter."

"We burned it."

"You should take what you have and leave," said Freddie. "Fly to New York for your next job. My cousin is ready for you— security at the Met is a joke."

The ghost shook his head. "I have to go back."

"Security will—"

"—not be a problem," said the ghost. "Robbed once, they think it's over. Who would be so bold? We hit the Kode Museum in Norway three different times."

"This…isn't…Norway," said Freddie. "It's not even Sweden. You don't want to listen, fine, but you're taking a risk. Which means I'm taking a risk."

"There are more pieces," said the ghost. "I'm not leaving without them."

"Or what?" Freddie stubbed his cigarette into the ashtray. The pack was empty.

"Or I have to answer to the Devil."

The name sounded like *Moh-gway*, and Freddie had heard it before. He was connected politically enough to know the myth was flesh and blood. A long arm that stretched all the way from Beijing through Hong Kong to the West. Long enough to reach all the way to San Francisco, grab Freddie by the neck, and strangle the life out of him.

"Go to New York and then return, get the other pieces on your way back to China, a month from now." Freddie wanted to sound more reasonable than antagonistic, but it wasn't in his nature. "They won't expect that."

The ghost shook his head, his eyes the color of blood. "I'm not done here."

Freddie sighed and rummaged through his desk drawer for more cigarettes. "I'm not getting you another helicopter."

"I won't need one," said the ghost. "Just find the girl."

13

Sergey held the girl tightly, worried she might slip from his grasp.

He brought the paintbrush to her cheek and turned his wrist counterclockwise to draw a red oval beneath her eye. His knuckles were turning white as he tried to hold her steady. He didn't want to repeat his mistake from yesterday, when he relaxed his grip and the girl fell and shot across the room before he could catch her.

The nesting doll wasn't much wider than a soda bottle, but the girl painted on its surface had taken a week to design and two days to paint. This was a special order, and Sergey wanted to get every detail right. He set the girl gently on the counter next to the other dolls, their pear-shaped figures gleaming in the overhead light.

Authentic *matryoshka* were nesting dolls in traditional Russian dress, girls with rosy cheeks, each successive doll getting smaller and smaller as the color scheme of their clothes changed. Sergey imported them from a cousin who ran a shop in Sergiyev Posad in Vladivostok.

Sometimes they were just nesting dolls. Other times they were filled with carefully measured quantities of illegal substances. Synthetic drugs, black market pharmaceuticals, and the occasional homeopathic remedy banned by the FDA. Nothing dangerous, just lucrative enough to improve the store's margins.

Special orders for locals, tourists, or visitors to the website—custom-crafted nesting dolls like this one—Sergey painted himself. He found it calming. Much more relaxing than dealing with his domineering sisters and extended family of gangsters.

When the bell mounted on the back of the door rang, Sergey wiped paint off his hands and put on his respectable shopkeeper face, but his expression broke into a savage grin when he saw who it was.

"Cape!" Sergey spread his arms in greeting. "*Moy brat*, it's been a while."

As Cape held the door, Sergey came around the counter and saw the woman. He instinctively glanced down to see if his fly was open. Paint stains on the pants but everything else was tucked into place. Sergey's tendency to think incessantly about sex whenever he wasn't painting often led to social missteps, and he didn't want to embarrass his friend before he even said hello.

"Sergey," said Cape, "this is Maria."

Sergey shook her hand and led them back into the store. Maria was mesmerized by the *matryoshka* standing shoulder to shoulder on shelves, in the window displays, arranged on tables.

Maria noticed the dolls drying on the counter. "Those are so…interesting."

Sergey gave an embarrassed shrug as Cape took a step forward to examine the dolls.

From left to right, the Mary Poppins story took shape, with a twist. Here were the children, Jane and Michael, the little girl glistening with wet paint on her cheeks. Then their parents, Mr. and Mrs. Banks, followed by Bert, the friendly chimney sweep.

The largest nesting doll was Mary herself, wearing a white apron, from the scene when a songbird visits the nursery. All the figures were meticulously detailed, as if the dolls had stepped out of the movie, with one exception.

Underneath the apron it was readily apparent that Mary Poppins was topless.

"You've got to be kidding," said Cape.

"You'd be amazed what people request." Sergey sighed. "This one is for an online customer. Last week they ordered a Peter Pan set, only they wanted Tinkerbell, well, you know..."

Cape's eyebrows rose. "You didn't."

"Of course not." Sergey shook his head. "We have standards. No kids, no animals in compromising positions, and—"

"—no naked fairies?" asked Maria.

"*Da*," said Sergey. "This is a family business." He retreated behind the counter.

"Speaking of the family business," said Cape. "I need your help."

Sergey's eyes darted to Maria. "Do you trust her?"

"She hasn't tried to kill me," said Cape.

"That's a good sign," said Sergey. "Your judgment must be improving."

Maria looked bemused. "How do you two know each other?"

"He saved my life," said Cape and Sergey simultaneously.

Sergey nodded and added, "We both got shot by the same person."

Maria laughed. "That's a story I'd like to hear."

"And I would love to tell it to you," said Sergey. "I was very heroic."

Cape said, "Maria is with Interpol—"

"—unfortunately," said Sergey abruptly, "I am not at liberty to discuss my past adventures." He turned to Cape with alarm and whispered, "Why are you, and your extremely well-dressed friend from Interpol…the international criminal police organization…in my store?"

"Relax," said Cape. "Maria is with the art crimes division."

"*Potryasayushchiy!*" Sergey rubbed his hands together. "That is not the family business."

"We're looking for someone," said Maria.

"Who?"

"A pilot."

"A dead Russian," said Cape.

Sergey listened as Cape told him what happened at the museum. He wondered how Cape knew so much about a crime that only happened hours ago but didn't want to ask questions in front of the elegant policewoman. He trusted Cape, who could have turned Sergey and his sister, Eva, over to the police long ago, but anyone tied to the Russian *mafiya* was rarely in the same room as someone from Interpol—unless that room happened to be a prison cell.

Sergey decided to save his questions for another time.

"My guess is the pilot wasn't part of the heist." Cape paused as if choosing his next words carefully. "They hired him to fly them in, but intended to kill him after the job was done. Once they crashed, there was no reason to wait."

Sergey saw where this was going. "The helicopter must have been stolen—"

"—or borrowed," said Maria. "Either way, he knew he was flying to a robbery."

"So he was bought," said Cape, "or blackmailed."

"Or was already a criminal," said Sergey. "You sure he's Russian?"

"No," said Cape.

Sergey drummed his fingers on the counter. "What do you want, exactly?"

"An introduction," said Cape. "We'll trace the helicopter, but that's a dead end if it was stolen. The better angle is to identify the pilot and work backward."

"*Khorosho.*" Sergey nodded as he glanced at his handiwork.

Mary Poppins smiled beatifically and gave him an encouraging look of approval. Sergey felt a sudden craving for a spoon full of sugar. He made a mental note to rent the movie tonight and buy his girlfriend a white apron.

Cape watched him but didn't say anything.

Sergey looked up from the counter and sighed.

"If I give you the name of someone I know, it can come back to me...or my sister. And some of my second cousins and uncles are not as gentle as our side of the family."

"I understand." Cape fingered a scar on his neck as if tracing a memory. "I met some of them, before I met you."

Sergey rubbed the dried paint on his fingers. "But if I give you a name that everyone knows...and a place...that might get you somewhere."

"Without leading them here," said Cape.

"A place?" asked Maria.

"In the Richmond District," said Sergey. "Many Russian immigrants there. Most are families chasing the American dream, but a few are exploiting it—and their neighbors. Those men you can find at a certain restaurant every Tuesday night."

"Today is Tuesday," said Maria.

"Why Tuesday?" asked Cape.

Sergey chuckled. "Russian gangsters are obsessed with *America's Got Talent.* The place has a wide-screen TV and great sound system. They bought it for soccer games, but on Tuesday night it's Simon, Heidi, and Howie."

"*¡Maravillosa!*" Maria clapped her hands together. "This is a wonderfully strange city. What is the restaurant called?"

"The Red Tavern," said Sergey. "On Clement Street in the Richmond."

"And what is the name that everybody knows?" asked Cape.

Sergey took another look at the Banks family and their magical governess, but they kept their own counsel. He'd have to take the next step on his own.

Step in time, step in time. Never need a reason, never need a rhyme.

"Maksim Valenko," he said to Cape. "This is a name that everyone knows, but nobody says out loud."

"Like Voldemort?"

"Exactly like Voldemort."

"I always wanted to be Hermione," said Maria.

Cape raised a hand. "Harry."

Sergey shrugged. "Ron."

Maria arched an eyebrow. "Who wants to be Ron?"

"He's good at chess," said Sergey defensively. "I like chess."

"So I whisper Valenko," said Cape, "and dementors appear and drag me off to Azkaban prison?"

"Much worse," said Sergey. "The Russian *mafiya* shows up and breaks your legs."

"Swell."

"Unlike Voldemort," said Sergey. "Valenko still has a nose, which he sticks into everybody's business. So if your dead pilot was connected, he'd have ties to Valenko."

Cape extended his hand and shook Sergey's. "Anything else?"

"Don't tell my sister about this." Sergey jutted his chin at the naughty nanny. "She thinks I've matured."

"I was never here."

"I don't even know your sister," added Maria.

Sergey leaned close to Cape and lowered his voice. "I like this Interpol of yours."

"She's not my Interpol," said Cape. "She's—"

"—Isabella Maria Diaz y Angelos," said Maria. "And it was *encantado*—lovely meeting you, Sergey."

Sergey blushed and asked, "Were you ever a governess?"

"Time to go," said Cape.

Before they reached the door, Sergey called out, "I know you don't like guns, but if you're going to see Valenko, you should bring a weapon."

"Don't worry," said Cape. "I'm going to bring a friend."

14

"You don't bring a friend to a meeting with your boss."

Peng pretended he didn't hear Yan, but as they stepped off the curb, she punched him in the shoulder. Peng took another step and stopped in the middle of the street.

He turned to Yan and put his hands on her shoulders. His fingers were long and delicate. Yan always thought that Peng might have been a pianist if he wasn't a painter and sculptor.

"You're not a friend," he said. "You're a coworker." Seeing the look on her face, he added, "Sorry, you are a friend, a very good one, but for the purpose of this meeting, you are an impartial coworker who can speak of my integrity."

"Not your best apology." Skepticism bent the corners of Yan's mouth. "Why should Niu listen to me? He's a dumb ox who runs an assembly line, and I am a lowly painter."

"You're the best background artist on the line," said Peng. "Nobody paints trees like you can, and Niu would be furious if you left. Our paintings would look like cheap knockoffs without your brush."

"They are cheap knockoffs," replied Yan. "That's the point. Why buy a real Van Gogh when you can buy an oil painting that looks like Van Gogh painted it himself, but which costs less than a poster? Look, it's a good business, and I'm not claiming to be a capitalist, but—"

"—shhhh." Peng looked to see if anyone was walking nearby. The village of Dafen was part of the Special Economic Zone of Shenzhen, what the government called a SEZ, but it was still China. "You always talk before you look, it will get you in trouble one day."

Peng glanced at the streetlight and the camera mounted below. He knew there was another camera five meters behind them, but the middle of the street should be a dead zone for audio surveillance. His mobile phone was turned off, so they should be fine, as long as a passing car didn't turn them into roadkill before they finished their conversation.

Dafen still had the feel of a village though it had grown exponentially since Peng was a child. A crowded jumble of factories, apartment buildings, and small shops, with most storefronts open to the street, their colorful creations propped in the windows or displayed on the sidewalk to entice passersby. Yet none of that charm was the basis for Dafen's cultural significance.

More than half the world's oil paintings came from this one village.

A handful of tradesmen moved to Dafen in the nineties to set up independent art studios. Over time they grew into production houses, massive art factories with artists sitting in a line, each recreating a different part of a known masterpiece by the Dutch Masters, French Impressionists, Spanish Surrealists, or any painter recognized globally.

Orders from museum stores and online art stores around the world, plus a growing middle class in China, drove demand. More artists moved to Dafen, initially trade painters who were content to add texture or background to a replica painting. Soon other artists arrived with bigger aspirations, and independent studios sold original art by local Chinese painters.

Tastes began to shift from West to East.

Chinese aristocracy, who once wanted forbidden Western art on their walls, were buying more Chinese art and antiquities. The floodgates opened after the central government declared that interest in Chinese culture before the revolution was no longer seen as decadent but rather patriotic. Sotheby's opened a joint venture in Beijing to sell lost Chinese treasures back to the Chinese.

Inside the Special Economic Zones, tech billionaires collected art like wine, building galleries and donating to museums to enhance their social status. Some were investing in emerging artists in hopes of discovering the next Rembrandt, a painter so admired around the world that other countries would finally look to China as a source of creativity instead of copies.

Peng dreamed of being that painter. Now he had put his future in jeopardy.

His foreman, Niu, had forbidden side projects. Peng was the factory's lead painter, responsible for the most iconic pieces, and Niu didn't want him distracted.

Without asking permission, Peng cut a deal with a small gallery where he knew the owner to keep 50 percent of anything sold. If he could earn enough to venture out on his own, Peng would leave the factory, but he had never missed a day of work.

He hadn't told anyone except Yan, and she wouldn't tell a soul. Peng wondered if the gallery owner had betrayed him, because now Niu was demanding to see him in his office.

"Maybe Niu doesn't know," said Yan. "Don't be so paranoid."

They crossed the street toward the factory at the center of a three-way intersection, where a main thoroughfare split into a Y-shaped juncture of two smaller roads. The ground floor was painted in bright, primary colors, but the upper floors were drab yellow. Once a textile factory, the building had large windows, good light for a painter's assembly line.

"When has Niu ever asked for a meeting?" Peng ran his long fingers through his long black hair. "If you can think of another reason why he summoned me, I'll stop worrying."

"Maybe he's giving you a raise," said Yan. "He's been so generous to us in the past."

Peng stopped in mid-stride and looked at Yan, who was struggling to keep a straight face. Her eyes started to water until she burst out laughing. Peng tried to scowl but couldn't hold it. He coughed, then giggled, then laughed until he had to bend down and rest his hands on his knees.

"Thank you." Peng was still wheezing as he stood.

Yan brushed his hair away from his eyes. "Don't worry, I'll be right outside the door."

"You wait in the hall." Peng nodded. "If he questions my dedication—"

"—you'll admit that you're selling your own paintings," said Yan. "And I'll come in and assure him it's only a hobby." She tapped Peng on the chest. "But if he does give you a raise, you owe me."

"I owe you already." Peng stared at the wide red factory door. "Let's go."

Normally the factory was bustling, but today it felt empty the instant they walked through the door, quiet even for a weekend. Their footsteps echoed on the stairs as they climbed to the second level, where Niu's office overlooked the main floor. At the top of the stairs was a broad landing and short hallway with a men's and women's bathroom on either side. The door to Niu's office was at the end of the hall.

Yan spoke in a low voice. "I'm going to wait in the bathroom until you've gone into his office, so he won't see me in the hallway. I'll count to twenty and then come and listen outside the door."

"Make it a hundred," said Peng.

"Okay," said Yan. "Leave the door ajar if you can, I really want to eavesdrop."

Peng waited until Yan slipped into the ladies' room before striding the length of the hall to rap on the office door. To his surprise it was unlatched and swung open from his knock. Niu sat behind his desk but didn't look happy to see Peng.

He looked scared.

Peng caught movement in his peripheral vision as he crossed the threshold. The man who stepped from behind the door was two meters tall, with close-cropped hair and somber eyes. He stared dispassionately at Peng but didn't come any closer. He was merely making his presence known. That was when Peng realized a fourth person was in the room.

A rustling behind the door preceded the appearance of another unexpected guest. That was how it seemed to Peng. The figure appeared as if conjured by an incantation.

Though Peng heard the swishing of robes, he did not hear any footfalls as the figure pushed the door closed and moved behind the desk. Peng was fairly sure the door didn't latch but hoped Yan had remained in the bathroom.

The figure was cloaked in black, a flowing *changsan* robe over loose pants. Gloves extended under the sleeves of the robe, leaving no skin exposed along the arms.

But the most unsettling thing was the face, because there wasn't any.

An executioner's hood covered the head, with no face visible within, which made Peng wonder if there was a mask under the hood, as well. His nervous brain jumped to an image of Darth Vader taunting Luke Skywalker.

His subconscious was still in a galaxy far, far away when the figure spoke fluent Mandarin in a digital rasp. The voice was an electronic tangle of discordant sounds, fused together by a microphone secured at the neck of the costume. Whoever or whatever was under the hood didn't want to be recognized by anyone.

"Peng, I'm so pleased to meet you," said the voice. "My name is Mogwai."

Peng tried to swallow but his mouth was dry.

"Perhaps you've heard of me?"

Peng nodded. Everyone knew the Devil existed, but meeting him was another matter.

"Your supervisor and I have come to an understanding," said Mogwai.

Niu didn't look like he understood anything. He looked angry and afraid.

The disembodied voice drifted across the room, and Mogwai took a step closer to Peng.

"From now on, Peng, you work for me."

15

"Remember, I work for you." Sally patted the covers at the foot of the bed until the cat jumped onto Grace's feet. "And now, I have to go to work."

"Let me come with you." Grace was up on her elbows with a scowl on her face.

A scowl is better than a pout.

Sally shook her head. "As my employer, never forget that my job is to keep you safe. The less you are seen, the safer you are...for now."

"Until you find the men who killed my uncle."

"Yes."

Sally was going someplace that wasn't safe under any circumstances, if Cape was serious about dinner with Russian gangsters. She kept that to herself while keeping her eyes on Grace.

"I don't want to be alone," said Grace.

Sally held out her hand and the cat rubbed its cheek against her fingers. "The cat will watch over you."

"We need to give it a name."

"I'm sure he has a name," said Sally, "we just don't know it yet."

"What was your teacher's name?" Grace ran her hand gently across the cat's forehead. "The one with the scar."

Sally didn't say anything for a minute. The memory of the name carried images of her childhood, from her first day at school to the day she left the Triads forever.

Student, assassin, pawn, avenger.

A thousand images flashed across Sally's memory, and the lightning scar was the thread that tied them all together.

"Xan," said Sally. "His name was Xan."

"Was he a good teacher?"

I'm still alive, and that was his job.

"Yes," said Sally. "He was good at his job." Sally stood and checked that the blinds were drawn. "Now go to sleep."

"I took a nap," said Grace.

"From which I woke you," said Sally. "And you were awake all last night. If you can't sleep, read a book. You saw the bookcase in the alcove?"

Grace nodded. "You have books in Mandarin?"

They were speaking Cantonese, but Sally remembered the schools in Hong Kong were teaching in Mandarin these days. "Yes, along with Cantonese, English, Latin, and Russian," said Sally. "A few in Spanish."

"Do you speak all those languages?"

"I try not to talk too much, but I did learn how to listen in all of them."

"Will you be leaving by the big door?"

"No," said Sally. "I have another way out. So if you hear someone at that door, stay inside, and stay quiet. Understood?"

Grace nodded, and Sally wondered if she was getting the balance right. Keep the child alert to danger but not scared. She turned to leave but hesitated.

"Grace, the pilot of the helicopter... Can you remember any of the words he said?" asked Sally. "What they sounded like?"

Sally had spent the afternoon trying to distract Grace from

the night before, but at this point, any clue might help. She was having dinner with a hunch. Grace frowned, her brow furrowed, then she looked at Sally and gave a tentative nod.

"Po-jal-sta," said Grace. "I don't know if it's a word, but that was the sound. He kept shouting it…again and again…" Grace's voice got quiet. "…when the helicopter started to burn."

Sally nodded but didn't say anything.

Grace asked, "That word, is it Russian?"

"Yes." Sally gestured at the cat. "Take good care of Xan."

Sally left without offering what the word meant, and Grace didn't press. It was simply what any man would say to someone about to burn him alive.

Please.

16

"Please tell me you have a plan," said Maria.

"No," said Cape, "but I have a reservation."

"I have plenty of reservations," said Maria, "including whether I should be seen with you in public."

Maria's tone suggested she was teasing, but as Cape drove along Geary Boulevard into the neighborhood known as Little Russia, he felt compelled to say, "If you want to wait in the car—"

"—I will give you the benefit of the doubt," said Maria, "and assume you're being gallant and not sexist."

"You have a career," replied Cape, "I have a job. There's a difference."

Maria cocked an eyebrow. "Meaning?"

"You have more to lose if things go south." Cape turned the wheel to swing past a garbage truck. "Even off duty and on vacation, you could lose your badge."

Maria was about to respond when she saw five golden onions on the horizon.

The Holy Virgin Cathedral grew larger as they approached 25th Street, its distinctive onion domes topped with crosses in the Eastern Orthodox tradition, three crossbeams with the lowest slanted at a slight angle off the perpendicular. The largest Russian Orthodox cathedral outside Russia, it dominated the otherwise unremarkable skyline of the Richmond District.

The façade was white, green, and red below the golden towers, with saints painted in the Byzantine style flanking massive wooden doors. It was a colorful anomaly in a neighborhood of stucco apartment buildings, small grocers, and restaurants.

Cape pulled alongside the curb opposite the cathedral and turned off the ignition.

"We got here early."

"You drive fast."

"I just knew where I was headed for a change."

Maria was admiring the cathedral. "I guess there really are Russians in San Francisco."

"You bet," said Cape. "The migration started after the Bolshevik business in the twenties, then a second wave after World War Two. The neighborhood is a mix of Russian, Chinese, Irish, and Vietnamese...a little bit of everyone from everywhere, but more known for its Russian influence because they got here first."

"You know your city."

"Helps with the job," said Cape. "San Francisco has a lot of diversity but isn't very integrated, so most of the underground economy—organized crime—breaks along ethnic lines."

"This is true in Spain as well." Maria studied the storefronts on their right, many signs displaying three languages. "The restaurant is close?"

"One street over, on Clement, next to a Chinese seafood wholesaler and a Mexican produce market," said Cape. "I don't want to arrive too early—"

"—so your friend can get there first." Maria took another

look at the Byzantine saints before locking eyes with Cape. "Or because you want to interrogate me?"

Cape held up his hands. "I stand accused."

"You said if I was on vacation—if." Maria pulled a long face. "You are suspicious?"

"Curious." Cape drummed his fingers on the steering wheel. "I know more about what went down in the museum, but you clearly know something about the thieves. And since we're about to have dinner with Russian mobsters, I thought maybe we should enlighten each other."

"In case only one of us gets out alive?" Maria's eyes danced. "Americans...so pragmatic."

"You said it, not me."

"*Cierto.*" Maria turned in her seat. "Have you ever been to Stockholm?"

"No, but I had an addiction to Swedish Fish."

"Are those like Gummi Bears?"

"Chewier," said Cape. "Not as sweet."

"How about Norway?"

Cape shook his head. "The hotspots I covered as a reporter were...well, hot...Scandinavian countries were too civilized to make headlines."

"No matter," said Maria. "During the summer of 2010, Swedish police got a call one night saying cars were on fire in downtown Stockholm." Maria ran her fingers through her hair as if drawing forth a memory. "But the cars were a distraction, with an added benefit of snarling traffic. While the police were busy putting out fires, thieves broke into Drottningholm Palace a few blocks away and stole several precious works of art, then fled by scooter to the waterfront. They escaped by speedboat before anyone knew there was a robbery."

"Professionals—"

"—who knew what they were after," said Maria. "In and out in less than five minutes."

"What did they take?"

Maria made a give-me-a-minute gesture. "Not long after, an equally daring robbery occurred in Bergen, Norway, at the Kode Museum. This time *los ladrones* took over fifty pieces, all from the Asian art collection. They broke in through a skylight."

Cape cocked an eyebrow. "Sounds familiar."

"The Chinese art collection at Cambridge was next." Maria counted off events with the fingers of her left hand. "Then, a few years later, a second break-in at the Kode in Norway. Over twenty objects overlooked during the first robbery. This time they vanished within two minutes."

"You think it's the same team."

"Burning cars were used in both Stockholm and the second Kode heist," said Maria. "The first time in Norway they came in through a skylight, which is what they tried here. That's no *coincidencia*; it's the same team."

"You knew they were coming," said Cape. "That's the mystery, but you haven't told—"

"—what is the expression?" asked Maria. "You show me yours?"

Cape's fingers drummed a silent tune on his steering wheel. "I have a client."

"Who was inside the museum."

Cape nodded. "That's all there is to say for now—"

"—because you don't really know me," said Maria. "And I'm the police."

"By any other name," said Cape.

"Fair." Maria pressed her palms together as if in prayer. "I'm getting hungry."

Cape checked his watch. "Let's give it ten minutes. Plenty of time for you to share the prophecy that brought you here."

"It's not magic." Maria pulled out her phone and thumbed through her photos. "The clues were everywhere." She scrolled to an album and handed the phone to Cape.

Catalog pages featured photographs of statues, paintings, incense burners, vases, and other items Cape could not identify. Next to each was a short description of the object, its provenance and current location. Some entries appeared in English, others in Italian, French, Spanish, and Chinese. The pages were apparently from different sources. Fonts varied and image quality was inconsistent.

"Auction catalogs?"

"And museum guidebooks," said Maria. "From all over the world."

Cape studied the images. "It's all Asian art."

"It's all Chinese art," said Maria. "Antiques from key periods in China's history."

"You think it's the same buyer?"

"You're thinking black market," said Maria. "Think bigger."

"Organized crime?"

"Bigger still." Maria pressed her fingers together. "Have you heard of China Poly Group? No reason you should have, unless you're with military intelligence or an art collector."

"Those two worlds don't usually overlap."

"It's a company," said Maria, "based in Beijing."

"Government affiliated?"

"Defense contractors," said Maria. "They make missiles, guidance systems, all sort of toys for the Chinese military. Latest estimates put their revenue over a hundred billion dollars."

"So it's a well-connected company." Cape already felt in over his head but now sensed an undercurrent of something much deeper. "What's that got to do with art?"

"What if art could be turned into a weapon?"

"That's a hell of a question," said Cape. "Now pretend I'm stupid, because I frequently am."

"Don't feel bad, I've been working on this more than a year." Maria looked across the street at the Byzantine saints, their expressions unwavering. "Consider what happened in Hong Kong. Student protestors arrested, tech billionaires gone missing, songs banned. Total suppression of political dissent."

Cape nodded. Sally rarely talked about her childhood but often spoke about current events in Hong Kong. "Keep going."

"Imagine what it's like on the mainland," said Maria. "What can you do to prove you're patriotic enough, more patriotic than your neighbor or political adversary?" Maria's eyes did their now familiar dance. "You could repatriate priceless Chinese art."

"Repatriate." Cape deconstructed the word. "Bring lost art home to China."

"This art isn't lost," said Maria. "It's hiding in plain sight in museums."

"Isn't the art in museums on loan from private collections, or bought from a previous owner?" Cape had visited museums his entire life and was surprised he'd never considered the angles. "Or found by archaeologists, or maybe—"

"—taken by conquering armies," said Maria. "China was invaded many, many times over the centuries. Mongolia, Russia, and Japan took their turns. England and France fought together during the 1900s. Spoils of war ended up in private collections and museums."

"Good content for The History Channel," said Cape, "but why Interpol?"

"My office became aware of China Poly when they launched a division called Poly Culture," said Maria, "a special group dedicated to reclaiming lost art. A task force was put together and started traveling the world. Delegations visited every major museum, asking permission to catalog their Chinese antiquities. They published the catalog online and updated it after each trip." Maria shifted in her seat and faced Cape. "At the same time, a new wave of Chinese billionaires began outbidding everyone at auction houses for historic art."

"Sounds expensive, but not illegal."

"Not at all," said Maria. "But you'll never guess what the task force did after they completed their catalog of all the museum collections of Chinese art."

"What?" Cape sat up straighter behind the wheel.

"They demanded all the art be returned," said Maria. "Immediately."

Cape shook his head in disbelief. "I bet the museum directors loved that."

"Awkward, to say the least," said Maria. "No one was ever brazen enough to ask."

"If a work of art was in the museum's possession for more than a century—"

"—who does it belong to?" Maria rubbed her hands together, excited by her own question. "Provenance sometimes leads to more controversy, not less."

"For example?"

"Say an antique was bought at auction after it was sold to the auction house by a private collector, who bought it from another collector, who was given the piece by their great-grandfather who fought in the war, who acquired it during a campaign in Southeast Asia."

"How far back do you go?" asked Cape. "There must be some precedent."

"There are conventions," said Maria. "Guidelines really, tacit agreements, but no one in the art world has dealt with a state entity before, not at this scale. And make no mistake, Poly

Culture is a state entity. Half their staff members come from military intelligence, no formal training in art or antiquities. Imagine if the CIA suddenly took an interest in Colonial art."

"If there's no legal precedent," said Cape, "the museums could just say no."

"Most of them did."

"And?"

"One by one, they all got robbed."

17

"You got robbed," said Beau. "Which means your security tape belongs to me."

The security officer had a handlebar mustache that wriggled nervously when he looked at his feet. "The museum director was quite explicit when he called."

"And said what, exactly?"

Beau looked relaxed in jeans and sneakers, but his eyes had the subzero glint of a veteran cop with a low tolerance for bullshit. His partner, Vinnie, leaned against the wall, looking more like the next cover of *GQ* than a police detective. His suit was cobalt blue, his tie gray silk, and his shoes as polished as Beau's stare. Vinnie had never seen anyone successfully stonewall Beau and clearly enjoyed watching the timorous walrus talk himself into a trap.

"You've got a helicopter sticking out your window," said Beau. "So you're not getting out of this room until we get some cooperation."

The three of them were squeezed into the security office on the ground level of the museum, a beige room with beige carpeting and a bank of monitors worthy of a casino. Vinnie figured there were at least thirty cameras on three-hundred-sixty-degree rotations. Below the screens was a control panel and phone on a long table, under which a bank of servers hummed contentedly.

"The director said he would prefer the museum's lawyers were consulted before any videotapes are shared with, um...the authorities...mmhhmm...with you." The security officer cleared his throat and looked longingly at the door. He was the day guard for a reason—because nothing ever happened during the day.

"Where is the director presently?" asked Beau.

Another throat clearing. "He's in Napa...at his vineyard."

Beau glanced at Vinnie. "He's at his vineyard."

"Nice," said Vinnie. "Maybe we should visit, deliver the warrant ourselves."

"It is a nice drive," said Beau. "Could be there in two hours if we hustle."

The walrus did a little two-step at the suggestion. "I don't think—"

"You have his cell number?" asked Beau.

"Of course," said the guard.

"Good," said Beau. "Because after we take you down to the station, you get one phone call."

"It's one of the perks," said Vinnie.

"Arrest...me?" The guard's mustache tried to escape from his face.

"Obstruction of justice," said Beau, "is a felony."

"Interfering with an investigation," said Vinnie, "includes delaying an investigation."

"And we're in a hurry," said Beau.

The guard swiveled his head between the detectives, indecision etched across his mouth.

"Let me give you some advice." Vinnie pushed himself off the wall, not a crease visible anywhere. "Go outside for a cigarette."

"I...I don't smoke," said the guard.

"Never too late to start," said Beau. "Does wonders for the lungs."

"Would you rather stay here?" Vinnie patted his jacket pockets. "While I find my handcuffs?"

The guard rushed to the door but froze when Beau's hand landed on his shoulder.

"Cue the security footage from last night before you go." Beau gestured at the monitors. "So we don't have to come outside and drag your ass back in here."

The footage they needed was sourced from three cameras and appeared on the monitors along the top of the array. Beau and Vinnie each took a chair and watched the prior night unfold.

"Damn." Beau smacked a hand on the table as Grace appeared in frame.

"How young do you guess she is?"

Beau shook his head. "Too young to witness a murder."

"No wonder the museum director is reluctant to share the footage. "

Beau scowled. "Asshole is more worried about a kid wandering around after hours, while his night guard is lying in pieces at the morgue."

"Wait...here it comes."

Silence as they watched Grace stand by the window as light from the helicopter illuminated the glass walkway. Neither Beau nor Vinnie looked away when the rotor blade flew from the tail of the helicopter. Within the confines of the security room, the airborne scythe traveled from left to right, spinning across screens on its tragic trajectory. Both detectives grimaced as the guard met his end, a grisly scene, even for veterans of homicide.

"You think the girl was with the guard?" asked Vinnie.

Beau nodded. "Family maybe."

Vinnie was about to say something but caught himself as figures emerged from the helicopter. The crash had damaged the camera in the hallway, so the screen on the left cut off suddenly, which would have provided a view from a second angle. Vinnie and Beau saw the figures as Grace would have, as they approached the gallery.

Two Asian men in black clothes, one stocky and the other tall. Smoke trailed alongside as they walked toward the exhibit hall, a fog that warped the air and blurred everything in its vicinity. When the two intruders entered the hall of Buddhas, each statue they passed shimmered and vanished, then reappeared in their wake.

"You seeing this?"

Vinnie found the button on the console that froze the playback, then struck the button like a man playing "Jingle Bells" on a piano to advance the scene one frame at a time. The aura expanded and contracted as it moved, a cumulous cloud gliding with purpose. Under the strobe effect of Vinnie's playback, the inchoate fog took on a tenuous shape. It became the silhouette of a man.

"Now that's clever," said Vinnie. "Some kind of electronic distortion?"

"Looks like a goddamn ghost," said Beau. "We can ID the other two, though."

"What we need is a witness." Vinnie used his phone to capture the faces of the men in black. "We should go to the security guard's place, pick up the girl."

"Yeah." Beau stood and pushed his chair to the side with his foot. "But five bucks says she's not there."

"Then where's the kid?"

"I don't know," said Beau. "But I know who to ask."

18

Sally asked to see the menu before requesting a table at the back of the restaurant.

She wasn't hungry, but standing near the entrance and pretending to browse the list of appetizers created an opportunity to surveil the room. Oil paintings and wood trim evoked a rich heritage, and the smells from the kitchen made guests feel warm before they removed their coats. The tables were narrow, the coffered ceiling white, and the walls were still deciding if they were red or orange.

Sally spotted a long table on the left, actually four tables pushed together to accommodate large men squeezed into small chairs. Their voices were raucous, their bearing bellicose, and the number of empty bottles was prodigious. A flat-screen TV was mounted on the wall above their table.

The restaurant wasn't busy, only two couples and a family of four. Tuesday being a slow night, the hostess was surprised when Sally asked to sit directly behind and across from the men.

Sally nodded at the television. "I like to watch while I eat."

The table of men glanced her way, but Sally didn't make eye contact. She had been trained to notice things without looking at them directly. Two men in particular tracked her progress from the hostess station until she sat at her table and spread the napkin over her lap. The two men's chairs were spaced farther apart than the others, so it would be easier for them to stand.

Those are the bodyguards.

The bodyguards sat on either side of a broad-shouldered man who sat facing the television with his back to Sally.

And that must be Valenko.

Sally gave the menu a cursory glance and ordered a steak medium-rare. She preferred vegetarian dishes or seafood but wanted access to the steak knife that came with her meal.

Her purse contained a few handy items for more intimate settings. A necklace that doubled as a garotte, a narcotic lipstick, and a perfume vial filled with acid strong enough to eat through most padlocks. From the look of the thick-necked men at the nearby table, Sally doubted those would be necessary.

The bodyguard on the right shifted in his chair, and Sally noticed the bulge under his right arm. He needed a better tailor or a smaller handgun.

He's left-handed.

Sally smiled as the waiter refilled her water glass, then she turned her attention to the television. *America's Got Talent* was in full swing. A dance troupe performed a scene from *Grease*, blindfolded. A big number with one dozen dancers, the potential for collisions was high.

It reminded Sally of her school days in Hong Kong.

For one of Sally's middle school classes, her instructors made the class traverse a maze of wooden poles, hopping from one to another without falling. The poles were ten feet high, and the ground was covered in sand, not soft enough to prevent a bruise but thick enough to avoid a break, and absorbent in case there was bleeding.

The final exam was to complete the maze blindfolded.

Sally thought the dancers did a pretty good job, and the *AGT* judges seemed to agree. The Russians banged glasses on the big table in unison and drank a shot of vodka. It was unanimous.

Cape was due to arrive halfway into the show, so Sally ate slowly. He was coming to have a conversation, but Valenko might not be in a voluble mood. Sally considered the body-guard's ill-fitting suit and assumed all the men were armed. She cut her steak, testing the edge of the knife, before turning her attention back to the TV.

The next act was about to begin.

19

"He said the final act was about to begin," said Peng. "The curtain will rise, and the world shall see the Middle Kingdom in all its glory."

"That's quite a sales pitch," said Yan. "But what does Mogwai want you to do?"

Peng took a deep breath to slow his pulse, still wired from his encounter with the Devil. He spoke in rapid bursts as his adrenaline sloshed up and down.

After Peng had left his supervisor's office, Yan hid in one of the bathroom stalls until everyone had left the building, including Mogwai. By the time she returned to Peng's apartment he was already there, hyperventilating.

Peng insisted they leave their phones behind and take a walk. Neither of them spoke until the lampposts and CCTV cameras gave way to a small park. With every step, Peng wondered what twist in fate had led to this moment.

"He spoke about lost art."

"That's it?" asked Yan. "The Devil appears to discuss art history?"

"It was sort of a one-way conversation," said Peng defensively.

"Details."

"I felt like I was listening to a speech," said Peng. "Mogwai talked about 'the century of humiliation' and the Opium Wars, then ranted about reclaiming our dignity to find our destiny, that sort of thing."

"Sounds like an article you'd find in *People's Daily*," said Yan, "but in a way, it makes sense."

"If it makes sense to you, please explain it to me."

"Why else come to Dafen?" Yan spread her hands to encompass the town. "The CCP never cared about history or culture until recently. Remember that fuss over the zodiac sculptures taken from the Summer Palace?"

"Of course."

Every student in China was taught the shame of the nineteenth century, when British and French invaders looted the emperor's Summer Palace. The grounds defiled, buildings burned, artwork stolen. The government left it in ruins as a cautionary tale.

"Whenever someone mentions the Opium Wars, I think of the palace," said Yan.

"I always thought it was ironic that the looted artwork only survived the Cultural Revolution because it was stolen from China."

"You're starting to think like a rebel," said Yan. "I like it."

Peng blanched. "That's not funny."

"You worry too much." Yan smiled. "Anyway, when two of the zodiac animals turned up in Europe—"

"—the government intervened in a private auction, right?"

"Exactly," said Yan. "China pressured France, where the auction was taking place, to return the sculptures. In exchange, the auction house got a license to operate in Hong Kong."

"That's global politics." Peng's lips twitched nervously. "I'm just a local artist."

"If the Devil is here," said Yan, "it has something to do with power. Anything that can become a symbol has influence. Art has been used to fuel patriotism before."

Peng looked skeptical. "Patriotism..."

"—another word for obedience."

"You need to watch what you s—"

"—tell me what Mogwai asked you to do, exactly," said Yan.

"Okay, but first...will you hold my hand?"

Yan stopped walking and stared at Peng. He walked a few more paces before he realized that his question had stopped Yan in her tracks.

"Wow," said Yan, "are you that shaken up?"

Peng gave a shy smile. "No, I just thought it might be nice."

"I thought we were friends."

"We—"

"—actually." Yan put a hand on her hip. "I almost forgot, we're not friends...you called us coworkers."

"You're not going to make this easy, are you?"

"Not a chance."

Peng took a step closer. "Let's keep walking." He took Yan's hand in his and added, "And I'll tell you everything."

"Is this your way of asking me out?"

Peng looked at the grass and didn't reply.

"Your hand is clammy," said Yan. "Are you nervous?"

Peng gave her a look. "Maybe."

"Don't be." Yan smiled and gave his hand a long squeeze. "I've only been dropping hints for a year."

Peng exhaled loudly, then laughed. "I hadn't noticed."

"Clearly," said Yan. "You're a great artist, but you need some help with social skills."

They found an unoccupied patch of grass suitably distant from anyone and sat cross-legged facing each other.

Yan gave Peng's hand another squeeze. "Now, tell me what happened."

Peng did his best to recount the entire conversation, but Mogwai had rambled and changed topics without waiting for a reply. Maybe the Devil didn't care about Peng's answers, since his only option was to have agreed.

The distortion of the mask and throat mike also made the voice hard to follow.

"It sounds like you're supposed to keep doing exactly what you're doing," said Yan. "Only instead of copying Western masters, you'll recreate Chinese classics."

"And sculptures," said Peng. "Mogwai talked a lot about statues."

"Was all the art he described historical?"

Peng nodded. "Why?"

"It's curious, that's all."

"I'll be working with someone else, an expert from Hong Kong."

"Another painter?"

"No," said Peng. "A professor."

"You've painted a thousand Rembrandts but never had to work anyone before."

"I know, that's what has me worried," said Peng. "What if I mess up?"

"Don't worry." Yan leaned forward and kissed him on the cheek. "You're the most talented person I know." She stood and extended her hand to help him up. "Let's go get something to eat."

"Are you asking me out?" Peng grinned.

"No, you are taking me to dinner. I'm just informing you of the fact." Yan smiled. "There's a difference."

"Was that our first kiss?"

"Absolutely not!" Yan looked dismayed. "That was a friendly kiss. If dinner goes well, you may kiss me later."

Peng quickened his pace but managed to refrain from skipping. It wasn't easy. "Are you going to make all the decisions in our relationship, Yan?"

"I haven't decided," said Yan. "Now, let's go to dinner."

20

"Before we go to dinner," said Cape, "I want to give you something."

Maria glanced across the seat and smiled. "Flowers?"

Cape looked bemused. "Are all Spanish women—"

"—this charming?"

"I was going to say—"

"—forward," said Maria, "or assertive?"

"Something along those lines."

"If you keep a man off balance," said Maria, "he'll never throw you off yours."

Cape reached across Maria and inserted a key into the glove compartment. "I know you like to be disarming, but I'd prefer that you were armed." He turned the key, popped open the compartment, and reached inside. Maria's eyebrows rose as Cape placed a pistol in her hands.

"I thought you didn't like guns."

"Guns don't bother me," said Cape. "I just don't like shooting people."

"Is that something you do often?"

"No," said Cape, "but it's been known to happen."

"It's better than getting shot," said Maria. "Wouldn't you agree?"

"That's why I have a gun."

"Which you gave to me." Maria turned the pistol over in her hands. "Very nice." The gun was black, six and a half inches long with a metal slide on a composite frame. "A 9-millimeter Heckler & Koch, subcompact model. Easy to conceal, good stopping power. You have good taste."

"You must work for Interpol," said Cape. "Most people would judge me for my car."

"I don't like convertibles," said Maria. "My hair is too long."

"The magazine release is ambidextrous," said Cape. "And there's an extra clip in the glove compartment if you want it."

"If I need an extra magazine," said Maria, "we're already dead."

"Agreed," said Cape. "I doubt you'll need it, unless we have to bluff our way out."

Maria released the magazine, checked it was loaded, then thrust it back inside the handle of the gun. "Why aren't you carrying?"

"Once we start talking, one of two things will happen," said Cape. "We'll either be having drinks with a bunch of Russians, or Valenko's men will search me before we get close. And if I don't have a gun, they'll assume you don't, either."

"*Sí*, you are right." Maria scowled. "Russians gangsters are the most sexist criminals on the planet. So are Russian policemen. Remind me to tell you about the time I kicked one in the *cojones* while on assignment in Moscow."

"A gangster or a policeman?"

"I was never sure," said Maria. "But he had it coming."

"Remind me to never piss you off."

"You have much better manners." Maria hefted the gun in

her hand. "We haven't even had dinner, and already you gave me a present."

"That's on loan," said Cape. "And I'm pretty sure it's illegal for you to have that, since you're off duty—"

"—and on vacation," said Maria. "It is definitely illegal. That's what makes it so fun." She racked the slide to load a bullet in the chamber. "Oh, if we get arrested, I'm afraid I'll have to say the gun is yours."

"I figured."

"Such a gentleman." Maria dropped the gun into her shoulder bag.

Cape pocketed his keys and checked his watch. "Hungry?"

"Famished."

Five minutes later they entered the Red Tavern.

Cape left his jacket in the car so it was clear he wasn't armed. Maria wore her bag over her right shoulder as they followed the hostess to their table. Maria sat against the same wall as Sally, who was two tables down, looking disinterested in their arrival.

Valenko never turned around, secure in his position. Confident in his men.

Cape sat across from Maria but turned his chair sideways, as if angling for a view of the television mounted on the wall. The two bodyguards made similar adjustments to their seating when Maria sat down, each keeping one eye on the new dinner guests and the other eye glued to their favorite show.

Cape ordered a bottle of the same vodka the Russians were drinking, along with two glasses. Maria suppressed a smile and pretended to glance at the menu. The closest bodyguard turned his head to keep them in his peripheral vision, but his attention was clearly on the screen in the corner. Things were getting tense on *America's Got Talent*.

A woman with a singing dog was halfway through her number.

The act was fairly simple. She accompanied the dog by playing the piano and joining in the chorus, but the canine crooner was the main attraction. It looked like they would make it to the finish until Mel B hit her buzzer so hard the other judges jumped in their chairs. Even Simon was startled by her savagery.

The Russian gangsters gave a collective sigh.

"Mel B is tough on singers," said Cape, more loudly than necessary.

The bodyguard on the right gave Cape a steely stare, but after a long moment, he nodded and said, "*Da*, she is a tyrant."

"Scary Spice." Cape raised his glass and drank. The Russian held up his own glass before turning his attention to the show's judges, who continued to argue.

Maria glanced over the menu. "What are you doing?"

"Trying to engage," said Cape. "Maybe making a fool of myself."

"You're very good at it," said Maria. "But don't you want to eat first?"

Cape glanced over his shoulder. "Only two or three acts before the show ends."

"And I thought you were a gentleman," said Maria. "You won't buy me dinner?"

"I bought you breakfast," said Cape. "And we don't have much time."

Maria lowered the menu and lowered her voice at the same time. "They will think it's suspicious if we come for dinner and don't order food." She smiled as the waiter arrived.

Cape glanced at Sally's table without looking directly at her. "The steak looks good."

"No, no, no," said Maria, eyes still on the waiter, who had one eye on the television. "We're going to share." She ran a finger down the menu. "We will have the Baltic herring, pelmeni, blinchiki with meat, and pirozhki with cabbage."

"I hate cabbage," said Cape.

"Then just eat the pirozhki," said Maria.

"What are blinchiki?"

"Another name for blini."

"That doesn't help."

"Crepes," said Maria. "They're like crepes."

"I love crepes," said Cape.

"Everybody loves crepes," said Maria.

"I like to think of them as pretentious pancakes."

"Do you always say whatever you're thinking?" asked Maria. "Or do you have filters?"

"Was that a rhetorical question?"

"Yes."

Maria handed her menu back to the waiter, who made a slow turn so he could catch the end of the latest act. A magician was sawing a woman in half, but his act had a twist.

The magician was using a light saber. He was dressed as a Jedi, and his assistant was Chewbacca. Otherwise the trick was familiar to anyone who'd seen stage magic before. The Jedi was about to use the Force to stitch the two halves of the woman back together when Howie hit his buzzer. The dejected magician wheeled the two separate halves of the woman off stage, her legs kicking indignantly. Chewbacca howled at the judges.

The Russians howled in sympathy with the Wookiee and banged the table. Cape drank a shot in solidarity and slammed his glass on the table. Maria followed suit, which garnered a look of approval from the bodyguard on the left.

"We have this show in Spain," said Maria.

"But it's not called *America's Got Talent*, is it?"

"You must be a detective," said Maria. "Spain is in the title, if that's what you're asking."

"Same format?"

"Identical." Maria spun the bottle of vodka to inspect the label. "I never knew it could be a drinking game."

Cape checked the TV. "Another drink and my judgment will be impaired." He pushed his chair back. "I'm going to say hello."

"You Americans." Maria put a hand on his arm. "Always in a hurry."

"Not always." Cape checked his watch. "But I am getting anxious."

"I keep forgetting you're not *policía*," said Maria. "By now your friend, the inspector—"

"—Beau."

"He's checked the security tape from the museum."

"Which means he's seen my client."

"I never thought of this before," said Maria. "For someone like you, speed is an ally. For me, every step requires deliberation. Tonight I would observe. Tomorrow I would engage. Each night, I would file a report."

"Procedures and process. It's linear for a cop." Cape shrugged. "You have all the resources. The only thing I have is momentum."

Maria's eyes sparked. "You are like a *colibrí*."

"Is that a crepe," asked Cape, "or a pancake?"

"It's a hummingbird." Maria's hand zigzagged over the table. "You go where you please."

"Then, please, let me go to the bathroom." Cape jerked his head toward the hallway at the back of the restaurant. "And put your hand in your purse."

Cape stood and strode casually past the tables, Russians on his left and Sally on his right. He could feel the bodyguards' eyes on his back as he entered a short hall that extended past the kitchen to the restrooms. After entering the men's room, he counted to sixty, guessing there were four commercials in the break. He wanted to return during the third.

He timed it pretty well.

Cape studied Valenko's profile as he approached the tables. A leonine countenance, thick black hair with streaks of gray flowing past his collar. The rugged look of an aging movie star.

Cape was almost at his own table when he gave Maria a sardonic grin and spun on his heel. He spread his arms as if seeing an old friend after years apart.

"Maksim." Cape took a step closer. "Maksim Valenko?"

All six Russians turned as one the instant Cape uttered the name.

The nearest bodyguard stood between Cape and his boss. Sally stood and headed to the ladies' room. The Russians ignored her.

Cape held his arms away from his sides and nodded at the television. The last commercial was running. "Place a bet on the final act?"

The closest bodyguard moved laterally so Valenko could make eye contact with Cape.

"We do not know each other." Valenko's voice was a bottomless pit filled with corpses.

"We don't," said Cape, "but I'll bet you the next act is a singer."

The nearest bodyguard muttered under his breath. "Dancers, it will be dancers."

Valenko's eyes darted to the TV. "What if it is?"

"You answer my questions."

"And if it's not?"

Cape shrugged. "You decide."

Valenko's eyes narrowed at the prospect of doing whatever it is that someone like him enjoys doing to someone who loses a bet. Cape suspected it involved pliers and a car battery.

Valenko gave a nonverbal invitation by canting his head at the nearest chair.

Then Cape made a terrible mistake.

He lowered his hands too quickly as he stepped forward. Whether it was from his own impatience or the vodka, Cape was off tempo in an orchestra where all the musicians were heavily armed. The closest bodyguard brought his hands up in a fighting stance and moved sideways to block a path to Valenko. Two men on the far side of the table shifted in their seats and slid their hands behind their backs.

The bodyguard closest to the hallway on Valenko's right was still seated. As he moved to stand, he pressed his right hand on the table with fingers spread wide to push himself up. His left hand began snaking under his jacket for his gun.

Cape heard the sharp click of a gun being cocked, but he couldn't tell whose it was. It sounded like entropy clucking its tongue, and he cursed himself for his clumsiness. The mood of the room was accelerating toward chaos.

Someone started yelling. All eyes swung to the bodyguard sitting on Valenko's right.

His head shook and his left hand banged on the table as he bellowed in pain. His gun clattered from his lap to the floor. It was obvious to everyone why he never managed to stand or point his gun at Cape.

His right hand was impaled by a steak knife.

The knife was embedded between the third and fourth fingers at the point where they branch upward from the back of the hand. The blade penetrated deep into the table so he couldn't pull it out. Blood pooled under his palm in arterial waves of claret.

Sally was nowhere to be seen. The hallway was empty. Cape hadn't moved.

Valenko's men regained focus and gave Cape their undivided attention. Every one of them pointed a gun at the lone detective. The first shot was a thunderclap in the small restaurant.

Cape remained upright.

The Russians stared at the bullet hole in the wall above their heads. Then they turned their heads toward the shooter without changing the position of their gun arms.

Maria stood holding the compact semiautomatic, the barrel whispering a trail of smoke.

Maria swept her eyes across the men until they lowered their weapons, then she aimed directly at the television. Everyone gasped in horror.

"Gentlemen." Maria smiled, but her bright eyes had gone hard. "Unless you want your show to be canceled, stop acting like a bunch of hyenas." She sat down but kept her gun up.

Valenko glanced at his incapacitated bodyguard, then turned his gaze on Maria before locking eyes with Cape. The corners of his mouth curled upward as the commercial ended and the *America's Got Talent* logo filled the screen. Once again he indicated the chair next to him.

This time Cape took a seat. All eyes looked to the television for an answer.

A moment later, a brother-sister duo took the stage and started to sing.

Valenko turned to Cape. "Ask your questions."

21

Grace kept asking herself the same question.

Could she leave and come back before Sally returned?

Grace couldn't sleep. Every time she started to doze, her uncle ran up the steps of the museum, waving her back from the window as the helicopter flew straight at her. Her day of training and the distraction that came with it had disappeared, gone with Sally, leaving Grace alone with the nightmare of her new reality.

She missed her uncle. She missed her dad. Memories were the only family she had left.

Grace felt a sudden yearning for a physical connection to her past. Something tangible, an artifact that proved she came from somewhere. From someone.

That once she had been loved, and not hunted.

There was a photograph. Her dad and her uncle together, years ago in Hong Kong. The two of them smiling as they pretend to fight over a bundle in her father's hands, her uncle laughing as he makes an exaggerated grab. The bundle is Grace. Strands of hair escape from the shawl, her face is obscured, but infant Grace is giggling at the grown-ups.

Her father gave Grace that photograph the day he smuggled her out of Hong Kong so she could recognize her uncle Han after so many years apart. Now it was the only evidence that Grace had ever had a childhood. She wanted it back.

This is a bad idea.

Grace got up from bed before the voice in her head got the upper hand. The cat had been curled at her feet and now lifted his head to open one eye. It stood and arched its back with a disapproving *mrrowll* as Grace tightened the laces on her shoes.

"Don't worry, Xan," said Grace. "I'll be back before Sally, so it will be our secret."

Xan licked his paw with the lightning scar and gave Grace a skeptical look.

"You can keep a secret, can't you?" Grace realized that a cat's loyalty could be bought, so she knelt and scratched Xan behind the ears until he started purring. "Keep the bed warm until I get back."

She crossed the wooden floor of the dojo and stopped before the vast wooden door. She worried exiting would be as puzzling as entering, but mounted on the wall was a circular handle roughly eight inches in diameter. It resembled a wheel on a ship's hatch.

Grace studied the door, recalling that it slid into the wall left to right from her current perspective. If the wheel matched the movement of the door, that meant turn the handle clockwise.

That's too easy.

Though she was inside the sanctum, Grace suspected there would be at least one twist. Exits should be quick, so she prayed there wasn't a puzzle or hidden latch. She took a step back and almost stumbled over the cat. Xan had followed and was vigorously rubbing against her legs.

"Not now, Xan."

Taking a deep breath, Grace stepped to the wheel and spun it counterclockwise. She closed her eyes as she gripped the wheel, tensed in anticipation of poison darts, electric shocks, or a fall through a trapdoor. Instead, she heard a click followed by a whirring sound as the half-ton slab of wood slid along its tracks.

The door was opening. Xan was first to exit, the cat bounding down the stairs before Grace could stop him. She knew he'd been out before and hoped he'd come back. Grace searched for a way to close the door, but after a moment, there was another click as the door reversed to slide back into place.

No turning back now.

Grace moved quickly down the steps to the street. From the shadow of the doorway, she looked left to right and got her bearings. Her uncle's apartment was only a few blocks away.

She stepped from the shadows, sparing a glance across the street. The old woman, Rushi, was minding the fish market, talking to a young couple at the entrance. The overhead fluorescents cast a sepia light across Rushi and her customers, making it look like a scene from a vintage postcard. Grace felt frozen in time and fought an impulse to run back up the stairs.

Grace shoved her hands in her pockets and walked with her head down. She went half a block, then waited for a car to pass before she crossed the street. It was dark but early. Most of the tourists were gone, but the street was busy enough for Grace to feel safe. The crowds were nothing compared to Hong Kong's, so she was able to glide along the ebbs and flows without making waves.

Ten minutes later she was standing inside the doorway of a building across the street from her uncle's apartment. Grace tried to remember clever tricks she had seen in action movies. Her imagination had turned this excursion into a secret mission, because if she didn't feel like a spy, there was every chance she might feel like a girl with a price on her head.

Which is precisely what she was.

Pedestrians came and went, but no one entered the building. Grace wished she was wearing a hat. She ran her hands through her hair to mess it up, pulling her long hair from the back across the sides of her face and over her eyes. She knew how that felt after she woke up each morning so didn't need a mirror to know how it looked. With a final shake of her head, Grace paused for a passing car and dashed across the street.

She crept up the stairs to the landing. Her uncle's apartment door was directly ahead, unobstructed by policemen or yellow tape. The red doormat was undisturbed. Her uncle told Grace that red was the most auspicious color since their apartment faced south. He also told her where the extra key was hidden, taped under the upper left corner of the mat.

Grace darted from the landing, knelt, and tore away the key. One turn of the deadbolt, then she slid the same key into the lock embedded in the doorknob. Grace slipped inside and pressed her back against the door, exhaling loudly.

The apartment was small and cozy, a modest one-bedroom with a convertible couch in the living room where Grace had slept. Diffuse light from a streetlamp cut across the rails of the fire escape outside the lone window behind the couch. The glow bathed the apartment in a crosshatch strobe that caught dust motes surfing the air currents displaced by the opening of the door.

Though Grace had been gone less than a day, the apartment felt abandoned.

Her eyes burned, but she blinked away the tears before they came. Grace knew it wasn't safe to linger. With a determined clench of her jaw, she turned on the lights and moved to the end table by the couch. The photograph was there, in an acrylic frame next to an alarm clock.

Grace rummaged under the couch and found her backpack, grabbed the photo and clock, and tossed them inside. She spotted a stuffed animal in the corner of the couch. It was a red rooster. Her uncle bought it from a local shop the day she arrived, a reminder of her birth year and something to hug if she ever felt scared at night. Next to the rooster was a worn baseball cap, with the insignia of the local baseball team that her uncle wore all the time. On the coffee table was an old book he had read to her, traditional Chinese legends and myths. Grace grabbed the rooster, hat, and book, then headed for the adjoining room and closet she shared with her uncle.

The doorknob began to rattle.

Grace froze in mid-step. The lock inside the doorknob was automatic, but she did not turn the deadbolt after coming inside. A scraping sound now accompanied the rattle. Someone was trying to slip the latch.

Grace scrambled over the back of the couch, backpack over her shoulder, and wedged into the small space below the window. She pressed her face against the floor and inched forward to peek around the leg of the couch.

The door swung open with a metallic groan. A man stood in the hallway.

Even before he came inside, Grace recognized the stocky man from the museum. She had seen that silhouette before, backlit by flames. He stepped across the threshold, and light from the window bounced off the gun in his waistband.

Grace held her breath. She felt like she was back in the museum, crouching in terror behind the Buddha. The man took another step, his head turning as he looked for the light switch.

A heavy tread on the stairs preceded a second figure

appearing in the hallway, much taller than the first. The stocky man jerked in surprise as a deep voice rumbled into the room.

"This isn't your apartment, is it?"

The shorter man stopped in mid-turn. His gaze shifted, and a pair of nervous eyes caught Grace peering around the couch. A cruel smile spread across his face as his hand began to slide along his belt toward his gun.

"Show me your hands," said the hallway baritone. "And I'll show you my badge."

Grace released the breath she'd been holding as the shorter man began to raise his arms.

Then he dropped into a crouch and spun on his heel. Lightning flashed in the hallway and thunder tore through the room. A hole the size of a fist appeared in the man's right shoulder.

Grace tasted blood as it splattered across the couch.

The stocky man fell backward. His gun slid under the couch as his head hit the floor.

The gun smacked Grace in the side and she yelped. Without thinking, she grabbed the pistol and shoved it into her backpack. She didn't want the gun, but at a primal level Grace didn't want anyone else to have it, either. Panic flooded her veins, and she lunged for the window.

A deep voice shouted at her, but blood was rushing in her ears and all Grace knew was her nails were breaking as she frantically tried to slide the window up and escape.

She rolled onto the fire escape. The night air was a cold slap that sent her running.

One flight of metal steps, a hairpin turn, down and around on her zigzag race to freedom. When she reached the platform at the bottom of the stairs, Grace spared a look over her shoulder. A large man leaned out the window, his skin dark and his head shaved. Around his neck was a lanyard holding a gold badge.

Grace grabbed the ladder and hung in space but was afraid to let go. Her fingers were petrified, and she was suddenly unsure if she should climb back up to the apartment or drop into the unknown. When her right hand slipped, the fingers on her left hand made the decision for her. She fell hard and tumbled across the alley behind the building.

Grace was still on her hands and knees when a new voice cut through the night. Two shoes appeared on either side of her shoulders as a man straddled her, pinning her down.

"*Zhù xiàlái.*"

Grace craned her neck and recognized the second man from the museum, the tall one. She choked back a sob. The man had just told her not to move, but her arms buckled and Grace worried she would fall on her face if she didn't stand up. She wished that Sally was there, but Grace was alone. Sally had told her to wait, and Grace didn't listen.

Then Grace remembered the lesson of the day.

If I get away, I've won.

Grace tried to control her breathing. She stared at her bloody hands and knew things could get much worse. She was too weak to resist, and the man standing over her seemed to be waiting for her to calm down and be still.

Maybe he's waiting for a ghost to appear.

That thought was all the motivation Grace needed. She rocked back on her knees, dug her toes into the concrete, and shot upward like an Olympic gymnast. Her tiny hands came together on impact, catching both testicles in a fist sandwich.

The man buckled as his face became an abstract painting of agony and rage.

Grace snatched her backpack off the pavement and ran. She

didn't look back until she made it across the street and ran two more blocks. No ghosts in sight, only couples exiting bars and merchants minding their shops.

She kept moving. With every slap of her shoes, she heard Sally's voice in her head, guiding her back to the loft. Grace had almost lost everything, and now she swore that she would never stop running.

Not until she won something back.

22

"You won your wager," said Valenko. "But if I may, I would like to speak first."

"Shoot." Cape remembered he was surrounded by guns and added, "Go ahead."

Cape sat on Valenko's left. The television was turned off, the game show over.

Behind the Russian mob boss, two men were attempting to pry the steak knife from the table without severing any arteries in the bodyguard's hand. The wounded man put his good hand in his mouth and bit down hard. Valenko paid them no attention.

"You are not *politsiya*." Valenko remained fixed on Cape as he tilted his head in Maria's direction. "But your colleague holds her gun like a cop, in a textbook stance, even when shooting my television."

"*Relajarse*, I only shot the wall." Maria had returned to her table because the food had arrived. Her gun lay on its side next to her water glass, the barrel pointing at Valenko. If tempers flared, Maria could pull the trigger in less time than it would take to grab her fork.

"And for that I am in your debt." Valenko seemed unperturbed, but his eyes caught the light as he smiled at Maria. It was the gaze of a lion caught in the beam of a safari guide's flashlight, right before the guide got eaten alive. "How do you like the *pelmeni*?"

"What are *pelmeni*?" asked Cape.

"Little dumpling," said Maria.

"I asked you not to use my pet name in public," said Cape.

Maria almost spit her water across the table.

"*Pelmeni* are dumplings stuffed with meat." Valenko was still watching Maria. "Did you get the veal or the pork?"

"Veal." Maria used her left hand to pop one into her mouth.

Valenko shifted back to Cape. "Your colleague has good taste." He waved at a waiter and said something in Russian. A moment later a plate appeared. He pushed it closer to Cape. "Try one."

As Cape bit into a dumpling, Valenko added, "*Pelmeni* is a Siberian staple. I grew up with it. Have you been to Siberia?"

"It's delicious," said Cape. "The *pelmeni*, not Siberia. I hear it's cold."

"The town where I grew up is called Oymyakon," said Valenko. "You have heard of it?"

Cape shook his head and swallowed his dumpling.

"It is the coldest place on the planet inhabited by humans," said Valenko. "Minus fifty degrees Celsius in winter."

"What's that in Fahrenheit?" asked Cape.

"Very cold." Maria called from the other table. "Can you boys skip the foreplay? I'm almost done eating."

Valenko ignored her. "Only five hundred or so families live there, so close to the Arctic Circle."

Cape felt like he was being tested. "Why do they live there?"

"That was a good question." Valenko smiled. "Most people ask if there are reindeer."

"Are there?"

"Naturally," said Valenko. "Reindeer is one of the meats we stuff into *pelmeni*."

"Is Santa okay with that?"

"We call him *Ded Moroz*," said Valenko. "Grandfather Frost. He doesn't use reindeer; his sled is a troika pulled by three magnificent horses."

"Do the horses fly?"

"They don't need to," said Valenko. "They gallop across the ice and snow faster than any reindeer could fly."

"Flying reindeer are pretty cool." Cape took a sip of vodka. "Admit it, our Santa is better than yours."

"Diamonds." Valenko's eyes glinted at the word. "That is the answer to your question. Oymyakon produces more diamonds than any place in the world, even Africa. That's why Russians were sent by Moscow to live with the locals—the Yukats—to mine for diamonds. Russians like my parents." He finished his vodka and poured himself another. "Go outside in January and you're dead in sixty seconds. The ground is permafrost, unstable when spring comes." His gravelly voice fell another octave. "The world beneath your feet may collapse at any moment."

"Is that a friendly warning," said Cape, "Or a metaphor?"

"It's a lesson I never forgot," said Valenko. "One I wished to share with you."

"Before I start asking the wrong questions."

"*Imenno tak*," said Valenko. "Just so."

Valenko smiled, and Cape became acutely aware of what it felt like to sit next to a man who had grown up in the coldest place on earth.

"I don't care about your business." Cape wrapped his hand around his glass but didn't drink. He glanced at Maria, and their only gun, then at the bodyguards who had more guns than

Maria had bullets. "I'm not a cop, and as far as you're concerned, neither is she."

Valenko gestured at the television. "You bet your life the last act would be a singer."

"I played the odds," said Cape. "And the last act was a magic trick...out of nowhere, a steak knife appeared in the back of your bodyguard's hand."

The two men behind Valenko finally pulled the knife free with a screech from the table and a squawk from the wounded bodyguard, who wrapped his bloody hand in a napkin.

"That was a good trick." Valenko watched the wounded man disappear through the kitchen door. "Now tell me, why risk coming here if you don't care about my business?"

"I'm desperate," said Cape.

"I'm hungry," said Maria.

Valenko and Cape turned in unison. They looked more astonished by Maria's appetite than annoyed at her interruption. She had finished the share plates without any help from Cape.

"Impressive," said Valenko. "Have the *chernosliv*." He gestured at the waiter. "Walnut-stuffed prunes covered in *smetana*."

Valenko held up a hand and answered the question before Cape could ask.

"Sour cream."

"*Suena deliciosa*," said Maria. She made a get-on-with-it gesture with her left hand. "Please, continue your dance."

"*Gracias*," said Cape. He turned to Valenko. "Where was I?"

"You were desperate."

"I still am," said Cape. "I need to find some people before they find someone else."

"Who are you?" asked Valenko. "How do you know my name?" He took another drink. "Why haven't I killed you?"

"I can't answer that last one," said Cape. "I'm a private investigator. Everybody knows your name; they're just too afraid to say it."

Valenko smiled, and Cape felt a chill as if someone had opened a door.

"And why should I help you?"

"Because someone lost a helicopter," said Cape. "And I think you lost a pilot."

Valenko's smile disappeared as he whipped around and called to the guard across the table to his right, a broad-faced man with close-cropped hair and a thick scar across his nose.

They spoke rapidly in Russian, calmly at first, but in answer to one of Valenko's questions the scarred guard grimaced. Valenko banged his hand on the table hard enough to make the vodka bottles jump.

Another terse exchange ensued before Valenko turned his arctic gaze on Cape.

"My nephew is a pilot."

"Not anymore." Cape gave an abridged version of the robbery gone wrong.

Valenko listened intently, the lines on his face getting deeper with every detail.

Cape finished by saying, "I need to find these men."

Valenko didn't speak for a long moment, his eyes on Cape but his attention elsewhere. The guard with the nose scar was making a call. No one moved as the one-sided conversation took place. When he hung up, his expression was grave.

Scar-nose said something in Russian that was barely a whisper. Valenko's hand squeezed his glass until his knuckles went white.

"My question stands," he asked. "Why should I help you?"

Cape anticipated this and omitted the most important part

of his story until now. "You should help because your nephew didn't die in the crash."

Valenko was a marble statue chiseled by rage.

"They burned him alive," said Cape.

Valenko's glass shattered in his hand.

He stared at his clenched fist as blood and vodka seeped between his fingers.

With stoic deliberation, he pulled shards of glass from his fingers in sync with each word of his answer. "I will find these men, and when I do, they will not be handed over to the police. Can you give me the same assurance?"

"The police are already looking," said Cape. "So am I, and so are you." He took his cloth napkin and laid it on the table near Valenko's hand. Wordlessly, Valenko wrapped his bloody fingers. Cape drained his own glass before speaking again. The burn in the back of his throat gave the words the edge they needed. "I don't care who finds these men or what happens to them, as long as they can't hurt my client."

"Who is your client?"

"No one you care about."

Valenko flexed his fingers. "We have an understanding with the Chinese on Grant Avenue and the Italians in North Beach. The yakuza in their enclave on Hemlock Street. The Chechens and Vietnamese, the Irish, even the Ukrainians." Valenko paused and looked around the table, making eye contact with each of his men. "We have...*arrangements.* Sometimes we import a product and one of our counterparts distributes that product while another provides protection. Depending on the product or service, we change roles and take different percentages. Most importantly, we pool resources to buy influence."

"Police and politicians on the payroll."

"So many politicians," said Valenko. "Politicians you can buy in bulk."

"Like toilet paper at Costco." Cape spread his hands. "I get it. You don't need me, and I might not need you. Just so we're clear, you're not my only line of investigation. You could have killed me before I sat down."

"Yet here you are."

"You have people on your payroll," said Cape. "I have friends."

"Friends."

"Cops you haven't bought. Headaches you don't need." Cape tilted his head toward Maria. "My famished friend has connections of her own. And the woman who turned your guard's hand into a fist-kabob tends to hold a grudge."

"Khorosho skazano." Valenko tossed the bloody napkin on the table. "We understand each other."

"I get the impression you didn't know the heist was happening."

"My nephew is…" Valenko paused, conscious of using the present tense, but he continued. "…impulsive. The men you seek must have approached him directly."

"Why not go through you?"

"I don't deal in stolen artwork."

"Even as collateral?" Maria called out. The fingers of her right hand tapped the table near the gun. Her plate was empty.

"You've done your homework." Valenko shook his head. "It's true, art can be better than cash on the black market, if you can sell it. I find the appraisals too contentious."

"The other men were Chinese," said Cape, "They took something from the museum."

"They took my nephew."

"Without asking."

"Da, that is what I don't understand," said Valenko. "You

say the thieves were Chinese. There is a man who runs Chinatown—"

"—Freddie Wang."

Valenko cocked an eyebrow. "It seems my name isn't the only one you know."

"I've crossed paths with Freddie before," said Cape, "inadvertently."

"If something gets stolen in this city, Freddie knows about it before it happens."

"He knew you'd find out eventually," said Cape. "Why not tell you he needed a pilot?"

"This is what concerns me."

No one spoke for a full minute.

Valenko took a new glass and filled it with vodka. Cape watched the pour, clear liquid riding up the sides, turning the glass into a lens that distorted everything.

Cape realized he was looking through the wrong end of the telescope.

"Maybe Freddie isn't the one who needed the pilot."

"Who then?"

"Why risk keeping you in the dark?" asked Cape. "Unless it wasn't Freddie's operation."

Valenko rubbed his hands together. "Someone told Freddie to keep this quiet."

"Someone else is telling Freddie what to do," said Cape, "in his city."

"Someone…" Valenko paused to consider the implications. "…from someplace else."

"Freddie wouldn't like that very much."

"Neither would I."

"He might even sabotage the operation by hiring a pilot with a dangerous uncle."

"He might." Valenko gave a half grin that was somehow warmer than his full smile. "Detective, you are much more clever than—"

"—yeah." Cape held up a hand. "I get that a lot."

"What do you propose?"

"That you take the bait," said Cape. "Stick your nose into Freddie's business, make waves, and flush these men into the open."

"And what will you be doing?" asked Valenko. "While I make waves?"

"Trying to surf."

23

The sea cucumber surfed along the surface of the water.

Grace studied the ungainly creature as it started to drift and ride the tiny waves emanating from the aerator in the fish tank. It wasn't much of a surfer. Grace pressed closer to the tank but still couldn't tell how it moved, where its eyes were, or why anyone would ever want to eat it.

Grace was hiding in the storeroom behind the seafood market, directly across the street from Sally's loft. Rushi had been sitting in her usual spot when Grace collapsed on the sidewalk at her feet. The old woman took one look at the girl with scuffed knees and bleeding hands before taking Grace by the hand and leading her to the back room of the market.

Rushi never asked what happened, she merely sat Grace in front of the reserve tanks and told her to study the animals. After a few minutes of silent sobs, it worked. The naiant wandering of the sea creatures was hypnotic. Her breathing returned to normal, her pulse slowed, and Grace didn't even notice when Rushi left her alone.

Rushi was back on her folding chair when Sally arrived.

"Hello, Āyí." Sally caught the expression on the old

woman's face as she gave her customary greeting. "What's good tonight?"

"I have a fresh catch in back," said Rushi. "Been saving it for you."

Sally nodded and headed to the back room. Rushi remained at her perch and watched the entrance to Sally's building.

Grace was studying an octopus as it meandered along the bottom of a tank. Its mottled texture shifted from brown to black to bloodred as it passed rocks and underwater ferns.

"An octopus is good at hiding," said Sally. "You clearly are not."

Grace started at Sally's voice but kept staring at the octopus as it squeezed into a crevice and vanished. That was a trick she'd have to learn.

Sally saw the blood splashed across Grace's cheek and noticed the absence of a cut or scratch. Someone else's blood. Sally took the young girl's left hand in both of hers and ran a thumb across the scraped knuckles and broken nails.

"Looks like we both had a big night."

Grace looked at Sally with eyes that had aged a lifetime since morning. Sally returned the gaze and held it long enough to find the little girl inside. She was still there, hiding behind that guarded look. Sally sensed a cataract of tears waiting to erupt and marveled at the girl's ability to hold it in check. Grace might be experiencing mild shock, or an adrenaline crash, but Sally guessed that stubbornness was the only thing keeping despair at bay.

Before Grace could stop her, Sally grabbed the backpack from the floor.

Sally's eyes narrowed in reproach as she zipped it open. "Is this gun yours?"

Grace shook her head.

"Your uncle's?"

Another shake.

"Did you handle it?"

"Only when I threw it in the backpack."

Sally gave the backpack a little shake to shift the contents. Without touching the gun, she grabbed the rooster and handed it to Grace.

"Birth animal?"

A contrite nod. "My uncle gave it to me."

Sally removed the photograph, fingers at the corner, and studied it. Neither of them spoke. Sally knew the baby was Grace without asking.

Sentimentality had been hammered out of Sally by instructors who told her that life began the day she entered the Triads. And yet Sally crossed an ocean to leave that school behind, and the only photographs she possessed were of her parents, taken during the first five years of her life. Those faded photographs gave Sally's faint memories of childhood a structure.

Sally remembered her parents' voices and often spoke to them in dreams, but thanks to those snapshots, she never forgot what they looked like. Sally zipped the backpack and looped it over her own shoulder. She handed the photograph to Grace.

"Am I in trouble?" Grace held the photograph in one hand and the rooster in the other.

"Bad men are after you, the police are looking for you, and there's a stolen gun in your backpack," said Sally. "Yes, I'd say you're in trouble." She tapped the photograph gently with a finger. "But you don't need any more trouble from me."

"I should have waited."

"Yes," said Sally. "That's another lesson for today."

"I remembered the first lesson," said Grace. "I got away."

"Then you won," said Sally. "Now, little rooster, let's go home."

24

"I'm not going home," said Wen. "I'm going to Dafen."

Bohai scratched the stubble on his chin. "The art village?"

Wen nodded. They were lying down in the barracks, lights out, but their beds were close enough to whisper. Most of the other workers were asleep.

"That's what the camp supervisor told me," said Wen. "The head guard was there, too, the one who brought me to the office."

Bohai nodded. "Biaggio, the ruffian who stutters."

"That's the one," said Wen. "The supervisor did all the talking. I'm being transferred."

The high windows pulsed rhythmically as rotating searchlights on the nearest fence penetrated the wired glass. Bohai's features were clearly visible in the intermittent strobe. He looked bemused.

"What did you say?"

"I asked if I could return to Hong Kong," replied Wen.

"And what did they say?"

"Biaggio smirked until the supervisor shot him a look," said Wen. "Apparently my patriotic reeducation isn't complete. Supposedly I'll have better working conditions."

"Maybe you'll get your own bathroom."

"Somehow I doubt it."

"Security might be minimal," said Bohai. "There are no labor camps in that region, it's too densely populated."

Wen watched the ghostly light wash the ceiling. "Why move me?"

Bohai rubbed his temples. "You taught art history?"

Wen nodded.

"You're going to an art factory," said Bohai. "It's the only explanation."

"But I'm not an artist," said Wen. "I can tell you who painted something, and when, or which sculpture came from which dynasty, but I can't paint or sculpt anything. Even my calligraphy is sloppy."

"The art factories make reproductions," said Bohai. "You'll be some kind of production line supervisor, or something like that. Dafen is big business, one of the special economic zones. You don't think communism pays for itself, do you?"

"No wonder they locked you up," said Wen.

"You should have heard the customers at my bookstore."

"I'm sorry I never visited your store when I was in Hong Kong."

"I think you would have liked it," said Bohai.

Wen gave a wistful look. "My wife would have told me to not buy anything."

"Oh?"

"I meant that as a compliment." Wen smiled. "She worked for the government."

"The professor and the patriot," said Bohai. "That's a television show I would watch."

Wen laughed. "Not as dramatic as you might think." He glanced at Bohai. "I'm worried about leaving here... I know that sounds crazy."

Bohai gave a wan smile. "I've enjoyed your company, too."

"If they're not going to release me..." Wen's voice trailed off.

"You'd rather not be alone." Bohai nodded. "You won't be alone, Wen. You'll meet other..." He almost said prisoners but added, "...workers. Just be careful what you say. You never know who's within hearing distance."

As if on cue, the man on the cot behind Bohai moaned and rolled over in his sleep.

"*Xié xie.*" Wen extended his right hand to reach across the gap between their beds. Bohai took the hand in both of his and gave it a squeeze. "I would have broken without your spirit."

"I hope you see your daughter again someday," said Bohai.

Wen inhaled deeply. "I thought you told me to forget her."

"I'm a liar," said Bohai. "I survive each day by lying to myself."

Neither spoke as they contemplated their divergent futures. The heavy breathing of exhausted workers filled the room, punctuated by an occasional whimper or nightmare twitch. Three bunks away, a heavyset man with apnea snuffled and rumbled as he turned on his side.

The ambient noise protected Wen and Bohai from being overheard, but it also kept them from noticing a macaque sitting on the ledge of the nearest window.

The monkey had been sent to spy on them.

Doctor Loh trained all the macaques to register human facial expressions, starting with primary emotions like joy, sadness, worry, and fear. By matching prisoners' photographs to an illustrated chart of mouths, eyes, and eyebrows, the doctor used a system of food rewards in a matching game. Monkeys matched facial expressions to photographs to report on which prisoners were acting suspicious.

The monkey in the window was named Junjie, which meant handsome. He should have been named Randy, because like all male macaques, he became uncontrollably aroused when a female macaque was nearby. Several were roaming outside the perimeter fence, and their scent carried. Junjie's olfactory sense, like his sex drive, was exceptional.

Doctor Loh chose macaques for their brains without considering their loins.

Macaques were among the most lustful primates on earth. Clear the air of female pheromones, and a male macaque could solve puzzles baffling to humans, but one whiff of the opposite sex and the same monkey masturbates like a teenage boy after a cheerleading contest. The average monkey would succumb to his urges four times an hour, eight hours a day.

Junjie was an above average monkey.

He was smart enough to realize his own facial expressions would be studied by the doctor when he returned to the lab, so when the matching game began, Junjie simply widened or narrowed his eyes as he scanned the prisoners' faces. He would furrow his brow and shake his head randomly. The doctor would feel satisfied that the inmates were not plotting a revolt, and Junjie would get his food.

Then he could resume jerking off.

Beyond hearing of the preoccupied primate, Wen's voice undercut the surrounding snores. "What about you?"

"What about me?" asked Bohai.

"The night classes are rote memorization of party doctrine. You know the speeches by heart, I've heard you recite them." Wen knew it was pointless to speculate but worried over his friend's fate. "When will they be satisfied that you've reformed?"

"There are always more phones to build," said Bohai, "and my fingers are nimble. Remember, you just went for a walk in Victoria Park, but I knowingly deceived party officials."

He smiled broadly. "You're a naïve protestor, but me? I'm a subversive."

"You sold used paperbacks."

"There is nothing more subversive than a book, my friend." Bohai's eyes flashed in the dim light. "But don't worry about me, I don't intend to stay here forever."

"You have a plan?"

"I have something better." Bohai sat up long enough to survey the surrounding cots. Then he rolled onto his side, right arm behind his back, hand moving as if he was scratching his buttocks. Before Wen could ask what he was doing, Bohai brought his hand to the front and held something low against the mattress. "I have pliers."

"How—"

"—don't ask," said Bohai. "Sometimes the guards are distracted when we work the fence. Remember the day of the movie?"

Wen considered the ramifications. "You said the fence isn't always electrified."

Bohai gestured at the milky light spilled across the ceiling. "When the searchlights break their pattern, you know the generator is down." He rummaged beneath the rough blanket and replaced the pliers in the crevice from whence they came.

Wen realized why Bohai had always walked slowly. He carried pliers between his cheeks.

"Be careful," said Wen. "Time it wrong and you could die."

"We all die," said Bohai, "But I won't let them kill me slowly."

Wen nodded. "I hope we see each other again."

"In this life or the next. Now get some sleep, Professor. Tomorrow, you go to make art."

"And you," said Wen. "Go make trouble."

25

"How much trouble?"

"How much trouble will Valenko make?" asked Cape. "Or how much trouble are you in, as an Interpol agent?"

"I hadn't thought about that second question," said Maria. "Let's order another drink before my answer ruins the mood." She caught the eye of a passing waiter whose grass skirt swished as he approached their table. His bare chest was covered by a lei of plastic flowers.

They sat in an underground bar at Maria's hotel, the Fairmont on Nob Hill. The hotel was a white-columned marvel built over a century ago, where diplomats and celebrities came to meet, and Tony Bennett once came to sing.

The Fairmont was incongruously also home to the Tonga Room & Hurricane Bar, a tiki bar renowned for decor that was gaudy, loud, and ludicrous. Waiters and waitresses wore grass skirts, drinks came in carved coconut cups, and the band performed on a floating island in the middle of a converted swimming pool. Claps of thunder and flashes of lightning were thrown across the room by camouflaged speakers and strobes. The tiki bar was a wormhole to a kitsch dimension, hidden in the basement of an otherwise stuffy hotel.

Maria loved it. When their coconuts arrived, she removed the pink umbrella and took a sip of her drink, holding the cup with both hands.

"This place is so perfectly American."

"You have a cultural theory to explain…" Cape gestured at the island band as they played Bing Crosby's "Mele Kalikimaka" with electronic gusto. "…all this?"

"I do." Maria pointed at the ceiling, above which sat the lobby of the hotel. "On the surface, this place is all business." Maria smiled as thunder boomed overhead. "But beneath the serious facade, fun awaits."

"You think Americans are fun?"

"Some more than others, granted." Maria swirled the ice around in her drink. "Spaniards still know how to laugh at themselves. Germans laugh at the French, usually behind their backs. The English laugh at each other, but most of Europe takes itself far too seriously."

"You chase crooks all over Europe; maybe that colors your perspective." Cape took a drink and winced at the sour cocktail. "But what would I know? I'm just a frivolous American."

Maria raised her glass. "Dinner was fun."

Cape tilted his mug in her direction. "If you'd shot the television instead of the wall, we'd be cut into little pieces and stuffed into *pelmeni*."

"How did you like it?"

"You shooting the wall?" asked Cape. "It was very dramatic."

"The *pelmeni*," said Maria. "Wasn't it delicious?"

"Honestly?" said Cape. "The vodka made my tongue numb."

Maria sighed. "I'm dodging the question, aren't I?"

"You don't have to answer," said Cape. "I'm used to a certain amount of trouble, but then again—"

"—then again?"

"I can shoot as many TVs as I want and not lose my job," said Cape. "I don't carry a badge and don't want you to lose yours."

One corner of Maria's mouth turned up. "You're very gallant for a—"

"—fun American?"

"The truth," said Maria, "is that I'm already in danger of losing my badge."

"Beau said your supervisor put you on leave."

"A suspension," said Maria.

"But you were right about the museum."

"That just makes it worse."

"Because it makes him look foolish?"

"Because it makes him look guilty," said Maria. "Or weak."

Cape mused over Chinese art disappearing from museums around the globe. "You think he's caving to political pressure."

"*Definitivamente*," said Maria. "When I outlined the case for coming here, he ordered me to Italy to retrieve a missing Rembrandt."

"In other words, he wanted you to investigate a crime that's actually happened versus one that might occur but hasn't yet."

"A bureaucrat's logic."

"Is the Rembrandt very valuable?"

"Compared to other paintings, *sí*." Maria shrugged. "Compared to other Rembrandts, not so much. Besides, it's just a Rembrandt—"

"—just a Rembrandt." Cape laughed.

"There's always a missing Rembrandt," said Maria. "He was one of the few masters famous in his own lifetime. Ran his studio like a factory, turning out portraits for wealthy patrons. There are so many paintings and sketches in circulation that Rembrandts have become a legitimate currency in the underground economy. Crime syndicates accept them for ransom, collateral, as investments for a rainy day. Fine art retains its value more than gold."

"As long as the provenance doesn't land you in jail."

"There are ways around that," said Maria. "Auction houses look the other way, buyers remain anonymous, museums pay the ransom."

"That's not why you're here, drinking fruity cocktails," said Cape. "Is it?"

Maria looked wistfully at the band. "I'm pulling on the tail of a tiger, a global syndicate of state-sponsored art thieves, and my boss wants me to chase down a lousy Rembrandt."

"How much influence does China have in Spain?"

The strobe of lightning flashed in Maria's eyes. "You ask very good questions."

"It's my only real talent."

"Interpol gives senior agents a lot of latitude," said Maria. "As long as I clear my cases, I can pursue as many leads as I want, especially on an investigation that cuts across borders."

"So when you were told to stay away from San Francisco you got—"

"—*enfadada*," said Maria. "Pissed off, enough to do some homework at the foreign office. China has been investing heavily across Europe for years, their 'belt and road initiative' that links all the major trading centers into a single network with access to China."

"Investment doesn't always mean influence."

"Except in politics," said Maria. "China manages or holds a stake in every major port in Europe...Valencia in Spain, Vado in Italy, Kumport in Turkey...and some of those are free ports."

"Free ports." Cape knew the term but couldn't nail it down. "A port that operates like a tax haven...or something like that."

"Close," said Maria. "A commercial port with a special charter that exempts it from taxes, inspection, or customs laws of the local country. Think of a free port as an embassy for a neutral, nonexistent country, only it's a working port. Very popular in the art world." Maria grinned savagely. "Especially the world of stolen art."

Cape reached for his coconut. "So if I have an art collection and don't want to pay taxes when I buy, sell, or move one of my paintings—"

"—and you want to keep it safe—"

"—I ship it to a free port—"

"—and keep it there." Maria rubbed her hands together. "Climate-controlled warehouses designed to hold the world's treasures. You can visit your painting, sell it to someone, or put it on a ship and send it home, all without stepping foot in the host country."

"Who pays for the ports?"

"Any country that wants access to the special economic zone of the free port," said Maria. "And the biggest investor outside the EU is China, so there's your answer about influence."

"But who are they influencing?" Cape took one of the discarded paper umbrellas and twirled it between his fingers. "In Spain, for example, who pays for the free port, besides China? Is it Germany or France or...?"

"EU trading partners," said Maria. "Most of Europe pays a share."

"Now I see why you went rogue." Cape tossed the umbrella onto the table.

"The countries that fund the ports," said Maria, "also fund Interpol."

"So you're investigating the people who pay your salary."

"*Seguramente,*" said Maria. "You see my dilemma."

Cape leaned back in his chair and didn't say anything for a minute.

The band got the room swaying to a sultry ukulele playing "What a Wonderful World."

"All your evidence is circumstantial," said Cape.

"Unless I can catch a thief."

Cape barely knew Maria, but he understood her. She had rushed into a burning building, and now the only way out was to fight her way through to the other side. The lightning strobes flashed, and Cape caught his own reflection in Maria's eyes as the band found its groove.

> *I see skies of blue,*
> *and clouds of white.*
> *The bright blessed day,*
> *the dark sacred night.*

"What a wonderful world, where you have to break the rules to enforce the law."

"That's the world you live in," said Maria, "am I right?"

Cape was about to reply when he felt a hand on his shoulder. It was a big hand, and the squeeze was none too gentle. Maria's eyes widened in recognition and amusement.

Cape followed the mahogany fingers up the arm to Beau's smiling face and flat cop stare.

"The lyrics in the last stanza make me think the songwriter didn't have kids." Beau grabbed a chair from a nearby table and sat perpendicular to the table. "Tell me how babies crying is wonderful."

"Nice to see you again, Inspector," said Maria.

"Beau is just fine, Maria."

Beau's voice was as deep as the thunder rumbling from the nearby speakers. His eyes scanned the room before coming to rest on the litter of umbrellas on the table. "What in God's name are you drinking?"

"It's vaguely disgusting," said Cape, "but tropical."

"Would you like one?" asked Maria.

"Absolutely not," said Beau, adding, "No, *gracias*."

"*El gusto es mio.*"

Beau flagged a waiter and ordered a beer.

"Maria thinks Americans are fun," said Cape.

Beau snorted. "You haven't been in town long enough."

"We met some fun people tonight," said Maria.

Cape nodded. "We had dinner with Maksim Valenko."

Beau almost spit his beer across the table. "No wonder you're guzzling umbrella drinks."

"His nephew was the helicopter pilot," said Cape.

Beau raised his eyebrows. "Not bad." He drained the rest of his beer. "You work fast."

"You're welcome."

"I would have found—"

"—a week," said Cape. "By the time you got the warrants, a week would have passed."

"I think those fruity drinks are making you defensive," said Beau. "Too much sugar."

"Are you off duty?" asked Cape.

"I'm drinking beer," said Beau. "Does that answer your question?"

"No," said Cape. "Am I talking to Beau or Inspector Jones of the SFPD?"

Beau took a long sip of his beer. "Yes."

Maria jumped in before Cape could reply. "Valenko was angry," she said. "Very angry."

Beau glanced at Cape and slowly shook his head. "Had to poke the bear, didn't you?"

"How did you find us?"

"You're changing the subject," said Beau. "Maria is staying at this hotel, Sherlock, and you're the only dumbass who drives a convertible in a city covered in fog."

"Why did you find us?" asked Maria.

"Wanted to share a couple of things," said Beau. "Three, actually." He waved for another beer. "Might help with your investigation...and mine."

"That's very generous," said Cape. "Some might say suspicious—"

"—or I could arrest you for obstruction," said Beau. "That's still on the table."

"Share away."

"Vinnie and I saw a ghost," said Beau. "And I shot a guy in the shoulder."

"That's only two things," said Maria.

"Why did you shoot him?" asked Cape.

"He was about to kill your client."

26

Tommy Chen wanted to kill the nurse.

He was in the hospital when he regained consciousness, the throbbing in his shoulder a painful reminder of how he got there. Tommy closed his eyes and visualized the little museum brat skulking behind the couch in her apartment. Almost within reach, until a freight train hit Tommy in the shoulder. He tried turning his head and almost fainted.

His chin bumped against a bandage the size of a watermelon. The bullet must have passed through his shoulder and out the back. The cop probably used hollow points, so Tommy counted himself lucky to have his arm attached to his body. Freddie Wang would pay the hospital bills, but Tommy would have to learn how to shoot left-handed for a while.

The painkillers were wearing off, and his thumb was sore from pressing the call button. He tried moving his right hand and heard a rattle. Pressing chin to chest, he saw his right hand handcuffed to the bed. No wonder the nurse wasn't in a hurry. There was probably a cop at the door telling her to stay clear until it really started to hurt.

Take a shot at one cop and they all hold a grudge. Didn't seem fair.

Beige curtains shifted from a chill breeze outside. Tommy found that odd, an open window in a hospital room, especially in a city where temperatures could drop twenty degrees in a day. His eyes fluttered and the needles tingling in his shoulder were getting sharper. He blinked to stay awake but his vision was blurry.

He pulled the call button closer and heard the cord smack against the bed frame. He dropped the button onto his lap and tugged at the cord, felt no resistance as it snaked over the covers.

No wonder he was languishing, the call button had been disconnected.

The breeze got even colder as something paler than the curtains drifted into the room. Tommy thought it was fog until it coalesced into the shape of a man. Tommy's eyes regained focus as the ghost appeared at his side.

The albino had a gentle smile on his face.

"You're awake." The ghost spoke softly in Cantonese, his red eyes shifting to the door. "There's a policeman outside."

Tommy nodded. "Figured."

"Now that you're awake…" The ghost reached under his white robes as if straightening his shirt. "…they'll want to get your statement."

"I haven't talked to anyone." Tommy shifted his weight to sit up.

"I know." The ghost extended a chalky arm. "And now you won't."

Tommy gasped as icy fingers pressed against the soft flesh at the base of his neck. He felt a slight pressure, followed by a sensation of something folding inside his throat, his larynx converted to origami. When he tried to speak, his voice sounded like paper tearing. A sibilant plea to an uncaring world.

"Tch-tch-tch." The ghost spoke soothingly. "It only lasts a

few minutes." His other hand emerged from under his jacket holding a syringe. "Under normal circumstances." He caught the fear in Tommy's eyes. "Don't worry, it's empty." He held the needle to the light and retracted the plunger. "Nothing but air, see?"

Tommy was now wide awake, the pain in his shoulder a mere nuisance compared to the adrenaline rushing through his veins. He tracked the ghost's long fingers moving assuredly along the length of the IV until they found the valve where medicine could be injected into the drip.

"It's unfortunate you got shot," said the ghost. "And worse that you got caught." He paused. "If this were any other crime, Freddie would see to your release and you'd get back to work." The ghost's rueful expression was etched in alabaster. "But you know what was inside that helicopter."

Tommy rasped in protest, but the ghost put a cadaverous finger to his lips.

"With the painkillers they give, who knows what you might say? A night in jail we could handle, you'd be out before the police connected the dots, but you landed in here." The ghost looked mournful. "And it's just too soon for anyone to know what we're really up to."

Tommy swung his arm sideways but the ghost wheeled the IV stand out of reach before it toppled.

The fluorescent lights seemed to dim until the brightest thing in the room was the spectral figure standing over the bed. "I'm telling you because I would want to know," said the ghost. "You didn't do anything wrong, you just...got...caught."

Tommy tried to bang his handcuff against the bed frame but the ghost had already inserted the syringe into the valve. With deliberate slowness, he pressed down on the plunger.

"I told you it was empty," said the ghost. "Nothing but air."

Tommy's eyes started to bulge.

"Air in an IV sends bubbles racing through the bloodstream." The ghost moved to the curtains and swung one long leg over the windowsill. "Delicate depth-charges inside your veins." Someone in the hallway began to turn the door handle. "The embolism that follows can cause cardiac arrest, or more commonly a stroke."

Tommy's eyes went flat as a thin line of drool ran down his chin.

"Zàijiàn, Tommy." The voice was a whisper of wind in an empty room.

The door opened. The uniformed policeman stepped inside to check on his prisoner, with the nurse close behind to check on her patient.

All they found was a corpse, still warm but cooling rapidly in the night air.

The ghost was nowhere to be seen.

27

"Your ghost is nowhere to be seen on the security tapes," said Beau. "But something's there, a distortion, a heat wave. Nothing when the other two are standing still, but every time they move, it's there."

"Why is it my ghost?" asked Cape.

"Who are the other men?" asked Maria.

"My partner's working to ID the tall one, but the shorter guy is Tommy Chen." Beau picked up one of the tiny umbrellas and jabbed it at Cape. "Who works for your old friend Freddie Wang."

"Why is he *my* friend?" asked Cape. "And why is it my ghost and not our ghost?"

"Two drinks ago…" Beau made a show of counting umbrellas. "…you admitted you had a client."

"An unnamed person of indeterminate age who may or may not appear in the museum security tapes," said Cape. "Who told me there were three thieves—"

"—not counting the pilot," said Beau.

Cape nodded. "Not counting the pilot."

"And when I said there were only two," said Beau, "you said that's because—"

"—the third is a ghost," said Maria.

"According to your client," said Beau.

"I don't have a client," said Maria. "In fact, I might be unemployed."

"I have a client," said Cape. "So I guess it is my ghost."

Maria placed her hand on Cape's arm. "We can share the ghost."

"Did you drink at dinner before you got here?" asked Beau. "Or are those dumbass tropical drinks that strong?"

"Yes—" said Maria.

"—to both questions," said Cape.

"Your client," said Beau, "I'd like to speak to her."

"She comes from a part of the world where they no longer trust the police."

"You mean anywhere?" said Beau. "Or everywhere?"

"I'll ask her," said Cape.

"Persuade her," said Beau. "You're good at that."

"On one condition," said Cape.

Beau waited.

"Drive me home," said Cape. "I've been drinking."

"Do tell."

"And let us see the security tapes," said Maria.

Beau looked at her, a smile and frown wrestling for control of his mouth. "Okay."

"And pick up the bar tab," said Cape.

"Not a chance."

"Worth a shot," said Cape.

"See you at police headquarters first thing."

"Umm...no," said Cape. "My office."

"Fine," Beau shrugged. "See you at eight."

Maria rubbed her temples. "Can we say nine?"

"Deal," said Beau.

28

"I'll make you a deal," said Doctor Loh. "Cooperate, and I won't cut your head off."

"Sounds like a generous offer." Bohai scratched his belly and looked around the room. "What did you have in mind?"

His surroundings made Bohai think of his bookstore in Hong Kong, which had a section dedicated to Western cinema and several titles on early Gothic horror. Doctor Loh's laboratory resembled a movie set from the 1931 film *Frankenstein*, starring Boris Karloff. Blinking lights, test tubes, surgical equipment, examination tables. The door was steel, with a circular lock like a submarine. Sporadic flashes of light emanated from a tunnel branching off the main chamber. The walls were unfinished stone.

Doctor Loh was standing by one of the examination tables wearing a white lab coat.

He was bald, save for a few strands of black hair jutting out like cat's whiskers on either side of his skull. Brown eyes were watery but bright behind wire-rimmed spectacles, set wide on a broad face with a long nose and small mouth. His teeth were uneven, sharp enough to strip insulation from wire or flesh from bone.

He smiled at Bohai like a carnival barker in a Ray Bradbury novel.

"I designed this laboratory myself."

"I can tell." Bohai never thought of Gothic horror stories as inspiration for interior design; then again, Orwell wrote cautionary tales, not instruction manuals, yet Bohai was trading pleasantries with a government-funded mad scientist. He rubbed his chin and continued to survey the lab as he stalled for time. "We haven't been properly introduced."

"You know who I am," said Loh with a wave of his hand. "And you're—"

"—a prisoner?"

"We do not use that term." Loh pursed his lips. "You are a worker at this facility."

"Not an essential worker?"

"How do you mean?"

"Well," said Bohai, "the guard pulled me off the production line to bring me here. So what I was doing must not be very important."

"All the work we do here is important."

"Important to whom?" asked Bohai. "To the party, the country, or the—"

"—people," said Loh.

"Ah, I was going to ask if it was important to the Western companies whose products we make," said Bohai. "I forgot about 'the people.'"

Doctor Loh's left eye twitched. Nothing like a game of doublespeak to unsettle a bureaucrat. Bohai took that as a good sign.

Every minute you keep him talking is another minute he doesn't cut you open.

Bohai had been surprised when the guard sent him in alone, but now it made sense. Doctor Loh clearly didn't consider inmates a threat. Most were so emotionally cowed or physically depleted that they put up no resistance. The outcome was inevitable whether they fought, pleaded, or accepted their fate.

"What is it you want to know?" asked Bohai.

"Your friend, Wen, left the camp."

Bohai nodded. "I will miss him."

"You admit you were friends."

Bohai shrugged. "We were friendly."

"Do you know why he was here?"

Bohai shook his head.

"He participated in a march, a protest against the government."

"Was it a peaceful protest?"

"It was unlawful assembly."

"We all did something before we came here," said Bohai.

"Just so," said Loh. "You ran a bookstore."

"Yes," said Bohai. "I like to read."

"Some books are dangerous," said Loh.

Sociopaths with scalpels are dangerous.

"Do I look dangerous?" asked Bohai.

"No." Loh studied Bohai from head to toe. "You are too subversive to release and too educated to work the fences. Your insouciant answers suggest you're inclined to tell the truth. And I happen to need a new lab assistant."

"What happened to the old lab assistant?" asked Bohai. "Was there an accident?"

"Of course there was an accident," said Doctor Loh. "What do you think the word 'experiment' means?"

"Something might go wrong?"

"Precisely." Loh waved an arm to encompass his underground lair. "What I do here is important, yet the guards are too stupid and clumsy, and the workers too ignorant or fearful." Loh smiled. "So that leaves you. The last man standing."

"Are you offering me a job?"

"I'm giving you responsibility."

Bohai scratched the stubble under his chin. "Do I have a choice?"

"Remember the option of having your head cut off?"

"When do I start?" asked Bohai.

29

Cape awoke with a start to the sound of someone snoring.

The buzz-saw breathing stopped as soon as he jolted awake, but Cape couldn't see the culprit because someone had glued his eyelids shut. He suspected it was the same scoundrel who'd pasted his tongue to the roof of his mouth.

With a Herculean effort, Cape pried his eyelids apart.

Grace sat at his feet, on the end of the couch, smiling.

"Would you like some tea?"

She held a steaming mug between her small hands.

Cape scooted backward on the couch until his back was against the armrest. That seemed to stop the spinning. He looked at Grace, then past her at Sally, who was walking on her hands like an acrobat at the far end of the room.

Sally wagged a foot in his direction by way of hello.

That's when Cape remembered that he'd asked Beau to drop him off at his office instead of his apartment. He must have called Sally on the way. His inebriated instincts reasoned it would be better to crash on the couch than crawl out of bed and drive to his office with a hangover. Now all he had to do was focus.

Cape got his tongue detached and asked, "What time is it?"

"Seven-thirty," said Grace. "Sally says you have just enough time to make yourself presentable."

Cape accepted the tea with a grateful nod. He had drunk Sally's tinctures before but this seemed particularly potent. His eyes started to water as soon as the steam drifted across his face. He peered at the bilious brew with a questioning look on his face.

"Do I want to know what's in this?"

"Something that smells bad," said Grace.

"It tastes worse than it smells." Sally moved closer on her hands, then snapped both legs forward and landed on her feet at the base of the couch. "But you'll be as sober as a sermon after you drink it."

"Swell....more like swill." Cape considered holding the mug for a while to let the warmth run up his arms, but the smell was overpowering. Grace watched him with unabashed fascination. Maybe she'd never seen anyone hungover before, but her stare felt like a dare.

Cape downed the drink in one scalding gulp.

His esophagus caught fire. Eyes and nose started to run a race that neither would win. His ears popped. Grace started giggling. Cape gasped and wheezed for a short eternity. Then his head cleared like a guilty conscience after confession.

Cape pulled a handkerchief from his pocket and wiped his nose. "Thanks, I guess."

"You snore," said Grace. "Very, very loudly." Her lips contorted as she tried to suppress a laugh. "You woke yourself up!"

"I was just pretending to snore," said Cape, "so anyone who snuck into my office would think I was asleep."

"You were asleep."

"See?" said Cape. "I even had you fooled."

Grace made a *humph* sound as Cape stood and crossed to

the cabinet behind his desk. One of the best things about this building was the shower in the first-floor bathroom, a relic of a dot-com era renovation. Thirty minutes later Cape no longer smelled like a distillery.

When he returned to his office, Maria was sitting on the couch talking to Grace.

The coffee cup in Maria's hand was big enough to irrigate Death Valley, but she looked much better than Cape felt. Sally leaned against the bookcase. Cape noticed she stayed within Grace's line of sight.

"Good morning," said Maria.

"*Buenos días,*" said Cape. "Get any sleep?"

Maria held up her free hand in a so-so gesture. "Grace was telling me about last night's adventure."

Cape turned one of his client chairs around and sat a few feet away from the couch. He wanted Grace to see all three of them without feeling crowded. As she told her story, it became clear to Cape that he needn't worry. Grace was not easily intimidated.

When her narrative arrived in the alley where her assailant got his balls kicked into outer space, Cape glanced at Sally. The corner of her mouth twitched, but the suppressed smile was visible in her eyes. When Grace finished talking, she tugged at a wrinkle on her pant leg and gave Maria a wan smile.

"You were brave," said Maria.

Grace caught Sally's eye. "I was impulsive."

"You are both," said Sally, "in equal parts."

"I'm seventy percent impulsive," said Cape. "Maybe seventy-five."

Sally turned to Cape. "What's the play?"

"You're not here," said Cape. "But you're nearby." He turned to Maria. "Beau talks to Grace about the museum, not last night."

Grace said something in Cantonese to Sally. Sally responded

quickly and shook her head, then turned to Cape. "She doesn't want to go to police headquarters."

"That's why we're meeting here," said Cape. "She won't have to."

Maria gave him a look. "Won't the inspector have to take her in, for protection?"

"That would be standard procedure," said Cape. "I don't think he will."

"Why not?"

Cape winked at Grace. "Just a hunch."

Beau arrived half an hour later with a laptop under his arm.

Cape met him at the door to the office and shook his hand. Maria was standing near the couch. The two client chairs had been arranged in front of the windows at the far end of the room. Grace was sitting in one of them, but she stood when Beau entered.

Sally was gone.

Beau handed the laptop to Cape. "This leaves with me. " He tapped a finger against the computer. "I watched it once, with Vinnie. He's using a screenshot to ID the second burglar, the taller guy. See if you recognize him—pretty sure he works for Freddie, too."

"Got it."

Beau reached into his jacket pocket and fished out a pair of headphones. "And wear these." He glanced in Grace's direction. "It gets noisy."

Cape walked Beau over to Grace and made the introductions.

Beau shook Grace's hand, which disappeared inside his grip. She craned her neck to look him in the eye, until he sat down and made it easier. Grace remained standing for a moment to study his face. Beau could look as impassive as an oak tree, his eyes as sharp as flint, but now his face was open and friendly, eyes reassuring. A born poker player and career cop.

"Are all policeman as big as you?" Grace asked as she sat down.

Cape cut in. "Inspector Jones is unusually large, because he has such a big heart."

Beau smiled. "I hear you saw a ghost."

Grace nodded.

"So did I."

Beau started to talk in a low voice. Better to whisper when telling ghost stories. Cape left them sitting knee-to-knee, silhouetted against the windows.

He stepped over to the couch and sat next to Maria, on her left. She already had the laptop open. She scooted closer to hand him one of the earphones, stretching the cord to insert the other in her own left ear. When he was ready, she pressed the space bar.

The image was split-screen, taken from multiple security cameras simultaneously. Playback started from the moment Grace stood transfixed on the skywalk, seconds before the helicopter crashed into the building. When the rotor blades snapped and flew across the gallery, Maria grabbed Cape's hand in hers, squeezing until his knuckles popped and the headless body of Grace's uncle fell out of frame.

As Maria released his hand, Cape flicked his eyes at Grace, but her attention was still on Beau. She did not see their shocked expressions so didn't relive her uncle's death vicariously. The scene unfolded on the laptop, two men following a chalky will-o'-the-wisp around the museum. In the frozen memory of the tape, Grace hid as tendrils of fog wrapped around a golden Buddha and lifted it from its pedestal.

Grace lunged as the ghost inside the fog moved closer. The chase ensued.

After Grace's flight from the museum, the end of the

recording was anticlimactic. The thieves checked the burning helicopter, returned to the gallery, then made an orderly exit from the main entrance and climbed into a waiting car.

"They didn't even bother to use a side entrance," said Maria.

"And they weren't in a hurry," said Cape. "They knew the response time—"

"—or they had a backup plan for a hasty retreat."

"No plates on the car."

Cape nodded. "One more time?"

Maria ran the video a second time. Cape tried to ignore all the boxes on the screen except the upper left, the one with the best view of the gallery. He noticed Maria's eyes were locked on the bottom right.

They ran the tape four times.

Cape felt Maria's body tense at key intervals, her posture different after the fourth viewing. They looked at each other. The glint in her eyes reflected the excitement he felt. The corners of her mouth turned upward. Clearly he didn't have as good a poker face as Beau.

Cape wondered if they had spotted the same thing.

He didn't have any answers, but there was one question that Cape was dying to ask.

"What's in the helicopter?"

He said it loud enough for Beau to hear. Grace stopped talking, and Beau's head swiveled around. If he was annoyed at the interruption, it didn't show. Cape figured Grace had told Beau all she could, and now he was having her go over certain details.

Beau said something softly to Grace, stood, and crossed to the couch. Cape made eye contact with Grace. She gave a small wave, then turned and glanced out the open window at the street below. Cape turned his attention to Beau and scooted along the couch until he pressed against the left armrest. She patted the worn leather and tilted the laptop in his direction. Maria slid over to make room on her right for Beau.

She tapped the screen with a manicured nail. "This is when they return to the helicopter."

Beau nodded.

"Why go back?" asked Cape.

"Make sure the pilot is dead."

"He was on fire," said Cape, "and stopped screaming."

"Definitely dead," said Maria.

"They wanted to make sure the helicopter was still burning," said Cape.

"Maybe." Beau rubbed the stubble on his cheek. "And the pilot wasn't the only witness, was he?" He tilted his head toward Grace to underscore his point, then said, "What the hell?"

Two empty chairs sat by the open window. A breeze was the only thing moving across the room. Grace had vanished.

Beau whipped his head around. No chance that she had snuck by him. The office door was closed, the room too narrow for her to have passed the couch unnoticed. He gave Cape a leaden stare.

"Goddammit, she's a material witness."

"Who?" asked Cape.

"I don't see anyone," added Maria.

Beau looked at Maria. "You're as bad as he is."

"She's much better," said Cape.

"Or much worse," said Beau. "But the kid—"

"—is only eleven."

"Exactly," said Beau, "that's why—"

"—she's safe," said Cape. "Child services can't protect her as well as Sally can." He paused and held Beau's gaze. "We both know that."

Beau made a low sound in his throat that may have signaled grudging assent. "Okay, Houdini, you made a girl disappear... any other tricks up your sleeve?"

"Just wait." Cape held up his hands and wiggled his fingers with a flourish. "You won't believe what happens next."

30

Doctor Loh wiggled his fingers. They looked crooked and arthritic.

"You're good with your hands?" he asked.

"Surely your monkeys told you," said Bohai.

Loh's narrow lips curled upward. "Would you like to meet one of them?"

Bohai forced a smile. "I'd love to."

The doctor stepped from in front of the examination table to reveal that it was occupied. A macaque was strapped to the frame, a metal collar around its neck bolted to the table. The monkey's yellow eyes were wide, its teeth bared. Bohai couldn't tell if it was angry or afraid.

"Come closer," said Doctor Loh.

Bohai shuffled nearer the table. The monkey was the size of a small child, and Bohai couldn't help but feel sympathy for the creature. Like their human counterparts, there wasn't much choice for them once they left this room.

He took another step, and his blood froze.

On the floor beyond the far side of the table sat a basket with handles on each side. It was almost a meter high, the kind you might use as a laundry hamper. From where Bohai had been standing, the basket appeared to be filled with balls, or maybe grapefruit, since there was a pinkish-yellow tinge to the round objects. Now he could see clearly what they were.

The basket was filled with the severed heads of macaques.

Bohai guessed there must be at least twenty, maybe more. Bearded chins, pink faces, tiny noses, and dead eyes. The doctor spread his hands apologetically.

"You know that old proverb," said Loh. "'Failure is the mother of success.'"

"It looks like you've had a great deal of success." Bohai looked at the macaque on the table. It was straining its neck to get a look at the basket. "But what are you hoping to accomplish?"

Loh took one of the heads from the basket and examined it, as if commiserating with an old friend. Hamlet with Yorick set the stage, and now it was Doctor Loh's turn to perform a soliloquy.

"We began by making them smarter." Loh took a second head from the basket and hefted it in his left hand. "Splice a few genes, sprinkle in some human DNA, and by the time the stitches are removed, you've got a monkey that can beat you at rock-paper-scissors."

Loh reached into the basket and took a third head, managing to spread the fingers of his left hand enough to hold two at once, with the original still in his right hand.

Turning to Bohai, the doctor gave an embarrassed smile and started juggling.

"The real trick," Loh continued, warming to his narrative, "was training them. Simple at first, mazes and puzzles. Then came facial recognition, hand signals, and some rudimentary responsibilities."

For every skill described, Loh tossed a head into the air, its slow arc drawing the eye until he caught it with the opposite hand. Both the captive monkey and Bohai followed the flying skulls with morbid fascination and a growing sense of dread.

Toss-catch. Toss-catch. Toss-catch.

"They are excellent observers," Loh continued. "Within limits."

"Limits?" asked Bohai.

"Everyone has limits," said Loh. "Even monkeys." He glanced down to verify his proximity to the basket, then raised his eyes to track the rhythm of his throws. "And in the case of macaques, the limits are very primal."

The doctor timed his next throws carefully as he lobbed the three heads back into the basket, enunciating each word in sync with each toss.

"Male...macaques...masturbate."

Bohai wondered if the doctor was expecting applause. "And that's a problem?"

"They do it incessantly." Loh wiped his hands on his lab coat. "Males are more easily trained than females but also more easily distracted. It turns out their drive cuts both ways." The doctor stepped back to his side of the examination table. "We use them as ancillary guards, but we discovered their limits in their loins."

Bohai worried he'd been brought to the lab to contribute gray matter to a monkey. He grimaced at the macaque strapped to the table. "What about this little guy?"

"Ah," said Loh. "This is Junjie, one of my best students."

Bohai considered the basket of monkey heads and wondered where the bodies were now. "You said that you began by making them smarter."

"See, you are too smart for the fences." said Loh. "Now observe." He extended his right hand toward the captive macaque and gently ran his hand along the top of its head. As

Loh's hand came down across the forehead, the monkey's eyes narrowed, its teeth bared, and it lurched against the bonds in a vain attempt to bite the scientist.

Bohai jumped involuntarily.

"You have good reflexes," said Loh. "So does Junjie. Notice his hostility?"

"You did decapitate quite of a few of his friends."

"Exactly," said Loh. "Which means both recognition and remembrance. Higher cognitive functions that might be encoded."

"Encoded?"

Loh rubbed his hands together. "About two years ago at Harbin University, a Chinese scientist working with an Italian neurosurgeon performed the first successful head transplant on a mammal."

Bohai glanced at the basket again. The rictus grins clearly found all of this hilarious. He really was trapped inside a Mary Shelley novel.

"Why?"

"Spinal cord injuries," replied Loh. "They tried it on paralyzed dogs and had some success. The reassembled dogs managed to walk before—"

"—they died."

Loh nodded. "But the reconstituted dog—with the old dog's head—recognized its master. The hybrid dog exhibited the old personality. It was the same dog, only with a new body. Remarkable, no?"

A new question occurred to Bohai, but he was afraid to ask. Loh noticed his expression.

"You're wondering where they got an extra dog's body."

Bohai nodded.

"That's why it's called an experiment." Loh shrugged. "Risk is part of the reward."

"Aren't you supposed to learn from your mistakes?"

"Oh, but we have," said Loh. "One theory is that more intelligent mammals have a stronger will to live, can reason their way through trauma. They had some success with primates in Harbin but were working with chimpanzees, not monkeys like Junjie."

The macaque on the table struggled against his bonds.

"See?" Loh pointed excitedly. "Recognition."

Bohai wondered how long this macabre hallucination could last before he ended up on that table. "Are there really that many spinal cord injuries?"

Doctor Loh studied him for a minute. "You know your chances of leaving this place?"

The corner of Bohai's mouth bent sideways. "I'm guessing zero to nil."

Loh nodded. "You are too smart, articulate, and pertinacious to go free. What might happen if you told the people in Hong Kong what goes on here?"

"You'd be famous."

"Famous and infamous go hand in hand," said Loh. "Anonymity lets me do my work."

"Which is what, exactly?" Bohai had read enough books on psychology to know that Loh was dying to share his secret. All it took was enough air and a well-timed push. "It must be very... important."

"I am a curator of cultural memory." Loh's eyes shone with fervor. "I bring continuity and stability to our society."

"I thought you were helping injured dogs walk again."

"You don't believe that."

"No, I don't." Bohai chose his next words carefully. "I don't believe our government cares about broken dogs."

"You're right." Loh spread his hands as if smoothing a wrinkle in the fabric of time. "Do you know how civilizations fall, why dynasties crumble?"

"Revolution?" Bohai shrugged. "Economic collapse?"

Doctor Loh shook his head. "Change in leadership."

"That's a problem?"

"Most certainly," said Loh emphatically. "Emperors get stabbed, dictators die in their sleep—"

"—people elect a new leader."

"You spent too much time in Hong Kong," said Loh. "Democracy is irrelevant."

"Why is that?"

"Because it's inherently unstable," said Loh. "When a leader leaves, stability is lost. Imagine if Alexander the Great had never died, what would have happened."

"We'd all be speaking Greek."

"Exactly!" Loh smacked a hand on the table, causing the monkey to flinch. "Continuity is control. Stability is power."

"'Ignorance is strength.'"

"Don't quote Orwell to me," said Loh. "We read the same books, you and I—we just came to different conclusions."

Bohai decided to stop pushing his luck. The doctor was a true believer. "You see a world—"

"—imagine if an aging Party official could transfer his consciousness to a newer, younger body."

"You mean his head."

"His mind."

Bohai visualized a man's head on a monkey's body, then a dog's. A Hollywood mash-up, *Animal Farm* meets *Pet Sematary*. Maybe a remake of *Mars Attacks*. His subconscious was going into overdrive, trying to make him laugh so he wouldn't start screaming. His skin wanted to crawl away from the next question, but he asked it anyway.

"The monkeys are proxies for Party members?"

"Not exactly," said Loh. "The macaques are stand-ins for prisoners. Better to lose a monkey than a worker."

"Of course."

"The prisoners are proxies for Party members."

Bohai shivered as a cold sweat ran down his spine. He thought of his coworkers who had visited the doctor and never returned. He always considered himself someone who hoped for the best but prepared for the worst, but this was far worse than anything Bohai could have imagined. He gripped the table as his legs buckled.

"Now you see why my work cannot be interrupted." Loh seemed bemused at Bohai's reaction. "Our most senior Party members…they are not young men."

Bohai tried to stand without the support of the table but flinched as he straightened his legs. The pliers he had jammed between his cheeks had slid forward and partially opened when he bent his knees. Now they were nibbling at his nuts like a hungry squirrel.

They were long-nosed pliers with chromium jaws, designed for tightening wire fences. He might have balls of steel, but Bohai's scrotum was sore. He grimaced as he stepped gingerly around the corner of the table.

"You look faint." said Loh. "Maybe you're not up for this kind of work, after all." The doctor pursed his lips. "Should I call the guard?"

"No, no, it's fine," said Bohai. "Haven't eaten anything…just a little lightheaded." He stepped to the doctor's side of the table and gestured at the macaque. "Tell me more about the transplant process…how far down on the neck do you cut?"

Loh brightened at the question, his guest's well-being never a concern, only an unwanted interruption. He gestured at the monkey's neck. "A dog's spinal cord is much simpler than a monkey's. For the macaque we have to make an incision much lower, past the sixth or seventh vertebrae."

"How long can the head stay alive," asked Bohai, "before you reconnect it?"

"Two minutes or less." The doctor spared a glance at his basket of death. "That's why you need to have good hands, and why I need you."

Loh shifted his attention to the pitiful primate named Junjie.

If it has a name, maybe it has a soul.

Bohai met the gaze of the monkey, whose yellow eyes stared back as if reading his mind.

Bohai winked.

Junjie blinked.

"I'll do it." Bohai turned to the doctor. "Where do you cut, exactly?"

"I'll show you." Loh leaned over the table. "Come closer."

Bohai stepped sideways, rubbing his right hand against his lower back as if to relieve an ache. He bent over the table to get a closer look.

Loh ran a bony finger along Junjie's neck just above the collar bone.

Bohai kept rubbing his back. "Show me again."

As Loh retraced the pattern on the monkey's torso, Bohai slid his right hand down his pants and gripped the pliers in his sweaty palm.

Loh finished his demonstration with a self-satisfied smile on his face. His eyes were small and wet behind his glasses.

"You need to be quick," he said. "And precise."

Bohai pushed against the table with his left hand, pivoting on his heel to build momentum into his swing. He was both quick and precise.

His right hand swung from behind his back in a sweeping downward arc. The chromium pliers caught the lights of the laboratory and sparkled like a vengeful fairy. Doctor Loh saw the glint of metal before his brain deciphered the shape of the long-nosed pliers. He jerked his head sideways, an instinctive lunge that saved his left eye.

Not that it mattered. The move turned his right eye into the bull's-eye instead.

The pliers shattered the doctor's glasses and plowed through his cornea. Aqueous humor splashed across Bohai's hand, but there was nothing funny about it. Bohai gritted his teeth and shoved the pliers deeper into the socket.

Loh clawed at his face and gargled a scream that died in his throat. He fell backward onto the floor, blood streaming from his eye in fitful spurts. His gnarled hands clutched the pliers as if he was trying to operate on himself.

Bohai stared at the prone figure, waiting for nausea to arrive, or an adrenaline crash to bring him to his knees. Bohai had never killed anything bigger than a spider and expected the weight to fall on him like an anvil. He took a deep breath and braced himself.

He felt free.

Guilt didn't knock on the door of his conscience. Remorse sent its regrets it couldn't come. Bohai's moral compass starting spinning like a ballerina. If his knees weren't so stiff, he would have started to skip.

For the first time since he arrived in this contemptible camp, Bohai wasn't afraid.

He looked at Doctor Loh's body. Followed its contours, searching for proof it had once been a human being, but all he saw was a fallen scarecrow in a lab coat.

Bohai wiped his hand on his pants and turned to face the

table. Junjie watched him anxiously, like a little boy who just caught Santa leaving a present under the tree.

Bohai smiled and said, "Let's get out of here."

He found releases for the collar and the straps holding the monkey's arms and legs. Bohai unbuckled each in turn, acutely aware that Junjie might tear his face off. Still, he had faith in their man-to-monkey alliance, forged by a common enemy and shared goal of escape.

To test his theory, Bohai offered a hand to the macaque as soon as the bonds were removed. Junjie didn't hesitate. He extended a furry hand and allowed Bohai to help him stand. The macaque froze for a moment, body tensed as he took in the smells and sounds of the room. Then he leapt from the table, landing next to the sprawled figure of the doctor.

Junjie looked at Bohai and blinked. Then the monkey started to urinate on Doctor Loh.

"No time for that." Bohai cuffed Junjie gently across the back of his tawny head.

Junjie made a chattering sound and finished his business.

Bohai considered the submarine door of the main entrance, grateful for its thickness. He doubted the guard could hear a thing, but there was no doubt a guard still waited outside. There was a side corridor leading away from the laboratory, its stone walls alive with flashing lights. As he took a tentative step in that direction, Bohai felt a small furry hand slip into his.

He looked at his primate-in-crime.

"You know a way out?"

Junjie gave a sharp-toothed smirk and led Bohai deeper into the tunnel.

31

The ghost moved deeper into the tunnel.

"How much farther?"

The currents of air beneath the streets of San Francisco were breathable but dank. The ghost's head almost brushed the ceiling, and his white hair floated around his shoulders. In the subterranean gloom it looked as if he was walking underwater.

"Almost there." Gerry Gao kept pace three steps behind the ghost. He was the tall man who had accompanied the albino on the helicopter in the botched burglary. Now he was the ghost's guide dog through the service tunnels around city hall. He held a camping lantern high in his left hand as they walked.

Gerry was roughly the same height as the ghost, lean and in shape, but he had no illusions about who was more dangerous. The ghost was also protected by the Triads, while Gerry was merely muscle on Freddie Wang's payroll. No contest. If things went sideways, Gerry was disposable.

"We should have a third man," said Gerry, not for the first time. "With Tommy in the hospital, you'll have to go inside by yourself if I keep watch."

"I work better alone."

The ghost ran his right hand along the curved stone walls of the tunnel as he walked. His fingers were skeletal but his hand moved assuredly. When Gerry had offered the lantern, the ghost had refused, even though he walked in front. Gerry also had a small flashlight in his pocket, but that was spurned as well.

Gerry wondered if the man's eyesight was poor, or better in low light.

That wasn't the only thing he was wondering. Before heading underground he'd asked Freddie about Tommy Chen's status at the hospital. All he knew was that Tommy got shot at that kid's apartment. Gerry had managed to stumble his way out of the alley after that rotten kid kicked him in the balls, so he didn't know how badly Tommy was wounded.

All Freddie would say was that Tommy was at the hospital. When Gerry asked how bad it was, Freddie said the same thing in that raspy voice of his.

He's at the hospital.

Badly wounded or barely a scratch? Alive or dead? Nothing, just Freddie's baleful, unblinking eye, making it clear no more information would be forthcoming. Tommy was disposable, just like Gerry. Get back to work.

"Here." Gerry jiggled the lantern to shift the glow to a service ladder on their right. "We just walked under the east side of Civic Center Plaza and across Larkin Street." He pointed at the curved metal rungs of the ladder set into stone. "This leads to a drain behind a monument that sits between the south side of the museum and the library. It's sort of a pedestrian street, probably packed with homeless at this hour of the morning."

Gossamer threads of light as frail as the dawn stroked the upper rungs of the ladder.

"Perfect," said the ghost.

"Not my business, but I think it's batshit to try this in daylight."

"I'm on a schedule."

I don't think the police care about your schedule, thought Gerry as he said, "Okay."

"It's very early," said the ghost. "And the museum is closed indefinitely. When we come back next time, we will need more men. But today is a one-man job."

"Come back." Gerry stopped short of the ladder. "There's a next time?"

The ghost nodded.

"How many times do you—?"

"—as many as it takes," said the ghost, pausing. "If all goes to plan, it will take only one more."

Gerry studied the lines of the other man's face, obsession etched in alabaster. The red eyes glowed in the lamplight. There was no upside to arguing, and Gerry could think of several spine-chilling downsides. He ran his free hand across his scalp as if trying to dislodge an idea.

All he came up with was a question.

"What do you want me to do?"

"Go back to Freddie," said the ghost, "and tell him to check in with Hong Kong on my delivery. If he ignores the time difference, we'll only lose a day."

Gerry nodded. "You want the lantern?"

The ghost smiled and shook his head. "I won't need it." He ascended the ladder effortlessly, as if his feet had never touched the ground. He blended with the shadows until the faint shower of light from the drain fell upon him. His long hair glowed like an eldritch halo.

Gerry turned and ran down the tunnel as if he'd seen a ghost, which he had.

The ghost ignored him as he pushed open the drain and climbed into the light.

32

The light was sallow, and the air was damp at the impound lot on Seventh Avenue.

A miasma of morning fog and car exhaust drifted from the Route 80 overpass down to the impounded cars. Cape walked back to his car and popped the trunk, grabbed a sweatshirt and a light jacket, then returned and offered both to Maria.

"You pick."

"Always a gentleman." Maria took the jacket.

"San Francisco weather." Cape pulled the sweatshirt over his head. "As welcoming as a cold slap in the face."

Maria held the jacket up to her nose. "How long has this been in your trunk?"

"What year is it?"

Maria smiled and pulled the garment around her shoulders.

Beau stepped out of the corrugated shack that served as the office and gave a parting wave to the officer inside. He crossed the lot, pointing over Cape's shoulder at another building toward the back. Beyond the ragged rows of cars confiscated by the SFPD was a larger structure with twin double-wide garage doors flanking a standard door that you'd see on a house. Beau jangled a set of keys as they wound their way past cars that had been towed or stolen and recovered. The cars looked lonely waiting for their rightful owners to drive them home.

Cape recalled a visit he'd made last year, after his car vanished from its spot at a dead meter. A budget shortfall was reason enough for the city to tow any vehicle left unattended, and Cape's glove compartment full of unpaid tickets made it quite a catch. It took a couple of days to figure out how to disable the security cameras long enough to steal his car back at four in the morning.

"Why bring the helicopter here?" asked Cape. "And not the airfield?"

"Forensics hasn't had a good look," said Beau. "The airfield is too far south of the city." He jerked a thumb over his shoulder. "Hall of Justice is two blocks away, a short walk for anyone working the case."

Beau selected a key from the ring and unlocked the main entrance to the makeshift warehouse. Inside were more cars, interspersed with other vehicles—ATVs, motorcycles, even a golf cart. The closest car caught Cape's attention, and he checked the insignia, then noticed the grill of the car on its left. His gaze moved laterally, cataloging the street value of the row.

"You've got a Bugatti, a BMW i8, a McLaren…"

"Welcome to the Fast & Furious showroom," said Beau. "All vehicles inside this shed are either part of an active investigation, or they're stupid expensive—or both." He rubbed his thumb against his fingers as if waving cash. "Cars like this on the open lot, that's too big a temptation behind nothing more than a chain-link fence. Last year some numbskull stole a car in the middle of the night, right off the lot, and that was just a piece of shit convertible."

"Shocking," said Cape.

"Imagine if these gems were on display," said Beau. "City would have to pay for a night guard…easier to build this shed."

They cut through the next row, and Beau pointed them toward the left rear corner of the room. A plastic tarp was taped to the floor, on top of which sat a jigsaw of scorched metal. The helicopter looked like an unfinished erector set abandoned by an impatient child.

The curve of the shattered cockpit and a bent rotor blade were suggestive of a helicopter, but other pieces were ragged strips of aluminum that might have been dumped from the back of a truck headed to the scrap heap. The tail was bent in places but surprisingly intact, the registration number still legible if you followed the numbers along the crooked contours.

Up close, the helicopter was much larger than Cape expected. Jutting from the side of the museum, its scale relative to the building had made it look like a standard helicopter, the type used by police or news channels to monitor traffic. This was much longer and broader in the belly, the extended cockpit wide enough to hold four men abreast, with plenty of room between.

As if reading his mind, Maria said, "This could carry a dozen men, counting the pilot." She studied the tail. "It's a Sikorsky, isn't it?"

"Yup," said Beau. "Sikorsky Blackhawk from the Coast Guard station at the airport."

"Stolen?" asked Cape.

"Borrowed without permission, for sure," said Beau. "Taken from a maintenance hangar the night before the robbery. Maybe they planned on returning it, or they intended to get inside the museum quickly and abandon it on the roof, or—"

"—no." Maria knelt behind the mangled cockpit to study the charred debris. "If they hadn't crashed, they would have needed to carry everything." Lying on her stomach, Maria took a pen from her pocket and began moving caramelized fragments of wood around the tarp. "They didn't get what they came for..." She stood and brushed the front of her pants. "...not yet."

Cape hadn't seen the pattern at first, but now he did. The sections of wood were part of a whole, puzzle pieces torn apart. Maria walked a few paces to her right and dropped to her knees again, then crawled to the center of the tarp. More detritus came together, speckled bands of gold and green now visible through the gray ash.

Beau grunted, impressed. "What are we looking at?"

Maria rose to her knees, opened her bag and fished around until she produced a small brush. "Okay if I—?"

"Forensics will be pissed," said Beau. "Be my guest—you're the one who works at the cultural heritage whatever-it-is."

"Crime division," said Maria.

"Art police," said Cape.

"*Está bien.*" Maria pressed her face next to the first pile of debris and started brushing. She swept the brush away from her body, holding her breath on the backstroke. She worked from the edges of the fragments toward their center, exposing just enough of the surface to reveal the faint outline of an image.

A grand building, white walls offset by subtle hues of pink and blue, the tiled roof curved in the style of palaces seen in classical Chinese paintings. Rolling green hills and a small lake in the foreground. Fog wrapped delicately around the foothills, which reminded Cape of San Francisco and gave the entire scene the aspect of a fairy tale. The canvas was ruptured and covered in jagged trails of blackened paint, as if an apocalyptic storm had come down from the fairy-tale mountains to tear the world asunder.

Maria scooted backward on her stomach and stood, a triumphant grin on her face.

"What is it?" asked Cape.

"And what was it worth?" asked Beau.

"Yuanmingyuan," said Maria softly. "Scenes from the Summer Palace." She turned to Beau. "It would be priceless, if it were real."

"What was that first word?" asked Cape.

"Yuan...ming...yuan," said Maria. "It was the summer palace for Chinese emperors during the Qing Dynasty, looted and burned during the second Opium War. Your friend Sally would know the story, anyone raised in China does. This painting, it's one of forty commissioned by the Qianlong emperor, each depicting a different view of the palace."

"You said priceless," said Cape.

"These paintings are the only surviving images of the palace grounds before they were destroyed," said Maria. "So the real ones have added cultural significance."

"You think it's a fake," said Beau.

"It has to be." Maria's eyes betrayed her excitement. She was in her element.

Cape was staring at the ruined painting, but his mind's eye was re-watching the museum get robbed one frame at a time. "Security cameras didn't show any paintings being moved."

"Not one," said Maria.

"The museum claims nothing was stolen." Beau rubbed his face in his hands.

"I'm not sure that's true," said Maria.

"Me neither," said Cape.

"But what if it is," said Beau, "as far as these paintings are concerned."

"If these weren't stolen," said Maria, "that means—"

"—they were already in the helicopter," said Cape.

"—so the thieves were bringing art to the museum," said Beau. "That's a twist."

"Which makes this a forgery." Maria bounced up and down on her toes like a sprinter warming up before a race.

Cape wondered if she was going to do a backflip next. Maria clearly felt not only excited but vindicated. He glanced at the deep-fried wreckage and recalled how quickly she'd pieced the painting together. Even for someone with a mental catalog of art like Maria's, that could only mean she already knew what she was looking for. The painting was too complex, the lines of the mountains too subtle. A puzzle champion with four arms couldn't have done it faster.

"This is the painting you warned your boss at Interpol about," said Cape.

"I got a tip," said Maria. "These paintings are normally part of a permanent collection at the Bibliothèque Nationale in Paris, the French national library. There was an attempted robbery there last year. The entrance the burglars tried to use was closest to the gallery where these paintings are displayed."

"They got away?" asked Beau.

"Empty-handed, but yes," said Maria. "On our recommendation, the library upgraded their security system the week before. The thieves didn't know."

"Nothing on the security footage?" asked Cape, guessing the answer.

"Just static and white mist," said Maria.

"What a coincidence," said Beau.

"As soon as I heard that four of the paintings would be on loan to the museum here," said Maria, "I had to come to San Francisco."

Cape hummed the tune to 'San Francisco, here I come' as he paced the length of the helicopter. Something Maria had said was poking at him like a rock in his shoe. When he reached the end of the helicopter's tail, he turned and asked, "When the museum in Norway got hit, the thieves only took a few pieces and disappeared?"

"*Sí*," said Maria. "Gone in minutes."

"Both times?"

"Every time," said Maria. "They are working their way down a checklist, one national treasure at a time."

"Checklist." Cape repeated the word, weighing it against the facts. "The art committee or task force you told me about...after they traveled around the world demanding their art back—"

"—the robberies began," said Maria. "And Interpol took an interest."

"They hit too many museums in too short a period of time," said Beau. "Bank robbers do the same thing, never know when to quit."

Maria nodded. "They know Interpol has the same list. It's only a matter of time until museums tighten up security. Then it's back to diplomacy."

"Which takes forever," said Cape. "So they brought their own counterfeit art."

"That's good," said Beau. "Damn good."

"It's brilliant," said Maria. "If the art is still on the museum floor, how can it be stolen?"

Cape knelt and looked at the cracked flecks of paint on the charcoal panel Maria had excavated. Where the gold paint hadn't melted, it was mottled, aged. Any sections of wood not burned revealed a rough-hewn frame, fine craftsmanship rich with imperfections that suggested another century, when power tools did not exist.

"The art you're talking about," said Cape. "Sculptures, paintings, bronze from hundreds of years ago—making a copy good enough to fool a museum can't be easy."

"For something as detailed and famous as this?" Maria considered the challenge. "It would take at least two people."

"Two?"

"A true artist," said Maria, "and a historian."

33

"You are a true artist."

"I'm just a mimic," said Peng, setting down his brush. "And you are too kind."

"I know something about art." Wen smiled at the young man standing in front of him, a prodigy who barely realized his own talent. "And you're an artist."

Peng nodded his thanks. When he first heard a professor was going to help, Peng took offense, but only a day into their relationship, Peng wondered how he had ever painted alone. Wen's knowledge of the materials, brushstrokes, and the history behind the painting changed how Peng approached the canvas. He could feel the image before he drew a single brushstroke. It felt like uncovering lost art rather than recreating it.

The only thing that troubled Peng about his older colleague was the man's appearance. Wen was tall and lanky by nature but looked malnourished. His eyes were bright but sunken. Peng knew the professor once taught in Hong Kong but was beginning to wonder where Wen had been before arriving in Dafen.

"Do you want to sit?" Peng gestured at two nearby stools. "It will take a few minutes to dry before we can add the next layer."

"My knees thank you." Wen pulled a stool closer. "It would be ideal for each layer to dry longer, but if we adjust the thickness of the paint as we go, it should work."

The two had been leaning over the worktable for over an hour, standing side by side while Peng added details to the painting. They were working on the second floor of the art factory in a room sequestered for this project. The supervisor was instructed to get anything they needed. They answered only to the Devil himself.

"Have you met him?" asked Wen. "Mogwai."

"Oh, yes," said Peng. His eyes darted to the corners of the room.

Though no cameras or microphones were visible, Wen took the hint and lowered his voice. "Perhaps we can go for a walk in the park before I must…" He hesitated, glancing at his calloused hands. "…return to my quarters."

Peng nodded, grateful for the change in subject. "I've never used paints like these." He gestured at the palette next to the canvas and the nearby mixing bowls. "Berries and copper, that's new to me."

"Actually, it's very old," said Wen. "Berries were used to make pigments, and the iron and copper content in paint was much higher. It's important to get the mixture right if you want the painting to look authentic."

"Will this fade?"

"That's the idea," said Wen. "It will age rapidly to look like the original. Animal fats and urine were used as an emulsifier. Fortunately, we won't be needing anyone's urine today. I would hate to piss on your painting."

Peng laughed. "Tell me more about what I just painted."

"*Nine Continents Clear and Calm*," said Wen.

"Nine continents," said Peng. "I thought there were only seven."

Wen smiled. "It's a reference to the emperor's private residence at Yuanmingyuan, one of the lost views of the Summer Palace. Commissioned in 1744 and painted by two court artists, Shen Yuan and Tangdai."

"I like that you know the artists' names," said Peng.

"Too often people remember the art but not the artist." Wen spread his hands. "You can't have one without the other."

"Have you always been interested in art?"

"I taught art history at university," said Wen. "I even met my second wife at a museum."

"Is she also—"

"—no," said Wen. "She worked for the city government but would visit the museum during her lunch break. It was free and a nice place for a walk. We continued to meet there for walks after we started dating."

"Some believe all art is political." Peng glanced at the painting. "I only see beauty."

"I could have used you on my side of the debate, during those walks with my wife."

Peng thought of his girlfriend, Yan, working on the factory floor. He thought about their last kiss and remembered they were supposed to go out for dinner. "Your wife, where is—"

"—dead," said Wen, more abruptly than he intended. He lowered his eyes. "I think she's dead."

"I'm sorry." Peng studied his companion and saw exhaustion in the lines of his shoulders but iron in his jaw. He could only guess what Wen had been through, and Peng wondered if he would be as stoic if their roles were reversed. "What was your wife's name?"

Wen blinked at the question, disarmed by the young boy's sincerity. Other than his friend Bohai, no one had taken any interest since he'd been arrested. He briefly wondered what Bohai was doing and hoped his mischievous friend was safe.

"Her name was Chu Hua," said Wen. "Though her name meant chrysanthemum, she always smelled like jasmine. She loved a perfume I couldn't afford." He made a bittersweet smile. "The truth is, our marriage wasn't going very well. Hong Kong was changing, not for the better. She worked for the local government and wouldn't hear of it when I suggested we do something. I was an idealist, and she was a realist. We argued a lot." Wen's expression turned rueful. "I met her right after my first wife died, maybe it was too soon. Now I'll never know if we could have worked it out."

Peng didn't know what to say. He never had a real girlfriend until recently, let alone a wife. The two men were silent for a minute until Wen sighed loudly, as if expelling as much sadness as he could in one breath.

Peng asked, "Should we start mixing the next batch of paints?"

Wen took a deep breath and nodded. "Yes." He stood and stepped over to the table, put a hand on Peng's shoulder. "Thank you." He gestured at a row of plastic containers. "Hand me the chalk and the linseed oil."

"Why do you think we're recreating this particular painting?" Peng grabbed the ingredients and made room on the table a safe distance from the canvas. He moved a mortar and pestle closer to where they were standing. "And why the crazy schedule?"

"Your guess is as good as mine," said Wen, "but whoever wants this painting is in a very big hurry."

34

The ghost seemed in no particular hurry as he emerged from the drain to walk among the homeless.

The semipermanent encampment numbered close to a hundred people and a dozen dogs. It radiated outward from the base of Pioneer Monument, a cluster of historic figures flanking a much larger monument that stood atop a stone column almost ten feet in diameter. The central figure was an eight hundred-ton sculpture of the Roman goddess Minerva, more commonly known by her Greek name, Athena. She was the goddess of wisdom and war, and standing twenty feet high, clearly wise enough to stay above the battle for human dignity occurring daily on the streets of San Francisco. Minerva's gaze took in city hall less than a block away, its opaque windows blind to the godforsaken throngs outside.

At Minerva's side was an enormous grizzly bear symbolizing the state of California. The flanking statues covered the points of the compass and dated to the late 1800s. Each told a chapter in the story of the pioneers who settled California. One dramatized the gold rush, two were female figures symbolizing commerce and plenty, though it wasn't clear which was which. The last plinth once featured a tableau of a missionary, a vaquero, and a Native American, but it was removed in 2018 after a city commission decided it was racist.

After its removal, one of the committee members accused another member of being racist, who then decried her colleague for being sexist, at which point everyone else on the committee took sides until it was agreed that everyone was racist but only some of them were sexist. That seemed to settle things down until the homeless moved in, the taxpayer-funded commission ran out of money, and everyone agreed that the rest of the statues, and the homeless, could stay where they were.

The ghost didn't know this city's history and didn't care to learn any of it. Politics bored him, though politics could sometimes be a means to an end. The ghost did not trust the communists any more than he trusted Hong King's government under British rule, but it was true that the Triads had more autonomy and ability to expand their operations since the handover to China in '97. There were over fifty clans in Hong Kong alone, only a dozen under routine surveillance.

The police were too busy monitoring student groups and quelling protests to bother with known criminal organizations that predated the founding of the city. Accommodations had been made, deals were struck, palms greased, and the underground economy grew.

The ghost didn't question the illicit nature of his work; it was all he had ever known, but his loyalties remained with his clan, not the ruling class. He would ally with anyone who got him closer to his goal, and remove anyone who stood in his way.

The people sleeping at his feet right now could have been the ghost in another life.

Abandoned at birth, an albino child was too much of an aberration for a culture built on conformity. The ghost would have died on the street if he'd been left on any other doorstep. He often wondered how many people had walked past the screaming bundle in the basket, eyes averted, until the door finally opened.

The Triads weren't known for their compassion, but they understood the concept of not fitting in. They had also perfected the art of shaping human flesh like steel. So the ghost was adopted by the heaven and earth society before he could crawl.

Raised as a son, forged as a weapon.

There was no name pinned to the basket in which they found him, no monogrammed blanket. They decided to call him Guǐ because he was white as a ghost and wailed like a lost soul. When he was older, some of the kids called him èmó, which meant demon, fiend, or devil.

He liked Guǐ better and made it his name. He was a ghost, a spirit. *Weren't we all?* And if ever he doubted it, all he had to do was look in the mirror.

Guǐ also liked that his name sometimes meant sinister plot or dirty trick. It made him feel clever, and in time he learned that being clever was not a characteristic all his classmates admired. Everyone in his school was expected to be strong, but he wanted to be smart. By the time he was ten, it was obvious which of his friends would follow and which ones would lead.

The men he had led here in San Francisco, those who joined him in the helicopter, they had not been clever. They were blunt instruments for a crime that hadn't turned out as planned. The pilot was cocky and tried to land on the roof instead of hovering as the ghost instructed. They could have been in and out within ten minutes, using the cable winch to haul the art into the belly of the helicopter.

Even the best-laid plans go up in smoke, and that night the ghost's had burned along with the pilot. Now he needed a new plan. Freddie Wang, that old cur, was probably right—he should hit the museum in New York, stay clear of San Francisco for a while.

Guï wasn't stubborn, but he wasn't patient, either.

He moved through the crowd considering the options and ignoring the stares. An old man sitting cross-legged on the ground made the sign of the cross as the ghost passed. The dog by his side started to whimper. Most of the people huddled together were sleeping, but those awake followed him with a mixture of wonder, fear, and fascination. Their eyes on his back felt like a familiar weight across his shoulders, one he had borne so long that it was more of a comfort than a burden.

The ghost stepped around the corner to face the main entrance to the museum. He looked around the square. No civilians in sight, barely any sounds of traffic, his only company the vagrant horde and the thin tendrils of fog dancing in the dawn.

The stone façade consisted of two levels rising from the top of the granite steps. The first level framed three mammoth doors, the primary entrances and exits during visiting hours. The upper part of the building was an open balcony broken into five sections by columns shaped in the Greek or beaux-arts style, a classical design suggesting the building had once been something other than an Asian art museum. Five giant tapestries hung between each set of columns, artfully decorated to promote the latest exhibits. Behind the tapestries were shadows, but Guï wondered if there were glass doors leading onto the second floor.

Could it be so simple?

The skylight and helicopter had seemed the obvious choice after their success in Norway. The doors on the ground floor were heavy, wired for alarms, and the side doors were metal. But the bottom of this ornate balcony was only twenty feet from the top step, and the space between the columns was vast, at least ten feet. That made the balcony itself almost sixty feet wide, plenty of room to maneuver.

The ghost spun on his heel to make a clockwise scan of his surroundings, then glided to the base of the building directly below the last column on the left. Unwrapping a coil of white rope from around his waist, he reached inside his *cheongsam*-style jacket and removed a grappling hook from one of his many hidden pockets.

Guï tied the rope assuredly through the eye at the base of the clawed hook, then took a step back from the wall and started spinning the rope like a lasso. His first throw did the trick, looping over the granite balustrade so the hook caught the rope on the backswing. The ghost remembered practicing as a boy until his hands bled. His instructors made the entire class do it again until everyone mastered the throw.

He tugged on the rope, then leaned back on his heels to make sure the hook was set. He climbed up the rope and scaled the balustrade in less time than it would have taken to ride the escalator. He unfastened the hook, retrieved his rope, and ducked behind the tapestry.

His light-sensitive eyes adjusted quickly. The balcony was deep, but light from inside the museum shone through the windows. There were five sets of glass doors, and they all opened onto the second floor of the museum.

Staying in the shadows, the ghost moved to the closest set of doors and ran his long fingers along the window casings, the seam where the doors came together. He took a thin strip of metal from inside his jacket, longer than a lock pick but too delicate for a car jam, and slid it carefully between the doors at eye level.

The ghost slid the metal in minuscule increments up to the

top of the window and then down, checking for wires. He met no resistance. That could mean nothing, because the base of the door could have pressure-sensitive buttons, or an electric beam might be mounted inside, since the doors opened inward from the balcony.

An undetected alarm would limit their time, but they only needed a few minutes, and the ghost was skeptical the security system extended to these windows. Museum security around the world was a joke. Alarm systems in banks, even in stores and homes, were far more elaborate than the bare minimum deployed at most institutional buildings.

This museum, like so many others he had robbed, was run by people who considered their world beyond reach. Complacent in their authority and smug in their belief they were entitled to the art they possessed simply because it was in their possession.

By that logic, the priceless paintings would rightfully belong to Guǐ as soon as he took them. And that would be very soon indeed.

35

"When is soon?" asked Grace.

"Soon is another way of saying not yet," said Sally.

"I want to walk on the rooftops again," said Grace. "That was fun."

"It was necessary."

"The policeman seemed nice."

"He is," said Sally, "but he's still a policeman, and they have to follow rules."

Grace made a face. "You mean the law."

"Sometimes," said Sally. "Other times, the phone on their desk rings, and they have to take orders from city hall."

"The government."

"Yes."

Sally let that sit. Grace had told her about the day she lost her parents, the protest in the park. Not easy to see the world without a filter, let alone at eleven years old.

"I'm just saying it might be safer," said Grace, "if I came with you."

"A rhinoceros couldn't get in here." Sally gestured around her loft and pointed at the sliding door. "The problem isn't someone getting in, Grace, it's you sneaking out."

Grace looked at the floor and fidgeted. "Robin wouldn't stay home."

"Excuse me?"

Grace looked up and held Sally's bemused gaze. "Batman always brings Robin with him. Captain America had Bucky, then later the Falcon. Aquaman has Aqualad."

"Aqualad?" Sally frowned. "You made that one up."

Grace looked indignant. "Flash has Kid Flash."

"You read too many comic books," said Sally. "Schools in Hong Kong have really gone downhill."

"I want to be safe," said Grace, "but I feel safer with you."

Sally's mouth twitched. The kid changed tactics as soon as she met resistance. A natural negotiator. Grace had all the characteristics of someone born in the year of the rooster. One of those was an ability to persuade others, in part because a rooster would never give up. She combined the stubbornness of a preteen with the guile of a poker player.

"I'm going to find the tall man from the museum," said Sally. "The one who tried to grab you in the alley."

"The one I kicked in the balls?"

"That's the one."

Grace took a deep breath. "The policeman said they were looking."

"I know where to find him," said Sally. "He works for..." She paused, trying to find the right words to describe Freddie Wang. She went with the comic book narrative. "...a villain."

"A supervillain?"

"Definitely not," said Sally. "He's an old, bitter man who steals from other people. There is nothing super about him."

"Then—"

"—that doesn't mean he's not dangerous," said Sally. "I live in the same neighborhood." She almost added "and once worked for men like him" but merely said, "And I know his men."

Grace made a last stand by appearing contrite, her voice resigned. "I understand."

Sally's mouth twitched again and she snorted, a laugh cut short. She felt as if she'd traveled back in time and was arguing with herself, or staring into a mirror.

You started much younger than she did, and no one gave you a choice.

After a pause, Sally said, "It's your decision, but whatever you choose, the same rules apply. You do exactly as I say, when I say it, or next time we're on a roof, I'll throw you off."

Grace nodded, her mouth a straight line.

"It may be dangerous."

Grace nodded again.

"Your call," said Sally.

"I want to go with you."

No one spoke, and neither blinked for a full minute.

"Okay, Kid Flash," said Sally. "Let's go catch a bad guy."

36

"The bad guy is dead," said Beau. "One of them, anyway."

Beau slid his phone into his jacket, thunderclouds forming on his brow. He looked at Maria without seeing, his focus somewhere else. She was still on her knees putting pieces of charcoal together and hadn't heard him. Cape had and walked over to his friend.

"Which one," asked Cape, "the guy you shot?"

"Yeah," said Beau. "Tommy Chen."

"He did try to shoot you."

Beau's eyes snapped into focus. "This isn't me feeling bad. If he'd shot me first, then I'd feel bad. And if I have to put someone down, you know me, I sleep—"

"—like the dead?"

"Exactly," said Beau. "But I was close, my aim was good, and I shot that stocky scumbag in the shoulder."

"He died in the hospital?"

Beau nodded. "A stroke. Happens sometimes after traumatic injury, the body throws a clot that pinballs its way up to the brain."

"How old was he?"

"Couldn't have been more than thirty-five."

"Anybody visit him?"

"Just the nurse," said Beau. "The cop stayed outside during his shift. Besides, I know the patrolman, and he's not bent."

"Convenient, Tommy dropping dead like that."

"Very," said Beau, "since we hadn't questioned him yet."

Both men watched Maria for a minute. She had completed two puzzles and was working on the third, her brush painstakingly slow. Most of the wreckage was oily ash, but she managed to find enough strips of color to make a faint constellation of art come to life.

Cape turned back to Beau. "Maybe it's coincidence, but it's fishy."

"I hate fish."

"I don't like salmon," said Cape, "but most other fish, I'm good."

"They all stink after a few days," said Beau. "Like this case."

"How about the other guy, the taller one?"

"Vinnie tagged him as Gerry Gao," said Beau. "He's going to bring him in today."

"You think Freddie is cutting any loose ends that lead back to his business?"

"Wouldn't you?" Beau patted his pockets to make sure he didn't forget anything. "If I leave you here with Indiana Jones…" He jutted his chin at Maria. "…think you can lock up?"

"Where are you headed?"

"To sit behind a typewriter," said Beau. "I shot the guy, so I do the paperwork."

"That's why I'm not a cop," said Cape. "When I shoot someone, all I have to do is go to jail." He crossed to Maria and knelt down, said a few words. She nodded and returned to her work. Cape rejoined Beau. "If you're okay with Maria closing up, I'll walk out with you."

Beau glanced at Maria. It was obvious she'd be at this for at least another hour.

"I'm useless here, clearly," said Cape, "so I'm going to try and answer a riddle."

"Which is..?"

"How do you catch a ghost?"

37

"That's an intriguing question."

"I knew you'd like it," said Cape. "But is it possible?"

Dumont Frazer rubbed his chin and worked his jaw as if the answer would emerge in the form of a bubble from his mouth. His black hair was streaked with gray, with an unkempt look that suggested his brush was actually his fingers. His eyeglasses reflected the overhead lights in a subtle semaphore of contemplation. His unbuttoned lab coat partially covered a T-shirt which featured a drawing of a man holding a blaster, the bold type proclaiming Han Shot First.

Cape had never seen Dumont without a lab coat and wondered if the scientist wore one when he went out to dinner, in case he wanted to experiment with his food.

The laboratory was a converted warehouse on a stretch of Market Street known for its street vendors, squalor, and empty storefronts. His door looked like a garage entrance to the adjacent building, so unless you knew Dumont was here, he remained invisible to passersby.

Long tables were covered with test tube racks, beakers, dismantled computers, tasers, miniature drones, car parts, and loose wires. Shelves were cluttered with clockwork devices, wooden items that resembled three-dimensional puzzles, and books on everything from organic chemistry to secret societies and historical weapons.

Everyone who knew Dumont existed came to him for help, even the police. The SFPD had become infamous for scandals involving mishandled evidence, lab accidents, and cases over-turned by ruined samples. Detectives and DAs who couldn't afford to lose a case found the money to hire Dumont.

Fortunately for Cape, the inventor's rates varied depending on his level of interest in a problem. Dumont held patents on several devices currently in use by the Pentagon and law enforcement agencies across the country, in addition to his patents for educational children's toys, so the only thing Dumont couldn't afford was to be bored. Cape tried not to disappoint as he described every detail of the museum heist and invisible thief.

When he had finished, the scientist was smiling. "That's very good."

"I don't have the video," said Cape, "but I can look into getting a copy."

Dumont waved a hand. "No need, I know how it's done."

"I was hoping to stump you for once."

"Oh, I like this very much," said Dumont. "Thank you for bringing it to me. It's just that I've seen it before."

"Where?"

"Hong Kong," said Dumont. "Everyone knows China built the largest surveillance state in the world, but most people don't realize a battle for privacy is happening on the streets of Hong Kong. It's not a war that makes headlines, and it's being fought primarily by students."

"Students?"

"China took the model adopted by Europe after the terrorist bombings—security cameras on every street corner—and weaponized it to monitor their own citizens. They make the chips used in half the security cameras around the world, but those chips were based on Intel and AMD chips sold here, then reengineered at university labs in mainland China. Your ghost is using technology that was invented at engineering schools, adopted by protestors, and sold on the black market."

"I've never heard of it before."

"It's coming," said Dumont. "China has a social rating system that tracks people across digital platforms. Maybe you've heard of it?"

"I thought Facebook was banned over there."

"This is very *Minority Report*," said Dumont. "It works across any social media, not just state-sponsored platforms like Weibo or when shopping on Alibaba. Using facial recognition, it matches your online behavior to where you go and who you see in the real world."

"In my case that's cat videos online and cops in the real world," said Cape. "You called it a rating system, why?"

"Someone uses a public restroom, a facial scan on their phone is required to unlock the toilet paper roll. Even tourists. So the government knows where you are at any given moment."

"You're kidding."

"Stay with me," said Dumont. "Depending on where and when you show up, you're given a score. A high score means you can travel on high-speed trains, attend a better school, or apply for coveted job. A low score means you're riding coach on a local train or denied a higher paying job."

"This is real," said Cape, his voice more resigned than skeptical. "Today?"

"It's almost five years old," said Dumont.

"I know things are censored in other countries, shit, even here," said Cape, "that's why I quit the newspaper business, but this is—"

"Dystopian?"

"I was going to use a smaller word," said Cape. "Scary."

"So what would you do?" asked Dumont. "If you wanted to steal your privacy back?"

"I'd become invisible," said Cape. "Like a ghost."

Dumont nodded. "Like a ghost."

Gesturing for Cape to follow, Dumont walked along a row of tables toward the far end of the warehouse. The overhead lights tracked their progress and illuminated their path as the lights behind them went dark. Dumont stopped in front of a table with a video camera mounted on a clamp. Cape waited while the inventor rummaged around a nearby shelf for a few minutes.

He returned and dumped a swatch of white fabric, tape, some wire, and a D battery onto the table. The battery was inside a plastic relay box to which wires could be fastened. Dumont's fingers were nimble, and soon he stitched together a net of wire and hooked it up to the battery.

"Watch this."

Dumont turned on the video camera and flipped the viewing screen out from the side of the camera, a two-by-three rectangle displaying an image of the table. He took the cloth and moved his hand in front of the camera lens, waving it back and forth like a flag. Cape followed the motion on the tiny screen.

"I see your white flag," said Cape, "and accept your surrender."

"Not so fast." Dumont spread the cloth on the table and laid the wire mesh over it. "Most fabric isn't good for carrying a current, but this is conductive cloth, fibers interwoven with strands of metal as thin as a hair." Tearing pieces of black electrical tape off a roll, he secured the net to the fabric. "Now, tell me what you see."

Dumont waved the cloth in front of the lens as Cape stared at the camera's viewing screen. The only thing visible was white mist.

The image stuttered, and Cape could suddenly see the cloth, then it vanished again, mere smoke wrapped around the scientist's fingers. The screen pixelated, then resolved into a clear image, the cloth plainly visible.

Dumont disconnected the battery and set his makeshift contraption on the workbench.

"You can see the limitations," he said. "To maintain the illusion, your ghost would have to carry a much stronger charge, attuned to a specific wavelength to disrupt the cameras."

"I could see your hand," said Cape. "Not all the time, but there were moments when it was visible. Is that because of the low current, or—"

"No," said Dumont. "That's the other thing your ethereal friend was wearing." He ran two long fingers across his cheek. "Topographical makeup."

"Like foundation," said Cape. "Or face cream?"

"Precisely," said Dumont. "The most expensive blush you'll ever buy. Nanoparticles are mixed into the cream to create invisible contours and angles on your skin. The same geometry as a stealth bomber, and not as clumsy as prosthetics. You still look like you, but to the cameras you either look like someone else—so there's no identity match—or your face distorts beyond recognition until it resembles—"

"—smoke."

"Yes."

"This should be on every criminal's Christmas list."

"Now that you know how it's done," said Dumont, "what do you want to do about it?"

Cape lifted the fabric with his right hand and rubbed it

between his fingers. "Can you make an outfit for me?" He thought about Sally and her need to keep Grace out of sight. "Or someone smaller?"

"Give me the measurements." Dumont turned off the camera. "Anything else?"

Cape hefted the battery. "How much power does it take to make a full suit work?"

The corner of Dumont's mouth did a mischievous mamba. "You have a plan."

"I have an idea." Cape handed the battery to Dumont. "How would you power it?"

"You could use a single battery pack, holstered on your waist." Dumont tossed the battery back and forth between his delicate hands. "But that would be heavy, throw off your balance."

Cape considered what little he knew of the ghost. Sally heard rumors of his existence. Grace said he walked like Sally. Like a cat. That meant he was dangerous, and he was trained.

"He'll need to move," said Cape. "Gracefully."

Dumont brought his palms together and rolled the battery between them. "Then I'd use four. Lithium batteries would be thinner, hold a charge longer. One pack behind each shoulder, one at the waist in front of the right hip, the last on the left hip, but on the lower back. The weight would be distributed evenly, so any movement would feel natural."

"Good," said Cape. "Perfect, actually." He patted his shoulders and hips as he imagined wearing his own rig. "Ready for the bonus question?"

"Always."

"Could you figure out a way to make it short-circuit?" asked Cape. "From a distance?"

Dumont Frazer looked like a twelve-year-old boy who'd just won the science fair. "I do enjoy it when you come to visit."

"That sounds like a yes."

"It depends," said Dumont. "Is the goal to make him visible to the cameras, or something else."

"Something else," said Cape. "I want him distracted."

"For how long?"

"You tell me."

Dumont set down the battery and drummed his fingers on the table. "It would only last a few seconds."

"I just need an opening."

"And it might take a moment to activate," said Dumont.

"Not ideal, but okay," said Cape. "What will it feel like?"

"I haven't built the device yet." Dumont blew out his cheeks. "This is all theoretical."

Cape smiled sympathetically but wasn't buying it. He knew Dumont had already designed the gizmo in his head. The inventor once gave him a sonic grenade that saved his life. Another time he'd discovered the chemical key that unlocked a mystery. The man had Da Vinci on one shoulder and Edison on the other, whispering into his ears.

"If you had to guess," said Cape, "theoretically."

"Ever stick your tongue on a nine-volt battery when you were a kid?"

"Sure," said Cape. "A jolt through your tongue."

"It might feel like that, multiplied," said Dumont. "Like the low voltage electric fences used on farms to keep cattle in the field. A sharp jolt."

"That might do the trick."

"There's another possibility," said Dumont. "Not as shocking, but it might serve as a distraction. Ever feel a laptop or mobile phone get hot when it's charging? More annoying than painful."

"Do I get to choose?"

"I'm afraid not," said Dumont. "I won't know how it works until I know if it works. Sending a wireless signal at the same frequency, from a distance of...what?" He raised an inquisitive eyebrow.

"Twenty feet?"

"This might not work," said Dumont.

"That's okay," said Cape. "I might not need it."

"When do you need this thing that you might not need," said Dumont, "which hasn't been invented yet?"

"Is that a rhetorical question?"

"You do keep things interesting." Dumont grinned. "I'll get started right away." As they walked back toward the exit, he asked, "Where are you going now?"

"Going to meet Sally," said Cape. "And catch a thief."

38

"Gerry Gao isn't a thief," said Sally. "He's more of a thug."

"What's a thug?" asked Grace.

"A bad guy," said Cape.

They were standing on the rooftop of an empty warehouse that once stored plumbing supplies for a wholesaler that went bankrupt the year before. When the recently elected DA announced he wasn't going to arrest anyone unless they killed someone, an undercurrent of seediness spread across San Francisco like mold. Drug dealers, hustlers, and car thieves moved in, and anyone who could afford to moved out, while those with real money drove across the Golden Gate and bought houses in neighborhoods with private security, gates, and good schools nearby. That turned neighborhoods like this one, once a mix of commercial and residential, into landscapes of desolation and decay.

The roof on which they stood was higher than the adjacent building, which happened to be a textile factory owned by Freddie Wang. From their vantage point, a short walk to either side of the roof would give them a clear line of sight to the front or rear entrance of Freddie's factory.

Cape, Sally, and Grace crouched behind a low wall that encircled the roof. In the center of the roof was a service door that led to an enclosed stairway. A fire escape ran down the back of the building. Freddie's building had a similar structure, but its brick face had small windows on the first floor and more expansive windows on the second, multipaned and continuous from the days when electricity was a novelty and natural light was critical for factory workers being able to see what they were sewing.

"How bad is he?" Grace asked as if trying to brace herself for what might happen. "He tried to grab me in the alley, but I think he just wanted to take me to his boss."

"His boss is worse," said Cape. "He's the real villain."

"But not a supervillain." Grace nodded. "Sally told me."

"Just an old bully who's willing to hurt people to get what he wants." Cape studied Grace's expressions and added, "We're not talking about Lex Luthor, here, or even Doctor Octopus or Green Goblin. Not that bad."

Sally groaned.

Grace visibly brightened. "Sally told me I shouldn't read so many comic books."

"That's like saying you shouldn't study Greek myths," said Cape. "Comic books are a cornerstone of any classical education."

Sally shook her head. "You're a bad influence."

"But not a bad guy." Cape winked at Grace, who giggled. "Or a villain."

"Showtime," said Sally quietly.

The sound of an engine preceded a car coming into view.

They crouched behind the wall and followed the car's progress as it pulled around the back of Freddie's building. The driver stayed in the car, but another man exited the shotgun seat and, after a cursory look around, opened the rear door. Freddie

Wang climbed out of the black Cadillac, a cane in one hand and cigarette in the other.

The last time Cape had seen Freddie was at his restaurant in Chinatown. During a brief and acrimonious exchange, Freddie smoked a pack of cigarettes, his ashtray overflowing by the time Cape asked his first question. No one knew Freddie's real age, and after that meeting Cape was convinced that even cancer was afraid of killing him. Freddie Wang sat at the center of a web with so many connections that half the city's politicians and most of the monied gentry would die with him.

Even Maksim Valenko didn't have that much clout. If Freddie left a void, the Russian would be first to fill it, but their mutual business interests had kept them in their respective corners of the city. Until now.

Cape was watching Freddie hobble to the back door when Sally gave a low whistle from the far corner of the building. She gestured with an open palm for Grace to lie flat. Staying low, Cape made his way across the roof and peered over the edge.

A blue Toyota hatchback was approaching the front of the building from the north, still a few blocks away but driving as if searching for an address, slowing and then speeding up in bursts. Traffic was almost nonexistent, and the streets were flat south of Market compared to the notorious hills of San Francisco found in midtown. The only other car on the same side of the street was a dark sedan, farther back but moving at roughly the same speed as the Toyota.

Cape turned and checked the other end of the street. Another car was approaching from the opposite direction, still three blocks away, a red car low to the ground. Cape couldn't tell but thought it might be a Camaro.

"It's not every day that Freddie leaves his restaurant," said Sally quietly.

"Too many people are looking for Gerry Gao," replied Cape. "Gerry leading them all to Freddie's doorstep isn't good for business."

"Did you mention to Beau that you were coming here?"

"Slipped my mind."

"Sure it did."

"He said Vinnie would track down the second thief," said Cape. "So telling Beau you had already identified Gerry might—"

"—piss him off—"

"—compel Beau to insist we stand down and let Vinnie do his job," said Cape. "In other words, if I ask and he says no—"

"—but you show up anyway—"

"—I go to jail," said Cape. "Or lose my license. But if I happen to be in the neighborhood..."

"It's a mystery you haven't lost your license before."

"Spider-man doesn't need a license," Grace whispered. She had crawled on her stomach to join them. "Can I look?"

Sally watched the cars. The nearest was still a block away. She held the edge of her hand against her nose. "From the bridge of your nose, that's all I want to see over the edge. And only for a second. Then back on your stomach and tell me what you saw."

"Can't believe you brought her with you," said Cape. "I'm impressed."

"That worries me."

"Not with you," said Cape. "I'm impressed with her."

Grace popped up like a gopher and was down in an instant. "Blue car driving close to the curb, dark gray car two blocks behind."

Cape glanced at the second car. "Not bad. I thought the sedan was black, but you're right, it's gray."

"Can I look again?" asked Grace.

"No," said Sally. "He'll be here soon."

"There's that word again," said Grace. "Soon."

They heard the nearest car roll to a stop, gravel on the road crunching beneath its tires. Cape and Sally watched as a tall man exited the rear passenger door and waved the car off with his right hand, in which he was holding his phone.

"That's the man from the security tape," said Cape.

"That's Gerry," said Sally.

As the car drove away, Cape glimpsed a sticker in its front window.

"He took an Uber," said Cape. "What an idiot."

"Unless Freddie gave him a bogus account," said Sally, "and a burner phone—"

"—which I doubt," said Cape. "If he's using his own phone, anyone could track him."

Gerry Gao wore nondescript beige pants and a long-sleeved white shirt under a brown jacket. The bulge on his left hip was suggestive, but to a casual observer he looked fairly forgettable until you got to his shoes.

"Forget his cell phone," said Sally. "All you need to follow Gerry are those."

A pair of running shoes in neon orange lit up the sidewalk as Gerry approached the building. They were emblazoned with a green swoosh on the outer side of either foot, a splash of purple on the heel, with soles as white as the clouds overhead.

Cape turned to Grace. "One thing about criminals is that most think they're clever."

"But they're wrong," said Sally. "Báichī."

Grace smiled, her face pressed against her hands, which were folded under her chin. "Can I look now?"

"No."

Gerry was walking unhurriedly toward the entrance to the warehouse.

"How did you know he'd come here?" asked Cape.

"I squeezed one of Freddie's underlings," said Sally.

"She means it," said Grace. "She literally squeezed him."

"How hard?"

"He'll never have children," said Sally, "but he's still breathing."

Cape watched as the gray sedan that had been following Gerry's Uber rolled past both buildings, then made a slow U-turn and pulled against the curb a block south. Gerry didn't seem to notice; he was looking at his phone. Cape caught a glimpse of the driver before a break in the clouds threw glare against the windshield.

"That's Vinnie."

"I wanted to get Gerry first," said Sally.

"You got here first, so congratulations," said Cape, "but if the police bring him in, all the better."

"Hang back?" asked Sally.

"Definitely," said Cape. "Vinnie was talking into the radio. Company is coming."

"They'll never hold Freddie," said Sally. "He'll deny he was here to meet anyone."

"Yep." Cape suspected Vinnie would wait for backup, and patrol cars wouldn't approach until Gerry went inside. He turned to take another look south and cursed under his breath.

"What is it?" Sally heard the roar of an engine.

The red Camaro was racing toward the factory.

Gerry glanced up from his phone but looked unconcerned, as if a strange car on a deserted street had nothing to do with him. He was probably so inured to working under Freddie's protection that the only thing he feared was getting on the wrong side of his boss.

The smoked windows on the Camaro made it impossible to see the driver, but Cape had a sinking feeling he knew who owned the car.

39

"Valenko bought this car, so you'd better not mess it up, Ely."

Ely ignored his brother and started rolling down the window. He didn't want glass to blow back and blind him when he fired at the guy on the sidewalk.

Pasha did have a point. When they told Maksim Valenko—the *pakhan* of the brotherhood, the boss of bosses—that they didn't own a car, he stared at them in disbelief. Ely and Pasha tried to explain that nobody their age owned a car in San Francisco. No place to park, and if you did have a car and managed to park on the street, your windows got smashed. Besides, who needs a car when you can hail a ride with your phone?

When Valenko asked how they planned on running down a rival gang member with an Uber, the two brothers stopped talking. The *pakhan* solved the problem by loaning them a car that belonged to one of his men. It was a fast, loud American vehicle that Valenko had bought the man as a gift, after a troublesome witness in a racketeering case vanished before the trial.

So the car had sentimental value to two men capable of making both Ely and his brother disappear. Pasha was the better driver and the only one with a license. That put Ely in the back seat as the shooter.

Their instructions were clear. Make trouble for Freddie Wang in a fashion impossible to ignore, and in a manner that demanded reprisal. Start a skirmish. Do not injure Freddie, but any of his men were fair game. No collateral damage or innocent bystanders.

Valenko didn't want to start a war, but he did intend to make a point.

And if Ely or Pasha saw either of the idiots who were in the helicopter with Valenko's murdered nephew, then by all means, scorch the earth.

"Ten seconds."

Pasha shifted the wheel to aim the car down the center of the street, rapidly closing the distance to the guy with the neon running shoes. This was definitely the tall guy from the museum. Valenko called in a favor to hack into the museum's security system and watch the tapes. One of the benefits of being in the Russian *mafiya* was their ties to the FSB, the foreign intelligence service that specializes in recreational hacking of social media platforms and disruption of energy grids across the United States. Compared to the mischief they made on a regular basis, finding a back door into a museum's firewall was a cakewalk.

Ely lifted the bazooka from his lap and tried to remember exactly how it worked.

The Miniman was a disposable, single-shot, anti-tank weapon designed by the Swedish military. This one was a Pansarskott m/68 which fired a 74-millimeter H.E.A.T. projectile, the acronym meaning high-explosive anti-tank. In other words, a missile capable of penetrating armor with the assuredness of a blowtorch melting ice on a summer day.

Ely wondered what it might do to the guy in the orange shoes.

It was bad enough this guy didn't lift a hand to save Valenko's nephew from being cremated alive. This guy deserved to suffer for buying those fucking shoes. Even from a distance the neon orange and lime green were burning Ely's corneas.

And that's how, one step at a time, taste and elegance walk out of the world, thought Ely.

"Ely, are you ready?" Pasha called from the front seat. "Ely!"

Ely ceased his ruminations on the soles of men.

"*Da, brat*, drive the car."

"I am driving, and we're right on top of him."

"Then slow down, so I don't miss." Ely lifted the meter-long tube to his shoulder.

"Did you notice that other car?"

"The gray one parked on the curb, what about it?"

"It's a boring sedan," said Pasha. "Might be *politsiya*."

"If it's police," said Ely, "then speed up as soon I fire."

"How about we keep rolling and try another time?"

"You want to tell Valenko we were scared off by a boring car?" asked Ely. "Can you even see a driver?"

"Not from this angle."

"Our windows are tinted," said Ely, "so he can't see us."

"He could identify the car."

Ely snorted. "A blind man could identify this car, it's a red Camaro."

"We could say it was stolen."

"*Da, my mogli.*"

"Then make it quick," said Pasha. "And don't miss."

The Miniman was surprisingly light. Once the device was positioned correctly on the shoulder, a plastic sight swung into place. Ely found the factory, then shifted the angle until he found his target at the corner of the building. He zeroed in on the shoes.

Ely curled his index finger around the trigger, leaned against the inside of the door, and extended the muzzle through the open window. *"Gotovy."*

The car screeched to a stop in the middle of the street. Ely glanced over his shoulder and realized the gray sedan was directly behind him. A man sat behind the wheel holding a radio in one hand while reaching under his jacket with the other.

Definitely police.

"We should drive away." Pasha had also seen the policeman. "Now." He swiveled in his seat but kept his foot on the brake. He slapped his hand against the steering wheel. "Now, Ely."

The dude in the orange shoes looked up from his phone.

"Get closer," said Ely, "so he can see the weapon. At least we can scare this *mudak* before we run like rabbits."

Pasha took his foot off the brake and stepped on the accelerator.

He meant to simply roll past the factory slowly, so their quarry could look down the long barrel of death and know it was only a matter of time. If they got picked up, they could claim it was a prank and be out of jail by morning. Valenko had more friends on the police force than the mayor. But Pasha wasn't used to driving and was acutely aware that every second they waited was another moment for the policeman to see their faces, though currently their backs were to him. How hard could it be to track a red Camaro carrying two men and a bazooka? Instead of tapping the accelerator, Pasha pounced.

The car didn't roll, it leapt forward. Ely, unbuckled, lurched backward from the door, involuntarily clenching his fingers to grab hold of something. The only thing in his hands was an anti-tank gun.

His index finger pulled the trigger before his brain could tell it to stop.

The rocket fired with an incendiary blast that ruptured the space-time continuum. Everything moved in slow motion, beginning with Ely's realization that he should have read the instruction manual more carefully. He forgot that a rocket launcher emitted a blast from the back of the tube as well as the front.

Newton's law fucked him, hard.

The right-side window exploded, shooting glass shrapnel at the cop's sedan. Chunks of safety glass bounced between the cars like popcorn as kinetic energy ran its course. Some pieces ricocheted around the interior of their car and pelted Pasha in the face. The Camaro swerved wildly as he tried to keep them on the road.

Ely dropped the spent tube onto the floor. His ears were ringing and his brother was cursing in a tinny voice from far, far away. As they zoomed past the factory, both turned in their seats to check for carnage.

There was a crater in the sidewalk where Gerry Gao had been standing. The building was unscathed. A thin ribbon of smoke curled from the base of the crater like a question mark.

The orange sneakers were nowhere to be seen.

40

Cape saw the orange sneaker hurtling toward his face and rolled out of the way.

The shoe hit the roof like a meteor, bounced, flipped, and tumbled onto its side with the sole facing Grace and the toe pointed at Sally. Cape had a view of the top, so he knew there was still a foot inside.

He kept that information to himself as he scanned the heavens for another fallen sole.

"That's an ugly shoe," said Grace.

Sally made eye contact with Cape. "No wonder someone threw it away."

Cape crawled over to the shoe and grabbed it by the toe. By the toes. He could feel the severed foot through the neon mesh. He threw it backhand over the side of the building.

Cape smiled at Grace by way of explanation. "It was hurting my eyes." He turned to Sally. "We need to leave...before we can't."

Sally nodded and motioned for Grace to follow. They crawled with their heads down until they reached the door to the stairs. Cape crabbed sideways to the back of the building and risked a downward look.

"Freddie's car is pulling away."

"He's a slippery eel," said Sally. "They'll never get their hands on him."

"I like crispy eel," said Grace. "We used to eat it all the time in Hong Kong."

"We can have some tonight," said Sally. "I know a place."

Sirens filled the air as they opened the door to the stairs and made their way to the ground floor. The abandoned factory retained its original floor plan. The front room had been used for assembly and retrofitting of plumbing supplies, pipe cutting, and repairs. A smaller room in back was divided into an office and an area for packaging and shipping. Cape and Grace waited near the back door while Sally slid through the shadows of the front room. By the time she returned, the sirens had reached peak intensity.

"The police are assembling outside the factory next door and stretching yellow tape around the crater in the sidewalk. Beau's partner Vinnie is barking orders right and left. Two patrol cars are blocking the road on either side."

Cape nodded. "They don't know what, or who, they'll find inside Freddie's building."

"They won't find Gerry," said Sally.

Grace sparked at the name. "Where did the bad guy go?"

"Everywhere," said Cape.

Grace frowned.

Sally shot Cape a look. "He flew…don't worry, we won't be seeing him again." She put her hand on Grace's shoulder. "We're going back the way we came, between the buildings, cutting across the next block and the one after that, until we're closer to the center of town." She turned to Cape. "Where did you park?"

Cape pointed in the direction Sally had described. "Four blocks."

"Shouldn't we talk to the police?" asked Grace.

"I will," said Cape. "Later."

"That's his job," said Sally, tilting her head toward Cape.

"What's our job?" asked Grace.

"Being sneaky," said Sally. "Think you can handle that?"

Grace nodded, and the three of them stepped outside.

41

Stepping inside another world is how Mogwai would describe the feeling of putting on the hood and mask. The black robes enveloped the body down to the ankles. The tinted lenses turned the world red and made reality feel disconnected and emotionally distant.

Maybe that was the idea.

Sometimes a feeling of detachment was useful, other times being inside the costume was claustrophobic. The microphone sewn into the neck to create the Darth Vader effect was held in place by a Velcro strap, and after an hour it would start to chafe and make swallowing difficult. The robes weren't so bad, a synthetic weave that regulated temperature and wicked away perspiration.

As a Party-approved specter of intimidation, Mogwai couldn't be seen to sweat.

The lenses were polarized and chemically treated to enhance light and reduce glare, so Mogwai could actually see better under low-light conditions, but peripheral vision was almost nonexistent.

The real discomfort, that sensation of an alternate world,

was the hood. It was hot and stuffy, so maybe that other world was Hell. The name Mogwai often translated as devil, but the meaning was not the same as in the West. It was best translated as demon, a kind of devilish character who tormented humans.

Some believed devils tempted human beings away from grace, so they could be dragged to the underworld. Here again, the cultural differences struck Mogwai as another example of why East and West rarely understood each other. Like the ancient Greeks, the Chinese once believed the underworld was simply a destination mortals shared after they died, whether they were good or bad. There were different levels to Hell, though not as Dante described. Taoists believed the entrance to the underworld was above ground, in Fengdu, still known as the Ghost City. Ancient Buddhists claimed there were 134 worlds of Hell, practically an Epcot Center for the dead.

Mogwai believed devils existed to keep people on the right path.

The modern world was decadent, designed to drag people down. Mogwai's job was to scare them back up. Popular culture was fueled by fantasies of self-fulfillment that ignored the lessons of history. From Roman caesars to Russian czars and Chinese emperors, great leaders built empires not by expanding their borders but by tightening their grip on their own country. Any tin-pot tyrant could invade another country, but the rare civilization that endured for centuries conquered the hearts and minds of its people.

Civilization was the perfect harmony between pride and fear. National pride was nothing more than our primal instinct for safety in numbers, and the greater the pride, the more an undercurrent of fear became necessary to keep it going.

The fear of being ostracized or isolated from the group. The fear of losing it all.

Mogwai knew how to strike the perfect balance between pride and fear. The key was to keep everyone off balance, a pendulum swing between the two. Some Party members believed people had to be ruled for the state to survive, but Mogwai wasn't one of them. Recruited as a child and trained by the state, Mogwai discovered a deeper truth. People wanted to be ruled.

Deep in their subconscious, people craved a return to childhood, a simpler time when choices were made for them. What to wear, what to buy, and most importantly, what to believe. A long look in the mirror revealed that undeniable truth inside all of us.

It was a blemish on the human condition as plain as the nose on your face.

This isn't about you. History is never about you. Neither is the future in which we'll all live. The only question is whether or not you will be a part of it.

Mogwai had given that speech a hundred times and never doubted a word. The evidence was irrefutable, and time was running out. The United States had squandered its influence abroad. Europe, once the epicenter of civilization, was nothing more than a doormat for the great powers to wipe their feet. The countries that defined the twentieth century had lost any sense of their own identities. There was nothing holding them together, which is why they were falling into chaos.

Mogwai existed to keep chaos at bay. A necessary evil for the greater good.

Mogwai was created by the fertile imaginations of the ruling class. Party records didn't credit the official who first came up with the idea, but there had been twelve Mogwais before now. Currently three different Mogwais were deployed across China.

One Mogwai was in Chengdu, one was in Hong Kong, and the third was here in Dafen.

Despite the Bohemian atmosphere, Mogwai liked Dafen. The village had a growing sense of pride because residents knew they were putting China on the world stage. Every painting was a performance, a political statement about which country had the highest standards, the lowest costs, the best talent. Every resident was working toward a common goal.

That might not be how Dafen saw itself today, but fear was a lens that helped people see things as they really were. Mogwai saw this city as a great portrait, and every resident as a living brushstroke in a much bigger picture.

And the picture Mogwai saw was China.

For decades paintings and sculptures were dismissed as decadent relics of China's imperial days. But as the middle class grew, so did the rate of civil disobedience. Everything that was built stood on a shaky foundation of coercion, not loyalty. Then one day someone on the Central Committee said something that shocked everyone out of their stupor.

People will never be loyal to a party, but they cannot deny their past.

The Party must become synonymous with China. People may swear allegiance to the government, but they take pride in their history, their art, their culture. Control culture and you control everything.

Culture was the enemy of chaos, and all you needed to create culture was a can of paint.

Mogwai thought about the extraordinary young painter, Yan, who clearly didn't recognize his own talent. Bringing the professor here to teach Yan classic techniques was one of Mogwai's better ideas. Making that happen hadn't been easy, but Wen was wasted in a labor camp. His vast knowledge belonged to everyone and needed to be shared.

One more day and the first phase of their project would be complete.

What they were doing would truly put Dafen on the map. Mogwai stood on the roof of the art factory and looked through the custom lenses of the mask at the village below. People strolled along the sidewalks, greeting their neighbors as they passed. Every person going about their business, serving a purpose visible only to the Devil.

Brushstrokes on a canvas.

It was a nice little town. All it needed was a bit more fear.

42

"I fear I haven't been much help."

"You haven't been any help." Maria smiled at Cape. "So get on your knees and make yourself useful."

Cape had returned to the car impound to find Maria on her hands and knees, soot covering her fingers and face as she meticulously sifted through the helicopter fragments. Her face was partially obscured by unkempt hair until she blew a strand away from her eyes.

"That's better," said Cape. "I couldn't tell if you were looking at me or the wreckage."

Maria laughed. "Art restoration is sweaty work, my friend."

"What are we looking at?"

"While you were gone, I went out and got a set of these." Maria handed Cape a paintbrush with a half-inch-wide tip. "Not ideal but good enough." She twisted her mouth and blew another stray bit of hair. "I also got coffee but didn't get any for you, *perdóname*."

"I'm not much of a coffee drinker."

"No wonder," said Maria. "The coffee in this city is *asqueroso*."

"Is that bad?"

"It's disgusting."

"You need to know where to go," said Cape. "Most places that make coffee to your taste are in North Beach or the Mission. Everywhere else it's—"

"—Starbucks," said Maria. "On every corner, that green siren with her smug smile."

Cape laughed. "She's smug because she knows you don't have a choice."

"Tell me, why do Americans burn their coffee?"

"We didn't vote on it," said Cape. "Not everything here is a democracy. There must be something in Spain you don't like."

"*Criadillas*," said Maria without hesitation. "They served them at school every Thursday when I was little."

"What are they?"

"Bull's balls." Maria held up her hands and made two ovals with her fingers. "Bull testicles are about the size of meatballs, but chewier."

"Sounds worse than a bad cup of coffee," said Cape. "Let me guess...*asqueroso*?"

"Very," said Maria. "Your pronunciation isn't half bad, by the way."

"I'm learning," said Cape. "Now teach me about this." He gestured at the carbonized debris on the tarp. "You've been busy."

Using her brush as a pointer, Maria walked Cape through her excavations. Still on their knees, they shuffled sideways from the front of the cockpit to the tail of the helicopter.

"To begin, we have two lumps." Maria indicated a blob twelve inches in diameter, gray with black edges. "That was plaster mixed with putty and wire mesh." She pointed at another misshapen mass glinting under the fluorescent lights. "This was bronze, or more likely a cheaper metal tarnished to look like bronze. You said Grace saw the thieves take something?"

"She's not sure if they kept it or put it back when they started to chase her."

"There could be others." Maria ran her fingers through her hair, adding more charcoal streaks to her temples. "I'll go through a catalog of the museum's exhibits and cross-check that against the Interpol list." She sighed. "Look at this mess."

The remaining rubble was indecipherable. Considering the conflagration warped the metal of the cockpit, Cape was amazed she'd found any clues at all.

"The paintings must have been at the rear of the cabin," said Cape. "How many?"

"There are four," said Maria. "That corresponds with the number on loan from Paris." She jabbed her brush at the first mosaic she assembled. Faint green lines and splotches of red broke through the ash, enough to reveal a pattern. "I'm pretty sure this is *Nine Continents Clear and Calm,* a view of the emperor's private residence." Maria took her phone from the back pocket of her jeans and scrolled through her photos, then handed it to Cape. "See the curve of the shoreline, here?"

Cape returned her phone. "You're connecting a lot of dots to get there."

"It gets worse." Maria waved her brush like a conductor's baton at the second jigsaw, a mere fraction of a painting. "I think this is *The Magnanimous World*...but it doesn't look very magnanimous." Maria pointed at the next arrangement. "That should be *Harmony with the Past and Present.*" She nudged Cape a couple of feet to the right. "And here we've got *A Diligent and Talented Government.*"

"Is that a painting or propaganda?"

"That's what art is," said Maria, "a trick of the eye to make us see the world differently."

"Never took you for a cynic," said Cape. "Can't the museum tell you which paintings they have?"

"I'm going there later," said Maria. "Want to come?"

"Absolutely," said Cape. "What about the Paris museum? They must know which paintings they shipped."

Maria shook her head. "I called a colleague in France to verify which of the forty paintings were on tour. Ten in total— four sent here and six to the Met in New York."

"Which paintings went where?"

"A courier was supposed to accompany the paintings to New York and deliver six to the Met while a second courier took the remaining four to San Francisco from JFK." Maria picked up a rag and wiped some of the grime off her hands. "But something went wrong."

Cape sat back on his haunches to rest his knees but didn't say anything.

"The courier from Paris arrived incoherent," said Maria. "They thought he was drunk, but the stewardess claimed he never touched a drink. The Met sent a team to meet the plane, they unloaded six of the paintings and brought them to Manhattan. They're still in boxes, scheduled for display next month."

"What about the flight to San Francisco?"

"The second courier missed his flight." Maria rubbed her hands together, more in satisfaction than to remove grit from her hands. "Passed out in an airport lounge."

"Drunk?"

"Maybe." Maria wobbled a hand from side to side. "He was seen drinking with a woman in the first class lounge. So had the courier in Paris. Neither woman boarded either flight."

"You think the couriers were drugged."

"Yes…maybe…it's a working theory."

"If I were going to steal priceless art, I'd try to take it in transit." Cape drummed his fingers against his palm, trying to find a rhythm to the riddle. "Wouldn't you?"

"Stealing is one thing," said Maria, "swapping it for a forgery is another. The cargo holds on planes are freezing, too risky. But if you knock out a courier and meet the plane before anyone else, then there's—"

"—no one to stop you," said Cape. "Tell me why art thieves don't do this all the time."

"Because museums take precautions."

"Such as?" asked Cape. "What happened when the plane got to San Francisco?"

"The Bibliothèque Nationale in Paris had called the French Embassy and requested a guard meet the plane and bring the paintings to the museum," said Maria. "Nobody knew he was coming."

"So the artwork made it, despite the hiccups." Cape almost tripped over his own train of thought. "But the thieves…our thieves…have tried to steal it before."

"Twice before," said Maria. "Remember the foiled attempt in Paris."

"They must really, really, really want these paintings."

"So it would seem," said Maria. "And for the last hour, all I could think about was that call with my French colleague. The French take art very seriously, and if the paintings got stolen on their watch, it would be an international incident."

Cape connected some dots of his own. "You said nobody knew the guard was coming."

The corners of Maria's mouth turned up. "You should work for Interpol."

"Thanks, but I have problems with authority," said Cape. "Or maybe the authorities have problems with me. That's it, though, isn't it? The real precaution museums take is—"

"—they don't tell anyone when the art is being transported," said Maria. "The timing is the most closely guarded secret, as precious as the art itself, but somehow our crooks knew the couriers, and they knew the flights."

"Somebody told them."

"*Sí*, it's the only explanation," said Maria.

"Who knew the itinerary?" asked Cape. "The people packing the artwork would only know the artwork was being transported. The couriers would find out, but they might only be told the details at the last minute. Flights could be booked, then changed…you could even send multiple crates, some of them empty, on different flights." Cape rubbed his temples. "So the only people with operational oversight, with real inside information are—"

"—the museum directors." Maria stood and brushed off her pants. "And didn't Inspector Jones—"

"—Beau." Cape rolled back on his heels and stood. "He said the museum director wasn't there when they checked the security footage and wouldn't come to the phone."

"Where was he?"

"Napa," said Cape. "Wine country."

"I've never been," said Maria. "And I like wine."

"Two good reasons to go for a drive," said Cape. "I'll give you the grand tour."

43

The macaque named Junjie insisted on giving Bohai the grand tour of the underground tunnels. Bohai implored Junjie to find an exit, but the monkey wasn't interested in leaving.

Bohai was speaking softly, conscious that male macaques can become combative quickly and with little warning. Junjie didn't seem agitated, he simply chattered incessantly in a combination of chirps, barks, and grimaces that were indecipherable to his human companion.

Bohai wished Doctor Dolittle was waiting around the next corner, but no such luck.

A tunnel branched away from the laboratory where Bohai had skewered Doctor Loh with his pliers, but as the corridor narrowed, it detoured into cul-de-sacs and small chambers carved from the bedrock. Most of these were storerooms for cleaning supplies or unused lab equipment.

"This is all very interesting," said Bohai, "but it can't help us escape."

Junjie hopped up and down, then pointed in two different directions.

"You're lost?" asked Bohai. "Are you trying to remember which room you're looking for in this maze?"

Junjie tugged on Bohai's hand and pulled him forward.

"I really hope you're not lost." Bohai didn't want to go back to the laboratory. There was only one exit from that room, and he was sure the guard still waited outside. He wondered how much time would elapse before the guard got curious, or if guards ever came inside to watch. And how often Doctor Loh took his meals. Bohai didn't have a watch but guessed it had been less than an hour since he decided to risk his neck to save a monkey's head.

The next room contained a small worktable and pegboard mounted on the walls to hold a variety of tools. On the table was a soldering iron and magnifying glass mounted to a small vise. Wires and circuit boards were scattered across the table. On the back wall hung several hand tools. Bohai mulled these over before choosing a pair of long-nosed pliers to replace the ones he'd left in Doctor Loh's eye socket. He slipped them into his pocket and turned to leave.

Bohai spotted a fireman's axe on the wall. Junjie chattered excitedly as Bohai pulled it free. The handle was slightly shorter than his arm, the head as broad as the length of his hand and very sharp. Bohai hefted the axe and nodded in approval.

"Okay, that was a good stop. Now can we get out of here?"

He didn't have to ask. Junjie pulled him along with a renewed sense of purpose. The tunnel narrowed, the caged lights overhead close enough that Bohai had to duck.

Sparse lighting and mottled shadows gave the stone an organic energy, as if the walls were pulsing and flexing as they passed. Bohai hunched his shoulders and followed his feral friend toward a bright light at the end of the tunnel. He felt like he was being reborn.

The tunnel opened into a vast chamber filled with white light.

The floor was circular and twenty meters in diameter, the ceiling incredibly high and conical in shape. They were standing at the bottom of an inverted funnel, the top barely visible. Rectangular LED lights were spaced evenly in a ring that encircled the wall three meters off the ground. The singular shape of the room and elevated lighting compelled an upward glance, and Bohai craned his neck to see what hid in the shadows above.

He was distracted by a chattering chorus, and for an instant he thought it was Junjie's voice echoing around the chamber. He looked to his left and discovered the underground prison of Doctor Loh.

Above ground was the labor camp where humans were watched by guards and followed by genetically engineered simian spies. That had been Bohai's world, but now he realized there was a second prison hidden below the camp. He stood before a wall of cages, each one holding a male macaque that had gone under the knife but had yet to complete its training. Bohai checked the rows of cages, only one of which was empty.

He pointed at the last cage, its door ajar, and turned to Junjie. "Was that one yours?"

Junjie grimaced and blinked rapidly. He was vibrating with tension and squeezed Bohai's hand as he walked the length of the cages, chattering excitedly at each macaque they passed.

The captives howled, gnashed their teeth, and chirped in reply. Their gazes varied from excited and hopeful to suspicious and scared. Some monkeys grabbed the bars to pull themselves back and forth, but the cages were securely mounted and didn't budge.

One of the monkeys at the end of the row began masturbating. The monkey next to him concluded that was the perfect response to a stressful situation. The monkey on his left took notice and followed suit.

Junjie leapt forward and banged on the bars. The onanistic offenders bowed their heads sheepishly and sat on the straw, contrite and attentive. Junjie screeched like a parrot. Bohai started to panic over the noise, until he realized the squawk silenced all the other macaques.

Bohai watched as Junjie walked the length of the cages, guttural sounds coming from deep in his throat. The other monkeys tracked him, their yellow eyes glowing in the shadows of their cages.

He's making a speech.

Bohai marveled at his own cluelessness. Everything he had done since coming to the lab was based on instinct. Only the monkeys seemed to have a plan.

Junjie finished his address and approached Bohai but kept his eyes on his fellow macaques. With a closing series of chirps and clicks, Junjie reached up and patted Bohai on his belly.

I might be shaped like the Buddha, but I feel like a monkey's pet.

Bohai realized he had just been blessed by his animal ally. Whatever happened next, he was under the macaque's protection.

Bohai stepped to the center of the room and looked up.

The room was not a perfect funnel. A notch had been cut into the rear wall, where a metal ladder was bolted into the granite. Bohai followed the rungs past the lights to the narrowing peak of the cone. A hatch with a wheeled handle was mounted in the ceiling.

Bohai estimated the distance and knew it led to the surface. He wondered if this was how freshly trained monkeys were released back into the camp, or if it was a service entrance for something else. Maybe both. He turned to the right and smiled at his good fortune, wondering if his nightmare was turning into a dream.

The wall opposite the cages was divided into two sections. The section nearest the tunnel held more pegboard and shelves. Bohai saw a tranquilizer gun, a jar full of darts, and a holster. There was also a flashlight, and next to that, a ring of keys.

Nearer the ladder, the wall was completely obscured by a massive generator. Dials, circuit breakers, and levers protruded from an array of gray boxes half-a-meter square, each stacked on top of the other to form a power station big enough to run the entire camp.

Bohai finally had a plan.

He turned to Junjie, who did a backflip and gibbered excitedly as he gestured at the keys.

Bohai walked back to the shelves, strapped the holster around his waist and loaded the tranquilizer gun. He heard chattering behind him and called over his shoulder. "This isn't for them, it's for the guards." Bohai wondered if the darts were potent enough to topple a grown man, but at least they would sting. He slid the flashlight into his pocket, then took the keys from the ring and approached the first cage.

The caged monkey was big for a macaque. He was crouched and ready to spring, muscles taut and eyes unblinking. Bohai took a deep breath as he spun the key ring to find the right fit.

Macaques were remarkably strong. Bohai had seen a monkey rip a man's ear off with no more effort than plucking a leaf from a tree. Their teeth could chew through flesh and bone as easily as chomping a piece of fruit, and their reflexes were twice as fast as a human's.

Bohai could never resist a big macaque attack.

He glanced at Junjie and said, "We could just leave, you and I."

Junjie wobbled from side to side and blinked. Bohai sighed.

This is your second life, make it count.

Bohai unlocked the cage.

One by one, he unlocked the cages, holding his breath with every turn of the key. The monkeys eyed him warily. Some focused on the gun at his waist, others on his hands or eyes. None attacked. When he was done, Bohai tossed the keys onto the worktable and stood in the middle of the room, arms extended, wondering if he was about to be ripped apart.

The macaques came out of their cages, some jumping down to the floor, others climbing, a few limping. They all moved closer. Junjie took the lead, and the monkeys pressed inward.

Fifty macaques radiated outward from Bohai, a seething mandala of hair, nails, and teeth.

Bohai looked down at the pinched faces and bearded chins. Many had jagged scars across their temples. Others were missing patches of hair. A few had lost an eye, and two had livid burns at the base of the neck. Bohai tasted salt and realized a tear had run down his cheek. Whether he cried for the monkeys or himself, Bohai couldn't say.

The monkey directly behind Junjie pushed forward and patted Bohai on the stomach.

Junjie moved aside and the others took a turn, each concentric circle of paws patting the man's belly and rotating clockwise, spiraling inward until Junjie was once again closest to Bohai.

Bohai looked upon his army with pride. Fifty grimaces of sharp yellow teeth returned the sentiment.

Bohai walked to the generator. He took the flashlight from his pocket, thumbed it on and pointed at the nearest wall to maximize the reflection. The time had come to throw the camp into stygian darkness.

Bohai slipped the circuit breakers and grabbed the largest of the levers. He yanked the handle down and heard a snapping sound followed by sudden silence. The humming of the lights, the buzzing of the generator, even the breathing of the monkeys came to a halt as the room went pitch black. Fifty macaques and their man exhaled loudly.

Junjie and his primate pals started chattering quietly.

Bohai pointed the flashlight at the ladder, then moved its beam up the wall until it landed on the hatch that led to the surface. He glanced over his shoulder and angled the light to look into the faces of his marauding macaques. He didn't have Junjie's natural oratory skills but felt something should be said before heading into battle.

"Okay, guys, we have a long night ahead of us," said Bohai. "The time has come to free the prisoners, rescue your friends, and burn this godforsaken place to the ground."

44

"This whole place almost burned to the ground last year."

"It looks so idyllic." Maria followed the contours of the hills as they drove west on Route 128 toward the wine country. "I read about the fires."

"Napa and Sonoma got hit hardest," said Cape. "People evacuated, homes lost." He pointed to the right, where a scrub oak topped a low rise. "There used to be a whole stand of trees there, leading down to the winery on the far side of the hill. Some wineries lost their harvest. The sky was filled with ash that carried all the way to Delaware."

"This state is bigger than Spain; it's hard to imagine."

"In San Francisco, the sun looked like the moon on a cloudy night, and the sky was orange for three months. It was like living on Mars."

"These fires," said Maria. "They happen often, no?"

"They've become an annual event in California. The year before, in the hills above LA, hundreds of homes were evacuated." As they followed a bend in the road, Cape gestured through the windshield. "You can see the firebreaks they've cut along the road, those deep ditches between the trees and the surrounding property. Some of the wineries even built moats to douse the sparks blown by the wind from other properties."

"The towns did this?"

Cape shook his head. "The state government was too busy arguing with the power company over who was responsible for clearing the brush, and the power company was too busy lobbying the federal government for subsidies of windmills that nobody wanted in their backyard. So the residents dug the trenches themselves."

Maria smiled. "You really don't like the government, do you?"

"I like governments just fine," said Cape. "It's politicians I can't stand."

"You trust me, don't you?"

"You do work for the government," said Cape. "Or governments, in the plural. Isn't that what Interpol does?"

"Everyone has to work for someone."

"I work for an eleven-year-old."

Maria tossed her head to get her long hair behind her again. Cape was driving with the top down, so every sharp turn or gust of wind pulled her hair across her face. Whether covered in soot or riding in a convertible with hair like Medusa, she always managed to look glamorous. Cape could barely find matching socks in the morning, so her effortless elegance was a constant reminder they came from two very different worlds.

"What are you thinking?"

"You came a long way for a lot of trouble," said Cape.

"I always thought that I worked for the artist, not the government." Maria shrugged. "Interpol happens to pay me to do it."

"That's a great job description."

"I once recovered a painting," said Maria, "a Rembrandt stolen from a museum in Sweden—"

"—the Swedes really need to lock their doors."

Maria laughed. "They learned the hard way—their museums are more secure these days."

"So you recovered this painting—"

"—a self-portrait," said Maria. "One of many that Rembrandt painted over the years. Anyway, I went undercover as an independent collector disinterested in whether it was obtained legally, and eventually I managed to buy it back from an intermediary."

"Catch the thieves?"

"Not at first, no." Maria pull a strand of hair from her eyes. "When you're trying to recover something priceless, undamaged, sometimes the best you can do is pay a ransom." She turned to Cape and smiled. "But I got the bastards three months later."

"That must have felt good."

"It did," said Maria, "but the thrill was in getting the painting back. When I was undercover, every night I'd look at a facsimile of the painting I kept in my wallet. I would stare into Rembrandt's eyes and ask him where he was."

"Did he ever answer?"

"Sometimes I would find a clue in the way he looked at me," said Maria. "It always felt like I was looking for a person, not a painting. Someone who desperately wanted to be found."

"Art-knapping."

"Exactly," said Maria. "Art should be seen, not hidden away."

"No argument here."

Cape glanced at the map on his phone. The museum director's house was two miles north. The road curved gently around a cluster of red willows and opened onto a stretch that ran between matching rows of ginkgo trees as yellow as an open flame. The only other cars on the road were a panel truck a quarter mile behind them and a Ford sedan about to pass, headed in the opposite direction.

"Do you have a plan?" asked Maria.

"Almost never," said Cape, "but I was wondering if you brought your Interpol badge."

"I'm off duty."

"Not today."

Maria laughed. "You are…" She paused, trying to find the right word. "…*incorregible?*"

"Same word in English," said Cape, "and thank you." With his left hand on the wheel, he gestured at the glove compartment with his right. "Do you mind handing me the gun? I want it in my pocket before we pull up the driveway, in case there are security cameras."

Maria popped open the compartment and removed the H&K. She pulled the slide back to make sure a bullet was in the chamber, then thumbed the safety before handing it to Cape. "You think that's really necessary?"

"If you were the director of a museum where a robbery took place, what would you do?" asked Cape. "Go to the museum immediately, or pretend it never happened?"

"Point taken," said Maria, "but that doesn't mean he's dangerous."

"I'm betting he's not," said Cape, "but I want him to think that I am."

"Please don't do anything impulsive."

"Says the woman who almost shot a television in cold blood."

"Those were Russian mobsters," said Maria. "This is the director of a major art museum. He is no doubt connected to people who are connected to my boss, and to his boss, and—"

"—all the other bureaucrats who forced you to take a vacation."

"*Precisamante.*"

"He's hiding in Napa," said Cape. "Which means he's got something to hide."

Maria sighed. "You're right."

"Coming here was your idea."

"It was our idea," said Maria. "And a good one."

"Want to wait in the car?"

"Not on your life."

"I didn't think so."

Cape began to turn off the main road but braked suddenly as a black Honda Civic sped from the intersecting street, tires drifting on the dusty asphalt until the driver swerved into his lane and passed them. Cape realized how narrow the side street was as he made the turn, barely wide enough for two cars. Five minutes later he turned again, this time onto a gravel drive lined with hedges twelve feet high.

A sign on the mailbox indicated this was the Beckett property. The hedgerow on the right was set back from a dirt path wide enough for two bicycles to ride abreast. Considering the length of the driveway, Cape wondered if the mail was collected daily by someone in a golf cart. The mailbox and house were so far apart they practically had different zip codes.

"Alistair Beckett," said Maria. "That's the man we've come to see."

"His name sounds expensive."

"He lives an expensive lifestyle." Maria pulled out her phone and scrolled through some notes. "Lives at his winery in Napa—this place—and keeps apartments in San Francisco, New York, and Paris. Sits on a few charitable boards…" Maria spread her fingers to enlarge the type. "…and recently divorced his wife of twenty years."

"How recently?"

"Less than a year." Maria squinted at her screen. "His ex-wife lives in LA near their daughter, who goes to UCLA."

Cape considered the property values in Napa and what it

might take to keep apartments in three of the most expensive cities in the world. "Where does Alistair's money come from?"

"He is the son of a son of a very rich man," said Maria. "His grandfather donated the collection that started the museum."

"No wonder he's the museum director," said Cape. "It's a legacy."

"He's the third Beckett to hold the position." Maria clicked off her phone. "I've heard of the grandfather; he was an influential and controversial figure in the art world."

"Why controversial?"

"Hundreds of pieces came from the grandfather's travels across Asia in the late thirties," said Maria. "When Japan invaded China at the start of the Second World War, anyone hoping to buy safe passage out of Shanghai agreed to sell family heirlooms for virtually nothing. Beckett's grandfather bought as much as he could for as little as the families would accept. Then after Pearl Harbor, Beckett returned to the U.S. and had another windfall. Japanese antiques dealers risked internment camps, so they sold everything and fled to Japan. In later years he collected art from India and Indonesia, but the bulk of his collection— the catalyst for the museum—was art acquired during wartime."

"So he didn't steal the art," said Cape, "but he got it for a steal."

"Yes." Maria's mouth moved as if she tasted something sour but swallowed it anyway. "If Beckett's grandfather hadn't bought the antiques, others would have. It was a buyers' market. The pieces would have been acquired by dozens of different people, displayed in homes or resold at auctions, scattered and lost to public view. Beckett was a legitimate collector and helped start a museum that brings thousands of people a year closer to a culture they know little about, and it helps others stay connected to a culture they left behind when they came to this country."

"You don't have to convince me."

"I think there would be a lot less empathy in the world if we didn't have museums."

"No doubt, but you sound like you're building a case for the defense," said Cape. "Something is bugging you."

"It's just ironic…" Maria's voice trailed off as her eyes followed the row of hedges running to the house. "Ironic that so many years later, someone is trying to steal the art back."

"Irony is just a coincidence holding a grudge."

"I don't believe in coincidences," said Maria.

"Neither do I."

They reached the end of the endless driveway.

A lone vehicle was parked to the left of the main entrance, a vintage MG convertible, blue with a black interior. It was the perfect car for a winding road or midlife crisis.

Cape made a slow doughnut on the gravel turnaround so his car was facing the exit. He and Maria climbed out, their doors closing in tandem with the solid *thunk* of an older, heavier car. Maria stretched her arms above her head and bent at the waist so her chin almost touched her knees. During her stretch, Maria kept her eyes on the front door, but no one emerged.

The house was a massive two-story Spanish villa with ochre walls, wide windows, and a tile roof. Cape wandered to the corner of the house and strolled on a lawn that needed water and a haircut. The ground sloped downward toward the back of the house and Cape saw the gentle slopes and even rows of a vineyard extending the length of a football field. Like the lawn, the vines needed tending, the ground was parched. Stray hoses had broken free of the irrigation system and lay curled on the ground like dead snakes. Cape doubted you could squeeze a glass full of juice from the few grapes that hadn't shrunk into raisins.

Cape glanced along the walls of the house and saw patches

of stucco in need of paint. One of the shutters on the second floor was askew. Scanning the ground, he spotted three curved tiles that had fallen from the roof. At first glance the house was a work of art, but on closer examination it was a fading masterpiece sorely in need of restoration.

"What are you doing?" Maria called in a stage whisper.

Cape walked back to the front of the house. "Looking for a motive."

"Find anything?"

"No dead bodies in the garden," said Cape, "but I'm guessing it was a costly divorce."

They walked across the gravel, every step crunching with the sound of breakfast cereal. Maria slid her badge from her pocket, and Cape adjusted his jacket so it didn't sag on one side from the weight of the gun.

The oak door was arched. A patterned window at the top matched the curve of the door. Set at eye level was a heavy door knocker in the shape of a dragon eating its own tail. The dragon didn't fit the Spanish motif, but it looked valuable. The patina spoke of age, and the dragon's eyes sparkled like onyx.

Cape didn't see a doorbell. He lifted the handle of the knocker and let go. It struck the base plate with a loud *clang*, and the door slid forward a few inches. It was unlocked and unlatched. The last person through the door had either been careless or in a hurry.

Cape looked at Maria, who shrugged. He pressed lightly with an open palm, and the door swung inward before bouncing back against his hand. Something in the foyer was blocking the door. Cape wrapped his right hand around the edge of the door and pushed. The gap was just wide enough for him to poke his head inside and take a look.

The first thing Cape saw was a shoe.

45

"Grab the shoe and twist it off."

Sally held Grace's right foot as she said the words, and on the last syllable rotated her hands counterclockwise in one fluid motion. The foot told the ankle to save itself, and the ankle told the knee it had better come along, and the knee told the hip that it was going to break unless it twirled in the air, and the rest of the body realized it had no choice in the matter.

Grace spun sideways and fell on her face a few feet away. Sally told her the mats would be removed from the wooden floor after she learned how to roll. Grace was glad they were still in place. She got her arms under her and stood, then gave a small bow and asked, "What if I was bigger than you?"

"That's why you're learning this now," said Sally. "You're still small."

Grace made a face.

Sally smiled. "It's okay. I'm still small, but I'm fully grown."

"I'm still growing," said Grace.

"I bet you'll be taller than me." Sally let her gaze drift around her loft, at the walls covered with training weapons, the high ceilings, the mats arranged purposefully around the floor. Of all the things she could teach Grace, it was hard to decide what was most important. If there was going to be an attempt on her life, it would happen within days, not months.

Time is the enemy of life. Control time and you will live. Lose control and you will die.

The voices of her childhood instructors whispered to Sally. Wounds turned into scars, but memories became lessons. They reminded Sally to trust her instincts.

"Remember the first lesson?"

"If I get away, I win."

"Right," said Sally. "If you avoid conflict, you've taken power away from your enemy."

"Enemy," said Grace, "you mean villain."

"Don't start with that," said Sally. "This move I'm showing you, it's for buying time to run away. Anyone who attacks you is likely bigger than you, yes?"

Grace nodded.

"Come over here," said Sally, "pick me up, move me three feet in the air, and drop me on the ground."

Grace's eyes went wide.

"What's the matter?" asked Sally. "Not strong enough?"

Grace's eyebrows came together and she stomped over to Sally. She wrapped her arms around Sally's waist and gave an oomph as she tried to get her back muscles into the battle, but Sally set her legs wide and wouldn't budge. Grace shuffled around and grabbed Sally from behind.

Sally pretended to stumble backward, then let momentum carry her. She heard a yelp as she fell on top of Grace, pinning her to the ground.

Grace cried out in a muffled voice. "Not fair."

"Life isn't fair." Sally rolled sideways and stood. "That's why you have to change the rules."

Grace accepted Sally's outstretched hand. "I can't pick you up—"

"—but you can grab my foot," said Sally. "Physics and gravity will do the rest."

"You think someone will try to kick me?" Grace sounded earnest, not afraid.

Sally considered who might be coming after Grace. The two men from the museum weren't a threat. One died in the hospital, and the other had his DNA blasted across the city by a bazooka.

But Freddie Wang had more men, scores of them, and he bribed or controlled enough businesses in Chinatown to put Grace under constant surveillance. She could hide here until the case was resolved, but Sally knew that criminals sometimes got away with murder.

You could kill Freddie.

The thought swept across her mind like a cirrus cloud and vanished just as quickly. Sally knew she could kill Freddie, and he knew it, too. But his insurance policy was bulletproof.

Freddie wasn't the dragonhead. He answered to people far, far away. Cut off his head and another would grow in its place. He ran drugs, gambling, and prostitution rackets from his restaurant in Chinatown and controlled the local tong gangs. He was a soulless bureaucrat, a garden snake with fangs. Freddie didn't give the orders, he just executed them.

What if you had something Freddie wanted more than the girl?

The idea was amorphous, a mere wisp of a thought. Sally shook her head and focused on Grace. "I think a larger opponent will have a hard time catching you because you're fast. Suppose it's a man about the size of Cape."

"That's a funny name," said Grace, "don't you think?"

"He'd agree with you," said Sally. "You should ask him about it...now focus..."

Grace stood up straighter.

Sally continued, "Your attacker is going to be heavier, with longer reach, so he might try to hit you or, if you're quick enough to duck, to kick or trip you."

"So I grab his foot."

"Yes," said Sally. "It's actually easier to take a kick than a punch if you're trained. Let your body move with the motion of the kick, use your arms to slow its momentum—remember to bend your arms. Then grab the foot, or the shoe, if he's wearing one. Shoes are good because they have heels, laces, lots of things to get your fingers around. Then twist like you're opening a giant ketchup bottle with both hands."

"I don't really like ketchup."

"Neither do I," said Sally, "but you get the idea."

"And then I run away?"

Sally nodded her approval. "You run away."

"When did you run away?"

The question caught Sally off guard. Their conversations were a constellation of small bits and pieces shared inadvertently in the context of something else. Sally knew all relationships were merely mosaics of smaller moments, the final picture not visible till the end, but this type of relationship was new to her. She hadn't spent much time around children, other than her students, since she was Grace's age.

"I was older than you when I left Hong Kong," said Sally. "But I lost both my parents when I was five."

Grace bit her lower lip. "My mother died when I was five, but my father remarried when I was nine."

"How was that?"

The corner of Grace's mouth twitched. "I still miss my mom."

Sally didn't say anything.

Grace looked at her hands. "Do you think my father is dead?"

"I don't know."

"I still talk to him as if he's alive."

"I talk to my parents all the time," said Sally.

"Do they answer?"

Sally tilted her head. "Usually by the time I finish the question, I know the answer."

"So maybe they do."

"Yes," said Sally. "Maybe they do."

"Who raised you?"

Sally thought about her own life's mosaic and tried to visualize a better picture for Grace. "A nanny, my caretaker from when I was little."

Who sold me to the Triads.

"And then you went to boarding school?"

"Yes," said Sally, "with lots of other girls."

Who were trained to be assassins, consorts, and spies.

"Was it nice?" asked Grace. "Your school?"

After I killed the dragonhead's son, it was time to leave.

"I liked the other girls," said Sally. "And learned a lot."

"You're a good teacher."

"Glad you think so," said Sally. "Because there's still lots to learn. We covered running, and today we practiced grabbing. The next two subjects will be hitting and gouging."

"What's gouging?"

Sally took her thumbs and pressed them against her own eyelids. "You put your strongest fingers, usually your first two fingers or thumb, and press against something soft…and keep pressing as hard as you can."

"That's gross."

Sally opened her eyes. "And effective." She extended the index and middle finger of her right hand and poked Grace in the shoulder.

"Hey."

Sally prodded Grace in the other shoulder, then hip, elbow, and neck. She took Grace's right hand in hers and pressed a thumb into the soft flesh where Grace's index finger and thumb came together. Grace yanked her hand away as if she'd been shocked.

"That felt like electricity."

"There are pressure points all over the body," said Sally. "That's how acupuncture works. And there are soft spots, like eyeballs."

"Yuck."

"I'll give you a chart to memorize," said Sally. "And a quiz tomorrow." She bowed deeply to indicate the lesson was over.

Grace returned the bow. "What are we going to do now?"

"Eat," said Sally, "and plan."

"What are we planning?"

"A robbery."

46

"Maybe it's a robbery."

Maria's mouth was very close to Cape's ear as she whispered. It made him want to whisper all the time, but the shoe on the floor had a foot in it, and unlike the last shoe he'd seen, a body was still attached.

"If it's a robbery," whispered Cape, "then my name is Rumpelstiltskin."

"I might have guessed," said Maria. "I have a hard time believing that Cape is your—"

"—you mind if we focus on the corpse in the hallway?"

Cape pulled his head back from the opening in the door and removed the gun from his pocket. He thumbed the safety off and kept his index finger straight along the slide and away from the trigger.

"What did you see?" asked Maria.

"A man's body," said Cape. "And unless he dropped a bottle of ketchup, a lot of blood."

"Is he moving?" asked Maria. "Maybe he's still alive."

"I forgot to mention what I didn't see," said Cape. "Parts of him are missing."

"Which parts?"

"Important parts."

"How important?"

"You could ask him," said Cape, "but I don't think he'd hear you."

"Because he's dead?"

"Because his ears are missing, along with the top of his head."

"He's probably dead, then."

"What have I been saying?"

They took a step back from the door and scanned the upper windows, but the shades were drawn and motionless. They listened intently, but the only sounds were somnolent bees and distant ravens.

"We should call the police," said Maria.

"Definitely," said Cape.

Neither of them reached for their phones.

Cape held Maria's gaze for a beat. "Since we have one gun between the two of us, let's circle the house before—"

"—we go inside."

Cape led Maria around the left side of the house. Nothing was visible through the windows save for expensive furniture and rare art. Every shelf held a sculpture or artifact. The walls were covered with paintings. Cape heard Maria gasp more than once.

The back of the house opened onto a broad lawn that sloped down to the forlorn vineyard. The rear windows revealed a sitting room filled with overstuffed couches, a grand piano, and more artwork, but the walls were sparsely occupied. Empty rectangles in a shade darker than the surrounding paint outnumbered the paintings.

"*Caro*," said Maria quietly.

"What?"

"You were right, the divorce was expensive." Maria counted the number of blank spaces on the wall. "Assuming the missing paintings are as valuable as the ones still on the walls."

Cape was anxious to return to the body in the hall but didn't want to be struck on the head with a candlestick by Colonel Mustard. Far better to know what was inside before barging through the front door. They moved quickly but carefully as they worked their way around the back. Neither robbers nor residents were visible through any of the windows. It was when they came around the right side of the house that they discovered who killed the man in the hallway.

Alistair Beckett sat in an armchair in the middle of his study.

He was wearing tan slacks, a sky-blue polo shirt, and brown loafers. His hair was more silver than black, his face handsome and tanned, his eyes dark brown. Beckett's head oscillated back and forth as if he was looking for something but was too tired to get up and search.

Two of the walls were covered by bookshelves. The wall behind Beckett was filled with art. A thin stream of blood ran from Beckett's outstretched fingers onto the carpet.

A shotgun lay a few feet away from the chair.

Cape and Maria moved soundlessly to the front door. Cape handed the gun to Maria, wrapped both his hands around the edge of the door and pushed slowly but deliberately until the gap was wide enough to pass through.

The walls looked like a Jackson Pollock painting. The cream paint was splattered with blood and other organic material that Cape preferred not to identify. The body was facedown, despite not having a face. Cape could tell from the profile that the flesh was gone down to the jawline, and the top of the skull lay in fragments near the door.

Cape wasn't a forensics expert but guessed the deceased had

been the first man inside. A ragged hole in the wall near the door looked like a miss from a shotgun that had punched through the plaster. The second shot must have blown the intruder against the door as it decapitated him. The body fell forward after the brains flew backward.

A second man never made it inside, and there was no car in the drive except the MG, which Cape assumed was Beckett's. The Honda Civic that spun onto the highway came to mind. Thousands of Civics on the road, fast enough for a getaway car, perfect for two men.

Blood radiated from the shattered skull like a lopsided halo. It had stopped pooling, so Cape felt they could avoid leaving bloody footprints if they were careful. He didn't mind disturbing evidence, up to a point, but becoming a suspect wasn't on his list of things to do.

A glint of metal was visible on the man's left side, where the arm bent at an unnatural angle. The butt of a small caliber semiautomatic—not something that needed their fingerprints.

It might have been smarter to enter through the back of the house, but Cape wanted as little noise as possible, and picking a lock or breaking a window didn't always go smoothly. Clearly, Beckett was inclined to shoot first and ask questions never.

Which meant he'd been expecting intruders.

Cape held up three fingers, then lowered them in turn. At three, he stepped lightly past the corpse and hurried down the hallway toward the study, Maria close on his heels. The house was silent as they passed an open door on the left. A glance inside revealed a dining room with an open archway in the far wall that led to the first room they had glimpsed from outside. The dining table was set but had the appearance of tableware arranged for its appearance, not daily use.

Two heavy candlesticks sat at the center of the table.

The door to the study was ten feet ahead on the right. Cape paused and felt Maria press close. Speed was their ally. It wouldn't take long for Beckett to grab the shotgun.

As they approached the door, Maria used her cop voice.

"Señor Beckett, we are coming in."

Beckett jerked at the sound but made no move to stand or reach for the shotgun. His head moved in a lazy arc, a backyard swing with one of its ropes cut. An empty bottle of bourbon lay on the carpet. Moist eyes focused on his unexpected guests.

Cape nodded in greeting and crossed to the shotgun. He nudged the barrel with his shoe until it was out of reach for even the most desperate lunge. He moved closer to Maria so Beckett wouldn't have to pivot his head. Maria had the gun down by her right leg, visible if you were looking but not the first thing you'd notice.

"Have you seen my phone?" asked Beckett.

"*Cómo?*" asked Maria.

Beckett swiveled his head from bookcase to bookcase. "My phone." He looked at Cape. "I can't find my fucking cell phone." Back to Maria. "You know, to call the ambulance."

Maria handed the gun to Cape and moved to the chair.

Beckett's shoulder was damp with blood. Careful to avoid any drops hitting her shoes, Maria gingerly lifted the edge of his polo and hissed between her teeth.

"Bastard got my shoulder before I found my mark." Beckett's voice was strong but hoarse. "A lot tougher than shooting skeet…" He trailed off until his eyes found his weapon. "…but hard to miss twice with a shotgun."

Cape made eye contact with Maria. "How bad, from an ambulance point of view?"

"No artery," said Maria. "A deep gash, but no bullet…I'd say no immediate danger. He could drip like this for hours—"

"—still," said Cape, "we can't—"

"—find my phone?" asked Beckett. "Neither can I." He jutted his chin toward an overturned end table. "I left it there, but damned if I know where it is now...used to be phones in every room...shit, I grew up with rotary dials, remember..?" Beckett's pendulum head found Maria. "You seen my phone?"

"I haven't." Maria stepped back from the chair. "But I'll look."

When Maria came closer, Cape spoke under his breath. "Five minutes, then one of us calls an ambulance."

"Agreed," said Maria. "Can you find a towel, maybe a cloth napkin from the dining room?"

Cape returned to the hallway and navigated his way to a bathroom. He ran cold water over a hand towel and grabbed another, then returned to the study. He put the dry towel against Beckett's shoulder, then took Beckett's good arm, bent it gently and laid the hand on top of the towel.

"Press down."

Cape draped the cold towel across Beckett's forehead and tilted his neck so it wouldn't fall. He noticed a sideboard and returned with another bottle of bourbon. Cape unscrewed the cap and offered it to Beckett, who nodded.

He held the bottle to Beckett's lips and tilted it slowly. When he started to pull it away, a sublingual protest sounded deep in Beckett's throat. When a third of the liquid was gone, Cape withdrew the bottle and tucked it between Beckett's uninjured side and the chair.

Beckett's eyes cleared almost imperceptibly. "You from the sheriff's office?"

Cape shook his head. "We're from the city."

"SFPD?"

Cape let that sit and didn't say anything.

"Who tried to kill you?" asked Maria.

"Probably meant to scare me," said Beckett, "but I wasn't taking any chances." His head listed to the side so he could see the shotgun. Somehow the towel stayed in place. "Man's got to defend his home, am I right?"

"You knew they were coming," said Cape.

"I'm not getting in a car with someone who points a gun at me."

"Is that what happened?"

"I got shot, didn't I?"

"Yes," said Maria, "you got shot."

Interviewing a suspicious suspect was a stamina game—ask the same question over and over, a slightly different way each time. Once you get an answer, throw them a curve.

"You were expecting them," said Cape.

"I expected someone," said Beckett.

"Because the museum heist went sideways," said Cape mildly.

Beckett blinked a few times but said nothing.

"The helicopter—"

"—at the museum," added Maria.

"No loose ends." Beckett squeezed his eyes shut and breathed through his nose. "They said no loose ends." His eyes opened wide. "You caught the crooks?"

Cape chose his words with the care of a fisherman picking bait. "We caught up with one of them, yes." Obfuscation is a detective's best friend.

Beckett sagged in his chair. "Guess he talked."

He was blown to pieces before we could question him.

"He did talk," said Cape.

He must have talked to someone, about something, when he was alive...he just never talked to us before he spontaneously combusted.

"Maybe you want to talk," said Maria, "while we look for your phone."

"My wife left me," said Beckett.

"We heard." Maria walked around the room examining the books and sculptures on the shelves, occasionally checking the carpet for a phone.

"You needed money," said Cape.

"Ex-wives are expensive," said Beckett. "So are wineries."

"Especially one that's not producing any wine."

"We had fires," Beckett snapped. "Maybe you heard?"

"So you told the thieves when the artwork would be delivered to the museum."

"You think they squeezed me into telling them." Beckett laughed, a cruel cough that lasted only a second. "Unbelievable... no, insulting...I am insulted...I am shot and I am insulted... and can't decide which is worse."

"I'd rather be insulted," said Maria.

"I get insulted all the time," said Cape.

"Maybe," said Beckett, "but you don't have my name."

"Alistair?"

"Beckett...the Beckett name...look back over the generations...we may be a lot of things, but we are never an easy mark...not to anyone...the only deals we make are the deals we make, understand?"

"That sounded vaguely like a confession," said Cape.

"Confession?" asked Beckett. "You a cop or a priest?"

"We're art lovers," said Maria.

"Really?" Beckett's bobblehead tilted at the wall of paintings. "Then take a gander at my gallery."

Maria scanned the wall. Cape gave it a cursory glance until he heard Maria curse. She looked like she'd seen a ghost.

"That's my painting."

Cape recognized most of the artists, not from any deep expertise but because the brush strokes were so iconic. The bold colors of Van Gogh and pointillist perfection of Monet competed for wall space with the abstract musings of Chagall and idyllic interludes of Renoir. Very few collectors could afford a wall like this.

Maria ignored them all save for one painting on the left. It was a Rembrandt, a self-portrait done sometime in his later years. Maria extended her hand like a supplicant but didn't touch the canvas.

"This is the Rembrandt painting I recovered," she said, almost inaudibly.

"Did you?" Beckett sat up straighter. The towel fell off his head but he took no notice. "Or didn't you?" His tone was playful, and his eyes had a smug glint.

Maria stepped to the side to look at the painting from an angle. She stared at the frame.

"It took months to find," she said.

"A painting was recovered," said Beckett, "but you're looking at the original."

"That's not possible—"

"—swapped for a forgery after they stole it." Beckett shrugged. "When this landed on the black market, no way I could pass it up."

"We had it authenticated," said Maria. "By two different experts."

"You see that Chagall?"

Marie and Cape found the vibrant canvas.

Beckett gingerly moved his good arm to lift the bourbon to his lips.

"That's not a Chagall," he said. "It was painted by Guy Ribes."

Maria muttered something in Spanish, each syllable dripping with acid.

"Who's Guy Ribes?" asked Cape.

Beckett watched Maria.

"He's a Frenchman," said Maria. "The most notorious forger of the last century."

"Wikipedia page and everything," said Beckett. "Still alive but retired."

"He retired because he went to jail," said Maria. "A condition of his release."

"He painted this Chagall?" asked Cape.

"He painted hundreds," said Maria.

"More," said Beckett. "The man was a savant, a chameleon. He could paint like Chagall, Picasso, Renoir, you name it, down to the brushstrokes. He would pass them off as lost paintings, undiscovered masterpieces found in private collections, sketches passed down through generations. He fooled auction houses, appraisers, galleries—"

"—and museum directors." Maria turned from the wall to look down at Beckett. "They greedily bought into the hoaxes, provided certificates of authenticity, and shared any profits from a sale or reaped the rewards of having the art in their gallery. Many were naïve, others turned a blind eye, some were—"

"—business partners?" asked Cape.

"Yes," said Maria. "Never caught but forever suspect."

Beckett raised the bottle and took another swig.

"Ribes wasn't a villain, really," said Maria. "He grew up poor, had a gift and saw a way to make a living. Most forgers are tradespeople, simple craftsmen working for crooks."

"Hundreds of paintings...by one forger?" asked Cape.

"Maybe more," said Maria. "His paintings got certified in catalogs, so there's no way of knowing how many are still out there. You could be looking at a Renoir in a French museum that was never actually painted by Renoir. But it's hanging in a museum with a plaque—"

"—which makes it real." Beckett sounded proud.

Maria was disgusted. "People believe anything a so-called expert says is real."

The corner of Beckett's mouth rose as he studied Maria. "Carabinieri Art Squad?"

"They are Italian," said Maria. "I am Spanish." She stepped forward and took the Rembrandt off the wall. "The Carabinieri TPC are a special branch of the police, while I…" Maria glanced over her shoulder. "…am a humble tourist."

"She's not very humble," said Cape, "but she is a tourist."

Maria shifted her gaze from the painting to Beckett. "The recovered painting, your alleged counterfeit—"

"—perfect forgery," said Beckett, "Carbon-dated paints, layered patina on the canvas, reclaimed wood for the frame."

"Who made it?" asked Maria. "Who painted the forgery of this Rembrandt?"

Beckett shook his head. "The people who made that are not retired, and they don't plan on going to jail."

"It's not a single forger," said Maria, "is it?"

"Let's just say the art business is now a manufacturing business, and leave it at that."

"An art factory," said Maria.

Cape played a card he didn't have. "Your partners sold you out."

"I might get charged for tipping off some art thieves about a shipment," said Beckett. "Big deal…I'll claim it was coercion, blackmail, extortion…my lawyer can mix-and-match…I've got bigger legal problems from my divorce…either way, I'm fucked."

"Then why would they come after you?" asked Cape.

"They wanted another way into the museum…an easy way in," said Beckett. "Giving up a date is one thing, giving them keys to the front door is another…my hands go into the cookie jar, that makes me an accomplice…thank you, but no, Perry Mason, you can kiss my ass. So here I sit, not only wounded but hurt, deeply hurt. I almost died defending my reputation."

"A guard died defending your museum," said Cape. "He was decapitated."

"I was in Napa."

Cape rubbed his temples. Beckett liked to talk, and they caught him off guard, but now he had regained his footing. He was drunk but answered questions like a man standing in the witness box.

"Who painted a copy of this?" Maria was practically shaking but held the Rembrandt steady. "Where…where was it painted?"

"Sorry," said Beckett, "this is when I ask to call my lawyer."

"You lost your phone," said Cape, "remember?"

"Then I plead the fifth," said Beckett. "They could hurt me."

"We could hurt you," said Cape.

"I'd like to hurt him," said Maria.

Beckett's eyes moved between them like a shuttlecock. "Who are you?"

"We told you," said Cape. "Art lovers."

"Real art lovers." Maria set the Rembrandt down carefully. "Not fake art lovers."

"What's real?" Beckett scowled. "You like the painting, it made you feel something, that's real. People want to believe. There's no such thing as a fake in the art world."

"You might qualify," said Cape.

"You think that bothers me?" said Beckett. "The art world is all make-believe…somebody decides Picasso's a genius, but your kid's crayon drawing of flowers is shit…why? You're a loser if you don't rig the game, because the rules are arbitrary. None of it matters."

"It matters to me," said Maria.

Cape caught Maria's eye. "Ready to go?"

"Please."

"Hey," said Beckett, "aren't you going to make the call?" He glanced at his wounded shoulder, where a red Rorschach test was spreading through the fabric of the towel.

"I don't want to use my phone," said Cape. "Caller ID and all." He tilted his head at Maria. "Do you?"

"Not a chance."

"Give us the passcode to the museum's security system," said Cape.

Beckett coughed. "What?"

"Did I stutter?"

"Go fuck yourself."

"Okay." Cape shrugged and turned to leave. "I hope you don't bleed out—"

"—that would be a dumb way to die," said Maria.

Maria and Cape moved toward the door. They were crossing the threshold when Beckett barked at them.

"Zero-one-two-three-four-five-six-seven-eight-nine."

Cape and Maria returned to Beckett's gallery room.

"You're not serious," said Cape.

"It's a ten-digit code," said Beckett, "those are almost impossible to crack."

"That's an ordered list," said Cape, "not a code."

"He did use every number on the keypad," said Maria.

"Oh, the pound key," said Beckett. "Almost forgot...you have to punch the pound key at the end."

"*Gracias*," said Maria.

"Unbelievable," said Cape.

"I gave you the code," said Beckett. "Now give me a phone."

Cape had noticed a bulge in Beckett's pants when handing him the bourbon. Beckett clearly loved to drink, but Cape doubted a gunshot wound plus alcohol triggered tumescence.

"Check your pockets, dumbass."

Beckett blinked and shifted in his chair. The bottle tumbled out of his lap onto the floor. What little bourbon remained spilled in a syrupy stream across the carpet until it merged with the dried river of blood.

"Son of a bitch." Beckett fidgeted until he could reach across his lap with his good arm to fish the phone from his pocket. "You must be a detective."

Beckett tapped his phone screen.

Maria picked up the Rembrandt and headed for the door.

"Hey," said Beckett, "you can't take that."

"Stop me," said Maria.

"Maybe you should call the police." Cape crossed to where the shotgun lay on the carpet. He got the tip of his shoe under the barrel and lifted his leg like a soccer player. The gun jumped into the air, parallel to the floor, and Cape caught it with both hands.

The slide made a *ca-chunck* sound as Cape racked a new shell into the chamber. He gestured with the barrel of the shotgun.

"That Chagall is a fake?"

Beckett stopped looking at his phone to watch Cape's every move. The barrel swung back and forth idly between the paintings until it landed on the forgery.

Beckett nodded. "It's still worth—"

The shotgun boomed with an Old Testament clap of thunder.

Maria clutched her painting so it faced her, to shield Rembrandt from the horror. Beckett shrank into his chair but failed to squeeze between the cushions and disappear. Cape's ears were ringing. He wrinkled his nose against the acrid tinge of spent powder to ward off a sneeze.

The Chagall was obliterated, a supernova of color collapsed into a black hole. Light from the adjoining room shone faintly through the shredded canvas.

"I don't think it's worth much anymore," said Cape.

"You c-c-c-cks…" Beckett eyed the shotgun and stopped in mid-curse, sounding like a man clearing his throat.

Cape racked the slide three times in rapid succession until the remaining shells kicked out of the breach onto the floor. Using his shirttail, he wiped his prints off the gun, then tossed it onto Beckett's lap.

Beckett caught it reflexively with a sharp cry as his shoulder tightened. "Wh—?"

"Just wanted your prints on it again," said Cape. "Thanks for the art lesson."

"And thanks for the art." Maria hefted the Rembrandt under her arm. "We'll show ourselves out."

Alistair Beckett sat in his armchair and watched them leave. He had a hole in his arm and a hole in his wall. And despite the bravado, he knew his reputation would get blown apart like the faux Chagall, once the headlines were written.

He looked from the phone in his lap to the gun in his hands.

From where he was sitting, both choices looked about the same.

47

"They look the same," said Wen. "Can you see any difference?"

"I painted it," said Peng, "so I probably—"

"—you're too modest," said Wen. "I taught art history for years and know the paintings of Forty Scenes of the Yuanmingyuan like my own reflection. These two are identical down to the smallest detail."

Wen stood over the table where Peng's version of the painting *Harmony with the Past and Present* sat alongside a high-resolution digital reproduction of the original. He had inserted colored pins at key junctures where brushstrokes changed direction or hues faded, subtle and almost imperceptible moments that demanded an artist's touch. The difference between a copy and clone came down to those details.

"They feel the same," said Peng. "So I guess you're right."

Wen studied the young prodigy. "You feel the painting?"

"I see them, of course, but, yes, when I finish a painting, it feels…" Peng blushed as he tried to find the words. "…it feels like…what is the name of this painting again?"

"*Harmony with the Past and Present.*"

"Exactly." Peng smiled. "That's exactly how it feels."

"The Greeks believed an artist was inspired by a muse who shared secrets from the past."

"My muse is my girlfriend, Yan. She works downstairs in the factory."

"That's the best muse of all," said Wen. "One you can take home."

"I could never have done this alone," said Peng. "I learned so much."

"You learn fast," said Wen. "This is the final painting of the four."

Peng took a long look at his handiwork before nodding to himself, satisfied. He moved the canvas to the opposite side of the table where packing materials had been arranged. A wooden frame, packing straw, twine, and cardboard.

The wall behind them was dominated by a latticed window which overlooked the factory floor. Long tables were arranged around stations for each section of a mass-produced painting. Artists and production assistants stood on both sides of each table, passing a canvas along as soon as their background, detail, or base layer was finished. Peng spared a glance to find Yan, but only her body was visible at the far end of the room. Her face was blocked by one of the hanging lights that extended the length of the factory. Peng turned his attention back to his painting and laid it carefully inside the wooden frame.

Wen came around the table to move a portable hot air gun away from the packing materials. It was a plastic appliance sold in craft stores to heat paints, soften clay, or shrink dry plastics. Peng had used it for matching textures between different sections of the painting. It was shaped like a pistol and powered by an electric battery in the grip.

"We don't want to burn your masterpiece," said Wen.

"No, we definitely do not want to do that."

"What do you think?" Wen held the hot air gun at arm's length in a pose worthy of an action hero. "Should I use this to break out of here?"

Peng glanced nervously at the door. "Don't you think they'll send you home, now that you've helped?"

"I honestly don't know." Wen lowered his arm. "I may not have a home to go back to."

"Maybe you'll stay here and work with me."

"Anything is possible." Wen tried to strike a positive chord, but it sounded flat to his ear.

He thought of his daughter, Grace, and how badly he wanted to see her. Wen acted like an optimist but was a realist at heart. For taking a selfie in a park, he had been sent to a labor camp. Now he was under house arrest at an art factory. Even if he could return to Hong Kong, he would be banned from teaching, his travel restricted, put on a list for the rest of his life.

That was no life for a little girl like Grace. With every brushstroke that his young friend made across this final painting, Wen had inched closer to a decision. Now he was at peace.

His daughter was safely out of the country. Only he knew where. The best way to give Grace a happy life was to take that secret to his grave.

When you've taken care of what you love most, all your fears melt away.

Wen finally understood the advice Bohai had given him on his first day at the camp. Forget your daughter. What Bohai really meant was that Wen should act in such a way that his handlers forgot he ever had a daughter. His hope was their leverage.

Wen was going to take away that leverage. He was going to die in this village.

"Are you okay?" Peng was staring at him with a worried expression.

"Yes…thank you." Wen smiled. "I just hope Mogwai is satisfied with your latest masterpiece."

"Speak of the devil and…"

Peng jumped at the sound of the digitized voice.

Wen clenched his hands and spun on his heel.

Mogwai was standing in the doorway. Black robes billowed in a draft from the hall.

Wen and Peng watched the figure glide across the floor. Mogwai slid between the two of them and stood at the edge of the table. Peng shuffled sideways so their shoulders didn't touch. A thin bead of sweat ran down his cheek into the collar of his shirt.

The faceless head tilted toward the painting.

"Peng, you have surpassed yourself."

Peng's eyebrows yo-yoed up and down a few times. "I… had…h-h-help."

"Of course you did." Mogwai's head swiveled toward Wen. "The professor."

Wen gave a modest nod of his head. "Where are the paintings being sent?"

Peng's eyes tried to leap out of his head. He couldn't believe Wen had the temerity to ask the Devil a question.

Wen smiled benignly as the bottomless hood tilted in appraisal.

"To a museum." Mogwai's digital rasp seemed to rise an octave.

Wen wrinkled his nose and took a deep breath. "It's a beautiful forgery, isn't it?"

Peng blanched at the word. *Wèizào.* For years he'd painted canvases for collectors and printed posters for dorm rooms. Replicas designed to democratize art. He should have realized they were working on something more sinister but had told himself the attention to detail was for realism, not deception.

Yan had said that he was naïve, and now Peng wondered if he was willfully so.

Mogwai's hands jabbed at the canvas. "This painting—"

"—you must plan on stealing the original," said Wen. "To bring back to China."

Mogwai didn't reply but a low, digital buzzing filled the space between them.

Wen tilted his head to match the angle of the hood, as if looking into the Devil's eyes. His nostrils flared as if he was about to sneeze. Then he smiled sadly.

Mogwai took half a step backward but was too slow. Wen reached out and tore the hood from the Devil's head.

Peng was surprised to find himself looking at a woman.

Wen was not at all surprised to be looking at his wife.

"I never liked that perfume," he said. "The jasmine is overpowering."

The woman who was Mogwai stood speechless, her *changsan* robe swishing as her hands dropped to her sides. Her face was a series of sharp curves, perfectly proportioned, flowing gracefully into full lips compressed in a line. Gossamer strands of gray were visible in thick black hair, which was tousled from the rapid removal of the hood.

"Hello, Chu Hua," said Wen. "I thought you died, but I see you've been reborn."

No one spoke. The artist, the prisoner, and the party official were inches apart but standing in three separate realities.

"This is awkward," said Peng. "May I leave?"

"Yes," said Wen.

"No," said Mogwai, the unearthly voice coming from a mere mortal. Chu Hua raised a hand to her throat and pressed the button to deactivate the microphone. "This is too—"

"—too what?" Wen was trying to stay calm, but his voice had

a gruff kick behind it. "Too important?" To his ears he was starting to sound like Mogwai. "Important to what, Chu?"

"All those walks in the museum," said Chu, "and you never understood." She jutted her chin at the painting. "This art you love so much, it belongs—"

"—we have a daughter."

"You have a daughter," said Chu. "I have a job."

"To recruit me?" asked Wen. "Or seduce me?"

"This isn't about you," said Chu in a practiced tone. "History is never—"

"—save me the speeches," said Wen. "You're only talking to yourself...again."

"You're only thinking of yourself, as usual." Chu gave a thin smile. "Say we'd never met...but one day I arrived at the university to ask about coming here voluntarily, to help the Party. What would you have said?"

"I would have said I already had a job."

"Teaching history...when you could be making history."

"It's my choice."

"No," said Chu. "It's not."

"And there it is." Wen shook his head. "You actually believe that, don't you?"

Chu took a deep breath and spoke in a practiced tone. "This isn't about you, Wen. Neither is the future in which we'll all live. The only question is whether you'll be a part—"

"—that day in Victoria Park," said Wen. "I had a brighter future in mind."

"I told you not to visit the park," said Chu, "but you wouldn't listen."

"I thought you died," said Chen, "and that it was my fault."

Chu smiled. "Now that you're a master forger, you must appreciate the power of deception."

Peng cleared his throat and shuffled nervously behind them. "Um, I'm leaving now, don't forget to lock up... Chu Hua, well, so nice to meet you..."

Wen started to reply but jerked sideways as his right hand brushed against his own leg. The hot air gun was still in his hand. When Mogwai first appeared in the hallway, Wen had clenched his fingers and inadvertently pulled the trigger.

Now the air gun was as hot as a soldering iron.

Wen looked at his wife but thought of his daughter. Chu was married to the state, and he was wed to his fate. He threw his arms around her and spoke urgently to Peng.

"Run."

Peng didn't have to be told twice. His eyes were sad, but his feet were not interested in long goodbyes. He gave a last look at his older colleague and was in the hall before Chu shook her arms free from Wen's embrace.

Wen shoved the air gun into the packing straw. It ignited instantly.

Flame spread like a rumor. The straw singed the paper on the worktable and scorched the edges of the canvas, licking its way around the wooden frame of the shipping crate. The oils in the special paints Wen had mixed were ferociously flammable.

Before anyone could move, the surface of the painting erupted in a vision of hell.

The Devil dove in headfirst.

Chu Hua swung her arms across the top of the painting in an attempt to brush the surface oils off the base layers. The light-absorbent materials in her devil's cloak were chosen for their obsidian gloom, not for safety, and she underestimated how hot the antique paints could burn. Flames wrapped around the gloves and climbed up her sleeves toward her face.

She stumbled backward and crashed into the window that

overlooked the factory. Glass rained onto the factory floor, tiny mirrors reflecting the panicked faces looking up at the flames.

Wen lunged and grabbed the collar of Chu's robe to tear it off before she burned, but the seams held fast. His knuckles brushed against her throat and activated the microphone. When she screamed, it was the Devil's voice that tore through the factory.

The hood flew from Wen's hand. Caught in the updraft from the inferno, it soared above the workers until it snagged on one of the overhead lights. It hung despondently, the discarded flag of a retreating army. Terrified workers whispered the Devil's name.

The lenses on the hood reflected the flames, burning eyes looking down on everyone.

The Devil's scream turned into a roar, echoed by the cries of everyone surging toward the exits. Peng made it to the factory floor and found Yan, who had run through the flames toward the stairs to save him. She grabbed his hand and they ran.

Black smoke billowed from the office window.

Wen pulled Chu away from the window ledge, but she panicked as she frantically tried to tear the burning gloves from her hands. She fell against Wen, and together they slammed into the table. Wen felt the shipping crate press against his spine and flames crawl up his back.

Wen managed to tear the zipper on the back of the cloak, and Chu Hua wriggled free of the robes. The discarded Devil lay at her feet, deflated and empty.

Wen looked through the office window to see if there was any path to the exit. All he saw was an incendiary archipelago running the length of the factory. Fallen embers ignited canvases, turned brushes into torches and turpentine into napalm. Oily smoke obscured his view, but not before Wen spotted his young friend, the prodigy, running with his girlfriend through the exit door. Running to a better life.

Wen looked at his wife and saw the flames reflected in her eyes. There was no escape for them. He wrapped his arms around the devil he knew, and after a moment's hesitation, she returned the embrace. Tears spilled from a well of regret and ran down his cheeks as his skin began to blister and burn.

Then all his fears melted away.

48

Grace felt something melt deep inside her, as if her heart had sprung a leak.

She fell to the floor with a gasp. Sally was at her side in an instant, kneeling to prop Grace into a sitting position.

Grace stared at Sally without seeing. Her face was flushed.

Sally rested a hand on the side of the young girl's face. Grace felt warm but not feverish, a rush of heat beneath the skin. The light in Grace's eyes was as distant as a dying star.

Sally had seen that look before.

When Sally was five she was in a car accident with her parents. She awoke in a hospital, scared and alone, but no one would tell her what happened. Only her caretaker, Li Mei, told her the truth.

Her parents were dead.

Sally already knew. No one had told her, but she knew. A string had been cut somewhere deep inside, and her heart was untethered for the first time in her short life. It wouldn't be the last, and it was a feeling she'd never forget.

She remembered how her face looked in the mirror, after Li Mei left her alone. That was how Grace looked now. Sally sat next to her on the floor. She held Grace's hands until the light in her eyes came back from wherever it had gone. Sally knew Grace didn't know what just happened, not yet. She just knew how it felt when it did.

They sat together in silence and waited for the earth to starting spinning again.

49

"You're spinning your wheels." Freddie Wang sucked his cigarette down to ash. "You needed four forgeries, now you only have three."

The ghost's eyes narrowed. "We go anyway."

Freddie took another cigarette from the pack and used it to point at the desk phone. "Beijing says at least two weeks before you get that last forgery, maybe longer." He leaned forward and lit the fresh cigarette with a desktop lighter shaped like a dragon. "Big fire at the art factory."

"How big?" The red eyes smoldered like hot coals.

"Didn't ask." Freddie shrugged. "Maybe you go to New York after all."

Freddie leaned back in his chair, his good eye sharp in the dim light. Two men stood behind his right shoulder, near the heavily curtained bay window. They shifted nervously as they followed the conversation. Their faces were obscured by the nicotine haze.

Victorian London didn't have as much smog as this office, and the ghost wondered if Freddie was allergic to oxygen. Of all the criminals with whom the ghost had done business, Freddie was one of the few not completely unnerved by his phantasmal appearance. The ghost was starting to enjoy the company of his hoary host. Perhaps Freddie had cheated death so many times that he lived beyond fear.

Despite this mutual understanding, each encounter made the ghost trust the old man less. Their partnership was going to end soon. Clearly not soon enough for Freddie's taste.

"I'm here to bring lost art back to China." The ghost pressed his pale palms together. "One way or another is no difference to me."

"Without the forgeries, the museum will know the art was stolen," said Freddie.

"Once we have it in our hands, it won't matter." The ghost shrugged. "Did you know one of the pieces we took from the museum in Norway is currently on display in Shanghai airport?"

"*Bù Kāiwánxiào.*" Freddie's milky eye narrowed. "Why didn't Norway take it back?"

"What's more important to a tiny country like that?" asked the ghost. "Good relations with China, or a piece of art that may or may not be the original sculpture that was stolen from their museum—a museum only visited by a small percentage of Norwegians."

Freddie nodded in appreciation. "They're too afraid to ask."

"You see why I'm unconcerned," said the ghost. "I'll place the three forgeries in the museum, and they'll believe they only lost one painting. Less of a scandal. They can write it off, make amends with the French museum that loaned it, maybe by sending the French something else in return. Not my problem."

"That wasn't the plan."

"You're speaking of someone else's plan, not mine." The ghost stretched his long arms and gestured at a statue sitting on the desk. It was a Buddha made of bronze with a piebald patina of gold. In an office cluttered with antiques, the sculpture was the only thing older than Freddie. "Besides, you already got your payment."

Freddie extended a clawed hand and stroked the Buddha's belly. "Good thing you snatched this from the museum before the cops arrived. Otherwise no more help from me, which means no help from anyone in Chinatown."

The sleeves of the ghost's robe slid down his forearms with a sibilant hiss as he pointed a bony finger at the two men at the back of the room. "Who are they?"

Freddie stubbed out his cigarette and waved the two men forward without turning around. They stood next to the desk, nervous eyes darting at the ghost whenever they thought he wasn't looking. In the diffuse light from the desktop lamp, it was clear they were identical twins.

Midthirties, dark eyes and long faces, average height. Both wore jeans, black T-shirts, and thin leather jackets. The only discernible difference was their hairstyles. One man had combed his hair back with no visible part, the other's head was shiny with gel, hair spiked in every direction.

Freddie made a careless gesture with his left hand. "This is Feng, and this is Fang—they will be helping you rob the museum."

The ghost looked them over. "Which is which?"

"Feng is the smart one," said Freddie.

"What about Fang?"

"Fang is his brother."

"Wonderful." The ghost ran his fingers through his long white hair to pull it away from his face and down his back. He looked at the two men. "Can you handle explosives?"

"No," said the man on the left, precisely as his brother said, "yes."

The ghost pointed at the man with the slick hair. "Fang."

Fang nodded.

The ghost turned his attention to the twin with the teased tresses.

"Feng, you are going to be the distraction."

"Pretty big distraction." Freddie coughed up some phlegm, then spat into a garbage can at his feet. "You asked for enough explosives to blow up half the city."

"Not your half, Freddie." The ghost smiled. "Don't worry."

"I look worried?" Freddie started to cast a baleful stare but lost interest.

"No, Freddie, you looked annoyed." The ghost brought his lower lip forward in a mock pout. His lips were the color of stale milk. "Rest assured, I'll be leaving soon."

"Not soon enough." Freddie tugged at the hairs protruding from a massive mole on his cheek. "What about the girl?"

"The little witness." The ghost sighed. "The one I asked you to find."

"I found her, remember?" Freddie blew a cloud of smoke into the space between them. "And lost two men."

The ghost shifted his crimson eyes to the twins. "Let's hope you don't lose two more."

"Is that a threat?"

"It's a promise." The ghost smiled and the room felt ten degrees colder. "I plan to take care of the girl myself. Your men don't have to be involved."

"We agreed," said Freddie. "No loose ends that can be tied to me."

The ghost plucked at a thread on the sleeve of his jacket. "Never."

"The girl is invisible," said Freddie. "Which means there's only one place she can be."

"How cryptic." The ghost rubbed his hands together. "I do love a mystery."

"You're not going to love this."

The ghost leaned back and listened as Freddie described how his network of informants had checked the SFPD database, child services, hospitals, even ICE, in case the girl was in the county illegally. Nothing. Then a rumor, barely a whisper. A Chinese girl matching the description was seen at a seafood market located across the street from a martial arts school.

Freddie knew who ran that school. So did everyone in Chinatown.

"Her name is Sally," said Freddie, "but in the community she's known as—"

"—Little Dragon." The ghost's eyes flashed with excitement. "The one who got away."

"You know her?"

The ghost shook his head. "By reputation only. We went to the same school, different campuses, different years. All the students were orphans, all the instructors members of—"

"—Triads," said Freddie.

"Exactly," said the ghost. "She left; I was disavowed. There aren't many graduates, and most of them are dead."

"We have an arrangement—"

"—let me guess," said the ghost. "You leave her alone, and she doesn't kill you."

Freddie spat into his garbage can. "Something like that."

"So if I kill her—"

"—there's no one between you and the girl," said Freddie. "And I can die happy."

The ghost steepled his fingers in front of his face, his eyes half-lidded as he contemplated the challenge. Tendrils of smoke seemed to freeze in midair until he exhaled loudly and opened his eyes.

"I'll do it," he said, "the night we steal the paintings."

"When are you going in?"

"Tomorrow," said the ghost. "Signs are good."

"What signs?"

"It's a full moon."

Freddie cackled and coughed. "You're starting to believe your own mythology. All that moonlight, you should worry about being seen."

"Plenty of people have seen me," said the ghost. "It's just that no one can ever believe it."

50

"I can't believe this."

Police Inspector Beauregard Jones looked more flummoxed than furious, but the bass notes in his voice carried an undercurrent of warning.

"Can't believe what?" asked Cape.

"That we're having this conversation."

"I'm trying to be a responsible citizen," said Cape.

"Responsible?" Beau held up a white paper cup with a delicately drawn blue bottle on the outside. "How much did you pay for this coffee?"

"Four bucks."

"For all the coffees or just mine?"

"Yours was four bucks." Cape raised his own cup. "So was mine." He jerked a thumb at Maria. "Hers was six."

"Extra foam," said Maria.

Cape nodded. "Extra foam."

Beau took a long sip and set his cup on the table. "This coffee is as black as I am. No milk, no foam, nothing fancy. Just coffee."

"What's your point?"

"Paying fourteen bucks for coffee is not something a responsible person would do."

"Blame the neighborhood."

They were sitting behind the Ferry Building at a round table that overlooked the bay. Maria sat to Cape's right and Beau's left. The chair to Cape's left was empty. Their table seemed to be cut in half, sunlight on one side and the shadow of the clock tower draped over the other.

The four-sided clock tower was 245 feet tall, each clock face twenty-two feet in diameter. Since 1898 the landmark stood ready to welcome visitors to San Francisco, though very few arrived by ferry. Most drove across the Oakland Bay Bridge, visible to the right and close enough for Maria to see California drivers give new meaning to the term passive-aggressive.

Container ships moved cautiously across the bay, notorious for its shallow stretches and cross currents. Sailboats cut across whitecaps on their way to the Golden Gate Bridge. Fog was only hours away, and the wind never left San Francisco alone.

"I'm coming to you with a tip," said Cape.

"No." Beau held up a warning hand. "You're about to tell an inspector in the Robbery & Homicide Division—that's me, in case you forgot—about a crime before it occurs."

Cape nodded. "A tip."

"It's more of a warning," said Maria.

"What you just told me—"

"—was only the beginning," said Cape. "You haven't heard—"

"—and don't want to," said Beau. "That wasn't a tip." He gave Maria a bemused look. "Or a warning. That was a confession."

"No, that was the preamble to a well-conceived plan," said Cape. "We're—"

"—going to be criminals."

"You haven't heard the rest of it," said Cape. "I admit, the plan assumes we don't get killed, or caught, or—"

"—seen," said Maria. "We can't be seen."

"Enough." Beau pushed his chair back from the table but remained seated. A container ship rode the waves over his left shoulder. "The museum is closed till further notice. Repairs could take months."

"We only need a few hours," said Cape.

"Knock it off." Beau shook his head. "You can't make me an accessory before the fact."

"Obviously," said Cape.

"That won't keep you out of jail," said Beau, "but it could cost me my badge."

"Jail?" asked Cape. "Who said anything about jail?"

"He did." Maria tilted her head in Beau's direction. "Just now."

"Somebody's paying attention," said Beau. "The policeman said something about jail...want to write it down?"

"I have a pen," said Maria.

"He doesn't need a pen," said Beau. "He needs to listen."

"Remember the last time I had a plan?" asked Cape. "I didn't tell you, and—"

"—you got shot," said Beau, "because it was a shit plan."

"It was worth the risk," said Cape.

"The city got sued," said Beau. "And a lot of fish died."

"Fish?" asked Maria.

"I'll tell you later," said Cape.

Beau spread his hands. "Maybe you should let the police handle criminal matters."

"What's your plan, then?"

"I'm a cop," said Beau. "We don't make plans. We just wait for horrible shit to happen, then we arrest somebody."

"He's not wrong," said Maria. "That's what we did at Interpol."

Beau caught something in her voice. "Did?"

"I turned in my badge," said Maria. "Well, I still have the badge, but I resigned."

Cape's eyebrows rose behind his coffee cup.

"Sorry I didn't tell you," said Maria. "I called my boss before I came here—to tell him something important—but before I got a single word out, he demanded that I fly home..."

Cape figured she'd called about the rediscovered Rembrandt, but he kept silent.

"...when he finished his rant, I asked how much pressure he was getting to drop my investigation." Maria's mouth did a cynical dance and settled on a smile. "He didn't answer, so I asked where the pressure was coming from...then he threatened my job. When he finally took a breath, I told him I quit."

Beau ran his hands over his clean-shaven head. "How'd he react?"

Maria shrugged. "He's probably relieved."

"He didn't say anything?" asked Cape.

"I don't know," said Maria. "I hung up as soon as I said the words."

"Damn." Beau's tone suggested the same idea had crossed his mind, more than once. He raised his cup of coffee. *"Salud."*

"What will you do?" asked Cape.

"I have connections at the Policia Nacional through my father," said Maria. "And friends in the Carabinieri Art Squad in Rome—I always wanted to live there."

"Sounds like a plan," said Cape.

"It's an idea," said Maria. "For now, I'm a tourist enjoying her vacation."

"That's funny," said Beau, "because most tourists go to Fisherman's Wharf, drive across the Golden Gate, climb Coit Tower, visit Chinatown—"

"—we visited Chinatown," said Cape.

"—what they don't do," Beau continued, sparing a glance at Cape, "is hang out with well-meaning reprobates who think they're Dudley Do-Right."

"Hey," said Cape.

"What is this Do-Right?" asked Maria.

"He's a Canadian Mounty," said Beau. "Always trying to save the day, but too stupid—"

"—it's a cartoon," said Cape. "It's an old cartoon."

"His horse is smarter than he is," said Beau.

"I don't have a horse," said Cape. "And I'm not Canadian."

"He's always blowing shit up," said Beau.

"Now you're thinking of Wile E. Coyote," said Cape.

"No, I'm thinking of you."

"Okay, that's fair," said Cape. "But this time, I don't plan on blowing anything up."

"It's true," said Maria. "That is not part of the plan."

"That's the problem with plans, isn't it? Somebody always changes them." Beau watched a container ship slide under the Bay Bridge, then turned to Cape. "You know, the coffee in the squad room is free."

"And it tastes like it."

"Then don't get caught," said Beau.

51

"If you get caught, you're on your own."

Maksim Valenko spoke slowly and clearly, not because he was a patient man, but because he suspected the men sitting across from him were morons.

Ely and Pasha sat side by side on a narrow couch. Their knees were touching and they fidgeted like wayward students in detention.

Their discomfort began the moment they were shown into the office. Valenko had yet to arrive, so Ely suggested they sit in the chairs opposite the desk. Pasha refused, convinced the most feared man in the Russian *mafiya* might decide to impale them with a letter opener. After all, Pasha argued, to escape the police after vaporizing the guy with the garish shoes, they had ditched the car Valenko loaned them. Was there any doubt Valenko had killed for less?

Pasha suggested they sit in the love seat set against the wall of the office, which faced the desk from a distance and sat adjacent to a side door. With backs to the wall, no one could sneak up and strangle them, and if they decided to run, the door was right there.

Unfortunately, the love seat was really an overstuffed chair intended for one average-sized Russian gangster, not two brothers with long legs and short attention spans. When Valenko stepped through the other door and took a seat behind his desk, they were climbing on top of each other in an attempt to squeeze between the curved arms of the chair. Now they were trapped, pinned in place like two insects on display.

"I cannot risk a war with our associates in Chinatown," said Valenko. "But Freddie Wang took my nephew, so I must take something in return."

"We understand, *Pakhan*," said Ely.

"Just tell us what to do," said Pasha, glancing at the door.

"The first man from the robbery died in hospital, which is just as well. You eliminated the other man." Valenko chose his words carefully. "And though your approach was…unconventional…it was thorough."

"Sorry about your bodyguard's car," said Ely. "We'll pay you back—"

"—or him back," said Pasha. "We can pay him back."

"We'll pay someone back," added Ely.

"Anyone, really," said Pasha. "Tell us who to pay and—"

Valenko held up a hand. The two brothers stopped talking.

Though his first language was Russian, Valenko spoke several others, and his English was superb because he read constantly. He understood the power of history and had taken to reading in his adoptive language, to learn what came before so he could shape what happened next. Recently Valenko had discovered a word in the course of his reading that perfectly described the two brothers sitting in front of him.

Muttonheads.

These two were muttonheads of the first order. Slow-witted but quick to act, eager to please and prone to action. They would throw themselves at any task and bring absolute havoc to any situation. Setting them loose would be like lobbing a grenade into Freddie Wang's restaurant without any consequence of direct reprisal.

"What I want you to do is fairly simple," said Valenko.

"We're good at simple," said Pasha.

"Clearly," said Valenko.

"Tell us who—"

"Revenge is a young man's obsession," said Valenko. "I am more interested in justice."

"Should we be taking notes?" asked Ely.

"Definitely not." Valenko pressed his index and middle fingers against his temples. "Freddie took someone from me, but the only way to hurt Freddie is to take something from him. He will certainly make another attempt on the museum, and when he does, I want you there to make sure it's a complete disaster."

"We're good at disasters," said Pasha.

Valenko smiled.

"I'm counting on it."

52

Freddie Wang counted to fifty once the ghost left his office. Then he did it again.

And again.

At two hundred, he turned to Feng. "Check the hallway."

Freddie wasn't superstitious but was exceedingly careful, if not paranoid. The ghost could hear better than a bat and move as silently as a wraith. Freddie couldn't risk any eavesdropping on what he was about to say.

Feng returned and Freddie gestured for the twins to sit across from him. He stroked the belly of the golden Buddha on his desk and studied them with his good eye.

"You realize who this man works for," said Freddie.

"The ghost?" asked Fang.

"He is pale, but he bleeds red," said Freddie. "Never forget that."

Fang looked skeptical but didn't say anything.

"He works for the Triads," said Feng. "Doesn't he?"

"No, we work for the Triads," said Freddie. "Look at it this way—the Triads are arms that reach across the Pacific, and the tong gangs—our gangs—are the hands that squeeze the lifeblood from this city. This relationship gives the Triads influence in another country without direct interference with our business in Chinatown. As long as we deliver their share on jobs they recommend, we don't have to reveal the secrets of our underground economy."

Freddie fixed his minatory gaze on Feng, hoping at least one of them was bright enough to see where this was going. Both brothers remained silent.

"The ghost is nothing but a mercenary," said Freddie. "He was excommunicated from the Heaven and Earth Society."

"Why?" Fang knit his brows together wondering what possible offense could get a person kicked out of a crime syndicate.

"No one knows," said Freddie, "and no one asks."

"Why haven't they killed him?" asked Feng.

"They tried, many times." Freddie's smile was not a pretty sight. His rheumy eye bulged in its socket. "After the ghost killed twenty of their men, the Triads made a deal. The ghost works for them, on a contract basis. They stay out of his way, as long as nothing he does interferes with their business."

Feng's eyebrows were twin arrows pointing up at his spiky hair. "Is he interfering with their business?"

That was the right question, thought Freddie. *Maybe there was hope for this one, after all.*

"Since we're an extension of the Triads," said Freddie, "one could argue that if the ghost disrupts my business, he is messing with theirs."

"We lost two men," said Fang, parroting what Freddie had said earlier.

"Yes, Fang, we have," said Freddie.

"That seems disruptive to me," said Feng.

"Me, too," said Fang.

Freddie rubbed his hands together. "Now that we see the

problem, a solution presents itself." He took a long drag on his cigarette and exhaled through his nose, a wizened dragon contemplating his next meal. "The ghost works for a Beijing firm that specializes in the retrieval of lost antiquities, but this is merely a sidebar for a much bigger business that deals in all sorts of things. Weapons sales, domestic surveillance, counterintelligence, and, occasionally, global economic disruption."

Two blank stares suggested Freddie had slipped into giving a lecture. He boiled it down to the simplest argument he could make, if only to practice what he would say in his own defense when Beijing called.

"Some believe this company, which claims to be independent, is merely an extension of the Chinese government."

"What do you believe?" asked Feng.

"I believe China should stay out of Chinatown," said Freddie mildly.

He ran his finger through a trail of ash and studied the brothers' expressions for signs of discomfiture. Feng was first to take the hint.

"What if something happened to the ghost?"

Feng was indeed the smart brother. Fang may be loyal, but Feng might be cunning.

"It might discourage other visitors." Freddie's guileful smile was yellow from decades of unfiltered cigarettes. "If there was an accident."

Feng shrugged. "We are dealing with explosives."

"Well, then," said Freddie, "be careful." His black eye glowed. "Be very, very careful."

The brothers nodded to Freddie and then looked at each other, silently confirming what they just heard. They moved to stand, but Freddie waved them back into their chairs.

"We're not done."

Fang and Feng glanced at each other again. Neither had ever been in Freddie's company for this long. His reputation suggested shorter interviews were best, with less chance of him changing his mind or his mood.

Feng took a deep breath. "How can we serve?"

Freddie pointed a bony index finger at Feng's head. "Change your hair."

Feng's eyebrows collided in consternation. Clearly Freddie didn't understand the work involved in getting the spikes to hold. It had taken Feng almost an hour.

Before he could open his mouth to object, Freddie waved his hand at Fang.

"Or his hair," said Freddie. "I don't care which."

"You want us to look the same?" asked Fang.

"You do look the same," said Freddie. "I want you to look identical."

"Why?" asked Feng.

"It will annoy the ghost, maybe even confuse him," said Freddie. "And anyone else."

"Who else?" asked Fang.

Freddie cleared his throat until the gravel in his voice settled lower in his chest. "You heard me speak of the Little Dragon?"

The brothers gripped the arms of their chairs and brought their legs together until their kneecaps were touching.

"You look like you're about to wet yourselves." Freddie traced a pattern in the ash on his desk. "She is not the target. I want her preoccupied, it's your job to distract her."

"How?"

"By hurting someone else."

"The little girl?" asked Feng. "I thought the gho—"

"—a man," said Freddie, "who's stuck his nose in my business one too many times."

"You want us to cut off his nose?" asked Fang.

"No," said Freddie, "I want you to hurt his whole body."

"What if we kill him?" asked Fang.

"Then he'll be dead," said Freddie.

"What's his name?" asked Feng. "And what does he do?"

"He's a private detective," said Freddie, "and his name is Cape Weathers."

53

"Cape is counting on you," said Sally. "And I'm counting on you."

"What do you want me to do?"

Grace knelt on the tatami mat an arm's length away, her expression resolute but unafraid. Sally marveled at the young girl's ability to catch whatever life threw at her. She had not only regained her composure, she seemed ready for anything.

Resilience was the art of looking ahead at what could be, not back at what might have been, but it took most people a lifetime to learn that lesson. Grace had both eyes forward as if there was nowhere else to look. Maybe that was because nothing could ever look the same after what she'd been through.

Sally knew it was only a matter of time before Freddie connected the dots on the missing girl. Though the loft was nearly impregnable, someone with sufficient firepower could break in eventually. That seemed unlikely, but if Grace really had seen a ghost, Sally suspected he graduated from her alma mater. A venerable institution that did a fine job with reading, writing, and arithmetic, but which excelled at teaching its students how to circumvent trip wires, avoid booby traps, and kill with their hands.

Sally could break into a place like this, which meant that he could.

"I have a present for you."

Grace eyed the racks of weapons on the dojo walls. "A sword?"

"No," said Sally. "I already gave you a set of tonfa sticks."

"But a sword is so—"

"—much more likely to cut your hand off," said Sally, "if you haven't been trained."

"When can I learn?"

"After you master the sticks, the staff, and the knife, we can try the sword."

"So next week?" asked Grace, a smirk hiding in the corner of her mouth.

Sally smiled. "I did tell you that roosters should be confident, didn't I?"

"And smart," said Grace. "You said roosters are smart."

"Well, Little Rooster," said Sally, "did I mention they're also impatient?"

Grace lowered her chin but kept her eyes up. She had mastered the eleven-year-old skill of being deferential and defiant simultaneously. "So next month?"

"That sounds like a goal," said Sally.

"Can I learn how to use the sword in your room?"

Sally raised an eyebrow. "The *naginata* is a cavalry weapon. Do you know how to ride a horse?"

"Not yet," said Grace. "But I was hoping you could teach me."

"I don't have a horse," said Sally. "Only a visiting cat."

As if on cue, the black cat with the lightning scar padded across the floor and nuzzled Grace's elbow before climbing into her lap.

"Hello, Xan." Grace stroked the cat's back as a thunderous purr filled the room.

"Come with me," said Sally. "Bring the cat."

Sally stood and walked to her room. The *naginata* was mounted high on the wall. The blade was almost as long as the handle, weighted to be swung easily from a saddle.

Grace stood to Sally's left. The cat strutted over to the bed and jumped onto the mattress. It curled into a crescent and swished its tail back and forth. Sally gestured at the sword.

The folds in the ancient metal shimmered like ripples in a pond under a full moon.

"This was the sword of the greatest samurai in history," said Sally. "A woman named Tomoe Gozen."

"I thought only men were samurai."

"That was the tradition," said Sally, "but in twelfth-century Japan, during the Genpei War, a woman broke tradition and became a great warrior."

"I never heard that story before."

"I've been thinking about that a lot lately." Sally reached up and carefully removed the sword from its brackets. "This sword belongs in a museum, where people can learn its history."

Grace stared at the long blade but didn't try to touch it. "Where did you get it?"

"Someone gave it to me," said Sally. "After they took it from a museum."

Grace furrowed her brow. "It was stolen?"

"It was taken." Sally hefted the sword. "So, yes." She placed the *naginata* gently in Grace's outstretched hands, supporting it until she was sure the weight wasn't too much. "I used to think a sword like this should be free."

"Free?"

"Used in battle," said Sally. "But that was foolish. It's Tomoe's sword, not mine, and I'm not her." Sally shook her head and smiled. "I wanted to be her so badly when I was your age, but as much as I would love to wield this sword, it doesn't belong to me."

"And you don't have a horse," said Grace.

"It was selfish to keep it as long as I have."

"What are you going to do?"

"Return it to the museum."

Sally extended her arms, and Grace returned the medieval weapon.

"May I come?" asked Grace.

"No," said Sally. "Are you sure you're ready to go back there?"

Grace took a breath before answering. "I don't know if I'm ready, but I'm ready to go."

"I'm not sure that made sense," said Sally, "but I know what you mean."

"I want to be brave."

"Bravery is the acceptance of fear." Sally set the sword carefully against the wall. "Do you know what *The Tale of the Heike* says about Tomoe Gozen?"

"Is that a book?"

"A very old book," said Sally. "It says 'she was a warrior worth a thousand, ready to confront a demon.'"

"A demon?"

"Yes," said Sally, understanding the nuances between Japanese and Chinese mythology. "Like a ghost."

Grace glanced at the sword before returning Sally's gaze. "She sounds badass."

"She reminds me of you." Sally ran hand through Grace's hair.

"Do you think the ghost will come back," asked Grace, "to the museum?"

"Yes." Sally held the *naginata* steady in her left hand. "He'll come because he's afraid."

"Afraid?" Grace's eyebrows did a little dance. "Why would a ghost—"

"—he's not a ghost," said Sally. "He's a man. And men are always afraid of something."

"Always?"

"Usually."

"So not always—"

"—it's what motivates them," said Sally. "Fear of not being strong enough. Smart enough. Attractive enough—"

"—yuck."

"Tall enough—"

"—he's very tall—"

"—or clever enough," said Sally. "Whatever it is, it's the same drive."

"What—"

"—failure," said Sally. "The fear of failure."

Grace chewed on her lower lip for a while before saying, "I got away from him."

Sally nodded. "Which means you won…and he lost."

"And I got away from his men."

"Which means what?"

"He failed," said Grace. "Twice."

"Think about that," said Sally. "The ghost failed twice—"

"—because of me."

"Because of you." Sally squeezed Grace's shoulder. "Which means he's afraid of you."

Grace stood a little straighter and squared her jaw. "So I shouldn't be afraid of him?"

"It's okay to be afraid, as long as you remember that you're scarier than he is." Sally smiled. "Think you can do that?"

Grace took a deep breath and nodded.

"Good," said Sally. "Now hold out your hands."

Grace extended her hands, palms up and pressed together.

Sally took something from inside her left sleeve and placed it within the bowl of Grace's hands. It was a box two-by-two inches wide and less than an inch high, made of a black composite material. In the center was a red button encircled by a clear plastic ring, through which wires and diodes were visible.

The question on Grace's face was easy to read.

"Cape asked a friend to build this," said Sally. "The button lights up when you press it."

"When should I press it?"

"The next time you see a ghost."

54

Cape Weathers had never seen a ghost, but he often spoke to the dead.

His parents had shuffled off their mortal coils, but he still gave them an earful from time to time. There was something about speaking to someone, if only in his imagination, that helped organize his thoughts. It kept him honest, as if the revenants of his imagination were calling bullshit any time he started talking nonsense.

Sometimes his thoughts ran to people he'd never really known. As a reporter, Cape had been a war correspondent for years before taking over the city's crime beat. After seeing too many people killed in faraway places, he returned home, only to find dead bodies piling up in alleys, dumpsters, and shooting galleries around the city. Most of the dead had been powerless in life, so Cape tried writing about the people in power who could help but chose not to—it wasn't long before he discovered the pen is not mightier than the sword when somebody in power owns all the ink. He traded his pen for a license to cause trouble.

Now he had trouble of his own.

His allies numbered less than the fingers on one hand. His

opponents were everywhere and nowhere. They had infinite resources and the world's largest surveillance state behind them. If Cape wasn't being watched, he was certainly being followed.

He was a hot potato in a cold war that had nothing to do with him or his friends.

As he drove away from Maria's hotel, Cape wondered what the man hiding in the back seat of his car would say about power, politics, and paintings.

Cape had driven Maria back to the Fairmont Hotel after their coffee with Beau. He spotted the tail as soon as he turned onto California Street. A black Honda three cars behind, weaving more than it should to give the driver a view past the intervening cars.

Cape retrieved the H&K automatic from the glove compartment as he pulled against the curb in front of the hotel. Maria cocked an eyebrow but kept the conversation on their plans. Cape left his car on the street and walked her to the lobby, where they agreed on a time and place to meet later. By the time Cape returned to his car, it had been unattended for less than five minutes.

More than thirty thousand car thefts or break-ins occurred in San Francisco each year. Five minutes was plenty of time for mischief, but Cape never would have guessed he'd find a man squeezed onto the floorboards of his convertible.

The intruder was facedown, body tense, entirely dressed in black. His arms were over his head, collar pulled high. It reminded Cape of a kid playing hide-and-seek, squeezing his eyes shut to make himself invisible.

This felt like a plan gone awry.

The stowaway's intentions were clear. A bulge at the hip might be a handgun or something equally unpleasant. A wise man would walk away, but Cape was an impetuous man with the mind of a curious child.

He wanted answers.

The Fairmont was built on the crest of San Francisco's steepest hill, where Mason Street and California Street intersect. Cape was tempted to release the parking brake and watch the car roll down California Street until it reached the bottom and crashed into the bay.

Pedestrians would get hurt, and Cape would be all alone with his questions.

The car was a 1967 two-door Mustang convertible, the original blue paint faded by the sun and bruised by the city. Cape didn't have the best luck keeping his cars out of the scrapyard, so he wasn't picky about the color. The best part of having a convertible was how easy it was to swing his legs over the door and get behind the wheel. This came in handy when he didn't want to make noise opening a steel door that groaned with age.

Cape started the car and accelerated down California Street before the man on the floor realized what was happening. The sudden gravity of a street angled at thirty degrees squeezed the man's arms against his sides, and his body tight against the back of the front seats.

Cape gunned the engine, gripped the wheel with his left hand and slipped his gun under his left thigh. It wouldn't interfere with his driving but would still be a quick grab.

"Hi there," said Cape. "You might think I'm talking to myself, or an imaginary friend, because I do that sometimes." He reached back and patted the man on the buttocks. "But I'm talking to you."

The car caught the light at Powell Street and almost bottomed out when the cross street flattened the angle of descent, but Cape pressed his foot to the floor and the Mustang leapt through the intersection. It landed on its front wheels with a jolt and sped toward the next light.

"Why don't you sit up front with me?"

No answer.

"I'm very friendly," said Cape. "And these are foam-padded, twin bucket seats."

With a muffled groan, the man in the back did a push-up, struggling against the downward force of their descent. The car bottomed out on Stockton Street and the man's arms buckled. His face slammed against the floor.

"My bad." Cape spared a glance in his mirror to see if he'd lost the rear bumper. He eased up on the gas but kept his speed above the limit. "Oh, I should mention that if you try to use that thing on your hip, I'll punch the gas and spin the wheel, and the car will flip. Your call."

The man in the back seat managed to get up on his knees. Cape made eye contact through the rearview and saw the man was Chinese, with jet-black hair and a clean-shaven, handsome face. A thin trail of blood ran from his left nostril. Cape switched hands on the wheel, grabbed a handkerchief from his pocket and handed it to his reluctant passenger.

"Looks like that last bump got you," said Cape.

The man's expression was disconsolate, someone who realized he'd misread the numbers on his lottery ticket and wouldn't be this week's Mega Millions winner, after all. With a scowl that was mostly a pout, he climbed into the front seat.

Now that his passenger was riding shotgun, Cape slid the pistol from under his leg and pressed it hard against the man's knee.

"I wouldn't even have to slow down, but you'd carry a cane the rest of your life," said Cape. "What's on your hip?"

Cape inched the speed up as they rocketed past St. Mary's Square, a small park below Grant Avenue with a playground and benches. The homeless had commandeered the benches. A handful of parents encircled the playground as a gaggle of kids climbed ladders, slid down slides, and ran through the sand.

Cape's passenger twisted in his seat with an audible sigh and gingerly slid something off his belt. Cape kept one eye on the road and his speed in sync with the lights. As they crossed Kearny Street, the car jumped like a dolphin, rocking them both back in the seats.

The man held a Taser in his open palm. It was the size of a TV remote, a black plastic rectangle with a contoured grip and two metal electrodes protruding from the end.

"Toss it." Cape pressed the barrel of the gun into the soft flesh above the man's knee, which made him jump. A moment later, a glance in the side mirror confirmed the Taser was scattered in pieces in their wake. Cape withdrew the gun from the man's leg, then shifted the pistol to his left hand so he could steer with his right and hold the gun out of reach.

"What's your name?" asked Cape. "Mine is—"

"—Cape Weathers, I know." He gave a disconsolate sigh. "Fang, my name is Fang."

"Your nose stopped bleeding, Fang."

Fang dabbed at his nose to confirm the observation. "Thanks."

"If you don't mind my asking, what was the plan?"

Fang shrugged. "We didn't realize you drove a convertible until we started following."

"We?"

"Feng and I," said Fang. "He's my brother."

"Where is Feng?"

Fang craned his neck. "He should be behind us, but you're driving so fast."

Cape let the car roll across Montgomery and checked the mirror. Two blocks up the hill, a Honda Civic cruised through a yellow light.

"Black Honda?" asked Cape.

Fang nodded.

Cape kept his speed up to make sure the Honda stayed at least a block away.

"Why drive a convertible in San Francisco?" asked Fang. "It's not practical."

"Neither am I," said Cape, "when it comes to cars."

"It must get cold when the fog comes in."

"Freezing," said Cape. "There's a hole in the top."

Fang studied the analog dials on the dashboard. "How old is this car?"

"Older than you," said Cape.

"Why drive something like this?"

"Clearly, you're not a car person," said Cape.

"My car has a roof."

"When I bought my first car," said Cape, "it was just like this, but hadn't been restored. A beautiful wreck—scruffy, a little damaged, in desperate need of attention. We had a lot in common."

"This is your first car?"

"No," said Cape. "That got hit by a nice old lady in a Buick. Nobody hurt, but my car was totaled. Another car of mine flipped and crashed, one got blown to pieces by Russian mobsters, one drowned in the bay…"

"Your insurance payments must be horrible."

"I've been buying the same car again and again for years," said Cape. "It keeps things simple."

Fang looked sullen. "Convertibles are stupid."

"So your plan was to hide in the back seat, stun me with the Taser, and then what?"

"I would drive your car," said Fang, "and Feng would follow in his."

"That's a terrible plan," said Cape.

"No, it's not," said Fang. "This is a dumb car."

"I check the back seat of any car I get into," said Cape. "Professional habit. Didn't you see *Goodfellas*?"

"The movie?"

Cape nodded. "Joe Pesci hides in the back seat of a car, then when the guy he's after gets behind the wheel, Joe Pesci kills him with an ice pick."

"I never saw it."

"Doesn't matter," said Cape. "Your plan was shit."

Fang sat up straighter, annoyed. "We didn't have a lot of time."

"Why the rush?" Cape checked his mirror before giving Fang a sidelong glance. "You work for Freddie Wang, don't you?"

Fang's mouth opened and closed, but he didn't say anything.

"Freddie is an opportunist," said Cape. "He's impulsive; that's his weakness."

"He doesn't like you very much."

"He's jealous of my rugged good looks," said Cape, "because he looks like Gollum."

The corner of Fang's mouth rose a fraction before he clamped it back into place.

Cape grinned. "You saw that movie, huh?"

"All three," said Fang. "I was Legolas one Halloween."

"So tell me I'm wrong," said Cape.

"Gollum has more hair than Freddie."

"Fair enough." Cape turned onto Sansome Street. The Honda didn't make the light but was close enough to see him make the turn. "Where were you going to take me?"

"Freddie's restaurant," said Fang.

"For lunch?"

"No," said Fang. "To the kitchen."

"Where the knives are." Cape wiggled the fingers of his driving hand.

Fang shrugged apologetically. "And the cleavers."

"That's not very nice."

"Neither is shooting someone in the knee."

"I said I was friendly," replied Cape. "I never said I was nice."

Fang sulked against the door for the rest of the block. As they crossed Sacramento Street, he turned sideways to face Cape.

"Would you really have shot me in the leg?"

"Absolutely."

Cape slid his right hand off the wheel and passed the gun from his left with a sleight of hand that would have made Houdini proud. By the time Fang registered the movement, the barrel of the gun was pressed into the side of his kneecap.

"Hey."

Cape pulled the gun away from the knee. Fang began to exhale until Cape swung the gun laterally and pressed the barrel into Fang's crotch.

Fang shimmied in his bucket seat but had nowhere to go. He froze.

"Your boss is a bad man," said Cape, "but you already knew that." He cocked the gun and pressed it harder against Fang's balls. "Unlike your boss, I don't enjoy hurting people, but I like being hurt even less." Cape cut his speed to within the limit, then checked the mirror to track the Honda as it closed the gap. "If I didn't care about getting blood on the upholstery, I would have shot you already."

Fang licked his lips as if they were suddenly dry. "I believe you."

Cape uncocked the pistol and moved it away from Fang's terrified testicles.

Fang sighed audibly as the car passed through the next two

intersections. Cape returned the gun to his left hand as smoothly as before.

"Tell Freddie I'll stay out of his business if he stays out of mine."

"I don't think he cares about your business."

"The feeling is mutual," said Cape.

Fang looked through the windshield as if noticing the city for the first time. "Where are you taking me?"

"Same place you were taking me," said Cape, "to Freddie's restaurant."

Fang looked over his shoulder for his brother's car. There was only one vehicle between them. "I don't think that's a good idea."

"Your notion of a good idea was to kidnap me," said Cape.

Cape turned left and coasted for a stretch, then took another turn, continually checking his side mirror to make sure the Honda was on his tail. Fang slouched in the passenger seat. The convertible made another turn onto Grant, crossing Bush Street to pass through the Dragon Gate that marked the southern entrance to Chinatown.

The gate was an ornate archway that straddled the road, topped by a green-tiled roof and flanked by smaller, matching gates on either side for pedestrians. Tourists took selfies as they passed through the gate without realizing they were passing into a parallel world. A vital part of the city by day, and by night a playground for Freddie Wang's tongs.

Of all the restaurants with Hunan in their name, Freddie's hired the rudest waiters and most unwelcoming doormen. A front for laundering money and organizing crime in plain sight, the restaurant discouraged tourists from staying late. Cape had no intention of staying at all.

He pulled the convertible against the curb between a hydrant and a No Parking sign, directly in front of the restaurant. The doorman was as big as a frost giant and glared at Cape with an icy stare. Fang had sunk so low in his seat that only his jet-black hair was visible over the side of the door. The doorman spotted him and doubled down on his gelid gaze.

Cape reached across the front seat and opened the passenger door. "Goodbye, Fang."

"Freddie will think I talked."

"Freddie will know you failed," said Cape. "Get your story straight."

"I hate this car."

"Next time," said Cape, "I'll shoot you in the leg and you can limp into Freddie's office."

"Thanks a lot."

"You're welcome."

Fang stepped onto the curb and slammed the car door. "I was being sarcastic."

"Tell Freddie that if he wants to find me, I'll be at the museum."

Fang's eyes narrowed at the mention of the museum, but he didn't say anything. He made a petulant kick at the car door, then turned and stomped up the stairs. He pushed past the frost giant, through the front door. He didn't turn to wave or bother to give Cape the finger. He simply vanished inside the restaurant as if crossing a threshold from which there was no return.

Cape suspected Fang wouldn't live long. He wasn't cut out for this line of work. Maybe his brother was, but even Freddie's best soldiers rarely lived long enough to collect a pension. Most were orphans or troubled kids, recruited before they realized they had a choice. It would be nice to believe that someone like Fang could get out of this life, but history said otherwise.

Cape knew he didn't stand the ghost of a chance.

55

The ghost knew he didn't stand a chance of getting through the wooden door of the dojo.

The sliding door to Sally's loft must be opened by a puzzle lock, but if stories of the Little Dragon were true, she had been trained by the Triads. That meant nothing was as it appeared. Feints and deceptions would be built into the lock mechanism. Designed to render any intruder inert at her doorstep.

The skylight looked more promising.

The ghost had climbed halfway up the fire escape before he noticed trip wires near the top steps. Gossamer strands that might have been invisible if not for the full moon. Whether connected to an alarm or camera or hidden hazards, the ghost couldn't guess, but the best way to overcome an obstacle was to avoid it. He returned to the street, crossed to the adjacent building, and climbed.

From the neighboring roof it looked like a hop, skip, and a jump. The gap between the two buildings was narrow, the alley barely wider than a car. The ghost took three long strides away from the edge of the nearby roof and leapt across the abyss. His white robes billowed like wings as his silhouette eclipsed the moon.

He landed on both feet and tucked into a roll without breaking his momentum. His shoes were soft-soled and made no more sound than a cat's paws.

The skylight was shaped like a tiny greenhouse. On the far side of the roof stood a water tower, its wooden barrel resembling a watchtower in the moonlight. The ghost stared at the water tower for a long moment before turning his attention to the skylight. He was enjoying the Little Dragon's obstacle course but was on a tight schedule.

He lifted one of the hinged panels of glass that led into the loft and saw the wires immediately. The opening was wide enough, but there was no way to avoid brushing those spider strands. The ghost reached inside the sleeve of his robe and removed a narrow metal tube about six inches long. When held in a closed fist, it could be used to strike pressure points and disable an opponent, but the ghost used it now as a simple stick. He reached down and snapped his wrist to strike the nearest wire.

A sudden rush of air followed by *thwut-thwut-thwut* and darts no bigger than dragonflies crisscrossing the space below. *Thunk-thunk-thunk* as they struck the walls. An acrid smell assailed the ghost's nostrils, bringing back school memories and the required course in the history of weapons. The darts were tipped with a paralytic used in the Amazon jungle for generations. The poison would not have killed him, but the fall after he lost his grip just might.

The ghost smiled. This was the most fun he'd had since coming to America.

He lowered a leg through the opening but pulled it back as if he'd seen a scorpion.

That was too easy.

The ghost replaced the tube and removed a small packet,

which he unfolded to reveal a fine white powder. Taking some into his palm like a pinch of salt, he leaned through the window and blew across the powder, dispersing it into the air.

The lasers were visible immediately. Emerald beams as thin as a heretic's prayer.

The ghost wished he had time to find an elegant solution. To come and go without a trace. Instead he took off his jacket, untying the fasteners at the waist, careful of the battery pack knitted into the fabric, and slid the loose material off his torso. His alabaster flesh glowed in the moonlight.

He dropped his jacket through the skylight and jumped in after it.

The jacket tripped the lasers. *Shuriken* flew from the walls, spinning wheels of death that shredded the jacket as it fell. The ghost watched it all in slow motion as he plunged through its wake. He landed on his left foot and bent his right leg at the knee to roll sideways before a weighted net fell where he had been standing an instant before.

Silence.

His own breath and the susurrus of distant traffic were the only sounds in the loft. The ghost turned slowly and looked around the training room. The racks held enough weapons to besiege a castle. The hardwood floors shone below the skylight and receded into darkness.

The ghost moved toward the door at the far end of the room but stopped mid-stride as something caught his eye. Something on the floor at the periphery of the circle of light.

Two green orbs locked onto the ghost's red eyes.

A black cat hissed a warning before melting into the shadows, moving toward a door at the far end of the loft. The ghost took another step and examined his perforated jacket. He would retrieve it later. For now, he had a feline to follow.

He strode bare-chested through the door.

A short hallway led to two open doors. The ghost stretched his senses and listened to the undercurrents of the space, as he had been taught as a child.

Door number two.

He was almost at the threshold when the girl burst into the hallway.

Grace slid on her knees across the wooden floor. Her head was level with his knees, arms at her sides. The ghost rolled onto the balls of his feet as Grace snapped her right arm forward, releasing the tonfa stick clutched in her hand.

The ghost shifted his weight and the stick sailed past his right ear, through his long white hair, before crashing into the wall behind him. He pivoted on his left foot and swung his right leg in a broad arc aimed at the girl's head.

Grace caught his shoe with both hands and twisted it sideways.

The ghost's body had no choice but to follow the momentum of his foot. His face slammed against the wall, harder than he would have expected. He tasted blood as stars appeared in his peripheral vision.

He was impressed.

The ghost pushed off the wall and shook his head to clear it.

The girl reached into her left-hand pants pocket, fingers flexing as if she was trying to squeeze something. Her eyes were wide, intense rather than scared.

The ghost had seen more fear in grown men than he saw in this girl.

He grabbed Grace by the arm and lifted her off the floor. Her hand slipped out of her pocket and she kicked wildly.

That's when the ghost felt the skin on his back tear apart into tiny strips of agony.

He spasmed and dropped Grace as the cat clawed its way up his back toward his neck. His right arm whipped behind his head and grabbed the cat roughly, ripping it free of his flesh. He felt blood ooze along his spine as he hurled the ferocious feline into the air.

The cat cartwheeled and caterwauled across the wooden floor before landing on its feet at the end of the hall. It hissed menacingly but kept its distance.

Grace had almost reached the training room when the ghost caught her by the hair.

She spun and tried to kick his shins, but the ghost yanked her hair sideways and slammed her head against the wall. Her eyes rolled back and she crumpled onto the floor.

The ghost stood for a moment catching his breath, feeling the acid burn of the cat scratches as he inhaled deeply through his nose. He grabbed Grace by the ankle and dragged her through the door of the dojo. Her black hair spread across the floor like a veil taken by the wind.

When the ghost reached the center of the training space, he released his grip. Grace's leg fell to the floor with a leaden thump as he bent to reclaim his jacket. The perforated fabric was still caught in the net, illuminated by the moon through the skylight.

Barbs woven into the ropes shredded the white cloth further as he pulled it free, but the jacket held its shape. Nothing had fallen from the hidden pockets in his sleeves. Mapping the punctures against his torso and the corresponding internal organs, he was acutely aware that his jacket would be dripping red if he had kept it on and rushed his entrance.

The wiring inside his jacket had been exposed but seemed intact. Not that it mattered. Even if the museum security cameras caught him this time, he would be gone from this city before they looked at the tape.

He shrugged the jacket over his shoulders, the edges of the gutted cloth rubbing against the fresh gouges on his back. The ghost tugged absently at a frayed seam near his collar as he considered the body at his feet and reflected on his last meeting with Freddie Wang.

No loose ends.

He should probably kill her now.

The ghost frowned. He had hoped for more of a challenge. A great battle. Something visible enough to spark a legend. After all, what was the point of doing horrible things if no one was witness to the horror? A reputation was earned, never given.

His musing ended when the ghost caught a glimpse of something just beyond the edge of the net, half in shadow and half-lit from above. Something he missed when he first hit the floor, displaced by the falling jacket. He took a cautious step into the light until the object was at his feet.

It was a little dragon.

Origami with such intricate folds that scales running across the wings and down the tail seemed to move as clouds passed overhead. It was three inches tall and four long, the dragon's head raised in defiance, the tail coiled like a spring.

The ghost snatched it from the floor with his thumb and middle finger, then turned it over in his hands. It was beautiful. On its left side, a single Chinese character had been drawn with a brush.

The ghost thought it resembled a human figure. At the top was a rectangle-shaped head with a cowlick and tiny cross for the face, standing on two jaunty legs, one foot thrust forward and bent at the ankle. Next to the figure was a sideways-*V* shape, perhaps an arm bent at the elbow. No one else interpreted the character in that manner—it was a series of lines that any

Chinese child could draw—but for the ghost it symbolized the only identity he'd ever known.

Guǐ.

The man called Guǐ had never known his real name. He was a ghost, a rumor, a phantom. And yet, the woman called Little Dragon knew he was real. She knew that he was here, now. And why. She knew that he could bleed, which meant she understood he was flesh and blood.

It made Guǐ feel almost human.

He unfolded the paper dragon. It was crafted from a map of San Francisco. A circle was drawn around the area near city hall, and a big *X* marked a spot he had visited twice before. The Asian Art Museum sat at the heart of the little dragon he held in his hand.

Guǐ smiled. It was time.

56

It was time for Cape to get ready, but as he drove away from Freddie's restaurant, he decided to take a detour.

Something was off. His encounter with Fang was a stark reminder that Beau was always right. No matter how good your plan might seem, someone or something always comes along to ruin it. Cape gave himself thirty minutes to drive and think, hoping the crisp wind off the bay would bring an epiphany instead of the fog.

It didn't.

Chiffon tendrils of white spread across the road as Cape turned west along the Embarcadero. Traffic was light near the mini-mansions of Marina Boulevard. Cape veered right onto Mason Street. A road less traveled at night, it abutted the small-est of the city's beaches, Chrissy Field. Long grass that crested the sand splayed across the road. The lights of the Golden Gate were visible through tenuous fog.

Cape heard the barking of a dog but couldn't find the animal or the owner. Whitecaps caught the moonlight as waves swept rhythmically onshore twenty yards to his right. There was no way Cape was not going to walk on that beach, if only for a few minutes. He checked his mirrors and looked for a spot to pull over.

That's when Cape realized he was still being followed.

The Honda was only a hundred feet behind him. Its headlights were off, but a break in the fog gave the moon a chance to reveal how careless Cape had been.

Fang was Plan A, which meant Feng must be Plan B.

Cape watched the Honda close the distance in his rearview mirror. The man behind the wheel looked identical to the man Cape drove to the restaurant. Either Fang and Feng were twins or Freddie was running a bootleg cloning operation.

Cape accelerated. The road was devoid of traffic. If he could get enough distance and speed, he could pull the parking brake, spin the wheel, and turn the car one hundred eighty degrees. He meant to play a game of chicken, but first he had to cross the road.

He never got the chance.

Cape spun the wheel and the tires screamed in protest as the car drifted in a tight arc. His left hand gripped the wheel tightly as the centripetal force pressed him against the door. He whipped his head around to spot the other car as his own changed direction.

The Honda was closer than expected, but that wasn't what worried Cape.

Feng was smiling. He was also driving with one hand. In his other was a small rectangle, its details blurred by speed and lost in shadow. Cape knew it was some kind of remote control, because he saw the red light flash as Feng pressed a button.

The explosion turned the world upside down.

The charge must have been magnetic, easy to place in a hurry. Feng had simply waited until his brother was out of the car and Cape was on an isolated stretch of road. The rest was timing. Cape's maneuver had given Feng the perfect opening.

The convertible was already spinning and skidding in a high-speed turn when the blast snapped the rear axle in half. It felt as if the rear of the car was slapped by a petulant giant.

Cape was shot from the car like a man from a cannon.

He was airborne and accelerating before he remembered he wasn't wearing his seatbelt. Cape flew backward to the apogee of his doom.

His car was growing smaller when the gas tank exploded and the convertible shuddered in a paroxysm of angry physics. The car flipped, sparks igniting the tarmac as it tumbled and burned.

Cape did an involuntarily backflip and was upside down when his car bounced off the road into the long grass, setting it ablaze. His rotation continued until he was looking straight down, parallel to the road, when gravity took him by the hand and pulled. Cape couldn't tell if he was going to land on the road, his car, or the beach. He just knew he was going to hit hard.

His descent seemed quicker than his ascension, and somehow more deserved.

57

Maria knew she deserved to get fired but it felt so much better to resign.

Her boss was *un imbécil,* but that was not why she burned bridges all the way back to Barcelona. She could have outlasted a bureaucrat with misogynist tendencies—he certainly wasn't the first Maria had encountered in her career. She knew her incessant insubordination was going to get her sacked eventually.

She resigned because she didn't know who she was working for, and that made her uneasy. Any organization like Interpol was subject to political pressure, but her boss had become a puppet. The wires moving his hands and the hinges opening his mouth might not be visible, but they were there, and Maria didn't want to spend her career trying to cut them.

Maria loved her job.

She never thought about art as mere stolen property. An expensive canvas taken from a well-endowed museum makes good headlines, but people never see the real crime. Like burning a book or censoring a newspaper, it chips away our humanity. One of the few things that brings people together is not only lost from view but expunged from memory.

Steal a painting and you erase an idea.

Maria believed that, and she wanted to work with people who felt the same way. She had been willing to put up with a lot to work in art crimes, but she wasn't willing to work for the people she was investigating. Even a master forger couldn't paint over a lie that big.

Maria paced around her hotel room, a tiny bottle of water from the minibar held loosely in her right hand. When she reached the window, she pivoted on her heel and caught Rembrandt staring at her. His expression hadn't changed since the last time they made eye contact. Maria raised her bottle in a toast to the Dutch master and resumed pacing.

She was anxious to get going. Cape should have arrived by now.

Maria smiled at the thought of her unofficial and unconventional colleague. He was impulsive but inspired, reckless but relentless. Had Cape been her partner at Interpol, Maria had no doubt he would've been fired long before she got the boot. She didn't know if he cared about art at all, but he cared enough about a little girl whom he barely knew to risk his life.

He was free to do whatever he wanted, yet he chose to do what no one else would.

The only time Maria ever felt that free was the moment she quit her job. She glanced at her open suitcase, where her Interpol badge lay on top of her clothes. She looked at the photograph of her younger self and saw a determined woman with big plans but little insight into how the world actually worked.

Maria picked up the badge, flipped it facedown, and checked her watch. Something was wrong. There was too much at stake to be late. She set her drink on the desk and looked imploringly at Rembrandt.

Rembrandt kept his mouth shut.

Thunk.

Maria jumped at the sound. Instead of knock-knock-knock, it was a dull thud against the door. She crossed to the peephole and contorted her right eye until it focused on the blurred figure in the hallway.

"*¡Mierda!*"

Maria unchained the door and tore it open.

Cape tumbled forward as if he'd been leaning heavily on the door. Maria caught him clumsily with both arms. They stood nose to nose just long enough for things to feel awkward and intimate simultaneously.

Cape sucked in his breath and winced, ruining the moment.

Maria retreated by a step but kept her right hand on his shoulder, holding him steady. Parallel crimson streaks raced from beneath his chin up the left side of his face, converging at his hairline, where a dried patch of blood congealed over a deep gouge. Two blue-gray eyes shone with intensity, pupils contracted from an adrenaline surge that hadn't yet waned.

His shirt was untucked and spotless, totally incongruous with the rest of his appearance. Maria slid her hand from Cape's shoulder and gingerly tugged at the front of the shirt until she could peer over the gap at his bare chest.

"Is that duct tape?"

"Yes." Cape swatted her hand away, but not before Maria noticed the ring finger and pinky on his left hand were taped together, encircled by the same color of duct tape that girded his chest. "They say it has a thousand and one uses."

"Such as taping dislocated fingers," said Maria.

"And securing broken ribs." Cape forced a smile, which only made the furrows on his cheek more livid. "Sorry I'm late."

"What happened?"

"I forgot to check my side mirrors." Cape gestured at the minibar. "Do you mind?"

"Good idea."

Maria stepped to the small refrigerator and returned with a pocket-sized bottle of whiskey. She poured three-quarters into a glass which she handed to Cape, then drained the remainder of the bottle herself. Cape sat on the edge of the bed, took a long pull, then hissed through his teeth on the exhale. He pressed his left hand against his side about halfway up his torso and took a tentative breath. The duct tape crinkled audibly, and Maria imagined it was the sound of bone grinding against bone.

"Turns out beach grass is very resilient," said Cape. "Nature's own trampoline."

"You look like you got mauled by a tiger."

"I got tricked by a twin." Cape gave a cursory description of his unexpected detour.

"You should have gone to the hospital," said Maria.

"I'd be there all night," said Cape. "Walked to my office instead."

"Is that where you got the tape?"

Cape nodded. "I got something else, too. A clean shirt and…" He stood shakily and pulled the H&K nine-millimeter from his waistband. "Dug this out of the sand, figured you'd want to borrow it again." Laying the compact pistol on the bed, Cape pulled up his shirt with the fingers on his left hand that could still bend. "And this was in my desk drawer." He reached behind his back with his right hand and produced another handgun.

It was a Ruger .357 revolver, chrome with a three-inch barrel. A squat, angry gun that looked like a bulldog and barked like a mastiff. Cape tossed it on the bed next to the semiautomatic.

"Now we both have a date for the evening." Maria took a step forward and picked up the H&K. In one fluid motion she hit the thumb release for the magazine and racked the slide, checking to see if there was a bullet in the chamber. She slid the magazine back into the butt of the pistol and clicked on the safety. She studied Cape for a long moment before saying, "But maybe we go tomorrow."

"No." Cape took the Ruger and holstered it at the small of his back. "They came for me today, which means they'll make their move tonight."

"You might be concussed."

"That would explain the throbbing behind my eyes."

"Then we should call Beau," said Maria. "The police—"

"—have to play by the rules," said Cape.

"The police could secure the paintings."

"Then the bad guys might leave town."

"Is that so bad?"

"They'd come back, only we'd never know when." Cape took a deep breath and grimaced as the tape strained against his ribs. He slowly exhaled, keeping his breath shallow. "They'd come back for something...or someone."

"Yes." Maria swept aside a rogue ribbon of hair and looked at Cape. He was doing a valiant job standing and not passing out, but she could see the strain on his face. Their eyes met, and she gave him a winsome smile.

Maria crossed to the side of the bed and stepped in close. Before Cape could react, she rolled onto the balls of her feet and kissed him lightly on the lips.

Maria was back across the room before Cape could blush.

"What was that for?" asked Cape.

Maria shrugged. "I'm going to call you Santo Jude from now on."

"Why?"

"He's the patron saint of lost causes," said Maria, "and impossible missions."

"Like Tom Cruise?"

Maria shook her head. "Not exactly."

"She's only eleven," said Cape.

"I know." Maria glanced at Rembrandt, who looked bemused and a bit jealous. "It was never about the art for me, either."

"It's a good plan," said Cape. "Don't you think?"

"It's a terrible plan," said Maria.

"Well," said Cape, "let's go find out."

58

"Let's go find out how it works," said Pasha.

"There isn't time," said Ely. "Isn't that what you told me?"

"Maybe we should just use a handgun." Pasha glanced at the weird weapon in the back seat of their stolen car.

Valenko had refused to loan them another car after they abandoned the red Camaro, so they stole an Audi Q7 from the parking lot at Whole Foods. Ely felt guilty their theft would force a busy mom to call an Uber to bring her gluten-free, organic, and responsibly sourced groceries home, but Pasha insisted they were in a hurry.

Ely had asked, "How do you know it's a mom's car?"

"Think about it, it's an Audi SUV—"

"—still, I'm just saying—"

"—parked at a grocery store—"

"—seems kind of sexist—"

"—in San Francisco."

"Maybe it's a dad's car," said Ely. "Or maybe there are two dads."

"Or two moms," said Pasha. "Who gives—"

"—exactly, there could be—"

"—who cares?" Pasha spun the wheel and caught the curb pulling out of the lot. "Say we stole a dad's car. Does that make you feel more inclusive?"

"I'm just saying you shouldn't generalize."

"I don't care if it's a mom's car, a dad's car, a car owned by two dads, a car leased by two moms, or a car driven only on Sundays by a group of nonbinary caregivers," said Ely. "I only care that it has four wheels, gas in the tank, and it's big enough to hold that monstrosity in the back seat."

Ely gave no rebuttal and remained silent until they approached city hall from the west.

When Pasha suggested they test the weapon, Ely was taken aback. "You said we were running late."

"I think we are," said Pasha. "We don't know when Freddie's men will arrive, so we might be early, too, but it's been dark for hours."

"Then what's the problem?"

Pasha pulled against the curb and killed the headlights.

To their right was city hall, a conical mausoleum where the hopes of a city lay buried. The lost souls of San Francisco held a midnight vigil in the public square, open flames flickering like forlorn fireflies in dozens of homeless encampments. Above them the lights of the dome shone red, casting a bloody pallor across the square.

Pasha shifted in his seat to look his brother in the eye. "The problem is...that thing in the back seat scares me."

"*Rasslab'sya, brat,*" said Ely, half-smiling. "It's more epic than the rocket launcher."

"That's what worries me," said Pasha. "Your missile not only blew up the guy in the ugly sneakers, it blew out the window of our car and almost killed a *politseyskiy.* If we kill a cop, even Valenko can't protect us."

"You told Valenko we would cause a disaster," said Ely. "That thing in the back seat is a portable act of God."

Pasha looked over his shoulder at the weapon. "Where did you get it?"

"Same guy who got me the bazooka," said Ely. "He went to high school with our cousin Damien, they played football together. He used to be a halfback, now he's an arms dealer."

"At least he got a good job," said Pasha. "Damien still lives with his mother."

"You really want to test the weapon?"

Pasha shrugged. "Explain how it works, so I know where not to stand when you use it."

"Nothing to worry about," said Ely. "Unlike the bazooka, there's no blowback with this thing. I'm not sure there's any kick, either."

"You're not sure...that's what worries me."

"Look." Ely stretched over the seat and grabbed the weapon with both hands, angling to avoid Pasha's head. He laid it across his knees and ran his hands across its sleek surface. "Isn't it cool?"

It resembled a ray gun from a Flash Gordon cartoon. A bulbous and contoured rifle with a space-age aesthetic that looked both fantastic and formidable. The grip and stock were a textured composite material; the barrel was made from a matte gray alloy that gleamed in the wan light of the car. Twice as wide as a shotgun but half as long. Near the trigger at the top of the grip was an arrangement of buttons in red, green, and blue.

"It looks like a toy," said Pasha. "What did you call it again?"

"Hold on, I wrote it down." Ely pulled a crumpled piece of paper from his pocket. "The U.S. military calls it a laser-induced plasma channel generator."

"Say that in little words."

"It shoots lightning bolts."

"Like Thor's hammer?"

"Exactly like Thor's hammer!" Ely rubbed his hands together. "Now you get it."

Pasha looked impressed. "That does sound pretty cool."

"It's very cool," said Ely. "This toy shoots a laser that rips electrons from air molecules to create a beam of pure plasma."

"How big a laser?"

"You know how a light bulb at home might be sixty or a hundred watts?" asked Ely. "The high-intensity laser generates fifty billion watts."

"*Bez shutok?*"

"No kidding," said Ely. "But it only works for short distances, maybe twenty yards, and takes a while to recharge between blasts."

"Lightning bolts." Pasha's eyebrows rose in admiration.

"Right?" Ely was giddy. "You want to hold it? It's lighter than it looks."

"We should give it a name."

"Like *Mjölnir*?"

"Is that Thor's hammer?"

"Yes, don't you remember from the comics?" asked Ely. "Or the movie?"

"I could never pronounce that," said Pasha. "When one of Freddie's bandits points a gun at me, am I supposed to shout, 'hey, Ely, electrocute this asshole with mee-ow—'"

"ME-OLN-ERE."

"Not happening."

"How about…the hammer gun?"

"Sounds like a nail gun," said Pasha. "Try again."

"The shocker?"

"Lame."

"Plasma pistol."

"Not bad," said Pasha, "but it's a rifle, isn't it?"

"Fine," said Ely. "Lightning gun…my final offer."

"Lightning gun?"

"Yes."

Pasha chewed on the name. "Hey, Ely, shoot that bastard with the lightning gun!"

"Not bad."

"I could say that," said Pasha, "but we can do better."

"Okay…let me think."

Neither brother spoke for two minutes. Pasha stroked his chin.

Ely finally broke the silence with a reverent whisper.

"The Bastard Blaster."

"Ely," said Pasha, "you're a goddamn genius."

Ely patted the Bastard Blaster with pride.

Pasha peered through the windshield at the constellation of lonely people dotting the square. "I don't think we can test it." He took his foot off the brake, eased off the curb with the headlights off. "Look, there."

"What?" Ely scanned the park but saw nothing unusual until he looked across the square at the Asian Art Museum.

Three figures approached the museum from the direction of a large monument to the right of the main building. They hadn't been there a moment before, as if three statues trapped on the monument had torn themselves free. Two of the figures were silhouetted by security lights shining down from the museum's balcony. The third figure glowed.

He was taller than the other two, illuminated from above by the full moon, which shone through a small tear in the night fog. Ely wondered if he was seeing things, until he turned and saw the expression on Pasha's face.

Pasha looked like he'd just seen a ghost.

59

The ghost looked from Feng to Fang and back again, silently cursing Freddie Wang.

The twins were truly indistinguishable now. Feng and Fang wore matching leather jackets over black pants, their handsome features impassive under identical haircuts, slicked back from broad, unlined foreheads with no visible scars or wrinkles. They could have emerged from a cloning machine.

Guǐ told himself it was a minor annoyance. He could shout one of their names and see which brother jumped, intimidate them into telling him who was whom, or give them a quiz to determine which brother had the quicker wit. Yet once he handed explosives to the supposedly smart brother, the ghost would have no way of keeping track of them when things were underway.

Freddie wouldn't openly sabotage the operation, but Guǐ should have known the choleric crime boss wanted him off balance. Freddie had been forced to play gracious host to an albino interloper from the Middle Kingdom.

Freddie's only kingdom was Chinatown, and he intended to keep it that way.

The ghost cared nothing for Chinatown. He cared little for Beijing, beyond what they paid him. Their newfound obsession with heritage was comical, given how often they rewrote history. He knew their precious art collection was nothing more than misdirection, a political smokescreen, but Guĭ had spent a lifetime seeing through the mist.

Now he stood in a city enshrouded by fog, but his path forward remained perfectly clear. Guĭ might be a killer and a thief but he had integrity. He would steal the art as promised, cement his reputation, abandon this backwater, and return to Hong Kong.

His original plan was to make this an elegant robbery. An incendiary distraction near Fisherman's Wharf would draw police away from the museum just long enough for the ghost to secure the paintings. In and out with style, just like Norway.

But Freddie's ego demanded he mark his territory. He clearly didn't believe the ghost answered to Beijing or the Triads, and he wanted to send them a signal. He wanted to play games.

Freddie failed to realize the ghost was very good at playing games.

Now that the heist had lost any subtlety, it made no difference if one brother was smarter. Both were expendable. Not only that, explosions could occur anywhere. Once things started to go boom, fire trucks would be dispatched. Police would come running but keep their distance until special units could be deployed. Minutes lost. Whether terrorists or gas leaks, explosions slowed things down just long enough for a thief to vanish in the night.

Freddie wanted the ghost to leave his city, fine. He would leave it in ruins. But first he had to deal with the problem of the Little Dragon.

The ghost had brought Grace to the museum and held her

now, not indelicately, in his arms. She regained consciousness once during the trip over, but pressure on the nerve cluster at the base of her neck put her down again. Hard to gauge with adolescents, but he estimated another fifteen to thirty minutes before she opened her eyes.

He looked at the three boxed forgeries on the ground to his left. They were light enough to hoist up to the balcony after he'd climbed the balustrade. He was originally going to enlist one of the brothers to help steal the real paintings, but now he didn't trust them at all.

Guï shifted Grace's inert body and hoisted her over his shoulder, then pulled the strap of the cloth bag slung over his back. He reached inside and removed three hockey pucks, then handed them to the twin on the left. The ghost grabbed three more, which went to the other brother.

Fang and Feng turned the disks over in their hands.

The hockey pucks had been hollowed out, the centers packed with C-4 plastic explosives. The side of each disk had a small red button connected to a fuse on a five-second delay. The blast that had turned the private detective's car into a flying hibachi was triggered by remote detonator, a much more sophisticated device. By contrast, these disks were makeshift grenades which demanded a delicate sense of timing and an ability to run very fast in the opposite direction.

The ghost smiled at the simplicity of his new plan.

Guï raised a cadaverous arm and gestured down the steps of the museum. With a dramatic flourish he extended a pallid finger across the square, over the heads of the homeless. He pointed directly toward San Francisco City Hall.

Fang and Feng followed his line of sight to the crimson dome.

"You see that building?" asked the ghost.

The two brothers nodded, wide-eyed, but didn't say anything.

The ghost pointed at the brother on his left. "I want you to blow it up." The other twin opened his mouth, but the ghost held up a pale palm. "You...will carry the forgeries and come with me."

"To do what?"

"You're going to blow up the museum," said the ghost. "From the inside."

60

From inside the museum, it was obvious to Sally why the helicopter thieves had thought it would be smart to break through the skylight.

She counted at least nine points of entry across various sections of glass at the Asian Art Museum. Windows made the building more welcoming and displayed the art in a natural light, but they introduced several vulnerabilities.

The helicopter had been brazen but unnecessary. Sally managed to climb onto the roof using a grappling hook and knotted rope. It wasn't easy but wasn't particularly hard, either.

The masterminds who recommended a helicopter clearly watched too many action movies or simply didn't know the city. Sally suspected the plan was to transport the stolen art quickly, and loading paintings into a van would leave them exposed on the street. That might be problematic in a town with routine police patrols, but San Francisco's budget cuts had led to a shortage of uniformed cops that kept the downtown streets deserted after dark.

Stores had been looted so incessantly that plywood covering the windows was installed permanently. Half the storefronts were empty and had been for over a year. The few businesses still operating downtown cut their hours so their staff could leave before sunset. The only people on the streets were those who had already lost more than anyone could take.

The city by the bay had become a ghost town.

Now all we need is a ghost.

Sally walked across the first floor of the museum, past the gift shop, until she came to the Wilbur Grand Staircase, a marble marvel of craftsmanship regularly featured in society pages and countless wedding photos. The staircase was broad enough for six people to walk abreast, each step shallow, so climbing to the second floor took much longer than taking the escalator on the other side of the museum.

The stairs were flanked by walls of amber marble. Overhead was an arched, coffered ceiling of illuminated hexagons. At the top of the stairs a golden chandelier overhung the second-floor landing.

A stone balustrade surrounded the staircase on three sides, low enough for anyone to peer over the edge. Sally held the ancient calvary sword at her left side and scanned the gaps between the banister's pillars as she climbed.

Cape was waiting at the top of the stairs.

"You're late," said Sally. "What happened?"

"There was a bonfire at the beach," said Cape. "I volunteered to be one of the s'mores."

"You're hurt."

"Yep." Cape glanced down the empty staircase, then back the way he had come.

"Where's Maria?" asked Sally.

"Finishing up in the security room, making sure the code also disabled the cameras from recording."

"This plan of yours—"

"—isn't going to work," said Cape. "I know."

"We're out of time," said Sally. "And you're hurt." She waited until Cape wheezed his next breath. "Badly."

"There's no downside to trying," said Cape.

"There's a downside to dying."

Cape ignored the jibe. "The plan had three parts—distract, delay, and capture."

"The capture part involved police cooperation," said Sally. "Which you don't have."

"I have a new plan," said Cape. "Distract, delay, and—"

"—kill."

Cape frowned. "I was going to say 'chaos.'"

"I like my plan better," said Sally.

"Let's focus on the first two parts of the plan, okay?"

"Let's check the gallery."

As they moved away from the staircase, Cape asked, "What's the big deal with these paintings again?"

"I thought Maria explained it already." Sally half-smiled. "Using little words."

"She did," said Cape, "but I might have been distracted."

"By her, or by the case?"

"No comment."

"Going to pay attention this time?"

"You can quiz me later."

"Nineteenth century," said Sally, "toward the end of the second Opium War. The Summer Palace is already being looted by foreign soldiers when a British contingent arrives in Beijing, thinking they are going to negotiate China's surrender. But things don't go as planned, and the emissaries are imprisoned and tortured."

"Ouch."

"Needless to say, the British don't take the news well."

"So they attack the palace."

"Not just attack," said Sally. "British and French troops

ransack the palace grounds, which were considered the pinnacle of Chinese culture at the time. Countless pieces of art, sculpture, jade, and silks looted or destroyed. The palace was so extensive it took four thousand men three days to trash the place."

"Maria said the art is scattered across more than fifty museums today."

"That's why it's such a big deal," said Sally. "Anything taken during the 'century of humiliation' is considered by the government to be the rightful property of China."

"Maria said the same thing, but why does a communist government give two hoots about artwork from an imperial dynasty?"

"They didn't—until they realized the people did."

"Portable patriotism."

"Yup." Sally nodded. "These paintings depict China when it was the envy of the world. Interest in traditional art was soaring when I lived in Hong Kong, and that was a long time ago."

At the mention of Hong Kong, Cape asked, "How's Grace?"

"At the loft."

"I said how, not where." Cape studied Sally's expression. "Not like you to second guess."

"My instinct was to keep her close," said Sally, "but if we're outnumbered—"

"—which is likely—"

"—and they bring guns—"

"—almost a certainty—"

"—then I don't want her out in the open."

"No one could break into your loft," said Cape.

"I could," said Sally.

"Not on the first try."

"Maybe."

"Besides," said Cape. "He'd come here first."

"That's what I thought," said Sally. "Now I'm not so sure."

61

Fang was not so sure that blowing up the city hall building was the best use of his time.

His brother was inside the museum with the ghost, a man who would not hesitate to abandon or kill either one of them to effect his own escape. Fang didn't work for the ghost. He worked for Freddie Wang, and his instructions were clear—appear cooperative but undermine the ghost at every turn. Come back to Freddie bearing gifts or don't come back at all.

Fang reached the bottom of the steps and crossed the street to the park that lay between the museum and city hall. He debated whether to stay on the street and walk half a block north around the grass, until he noticed a path which ran straight through the center of the square. Ribbons of fog disintegrated when they hit the stone. The grass was crowded with sleeping bags and bonfires, but the cement trail was unobstructed.

Somewhere overhead was a full moon, but it was a diffuse gleam behind the downy fog. Fang imagined God pressing a pillow over the face of the city, a mercy killing before a fresh start.

A muffled voice called from the shadows as Fang passed the

first bench on the right. Fang was startled but unafraid since he was holding three bombs. He paused mid-stride to scan both sides of the path. A pile of clothes on the nearest bench shuffled with a low moan.

A man more gray than pale sat up, rubbed his scraggly beard, and stared at Fang.

"Whatcha doin'?"

The voice was hollow, as if the lungs couldn't be bothered to send enough air past the vocal cords. The figure was so non-threatening that Fang ignored any instinct to brush off the stranger or walk away. Instead, he answered truthfully.

"I'm going to blow up the city hall building."

"Got a name?" The man swayed as if caught in a breeze that Fang couldn't feel.

"Fang—"

"—m'name's Frank."

"I'm in kind of a hurry, Frank."

Frank scratched his beard, then raised both hands and ran his nails back and forth across his scalp. "Need any help?"

Fang glanced over his shoulder at the museum and wondered what his brother was doing. He looked across the square and tried to guess how long it would take to walk there, climb the steps, then find a way inside. Security was always lax in these old granite buildings, and city officials never worked nights or weekends, but that didn't mean a back door was left open for his convenience. He could lob a hockey puck through one of the windows, then run back to the museum to help his brother.

Then again, anyone could throw a hockey puck through a window.

Fang gave Frank an appraising look before saying, "Sure, that would be great."

Frank scratched his beard again and stood. Half the rags fell away onto the bench; the others were draped over his shoulders like memories he couldn't quite shake. "Let's go."

The two walked along the path a few feet before Frank tapped Fang on the shoulder and disappeared into the shadows. He returned a moment later accompanied by a younger man whose rust-colored hair peeked from under a gray hoodie.

"Who's this?"

"Billy wants to help, too."

Fang shrugged and kept walking. Twenty feet later a similar scene played out. Frank faded into the gloom, whispers and murmurs followed, then he reappeared with a friend in tow.

By the time Fang had gone halfway across the park, he led a nomadic band of two dozen discarded souls, their eyes locked on the blind, closed windows of city hall. Fang didn't know how they ended up here, whether through some failure in the system or some fault of their own, but he could hear in the rhythm of their steps a dogged determination to confront the building ahead, even if it was empty.

Fang stopped and turned to face the group. He had gone far enough.

Frank stood closest, his eyes bright. Fang handed him the hockey pucks and explained how the buttons worked. He pointed out the plastic explosive and made it clear that dropping or throwing the disks before you were ready was a bad idea. He ran through it a second time to make sure nothing went boom before he could return to the museum.

Frank passed the second bomb to a small woman standing on his left.

"This is Maggie, she used to be a softball pitcher."

"That's great." Fang smiled awkwardly at Maggie, who gave him a thumbs-up.

Fang felt like he should say something—make a speech,

inspire the troops—but the threadbare throng looked to Frank, not him.

"Well, thanks for the help," said Fang.

"Thanks for the opportunity," said Maggie brightly.

A murmur of assent swept through the ranks.

"Thanks for the plastic explosives." Frank held out his hand. "See you on the other side."

"Yes," said Fang as he shook hands. "See you on the other side."

62

Grace swam to the other side of consciousness with a sudden rush of adrenaline.

Her eyes shot open, and her nostrils flared as her lungs sucked in as much oxygen as they could. She had a sense of being fully awake with no recollection of how, why, or when she'd fallen asleep.

Then she remembered.

Grace heard blood rushing in her ears and a rhythmic tattoo against her skull as her pulse quickened. She took another deep breath and told herself not to panic, but the room started spinning. Then the room started swinging back and forth, and Grace realized why she was so disoriented.

She was hanging upside down.

A rope had been tied around her right ankle. Grace was suspended ten feet off the floor. Her arms were akimbo, her long hair pointed at the floor, her left leg dangled at an awkward angle. Her right leg was numb where the rope encircled her ankle, and her arms felt thick from gravity's pull on her blood.

She closed her eyes and took two more deep breaths, then

opened them and twisted her neck slowly, trying to get a glimpse of her surroundings without swaying.

She was in a gallery at the museum. Grace recognized it instantly from the late nights with her uncle. This was where all the special exhibitions were held, artwork on loan from other museums or private collections.

It was a large room, a square twenty meters wide on each side. Paintings were hung in curated groupings on each of the walls. The floor was a choreographed maze of pedestals, false walls, and tables adorned by pottery, sculptures, and religious artifacts made by people long dead for cultures lost to time.

Grace bent at the waist and tried an inverted sit-up to reach her ankle, but she could see how elaborately the knot had been tied. She wished she had a pocketknife or sword from Sally's dojo. She patted her pants pocket and realized she did have something. The button Sally had given her was still there. It hadn't worked at the loft, but maybe she hadn't pressed hard enough. She worried nothing could hurt a ghost, but it gave her a sense of satisfaction to not have lost it.

Grace swiveled her shoulders to rotate clockwise, craning her neck in all directions.

Empty space...paintings...marble floor...teapot...rhinoceros...vase...more paintings.

Grace was nearest the east wall, mere feet away from four paintings she recognized from a history lesson at school. Views of the Old Summer Palace. She wracked her memory for the name of the closest painting. Something about the past and present. She stretched her arms toward the painting, wondering if she could swing closer to the wall.

Her center of gravity shifted as she started to spin. Panicked, Grace flapped her arms like wings, hoping to counter the rotation. She froze when she heard footsteps. Someone was coming, but she couldn't tell from which direction.

All Grace could do was swing back and forth, a solitary pendulum with nowhere to hide.

63

There was nowhere to hide beyond the shadow of city hall, so Ely and Pasha felt relieved when Freddie Wang's soldier stopped in the middle of the park to confer with his homeless allies. When he turned and headed back to the museum, the Russian brothers bumped fists in the dark.

"*Prevoskhodno*," said Ely. "All clear."

Pasha gestured at the threadbare throng headed toward the building.

"What about them?"

"Not our problem," said Ely.

Pasha peered across the park at their receding nemesis as he climbed the steps of the museum. "Let's wait till he goes inside, then count to ten and follow."

But Ely was already walking briskly along the perimeter of the park.

Pasha jogged to catch up. "*Pritormozi brat.*"

"We don't want to miss any of the fun," said Ely.

Their quarry stepped through the front doors as if the museum was open to the public. Pasha marveled at the deserted streets but knew this had become the rule and not the exception for nonresidential neighborhoods. The city barely had enough cops to watch the neighborhoods where the politicians lived.

Pasha glanced at the ray gun in his brother's arms as they walked.

"You sure you want to use that thing?"

"What are you worried about?" Ely raised the Bastard Blaster heroically over his head.

Pasha pointed at the weapon. "That's what I'm worried about."

"Relax, brother," said Ely. "What could possibly go wrong?"

64

Maria tried counting all the things that could possibly go wrong and gave up after she reached a dozen. She may have quit Interpol but couldn't stop thinking like a detective.

There were too many variables in this case—and far too many players—to control the outcome. Maria was trained to plan for every contingency, cut off every escape, and follow every lead to its logical conclusion. Work the angles, set a trap, and execute.

That was a case, but this was a circus.

Maria liked the circus, but she was starting to feel like a trapeze artist without a net. She glanced around the security room, double-checking each monitor to make sure none of the cameras were recording.

That's when she noticed the figures moving rapidly across the screens.

Two men coming in through the front door, one holding a bulbous rifle. Another man rode the escalator on the far side of the museum.

Maria spotted a fourth man crossing the main floor, heading toward the staircase. He must have entered through the exit door located near the security room she was in now. If he took the stairs, that would put him close to the special acquisitions gallery on the second floor.

Maria glanced at the monitor covering the gallery and froze.

Grace was spinning at the end of a rope. Cape and Sally were in the hallway near the entrance. And inside the gallery, moving toward the girl, was a white cloud of smoke.

Maria was still a cop at heart.

She ran to the end of the control panel, grabbed the phone, and dialed 9-1-1. She didn't bother to wait for the dispatcher. She left the receiver on the desk and the phone off the hook. Then she thumbed the safety off her gun and opened the door.

65

Ely and Pasha opened the museum door in time to see Fang reach the top of the escalator.

Fang stepped onto the second floor landing, turned toward the galleries, and glanced over the railing as he walked. He spotted Ely and Pasha coming through the main entrance.

Fang and Pasha made eye contact.

Pasha cursed under his breath.

"I told you we should have counted to ten before we followed him."

"Too late now, brother." Ely squinted at a button on the grip of his rifle.

Fang drew a handgun from behind his back and took aim over the balcony.

"What are you waiting for?" Pasha smacked his brother on the back. "Blast that bastard!"

Ely lowered the rifle, grabbed Pasha by the sleeve and yanked him sideways, pulling him diagonally across the lobby to a corner behind the escalator. They were out of Fang's line of sight but could hear him muttering in Chinese as he tried to decide whether to continue to the galleries or descend the escalator and start shooting.

"We're sitting ducks," said Pasha. "Why didn't you blast him?"

"It's charging," said Ely.

"Charging?"

"It takes a lot of power, Pasha." Ely checked to see if the green light was illuminated. "Why didn't you draw your pistol?"

Pasha looked at his shoes. "I left it in the car."

"What?"

"I got distracted, okay?" Pasha kicked at an imaginary rock. "The people in the park—"

"—where is it?"

"Underneath my seat," said Pasha. "Where's yours?"

Ely cradled the rifle like a newborn. "I have this baby."

Pasha scowled. "If that doesn't work, I'll kill you."

"If this doesn't work, we're both dead." Ely craned his neck to peer at the balcony without exposing his body. "He hasn't come down…do we follow?"

"No way, he's got the high ground." Pasha pointed across the lobby toward the back of the museum. "Stay close to the wall, there's a staircase in back."

They left the main entrance and escalator behind and were passing the gift shop before they noticed a man standing directly ahead of them. He was about twenty yards away, his back to them, facing a woman who was pointing a gun at him.

The man's right hand was raised as if he'd been frozen mid-throw.

Ely and Pasha stopped in their tracks as the woman caught sight of them. Without changing her aim, she jutted her chin in their direction.

"*Quien son ustedes?*" she asked. "Who the hell are you two?"

Pasha leaned closer to Ely. "I think we should answer her—"

"—she's very attractive," said Ely, "and stylishly dressed—"

"—and she has a gun." Pasha raised his voice. "I'm Pasha, this is Ely."

"Hi, Pasha and Ely, I'm Maria." The woman tilted her head but the gun never wavered. She held her shooting stance like a cop. "What brings you to the museum?"

"We work for Maksim Valenko."

If raised eyebrows were any indication, the woman recognized Valenko's name.

It also got the attention of the man striking the Statue of Liberty pose. His raised arm didn't move but he twisted his head like an owl and looked over his shoulder.

Ely elbowed his brother and hissed under his breath. "That's the Asian guy from the escalator."

"How'd he get here so fast?" asked Pasha. "He's not even out of breath."

"He looks very fit," said Ely, "maybe he has a good cardio regimen."

"No way," said Pasha. "We were walking pretty fast, and he'd have to come downstairs."

"Maybe he's a clone."

"There aren't any clones, *tupoy*," said Pasha. "Maybe he's a twin."

"Same thing."

"Wait," said Pasha. "What's that in his hand?"

The man was holding a black disk.

From Ely's vantage, the man's thumb was plainly visible, sliding back and forth over a red button on the side of the disk. The woman named Maria couldn't see the button, which meant she didn't notice when the roving thumb pressed down, the skin under the nail turning pale from the pressure.

When the red light started to flash, Ely was the first to react. "Pasha, *move*."

The man with the hockey puck pivoted on his left heel and threw sidearm directly at the Russians. Pasha scurried to the left while Ely lunged to the right.

Maria fired. The shot went wide and ricocheted off the marble floor.

The echo bounced between the stone walls like a racquetball. Ely wondered fleetingly if Maria was a cop, and if she'd been reluctant to shoot a man in the back. Maybe she aimed for his leg and missed. Either way, she missed.

Ely scrambled on his hands and knees into the gift shop.

The hockey puck slid down the middle of the floor. The red light blinked faster.

Pasha crouched against the wall on the left. Ely slid under a table filled with calendars. When the disk reached the spot where they'd been standing—the midpoint between them—it exploded. The acoustics of the lobby turned the blast into a concussive wave of pure pressure.

Glass shattered on either side of Ely, bouncing like raindrops off the marble floor. Pasha tried to stand but staggered against the wall and pressed his hands to his ears. Maria fell to one knee. She swayed but held the gun steady in her right hand while the other hand cupped her left ear.

Maria tried to get a bead on the bomber, but he started running the moment he made the throw and disappeared up the broad staircase before she could take a second shot.

A second explosion reverberated from somewhere far away. It sounded like thunder. Ely wondered if it was raining outside, then worried he might have a concussion.

Maria lowered her gun, spared a last glance at the Russians, then stood shakily and followed up the stairs. She disappeared from sight, her footsteps echoing off the marble walls, but Ely could barely hear them over the ringing in his ears.

66

Cape didn't hear any footsteps because the echoes of the gunshot and the boom from the explosion were still reverberating around the museum.

The ragged sound of his own breathing didn't help. His broken ribs had turned into saws.

He started to turn away from the gallery toward the stairway when Sally's hand closed around his arm like a vise. Her expression was a warning to keep his mouth shut.

Sally was one step ahead, at the threshold to the special exhibitions galley. Cape moved sideways at an oblique angle to glance over Sally's shoulder into the room, expecting to see a theft-in-progress.

He didn't expect to see Grace hanging upside down.

She was twenty feet away, ten feet off the ground near the east wall, spinning slowly. Between the door and Grace was a low table on which a variety of teapots were displayed, each carved into the shape of an animal from the Chinese zodiac. Four feet beyond that was a pedestal five feet high supporting a stone carving of a rhinoceros.

As she rotated away from the wall, Grace caught sight of

Sally and frantically waved her arms to slow her rotation, but that didn't seem to work. Sally raised a finger to her lips before they lost eye contact. Grace nodded and remained silent as she rotated clockwise.

Sally took a step back from the door and pressed her lips against Cape's ear, careful to keep the curved blade of the *naginata* at arm's length.

"There's someone in the gallery."

Cape's whisper was barely audible. "Someone who isn't upside down?"

Sally nodded and extended the index and middle fingers of her free hand, inverting them to represent a human figure. She pantomimed a makeshift plan, interrupting her own narrative periodically to point at herself or Cape. It took less than a minute, but by the time she finished, they could hear the faint echoes of footsteps on marble stairs.

"We don't have much time," said Cape.

Sally's expression was grim. "Neither does Grace."

67

Grace's expression was grim, but she looked happy because her frown, like the rest of her, was upside down.

Cape could only imagine his own expression as he clenched his jaw against the serrated agony of his ribs. Once he charted a clear path across the gallery floor, he plowed forward as fast as possible, acutely aware that he was racing Sally. His legs fought a losing battle with gravity.

Gravity needed a win, because Sally was kicking its ass.

Cape ran diagonally toward Grace while Sally took two loping strides to the left, bouncing on her toes like a high-jumper approaching the bar. She held the long sword parallel to the floor as she sprang onto the low table, landing on her right foot in a narrow space between two teapots. Without losing momentum or touching the table with her other leg, Sally leapt onto the small pedestal, somehow finding purchase for her foot without wrecking the rhinoceros.

Then Sally debunked Newtonian physics altogether.

Cape was keeping pace when she launched herself off the pedestal. Her body flattened as her leg snapped back, the long sword extended like a spear as she vaulted higher. At the apex she bent at the waist, rolled into a forward somersault, and swung the *naginata* sideways.

The blade was a silver whisper that sent a chill down Cape's spine. He marveled Sally hadn't severed the girl's foot at the ankle. Sally landed on both feet, bounced like she had springs in her heels, and kept running deeper into the gallery.

Cape fell to his knees like a supplicant directly beneath the plummeting girl.

Grace tried to do a sit-up in midair, instinct telling her to protect her head, but she was still inverted when Cape caught her. He fell backward to dissipate the momentum, his legs bending at angles that made his knees want to look for another job.

His skull banged against the marble floor as Grace's head bounced off his broken ribs like a toddler on a trampoline. Cape saw stars as he craned his neck sideways to get a closer look at his catch. Grace's smile was right-side-up despite the fear in her eyes.

She rolled off his chest and one of her knees caught Cape across the bridge of his nose.

"I'm s—"

"—don't worry, it was already broken." Cape rolled onto his side to get his knees under him and stand, but the added weight against his ribs sent him coughing and wheezing like an asthmatic at an anthrax party.

By the time he got it under control, Grace was patting him on the back.

"Did you swallow something bad?" she asked.

"Only my pride," said Cape, gasping.

"Thanks for catching me."

"Thanks for dropping in."

Grace spun around, looking for Sally. "We have to leave, there's—"

"—someone else here."

Cape stood on wobbly legs and rested a hand on Grace's shoulder. He nudged her sideways and put himself between her and the gallery entrance.

Grace had been looking in the other direction, trying to see past the exhibits to spot Sally, but now she glanced at Cape. She followed his gaze and realized why he had shifted their positions, and why his other hand was drifting slowly toward the gun on his belt.

A man was standing at the entrance watching them. He had malice in his eyes and hockey pucks in his hands.

"That's Fang." Cape raised his voice so the man could hear. "Or Feng, it's hard to tell."

"You should be dead," said the man.

"I get that a lot," said Cape. "Feng?"

The man nodded.

"What does he want?" asked Grace in a whisper.

"Me, dead," Cape said under his breath. "Aren't you paying attention?" Then, more loudly, "I'm glad it's you and not your brother."

"Why?" Feng moved his arms fractionally and shifted his weight to his rear foot.

"I kind of like your brother," said Cape. "And you killed my car."

Feng's right arm swung away from his side but stopped moving when he saw the gun. Cape cocked the hammer on the revolver. The metallic click was unexpectedly loud in the cavernous space.

If this encounter had occurred the day before, Cape might have appealed to Feng's sense of reason by saying how reluctant he was to shoot someone, or by mentioning how unsympathetic Feng would seem if he threw a bomb across a room full of priceless antiques at a girl less than half his age. But a lot had happened in the last twenty-four hours.

Cape's car was dead. His ribs were broken. An eleven-year-old got hung upside down like a duck in a restaurant window. Cape sighted down the barrel and increased pressure on the trigger.

With his eyes on Feng, he spoke quietly to Grace. "Get ready to ru—"

A boom followed by a crash made Feng flinch before Cape could fire.

Cape felt Grace tugging frantically at his shirt. He eased his finger off the trigger but kept the hammer back and the Ruger raised as he traced the sound of the crash to a fallen column and shattered vase.

Standing among the shards of porcelain stood Sally. Her right arm was holding the cavalry sword like a javelin. Her left arm was bleeding. She backed toward them, feet sliding noiselessly across the marble floor.

Ahead and to the right of Sally, something moved behind a row of life-sized statues of mythological deities and demons. It was difficult to discern a definite shape as the shadows shifted between the statues. Cape had a vague sense of flowing robes and white mist.

Then he saw the ghost.

Cape felt cold fingers run across his scalp. He wasn't superstitious but couldn't deny the pale poltergeist brought a chill to the room. A primal reaction to seeing a figure from folklore manifest in the real world.

Sally pivoted slowly so her right foot was behind her and her left closer to the ghost. She angled the sword so it pointed toward the floor at a thirty-degree angle. The ghost's right arm shot forward, the cuff of his robe billowing and flaring from the motion.

A flash of silver flew past his open palm as a long ribbon emerged from his open sleeve. The triangular blade at the end of the ribbon flew at Sally's face like an angry arrow. Sally leaned back as if she was doing the limbo as the blade flew over her head.

The ghost spun his wrist to make the ribbon snap like a whip, which made the blade spin like a medieval flail. Sally twisted her hips and swung the *naginata* across her body.

Her blade caught the ribbon but didn't cut through.

Before the ghost could react, Sally spun her sword, yanking him closer. The ghost staggered, smiling as he regained his footing. He looped the ribbon around his wrist and tightened his grip. It was a tug-of-war to determine who would be left standing once the blades were freed.

A test of balance had begun.

Cape sensed movement on his left and realized too late he'd been distracted by the battle. Watching the wrong bad guy. He turned in time to see Feng whip his arm in a sidearm throw.

Even if Cape shot Feng, it was too late. The black disk with the flashing red light slid across the floor as if the marble was a sheet of ice.

Cape wondered how many seconds they had left before they died.

68

Maria wondered how many seconds she was running behind the mad bomber as she reached the landing halfway up the stairs. She also wondered how many bombs he had left.

He had turned right at the top of the stairs and disappeared without looking back. Maria worried he might throw another bomb down the stairs, but either he figured his lead was sufficient or he was saving his explosives for something else.

Maybe he was arrogant enough to believe she was too shaken from their first encounter to give chase. Unlikely, but just the thought of being underestimated pissed her off.

She took the remaining stairs two at a time.

At the upper landing she stopped and crouched behind the balustrade, pausing long enough to control her breathing and peer around the stone wall. The second-floor corridor led to a large open door, which must be the entrance to the special exhibitions gallery. Inside the gallery she could see the bomber, only he wasn't moving. Faint echoes made her think he was speaking to someone, but he stood as if frozen in place.

Maria moved cautiously around the balustrade and jogged quietly toward the gallery, staying close to the wall. She heard the smack of shoes on the stairs behind her and remembered the two Russians. Clearly, they were also undeterred by the gangster's grenades.

It seemed everyone had unfinished business with Freddie Wang's soldiers.

A voice inside Maria's head demanded to know what the hell she was doing, rushing headlong into danger. She was deliberately putting herself between two opposing forces, Chinese gangsters ahead and Russian mobsters behind. If they both decided she was a bigger threat, Maria was the meat in a murder sandwich.

There were two women named Maria, it seemed. The Maria who came to San Francisco less than a week ago was bold, even impulsive, but never reckless. She would spend days behind her desk, filling in all the necessary paperwork to get warrants, tactical support, and, if necessary, a strike team.

Maria decided that version of herself had a much better chance of staying alive, but she wasn't really living. Process and procedures took spontaneity off the menu, and now that the second incarnation of Maria had a taste of adventure, she was hungry for more.

She glanced over her shoulder, but no one crested the stairs. Maria figured at least half a minute before the Russians joined the party. She moved at an angle toward the gallery door.

She was twenty feet away when she got a sickening sense of déjà vu.

The bomber pivoted on his heel and swung his arm sideways. Maria saw the disk fly from his hand, the red light blinking, and wondered who was the target. Deep in her gut, she already knew the answer. Maria sprinted toward the door.

She counted down the seconds, but Maria feared Cape had finally run out of time.

69

Cape knew he had run out of time but prayed he hadn't run out of luck.

There was nowhere to hide in the open space of the gallery. Even without broken ribs, he could never outrun a skating hockey puck. All he could do was play goalie.

The trick was staying between Grace and the blast.

Cape looked for a pedestal or statue big enough to work as a shield, but even the rhinoceros sculpture was tiny. When the disk was halfway across the room, he decided the only defense was a good offense. Cape shoved Grace behind the table displaying the teapots. Then he ran directly at the bomb.

The flashing red light on the disk beckoned like a siren with a switchblade. Cape met it halfway to the door.

Feng was thirty feet away. There was no way to bend and grab the disk while running, so Cape did the only thing he could manage. He planted his left foot and kicked with his right.

The inside of Cape's shoe hit the hockey puck like a slapshot and sent it airborne.

Feng froze in disbelief. Cape tore his eyes away from the flying bomb and ran. He stumbled, caught his knee against the low table, and crashed across the top, turning teapots into ceramic shards.

Cape fell onto the floor next to Grace and rolled to cover her head with his arms. He was tall enough for his feet and the top of his head to extend beyond the edges of the table, so he caught a glimpse of Feng as the hockey puck reached its goal.

The disk struck Feng in the solar plexus.

He caught the puck with both arms, trapping it against his stomach at the precise moment the red light stopped blinking. Cape locked eyes with Feng as time ran out.

The blast punched a hole in Feng the size of a dinner plate.

The compression against his torso and shape of the charge channeled the blast into a perfect circle. Feng's insides went outside by way of his back, exiting the gallery through the main entrance.

For a macabre moment Feng just stood there. Then he fell on his back in a crumbled heap of charcoaled chagrin.

"Yuck."

Cape glanced down to see Grace peering around the corner of the table. He extended his arm to block her view with his open palm.

"Don't look."

"Too late." Grace pushed his hand away and scrambled to her feet. "Besides, I'm almost twelve." Cape groaned and rolled onto his stomach. It took a second to get his knees under him.

They both looked toward the spot where Sally and the ghost had been moments ago. Neither was visible, but sounds of a struggle echoed behind the row of statues at the back of the gallery. Cape's skull was buzzing from the concussive force of the blast, but he could still hear, and he didn't like the sounds of ragged breathing and feet slapping against the marble floor. He had never known Sally to struggle against an opponent.

The thought was a cold hand wrapped around his spine, trying to hold him back. Cape knocked it aside and started to move. Maria ran into the gallery, and Cape felt the same hand wrap around his heart.

Maria was covered in blood.

Their eyes met and Cape realized her expression was worried, not pained. The blood wasn't hers. Maria smiled in relief as she saw Grace.

"What happened to you?" asked Cape.

"I got hit by a spleen," said Maria. "Nice kick, by the way. You should play football."

"You mean soccer."

"I refuse to call it that." Maria looked over her shoulder at the hallway. "We're about to have company…Valenko's men."

Cape's eyes darted to the back of the gallery, where shadows fought behind a row of stone gods. "Can you cover the door?"

Maria nodded.

Cape drew his gun and started to move. Grace stayed by his side. He paused mid-stride, intending to send her back to Maria, until he remembered that heavily armed Russians were on their way.

The truth was that Grace wasn't safe anywhere. Not with Maria, not hiding in the loft, and not running next to Cape.

She would never be safe until they ended this.

70

Sally wondered how this was going to end.

She spent her childhood training in the martial arts, from the age of five until the moment she left the Triads. Her parents were taken along with her innocence, but she never felt alone. Death was her constant companion.

Death stayed close during her years of treacherous training, and Death opened her eyes to the betrayal that had brought her to the Triads. Even after she left, Sally knew her ally never left her side.

Now wounded and bleeding, Sally realized Death had many friends, and she couldn't help but wonder if the grim reaper played favorites. This battle felt like a stalemate until Sally lost ground to the ghost and a lot of blood along the way. It only made sense that she wasn't the favorite anymore. Sally had changed, but Death was constant.

The ghost was as expertly trained as Sally, and though she hated to admit it, he was stronger. He had the advantage of height, weight, and reach, and unlike most men, he didn't lean on them for confidence. He used them for leverage.

He pulled Sally off balance several times during their tug-of-war, and being off-kilter was fatal in martial arts. Only by lunging and retreating, spinning her sword, and slackening her grip, was Sally able to regain her footing and keep her distance.

The long ribbon with its deadly blade had finally been cut. It lay on the floor between them like a severed tentacle. The instant it fell, the ghost reached behind his back with his left hand and snapped his arm sideways, hurling three razor-sharp flying stars at Sally's head. She twisted sideways as two sailed past, but the third *shuriken* bit deep into her arm.

The ghost wounded the same arm previously with his flying blade, but now Sally felt the burn subside and wondered if he dipped his *shuriken* in narcotics. The ghost wouldn't hesitate to tip the scales by handicapping an opponent. Sally stepped sideways, careful to avoid a congealing puddle of her own blood, and tried to use her injured arm while she still could.

She kept a ten-foot radius between her and the ghost. The embers of his eyes glowed with amusement, as if this was the most fun he'd had in a long time. He mirrored her movements and kept his eyes on hers. As Sally circled, he bent his left arm as if preparing another throw, though his skeletal hand was empty.

Sally dropped into a crouch, her left hand brushing her waist before sweeping outward in a broad arc. Her fingers were tingling and would be numb soon, but she still had enough dexterity to return the kindness shown to her. Three metal darts flew from her hand like silver dragonflies.

One sailed past the ghost on his right. The second cut a thin gash across his left cheek, and as he spun on his heel, the third caught him in the left shoulder at the joint. He staggered backward and grimaced, a Bela Lugosi smile of agony and admiration.

"I understand why you left the society." The ghost moved counterclockwise in their tight circle, his ruby eyes full of mirth and malice. "But what I don't understand is why we're on opposite sides."

"You're wondering why I should care about a few stolen paintings." Sally shifted her stance to compensate for the heaviness of her left arm. "I didn't, not until you tried to kill a friend of mine."

"I've heard the stories." The ghost rotated his left shoulder, where a red orchid was seeping through the white of his jacket. "What you did for the Triads."

Sally bowed her head. "Your resumé isn't too shabby."

"Then tell me, Little Dragon," said the ghost. "Do you really believe saving a little girl will wash the blood off your hands?"

"I don't mind blood on my hands," said Sally, "as long as I'm the one who puts it there."

Sally spun the *naginata* like a baton until it was a whirlwind. She didn't want the ghost to know from which position she would attack.

The ghost attacked first. He seemed to withdraw from the spinning sword until he rolled forward on the balls of his feet. His left arm moved so quickly it was a blur. A second flying blade emerged, attached to a red ribbon flowing from his sleeve like a river of blood.

Maybe he is a ghost.

Sally had never seen anyone move that fast, especially someone with a wounded shoulder. She almost fell backward, barely catching herself with the hilt of her long sword. She began to regain her balance but heard the whistling of the blade on its return and collapsed onto one knee as it whooshed over her head. Severed strands of her black hair fell to the floor.

The ghost swung his left arm faster and faster, turning the blade into a scythe, seemingly oblivious to the crimson on his robe. He swung the weapon just fast enough to keep the blade aloft as he guided it lower and tighter.

The scratch on his cheek beaded red as his parchment skin tightened in concentration.

Anything that bleeds can be killed, even a ghost.

Sally had to strike before she got shredded, but the ghost held the high ground. She braced her right foot and shifted her weight from her left knee, looking for an opening, but it was like staring into a spinning fan. She could feel the breeze from the blade as it got nearer her head.

That was the moment Sally heard the squeak of sneakers running on marble.

She recognized the diminutive footsteps and wanted to turn, but Sally kept her eyes on the specter in front of her. She adjusted the grip on her sword and tensed the muscles in her legs.

As she prepared to jump, Sally wondered if she was about to die with Grace.

71

Grace almost died when she saw Sally bleeding.

The red streaks across Sally's clothes felt like cuts across Grace's heart. She started to move, but Cape put a heavy hand on her shoulder.

"You'll get her killed."

He and Grace had rushed past the row of statues before realizing how expansive this part of the gallery was relative to the area where they had left Maria. They slid to a stop twenty feet from the fight, with Sally between them and the ghost. The wrong position at a critical time. The long row of scowling gods and leering demons looked down on them, stone sentinels bearing witness to their failure.

Cape raised his gun and cursed under his breath.

Grace was terrified what would happen if Sally moved when Cape pulled the trigger. The spinning ribbon and oscillations of the ghost made it impossible for Cape to get a clear shot, even though Sally was on her knees. Grace felt her mouth go dry and palms start to sweat. She rubbed her hands up and down her thighs and tried to breathe.

Grace cried out as the heel of her right hand caught against a sharp edge.

She frowned and slid her hand gingerly into her pocket. Between hanging upside down and watching a man explode, she had forgotten about the plastic button. She tugged it frantically from her pocket with her right hand while smacking Cape repeatedly with her left.

Without lowering his gun, Cape spared a glance and realized what she was holding.

"*Push it.*"

He didn't have to tell her twice.

72

Twice Grace pressed the button with both thumbs, as hard as she could.

Nothing happened.

Sally found an opening and shifted her weight. The ghost saw her tense and retreated a step. Cape lined up a shot and gripped the revolver with both hands, one eye closed.

Sally vaulted into the air. The ghost crouched and raised his arm to swing his blade on an intercept course with Sally's neck.

Grace shook the plastic box and pressed the button a third time.

The button glowed red and Grace felt a buzzing in her palms. The ghost glowed with electric light that danced up his sleeves and down his torso, tracing the wiring in his jacket.

Rivers of neon flowed from shoulders to hips, and the ghost spasmed involuntarily, his face contorted with rage. His shoulders became rigid, his arms flew backward, and the spinning blade missed its mark.

Sally soared and swung her sword in a savage arc.

The long, curved blade of the *naginata* caught the ghost at the base of the wrist. His left hand spun through the air as if waving goodbye.

Without the ghost's gaunt fingers clutching the ribbon, the blade flew across the room and landed in a heap at the feet of an uncaring god. Sally landed in a crouch behind the ghost and pivoted for another swing.

The ghost spun on his heel, a geyser of blood marking the circumference of his turn. Before Sally could finish her swing, a roundhouse kick from the ghost's right leg struck her shoulder, knocking her off balance.

The ghost scurried behind the nearest statue, which was an aristocratic female figure holding a fan in one hand and sword in the other. Cape took a shot and the goddess lost her nose.

The ghost disappeared. Sally ran after him, with Cape and Grace in close pursuit.

The ghost darted between exhibits with a speed that belied any injury, dodging pedestals and leaping over tables as if they were hurdles. The electric aura dissipated, but his white robes were charred where wires had singed the fabric. He sprinted toward the gallery exit without looking back. He clearly intended to fight another day.

Sally closed the gap to less than ten feet. Cape and Grace were twenty feet behind. The ghost crossed the threshold and headed for the main stairway.

That's when he saw Maria, flanked by two Russians.

They stood left of the gallery entrance, immediately visible in the broad hallway, with its bright marble walls and well-lit vaulted ceiling. The ghost seemed to glide across the stone floor as he accelerated toward the main staircase.

Maria didn't even try to raise her pistol. By the time she could line up a shot, he'd be gone. She turned instead to her two companions, waiting for her cue.

Maria nodded, and Pasha smacked his brother fiercely on the arm.

"Ely, blast that bastard."

Ely held the rifle against his waist like a cowboy in an old Western. He pivoted slowly to track the movement of the ghost and, after a quick glance at the buttons on the grip, pulled the trigger. A primordial bolt of plasma erupted from the barrel.

The streak of lightning scorched the air to ozone.

It was impossible to look directly at the energy beam and just as hard to aim. Ely yanked the jagged beam across the marble as if dragging an electric snake by its tail.

Sally skidded to a halt. Cape and Grace did the same. There was no way to get closer without being boiled. The ghost ran, and Ely rotated his hips to sharpen his aim.

If Ely released the trigger, the gun would have to recharge, and already the beam was sputtering and shifting from white to blue to orange.

The ghost reached the balustrade at the top of the stairs. Without slowing down, he placed his right hand on the top of the stone banister and vaulted sideways.

At the apex of his jump, lightning finally struck.

The ghost seemed to freeze in midair as light enveloped him in a perfect sphere. His right arm was braced against the marble in mid-vault, his legs horizontal in anticipation of the jump, flexed and ready to land on the stairs below. His left arm was extended away from his body to counterbalance his momentum, the absence of a left hand a minor affront to symmetry. The ghost was an incandescent silhouette inside a bubble about to burst.

Everyone in the hallway held their breath. The buttons on Ely's gun switched from green to red. The chandelier overhead seemed to flicker and fade.

The ghost went supernova.

The explosion was soundless, as if it occurred in space. The orb with the ghost at its epicenter expanded until it encompassed everyone in the hall. Then the brilliant bubble exploded into a billion photons too fragile and weak to do anything but fade into memory.

No one could see for several seconds.

Ely was paying a bigger price for looking at the beam while aiming. He dropped the plasma rifle at his feet and rubbed his eyes with the heels of his hands. Cape and Sally were blinking spots away as they made it to the banister. The marble was hot to the touch.

Cape looked over the side, and Sally started down the stairs. The ghost was gone.

73

"We need to be gone."

Cape's eyesight had yet to return to normal, but his hearing was good enough to register the sirens. An all-too-familiar doppler whine indicated they were coming fast and getting closer.

Sally looked up from the stairwell below. "Get Grace out of here."

Cape wanted to argue but knew the futility of trying to get Sally off a scent. He blinked spots from his eyes and tracked her progress. There was no body, only a charred remnant of white fabric on the first landing. He called to Sally before turning away from the stairs.

"Two minutes."

Sally's voice carried from below. "Five."

Cape intercepted Grace before she could run down the stairs. "Forget it." Grace made a harrumph sound that belied her age until Cape added, "I need your help getting everyone out of here." He turned to Maria. "Thanks, by the way."

"Not me." Maria spread her arms expansively. "Thank Pasha and Ely."

Cape nodded at the brothers. "That's quite a gun."

"It's a bastard blaster," said Pasha.

Ely squinted and gave a thumbs-up. His eyes were watering profusely.

Maria headed back toward the special exhibitions gallery. Cape caught up to her.

"We have to leave, or your visit to San Francisco could become an extended stay behind bars."

"I have to check something," said Maria. "Then we leave."

Cape turned to Pasha and Ely. "You work for Valenko?"

They both nodded.

"He owes me a favor." Cape saw Maria's right eyebrow shoot upward. He bent to retrieve the plasma rifle from the floor and handed it to Ely. "How long till this thing recharges?"

Ely pressed the buttons on the side of the rifle. "Five minutes maybe?"

"Perfect," said Cape. "Go outside and hide in the shadow of the building. When the police arrive, light up the sky."

Pasha frowned. "Sorry?"

"If you can distract them or get them talking on the radio, you'll buy us time."

"But don't get caught," said Maria.

"That's right," said Cape. "Do not get caught. As soon as you have their attention, run."

"And don't hurt any police," added Maria. "Or blast anyone with that lightning gun."

"I told you lightning gun wasn't a bad name," said Ely.

"I still prefer bastard blaster," said Pasha.

"Agreed," said Ely, "but as a backup—"

"—it's a great name," said Cape, "but it's time to go."

Pasha turned to Maria and bent one knee as if genuflecting. "Goodbye, Maria."

Ely mimicked the move. "We will m—"

"Now," said Cape.

"Goodbye, boys." Maria kissed each of them on both cheeks. *"Muchísimas gracias."*

Pasha and Ely practically skipped down the stairs.

Cape jogged next to Maria as she headed for the gallery, Grace alongside.

"How did you get them to cooperate?" asked Cape.

Grace smiled at Maria. "I think they're crushing on you."

"Not at all," said Maria. "'The enemy of my enemy—'"

"—is my friend.'" Cape gasped as a rib took a stab at his lung.

"I implied that I still worked for Interpol," said Maria, "and could grant them immunity."

"And you give me a hard time." Cape slowed his pace to walk the rest of the way. Maria and Grace went on ahead. As soon as Maria crossed the threshold, she began cursing in Spanish. When Cape reached the entrance, he understood why.

The first three paintings of the Summer Palace hung as before, unmolested and undisturbed. The fourth, *Harmony with the Past and Present,* was missing. There was no harmony, and no past. Only the present, where Maria stood swearing at a bare rectangle on the wall. Cape counted to twenty before interrupting.

"Time isn't our friend."

Maria turned, her dark eyes alight with anger. "How di—"

"I was so worried about Feng," said Cape. "I forgot about Fang."

Maria's nostrils flared as she took a deep breath to unleash another stream of invectives, until she made eye contact with Grace. Maria looked at the young girl for a long moment before glancing back at the blank space on the wall. Then Maria exhaled, as if she'd been holding that breath her entire life and realized now it was okay to let it go.

"We got what we came for," she said. "Let's go home."

74

Going home for Freddie Wang was as easy as climbing the stairs.

That's because he lived where he worked, in the restaurant where he kept his office. The older Freddie got, the more paranoid he became, and not without reason. After several failed assassination attempts by erstwhile rivals, Freddie converted the top floor of the restaurant into his office and living quarters.

It was too early in the day for tourists, so Freddie dined with Fang in a booth on the main floor of the restaurant. The young man had lost his brother the night before, and Freddie reassured him that Feng's sacrifice would be honored in the next life and rewarded in this one. That was Freddie's way of saying that Fang would be given both his share and that of his dead brother for what he delivered.

Fang came directly to the restaurant from the museum. He delivered three forgeries, still in their packing crates; one original painting, still in its frame; and a severed hand.

Freddie wasn't sure why Fang had brought him the hand, but he appreciated the gesture.

As soon as Fang was fed and done talking, Freddie lit a fresh cigarette and smiled. Nothing had gone according to plan, but things could not have turned out better. Freddie now possessed three forgeries indistinguishable from the original paintings. He also had the original of the fourth painting that completed the set. And the best part? The only expert capable of telling a forgery from an original had died in a factory fire in China.

Four paintings would be shipped to China, and no one on the receiving end would ever suspect three were fake. Freddie was merely returning the forgeries they provided, an inside joke he would never tell. His obligation would be fulfilled, his bank account would be full, and both the Triads and their handlers in the central government would leave his city alone.

Freddie scribbled a phone number on a napkin and handed it to Fang, who departed with a quick bow. The paintings would leave on a charter flight in less than an hour.

When the cigarette burned to ash Freddie rose from the table. He was tempted to visit the kitchen and check the industrial freezer where the albino hand had been stored. To avoid unnerving the kitchen staff every time they opened the freezer, the hand rested inside a rectangular wooden box that once held chopsticks. It reminded Freddie of a little coffin.

Freddie didn't know why he kept the hand and resisted the urge to take a look. There was a gnawing feeling in his gut that one day someone might come looking for it. On that day, Freddie didn't want to show up empty-handed.

He waved his apprehensions away and left the dining room. The real prize was waiting in his office, the bronze Buddha covered in gold that was stolen by the ghost on the night of the helicopter crash. The museum could afford to lose a painting on loan from another museum, but the Buddha was priceless.

Freddie was more of a capitalist than he was a Buddhist, so possession was its own reward. The statue sat on his desk as a daily reminder that a cunning man could always get what he wants even when plans went awry.

Freddie climbed the steps as swiftly as his decrepit knees would allow. By the time he unlocked his office door and deactivated the alarm, he was desperate for another cigarette. He made a beeline for his desk but froze in mid-stride and forgot all about his craving.

The Buddha was gone.

In its place were two small animals. Freddie squinted to focus his good eye and saw they were made out of paper. An origami dragon of such intricacy it might have been alive. Next to the little dragon, folded with the same precision, was a little rooster.

Freddie sat down heavily and reached for his cigarettes. Though he would never admit it, deep down he knew this wasn't his city. Not anymore.

75

"This city of yours is not at all what I expected."

"The postcards can be deceiving," said Cape.

"*Verdaderamente.*" Maria ran her hands through her hair and turned it into a stretch, tilting her head back to soak up the warmth. The sun was winning its afternoon battle with the fog, but thick clumps of cotton were gathering around the Golden Gate. It was just a matter of time before the breeze across the bay cut the temperature in half.

The bench where they were sitting gave a clear view across Marina Green. Frisbees, kites, and volleyballs took turns flying above the grass with the seagulls. Sailboats on the bay wrestled with the wind to circle Alcatraz. A container ship drifted lazily under the bridge, and Cape couldn't help but wonder what cargo was hidden inside.

The fresh air was a caressing hand that made the night before seem like a fever dream, but Cape still had the copper taste of blood in the back of his throat. A vague scent of lightning tinged his nostrils. On the bench next to him was a discarded copy of the *San Francisco Chronicle*.

The headline simply read, BOMBING AT CITY HALL. The

page one story described the attack as a coordinated assault against democracy, according to the mayor, masterminded by his political opponents. The mayor had spoken on the record from his house in Napa and wouldn't be returning to the city until repairs were made to the building, but to maintain public confidence he recommended raising taxes to create a "war chest" in case of future incursions. He also recommended donating generously to his reelection campaign. There was no mention of the museum beyond a reference to the original robbery in an article on page ten about surging crime downtown and its effect on the tourist trade.

Cape had thrown the paper down as soon as he read it.

Maria turned to look at him. "You're the one who warned me about politicians, so don't tell me you're surprised. Besides, we didn't want to make headlines."

Cape nodded but his eyes were locked on Sally as she circumnavigated the park with Grace. They were fifty yards away when Cape lowered his hand from his eyes and blinked against the sun to focus on Maria.

"Thanks for making those calls."

Maria shrugged. "I still have some friends in faraway places, but even with connections at Interpol, it's impossible to know if the information is reliable. Law enforcement in China isn't known for sharing."

"What does your gut tell you?"

"Her parents are dead," said Maria. "Grace is an orphan."

"Yeah."

"Sally reacted as if she already knew," said Maria.

"Sally is not someone surprised by bad news," said Cape.

"What about you?"

"I'm only surprised by good news."

"That's not what I meant," said Maria. "How are you feeling?"

Cape pulled up his shirttail to reveal green medical tape stretched across his ribs. "Hospital issue, doctor applied."

"The neon green is very stylish," said Maria. "Much better than duct tape."

"The ribs are cracked, not broken," said Cape. "Apparently there's a difference."

"You need a vacation."

"You're not the first person to say that," said Cape.

"You talked to your friend, the police inspector?"

"Right up until he hung up on me."

"Does he want you to come in for questioning?"

"Officially, yes." Cape stretched out his legs and looked toward Alcatraz. "Unofficially, Beau suggested I leave town for a few days."

Maria nodded. "Did he say anything else?"

Cape suppressed a grin. "You mean, did he say anything about you?"

"*Sí, quizás.*"

"He mentioned that someone disabled the museum's security cameras—"

"—you're welcome," said Maria.

"And that same person dialed 9-1-1 from the control room…"

"Mm-hmm."

"…but the police were told to converge on city hall, because that's where their paychecks get signed."

"So there was no one at the museum to arrest by the time they got there," said Maria. "How sad."

"Tragic," said Cape. "Beau has a dead body and a mayor who doesn't give a shit."

"And he's angry with you?"

"Conflicted," said Cape. "It's not like I didn't try to warn him."

"There is a corpse."

"Beau already identified Feng—or what was left of him—as one of Freddie Wang's foot soldiers, so that's a line of inquiry that will lead nowhere. A bulletin has been issued for two men spotted near the museum shooting lightning bolts at trees, but the most they could get is attempted arson."

"You must have told him about Grace."

"That's the reason I'm not in an interrogation room," said Cape. "The only charge that would stick—if there was any interest in placing us at the scene—is trespassing. Everything else is conjecture without corroborating testimony. Said another way, I'm a big waste of his time."

"I wish I could have spent more time with Inspector Beauregard," said Maria. "He sounds like a good man."

"Better than this city deserves," said Cape. "You sound like someone whose vacation has come to an end."

Maria half-smiled. "I have a new job."

Cape raised an eyebrow. "Italy?"

"Not the Carabinieri, but yes, Italy," said Maria. "As of today, I am self-employed."

"Let me guess," said Cape. "Art retrieval?"

"Among other things," said Maria. "You can make a good living finding lost things, especially things that have been underwritten by an insurance company for millions of dollars."

"Like a stolen Rembrandt."

"*Exactamente.*" Maria sounded wistful as she added, "Which you helped find."

Cape shook his head. "I wouldn't know the difference between a Rembrandt and a black velvet Elvis without a crib sheet."

"I could teach you," said Maria.

Cape shifted on the bench to take a long look at Maria. Her smile didn't waver, and her eyes never blinked. "Are you offering me a job?"

"You're good at finding people," said Maria, "and I'm good at finding things."

Cape didn't say anything. He didn't know what to say.

"Transporting priceless art by yourself isn't easy," said Maria. "I could use a partner."

Cape let his eyes drift across the park until he found Sally. She and Grace had rounded the corner and were twenty yards away, walking toward them. They were holding hands.

"I have a partner," said Cape. "But I could use a vacation."

"How much did you get paid for this case?"

"Twenty-five cents."

"Then how about a working vacation?" Maria smiled. "Italy is lovely this time of year."

Cape laughed and held out his hand. "Deal." Maria took it warmly and they shook.

Sally and Grace arrived at the foot of the bench.

"What did we miss?" asked Sally.

"I'm going on vacation," said Cape.

"You never go on vacation."

"Figured I'd try," said Cape. "What's the worst that could happen?"

"You could blow something up in another country," said Sally. Maria laughed.

Cape turned to Grace and asked, "How about you?"

"I'm going to move in with Sally."

"Someone has to take care of the cat," said Sally.

Cape made eye contact with Sally before turning back to Grace. "I think that's a great idea."

"Will you come visit?"

Cape held out his hand. Grace took it firmly in hers and they shook.

"Deal."

Epilogue

Bohai made the only deal he could to escape Hong Kong.

At the time he was desperate. Now, months later, he was grateful.

The captain of the fishing boat recognized a fugitive when he saw one, but Bohai wasn't naïve enough to walk into a trap. Bohai spent the week prior visiting stalls in the Aberdeen Fish Market on Shek Pai Wan Road, befriending merchants and listening to gossip. Fishmongers were garrulous by nature, accustomed to haggling and telling stories to pass the time.

Bohai was affable, and his pet monkey, Junjie, made them laugh.

Casual conversation turned to conspiratorial whispers of people being smuggled out of Hong Kong. Rumors of fishing boats that made the crossing to Taiwan but never returned. It was a long trip for a small boat, but a larger vessel could never sneak past the patrol boats that cruised along the mainland harbors.

Bohai found a fisherman willing to take him on as a member of the crew.

The day they set off from Aberdeen Harbor, Bohai worried

over the rough seas until the captain explained it was easier to veer off course and disappear when skies were gray and rain was heavy. Bohai spent the next week vomiting over the side of the boat but never complained. It was only a year ago that a desperate man attempted the crossing in a rubber dinghy but got captured three days into his journey. Bohai counted himself lucky every day they sailed east with no other ships in sight.

Now he smiled at the memory of that hazy morning when the coast of Taiwan came into view. The captain waited until sunset to join the other fishing boats bringing their day's catch into the Port of Anping.

The crew unloaded their cargo, and Bohai stayed ashore. Junjie never left his side.

The little macaque had been fiercely loyal, and Bohai never doubted he would be dead or imprisoned if not for his genetically enhanced friend. Junjie could sense when someone was following them or merely taking an interest. He could smell their suspicion.

Once in Taiwan, they made a cautious week's journey to Taipei, where Bohai had contacts waiting. Another month to get identification papers, during which time Bohai scouted locations in the Da'an District, where he could begin another life. Now he stood behind the cash register of his new bookstore, grateful for second chances and wistful over lost friends.

The high shelves were crowded with daily newspapers, monthly comics, and books new and used, organized by language and genre. Junjie grabbed two volumes off the counter and hopped to the nearest shelf, happily restocking while Bohai stuffed an envelope full of cash. The fisherman kept his side of the bargain, and Bohai would keep his—half his income for a year seemed a small price to pay when so many others had paid with their lives.

Bohai finished counting and glanced idly at the open newspaper on the counter.

For weeks he'd been following stories of an underground artist who recently emerged in China. Paintings appeared on factory walls, subways, sidewalks, and buildings all over the country, yet no one knew the identity of the artist. The art was beautiful, unconventional, and subtly subversive. The official government stance was one of stern disapproval, while the public waited eagerly for the appearance of the next work of art.

They were calling him the Banksy of Asia. Many believed he was a young painter from the art village of Dafen; others insisted it was a couple, a man and woman with complementary styles. The newspaper Bohai was reading suggested something bigger, a movement begun in Dafen that had grown into a vast underground network of artists working in concert.

That last scenario gave Bohai a deep sense of satisfaction that bordered on hope.

Junjie leapt onto the counter and chattered excitedly. Bohai was glad to have a friendly face from his past life, albeit an unexpected one. He thought of his friend, Wen, and so many others left behind.

Bohai looked around his store at books from all over the world. He knew better than most that the best way to keep someone's memory alive was to tell their story. Pushing the newspaper aside, he reached under the counter and grabbed a sheaf of paper. Junjie handed him a pen.

With a macaque at his elbow and a smile on his lips, Bohai began to write.

Read on for an excerpt
from **Boxing the Octopus**,
another exciting Cape Weathers Mystery!

1

As he suspected, the village was full of misery, fear, and blood.

The Doctor adjusted his headphones, cranking the volume. After visiting the first two villages, he couldn't get the sounds of dying out of his head.

Nothing a little Katy Perry or Ariana Grande couldn't fix.

It wasn't his fault these people were born on the ass end of the planet. One thing he'd learned in medical school is life is cheap, and not everybody gets to live in the first world. Or even in the same century.

There were over a hundred cities in China with populations in excess of a million people, but this wasn't one of them. After a three-hour drive from the urban sprawl and pollution of Beijing, the Doctor crested a mountain range at the border of Hebei province. The Toyota Land Cruiser barely fit on the dirt track running to the village from the main road, the terrain as inhospitable as the surface of Mars. Some of the homes were only accessible by foot.

The Doctor stepped gingerly into the temporary structure erected on the outskirts of the village. The cots were full, most of them occupied by young children and their grandparents. As cities grew and jobs disappeared from rural China, many teenagers and able-bodied adults left family behind in the villages and headed to the nearest city, in hopes of bringing prosperity back home one day. The Doctor knew that day would never come.

These people were dead before they were born.

One of the nurses handed him a clipboard, but the Doctor already knew what it would reveal. He didn't have to take off the headphones or listen to her nervous voice explain that everyone who took the placebo was doing fine, but over twenty percent of the patients who took the new drug were writhing in agony, blood seeping from their ears, eyes, and nose.

Three weeks to the day since the drug was ingested. Just like the trials in Tunisia and Angola.

Two more sewers where years of work and millions of dollars got flushed down the drain.

The Doctor thumbed the controls on his phone and skipped over Beyoncé to find a better tune. He needed a new playlist. Beyoncé was overrated, and he desperately needed to cheer the fuck up.

He stepped outside onto the barren earth and stood under the unforgiving sun. The Doctor didn't want forgiveness, and the irony that this place was hot as Hell wasn't lost on him.

As his SUV bounced along the rutted road and the village shrank in his rearview mirror, he passed the convoy of mercenaries coming from the opposite direction. They were late, and he wasn't going to wait around to give them instructions. This was the third village, and they knew the drill. After Tunisia, the Doctor made sure they brought enough propane to keep the burn pit going for days.

…you just gotta ignite the light, and let it shine…

It was almost as if Katy Perry had written that song just for this moment. The Doctor hummed along as he grabbed the satellite phone from the passenger seat. The song would be over soon, and he needed to make a phone call. He kept his eyes on the road ahead as he dialed, not sparing another glance in the rearview mirror.

He had witnessed enough death for one day.

2

No one should witness his own murder.

The thought didn't occur to Hank because he had other things on his mind.

His partner was fifteen minutes late. Not the end of the world if you're giving someone a ride to the airport, but a very big deal when you have five million dollars in your vehicle.

Time to go, Lou.

The armored car squatted on the pier, its fat tires clutching the broken asphalt. San Francisco Bay sloshed lazily in his side mirror, and the engine vibrations threatened to rock Hank to sleep. Coffee wasn't an option unless he felt like pissing in a bottle, and his aim wasn't what it used to be.

Hank fingered the cross around his neck and considered asking God to find his partner or grant him the divine power of telepathy so he could summon the dipshit from the other side of the pier.

Where the fuck are you?

Lou didn't answer. Neither did God.

The backside of Pier 39 was almost deserted, only restaurant employees cutting behind the buildings where they worked.

Although this access road was quiet, Hank knew the main thoroughfare of the pier was buzzing this time of day, clogged with families from a dozen countries navigating an obstacle course of souvenir shops and chain restaurants on their quest to find the sea lions swimming at the end of the pier.

Visited over ten million times a year, Pier 39 had become San Francisco's leading tourist attraction, and none of the locals could understand why.

For Hank the pier was simply a job. It was also proof that even a natural beauty like San Francisco could look like a tramp if you dressed her like one.

He had parked along a narrow strip of asphalt running behind the pier, in the shadow of a crooked line of buildings on the east side. This was the last stop before the pier opened onto the street and he drove to the bank.

To his right, the rear entrances of the merchants, and on his left, a wooden railing to protect drunken tourists from falling into the adjacent marina. Sailboats, motorboats, and skiffs bobbed gently in the current from the bay. Hank caught the smell of dead fish every time he breathed through his nose, even though he couldn't roll down the windows in the armored car.

Hank twisted in his seat and looked to the uppermost level, almost directly above him. A lone window, curtains open, but no sign of movement.

She's minding the store. Doesn't have time to wave at you, dumbass.

Hank smiled and felt himself relax. Maybe Lou had found himself a girlfriend on the pier, too. There was a reason Hank preferred making the pickups instead of waiting in the car, but today was his turn to drive.

He glanced at the sloping driveway at the front of the pier, scanning traffic like he was trained to do. Taxis and cars drifted past, a monotonous blur of color.

A forklift emerged from the back of an eighteen-wheeler parked on the shoulder of the main road. The semi was too heavy for the pier, so the forklift turned off the street, boxes stacked high, and headed down the ramp. Hank had parked closer to the marina railing than the stores, so there would be plenty of room for the narrow forklift to pass. His only job was to sit tight.

Hank watched the forklift bounce and shimmy toward him.

A UPS truck followed a moment later, just narrow enough to fit on the ramp. The driver angled to avoid scraping the undercarriage, and Hank got a clear view of the man behind the wheel.

It was Lou.

It took a second to register a familiar face in a confusing context. By the time it clicked, there was nothing Hank could do.

The forklift spun violently against Hank's front bumper, the steel arms sliding beneath the armored car. The boxes were empty, collapsing and temporarily obscuring Hank's view. A metallic scream rose with the arms of the forklift. Hank's world swooned as his front wheels left the surface of the road.

As the broken boxes fell to the ground, the forklift driver leapt from the cab and ran toward the main road. His work was done.

Hank locked eyes with Lou as the UPS truck slammed mercilessly into the back of the forklift, driving it under the armored car like a wedge. The car reared backwards, balancing on its rear wheels for a sickening instant before flipping onto its roof.

The day wasn't supposed to go down like this.

Sparks flew as the car skidded across the asphalt and crashed through the wooden railing at the end of the pier. Free fall, and then the armored car struck the water. Hank bit through his tongue, the blood tasting like an unpaid debt.

He was upside down and sinking, and he couldn't roll down the window. Boats sloshed into view through the windshield. He threw his weight against the door but only a small gap appeared. Water poured in, drowning any hope of escape.

He tried to take a deep breath, but the frigid water had other ideas. Reflexively, Hank reached for the gun on his hip, but the small part of his brain still working remembered the glass was bulletproof.

The car hit bottom twenty feet down, the water green and murky.

Dashboard lights reflected off the windows, transforming them into mirrors. The only thing Hank could see was himself. He stared at his reflection as the water rose, a lone witness to his own fear.

By the time the water crested above his chin, it was a face he barely recognized, wearing an expression he'd never seen before.

He looked like a man who didn't want to die.

Acknowledgments

Writing a mystery is like painting an impressionist landscape using your subconscious as the brush. You hope the story that was in your head is now on the page, but the only way to be sure is to ask someone you trust to look over your shoulder, which is why I count myself lucky to be working with the brilliant bibliophiles at Poisoned Pen Press and Sourcebooks. Diane DiBiase is an editor extraordinaire whose keen eye and endless encouragement turned my manuscript into a book. Beth Deveny did the impossible (again) by making sure none of my mistakes were ever seen in print. Eternal thanks to the legendary Barbara Peters for giving me the courage to face the terror of the blank page, to Rob Rosenwald for giving me a home so long ago, and to Dominique Raccah for welcoming me to the Sourcebooks family. Finally, thanks to Clare and Helen for storytelling suggestions, to Kathryn for ongoing inspiration, and to readers and booksellers everywhere for loving books as much as I do.

About the Author

TIM MALEENY is the bestselling author of the award-winning Cape Weathers Mysteries including *Stealing the Dragon* and *Boxing the Octopus*, a series *Booklist* describes as "smart, snappily written, energetic mysteries starring an engaging hero." Tim's standalone thriller, *Jump*, was called "a perfectly blended cocktail of escapism," by *Publishers Weekly*, and his short fiction has won the prestigious Macavity Award. "If comic crime fiction is your thing, Maleeny delivers in spades," says the *Irish Times*. A former resident of San Francisco, Tim currently lives with his family in New York City, where he is writing diligently whenever he isn't busy procrastinating.